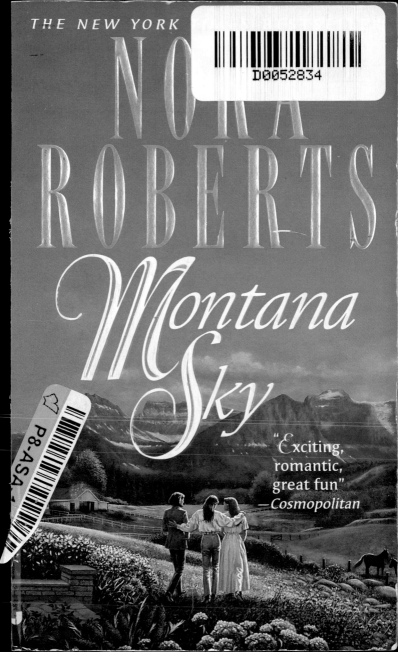

NORA ROBERTS

Montana Sky

"*Exciting,
romantic,
great fun*"
—*Cosmopolitan*

"Her stories have fueled the dreams
of twenty-five million readers."
—*Entertainment Weekly*

Also by
NORA ROBERTS...

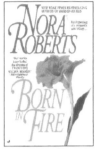

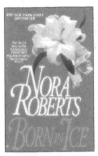

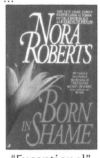

"Compelling"
—*Publishers Weekly*

"Exceptional"
—*Publishers Weekly*

"Captures the charisma and
earthy charm of Ireland"
—*Publishers Weekly*

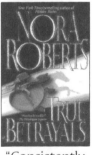

"Consistently
entertaining"
—*USA Today*

"ROBERTS IS INDEED A WORD ARTIST,
painting her characters with vitality and verve."
—*Los Angeles Daily News*

MONTANA SKY

"A TENSE ROMANTIC TALE . . . Nora Roberts just keeps
getting better and better."   —*MILWAUKEE JOURNAL SENTINEL*

"A RICH NARRATIVE . . . Roberts balances the tension . . .
with three romances, crackling dialogue, and a snappy infusion of
humor."   —*PUBLISHERS WEEKLY*

"If it is PASSION, SUSPENSE, AND EMOTIONAL POWER
you want, *Montana Sky* has them all."   —*TULSA WORLD*

TRUE BETRAYALS

*A thrilling story of family secrets and unexpected passions, set against
the high-stakes world of championship Thoroughbred racing...*

"AN ABSOLUTELY TERRIFIC SUMMER READ."
—*THE ORLANDO SENTINEL*

"A FAST-PACED, ENGAGING TALE of envy, greed, and
romance . . . another winner for this popular author."
—*PUBLISHERS WEEKLY*

"With the kind of savvy that would do Dick Francis proud,
Roberts gives you a peek at the sabotage and skulduggery the
horsey set is capable of when the stakes are high."
—*CHICAGO TRIBUNE*

continued on next page...

HIDDEN RICHES

In the intriguing world of antique dealing, Dora Conroy discovers the price of breathless desire—and the schemes of an obsessed killer...

"A HEROINE WHO WILL CHARM READERS."

—*USA TODAY*

"Roberts keeps us sensuously engrossed in a suspenseful romance."

—*KIRKUS REVIEWS*

"A SURE WINNER!"

—*LIBRARY JOURNAL*

PRIVATE SCANDALS

Behind the scenes of a television talk show, young and ambitious Deanna Reynolds is about to learn the price of her success...

"TOP-NOTCH . . . First-rate reading."

—*RENDEZVOUS*

"A FUN READ!"

—*PUBLISHERS WEEKLY*

HONEST ILLUSIONS

Nothing is as it seems in the world of a carnival—as Roxy Nouvelle discovers when a charming con man steps into her life...

"ROXY AND LUKE WILL STEAL YOUR HEART."

—CATHERINE COULTER

"A GENUINE PAGE-TURNER. I loved it!" —JANET DAILEY

"A CAPTIVATING STORY. You'll fall in love with these wonderful characters just as I did."

—JULIE GARWOOD

Don't miss Nora Roberts's exquisite trilogy of the Concannon sisters of Ireland—women of ambition and talent, bound by the timeless spirit and restless beauty of their land.

BORN IN FIRE

Maggie Concannon is a glassmaker whose stunning works reflect her fiery spirit. One man sees the soul in her art—and the need in her heart for a gentle love to heal her dark past...

"Refreshingly realistic [and] compelling." —PUBLISHERS WEEKLY

"Roberts's unique characters come to life through their wordplay and tempers . . . [a] fast-paced novel set in the Irish countryside."
—SCHOOL LIBRARY JOURNAL

BORN IN ICE

Brianna Concannon always enjoyed the cool quiet of her inn during the winter months. And her guest enjoyed the cold solitude of his life, burying a painful memory. But sometimes fate takes an unexpected turn...

"Captures the charisma and earthy charm of Ireland and the gentleness of its people." —PUBLISHERS WEEKLY

"Full of excitement, romance, and a unique twist that makes you wish it would go on and on." —WINTER HAVEN NEWS-CHIEF

BORN IN SHAME

American artist Shannon Bodine learned the identity of her real father: Thomas Concannon. Reluctantly she traveled to Ireland to discover her true roots—and the possibility of a love that was meant to be...

"With prose that's lively and compelling, Roberts creates exceptional characters whose relationships with each other develop and grow and live on in the reader's imagination and heart." —PUBLISHERS WEEKLY

"A memorable love story . . . a stirring end to a fine trilogy."
—RENDEZVOUS

"The incomparable Nora Roberts brings this magnificent trilogy to a highly satisfactory conclusion." —ROMANTIC TIMES

MONTANA SKY

NORA ROBERTS

JOVE BOOKS, NEW YORK

This Jove Book contains the complete text of the hardcover edition. It has been completely reset in a typeface designed for easy reading and was printed from new film.

MONTANA SKY

A Jove Book / published by arrangement with the author

PRINTING HISTORY
G. P. Putnam's Sons edition published March 1996
Jove edition / May 1997

The Putnam Berkley World Wide Web site address is
http://www.berkley.com

ISBN: 0-515-12061-8

A JOVE BOOK®
Jove Books are published by The Berkley Publishing Group,
200 Madison Avenue, New York, New York 10016.
JOVE and the "J" design are trademarks
belonging to Jove Publications, Inc.

PRINTED IN THE UNITED STATES OF AMERICA

10 9 8 7 6 5 4 3 2 1

To family

The world stands out on either side
No wider than the heart is wide;
Above the world is stretched the sky,—
No higher than the soul is high.
The heart can push the sea and land
Farther away on either hand;
The soul can split the sky in two,
And let the face of God shine through.
But East and West will pinch the heart
That can not keep them pushed apart;
And he whose soul is flat—the sky
Will cave in on him by and by.

—Edna St. Vincent Millay

PART ONE

AUTUMN

The beautiful and death-struck year

—A. E. Housman

ONE

Being dead didn't make Jack Mercy less of a son of a bitch. One week of dead didn't offset sixty-eight years of living mean. Plenty of the people gathered by his grave would be happy to say so.

The fact was, funeral or no funeral, Bethanne Mosebly muttered those sentiments into her husband's ear as they stood in the high grass of the cemetery. She was there only out of affection for young Willa, and she had bent her husband's tired ear with that information as well all the way up from Ennis.

As a man who had listened to his wife's chatter for forty-six years, Bob Mosebly simply grunted, tuning her and the preacher's droning voice out.

Not that Bob had fond memories of Jack. He'd hated the old bastard, as did most every living soul in the state of Montana.

But dead was dead, Bob mused, and they had sure come out in droves to send the fucker on his way to hell.

This peaceful corner of Mercy Ranch, set in the shadows of the Big Belt Mountains, near the banks of the Missouri, was crowded now with ranchers and cowboys, merchants and politicians. Here where cattle grazed the hills and horses danced in sunny pastures, generations of Mercys were buried under the billowing grass.

Jack was the latest. He'd ordered the glossy chestnut coffin himself, had it custom-made and inscribed in gold with the linked *M*s that made up the ranch's brand. The box was lined with white satin, and Jack was inside it now, wearing his best snakeskin boots, his oldest and most favored Stetson, and holding his bullwhip.

Jack had vowed to die the way he had lived. In nose-thumbing style.

Word was, Willa had already ordered the headstone, according to her father's instructions. It would be white marble—no ordinary granite for Jackson Mercy—and the sentiments inscribed on it were his own:

> *Here lies Jack Mercy.*
> *He lived as he wanted, died the same way.*
> *The hell with anybody who didn't like it.*

The monument would be raised once the ground had settled, to join all the others that tipped and dotted the stony ground, from Jack Mercy's great-grandfather, Jebidiah Mercy, who had roamed the mountains and claimed the land, to the last of Jack's three wives—and the only one who'd died before he could divorce her.

Wasn't it interesting, Bob mused, that each of Mercy's wives had presented him with a daughter when he'd been hell-bent on having a son? Bob liked to think of it as God's little joke on a man who had stepped on backs—and hearts—to get what he wanted in every other area of his life.

He remembered each of Jack's wives well enough, though none of them had lasted long. Lookers every one, he thought now, and the girls they'd birthed weren't hard on the eyes either. Bethanne had been burning up the phone lines ever since word came along that Mercy's two oldest daughters were flying in for the funeral. Neither of them had set foot on Mercy land since before they could walk.

And they wouldn't have been welcome.

Only Willa had stayed. There'd been little Mercy could do about that, seeing as how her mother had died almost before the child had been weaned. Without any relations to dump the girl on, he'd passed the baby along to his house-keeper, and Bess had raised the girl as best she could.

Each of the women had a touch of Jack in her, Bob noted, scanning them from under the brim of his hat. The dark hair, the sharp chin. You could tell they were sisters, all right, even though they'd never set eyes on each other before. Time would tell how they would deal together, and time would tell if Willa had enough of Jack Mercy in her to run a ranch of twenty-five thousand acres.

She was thinking of the ranch, and the work that needed to be done. The morning was bright and clear, with the hills sporting color so bold and beautiful it almost hurt the eyes. The mountains and valley might have been painted fancy for fall, but the chinook wind had come in hot and dry and thick. Early October was warm enough for shirtsleeves, but that could change tomorrow. There'd already been snow in the high country, and she could see it, dribbling along the black and gray peaks, slyly coating the forests. Cattle needed to be rounded up, fences needed to be checked, repaired, checked again. Winter wheat had to be planted.

It was up to her now. It was all up to her. Jack Mercy was no longer Mercy Ranch, Willa reminded herself. She was.

She listened to the preacher speak of everlasting life, of forgiveness and the welcome of heaven. And thought that Jack Mercy would spit on anyone's welcome into a place other than his own. Montana had been his, this wide country of mountain and meadow, of eagle and wolf.

Her father would be as miserable in heaven as he would in hell.

Her face remained calm as the fancy coffin was lowered into the newest scar in the earth. Her skin was pale gold, a legacy from her mother and her Blackfoot blood as much as the sun. Her eyes, nearly as black as the hair she'd hur-riedly twisted into a braid for the funeral, remained fixed on the box that held her father's body. She hadn't worn a hat, and the sun beamed like fire into her eyes. But she didn't let them tear.

She had a proud face, high cheekbones, a wide, haughty mouth, dark, exotic eyes with heavy lids and thick lashes. She'd broken her nose falling off an angry wild mustang when she was eight. Willa liked to think the slight left turn it took in the center of her face added character.

Character meant a great deal more to Willa Mercy than beauty. Men didn't respect beauty, she knew. They used it.

She stood very still, the wind picking up strands from her braid and teasing them into a dance. A woman of average height and tough, rangy build in an ill-fitting black dress and dainty black heels that had never been out of their box before that morning. A woman of twenty-four with work on her mind, and a raging, tearing grief in her heart.

She had, despite everything, loved Jack Mercy. And she said nothing, not one word, to the two women, the strangers who shared her blood and had come to see their father buried.

For a moment, just one moment, she let her gaze shift, let it rest on the grave of Mary Wolfchild Mercy. The mother she couldn't remember was buried under a soft mound of wildflowers that bloomed like jewels in the autumn sun. Adam's doing, she thought, and looked up and into the eyes of her half brother. He would know as no one else could that she had tears in her heart she could never let free.

When Adam took her hand, Willa linked fingers with his. In her mind, and heart, he was all the family she had now.

"He lived the life that satisfied him," Adam murmured. His voice was quiet, peaceful. If they had been alone Willa could have turned, rested her head on his shoulder, and found comfort.

"Yes, he did. And now it's done."

Adam glanced over at the two women, Jack Mercy's daughters, and thought something else was just beginning. "You have to speak with them, Willa."

"They're sleeping in my house, eating my food." Deliberately she looked back at her father's grave. "That's enough."

"They're your blood."

"No, Adam, you're my blood. They're nothing to me." She turned away from him and braced herself to receive the condolences.

NEIGHBORS BROUGHT FOOD FOR DEATH. THERE WAS NO stopping the bone-deep tradition, any more than Willa could have stopped Bess from cooking for three days straight to provide for what the housekeeper called the bereavement supper. And that was a double pile of horseshit in Willa's mind. There was no bereavement here. Curiosity, certainly. Many of the people who packed into the main house had been invited before. More, many more, had not. His death provided them entry, and they enjoyed it.

The main house was a showplace, Jack Mercy style. Once a cabin of log and mud had stood there, but that had been more than a hundred years before. Now there was a sprawling, rambling structure of stone and wood, of glistening glass. Rugs from all over the world spread over floors of gleaming pine or polished tile. Jack Mercy had liked to collect. When he'd become master of Mercy Ranch he had spent five years turning what had been a lovely home into his personal palace.

Rich lived rich, he liked to say.

So he had. Collecting paintings and sculpture, adding rooms where the art could be displayed. The entrance was a towering atrium, floored with tiles in jewel tones of sapphire and ruby in a repeating pattern of the Mercy Ranch brand. The staircase that swept to the second floor was polished oak, shiny as glass, with a newel post carved in the shape of a howling wolf.

People gathered there now, many of them goggling over it as they balanced their plates. Others crowded into the living room with its acre of slick floor and wide curve of sofa in cream-colored leather. On the smooth river rock of the wall-spanning fireplace hung a life-size painting of Jack Mercy astride a black stallion. His head was cocked, his hat tipped back, a bullwhip curled in one hand. Many felt that those hard blue eyes damned them as they sat drinking his whiskey and toasting his death.

For Lily Mercy, the second daughter Jack had conceived and discarded, it was terrifying. The house, the people, the noise. The room the housekeeper had given her the day before when she'd arrived was so beautiful. So quiet, she thought now as she moved closer to the rail of the side porch. The lovely bed, the pretty golden wood against the silky wallpaper.

The solitude.

She wanted that now, so very much, as she looked out toward the mountains. Such mountains, she thought. So high, so rough. Nothing at all like the pretty little hills of her home in Virginia. And all the sky, the shuddering and endless blue of it curving down to more land than could possibly exist.

The plains, that wild roll of them, and the wind that seemed never to stop. And the colors, the golds and russets, the scarlets and bronzes of both hill and plain exploding with autumn.

And this valley, where the ranch spread in a spot of such impossible strength and beauty. She'd seen deer out the window that morning, drinking from a stream that glowed silver in the dawn. She'd heard horses, the voices of men, the crow of a rooster, and what she thought—hoped—might have been an eagle's cry.

She wondered whether, if she found the courage to walk into the forest that danced up those foothills, she would see the moose, the elk, the fox that she had read about so greedily on the flight west.

She wondered if she would be allowed to stay even another day—and where she would go, what she would do, if she was asked to leave.

She couldn't go back east, not yet. Self-consciously she fingered the yellowing bruise she'd tried to hide with makeup and sunglasses. Jesse had found her. She'd been so careful, but he'd found her, and the court orders hadn't stopped his fists. They never had. Divorce hadn't stopped him, all the moving and the running hadn't stopped him.

But here, she thought, maybe here, thousands of miles away, in a country so huge, she could finally start again. Without fear.

The letter from the attorney informing her of Jack Mercy's death and requesting her to travel to Montana had been like a gift from God. Though her expenses had been paid, Lily had cashed in the first-class airfare and booked zigzagging flights across the country under three different names. She wanted desperately to believe Jesse Cooke couldn't find her here.

She was so tired of running, of being afraid.

She wondered if she could move to Billings or Helena and find a job. Any job. She wasn't without some skills. There was her teaching degree, and she knew how to use a keyboard. Maybe she could find a small apartment of her own, even just a room to start until she got on her feet again.

She could live here, she thought, staring out at the vast and terrifying and glorious space. Maybe she even belonged here.

She jumped when a hand touched her arm, barely stifled the scream as her heart leaped like a rabbit into her throat.

Not Jesse, she realized, feeling the fool. The man beside her was dark, where Jesse was blond. This man had bronzed skin and hair that streamed to his shoulders. Kind eyes, dark, very dark, in a face as beautiful as a painting.

But then Jesse was beautiful, too. She knew how cruel beauty could be.

"I'm sorry." Adam's voice was as soothing as it would have been if he'd frightened a puppy or a sick foal. "I didn't mean to startle you. Iced tea." He took her hand, noting the way it trembled, and wrapped it around the glass. "It's a dry day."

"Thank you. I didn't hear you come up behind me." In a habit she wasn't even aware of, Lily took a step aside, putting distance between them. Running room. "I was just . . . looking. It's so beautiful here."

"Yes, it is."

She sipped, cooling her dry throat, and ordered herself to

be calm and polite. People asked fewer questions when you were calm. "Do you live nearby?"

"Very." He smiled, stepped closer to the rail, and gestured east. He liked her voice, the slow, warm southern flavor of it. "The little white house on the other side of the horse barn."

"Yes, I saw it. You have blue shutters and a garden, and there was a little black dog sleeping in the yard." Lily remembered how homey it had looked, how much more welcoming than the grand house.

"That's Beans." Adam smiled again. "The dog. He has a fondness for refried beans. I'm Adam Wolfchild, Willa's brother."

"Oh." She studied the hand he offered for a moment, then ordered herself to take it. She could see the points of resemblance now, the high, slashing cheekbones, the eyes. "I didn't realize she had a—That would make us . . ."

"No." Her hand seemed very fragile, and he let it go gently. "You shared a father. Willa and I shared a mother."

"I see." And realizing that she'd given very little thought to the man they'd buried today, she felt ashamed. "Were you close, to him . . . your stepfather?"

"No one was." It was said simply and without bitterness. "You're uncomfortable here." He'd noticed her keeping to the edges of groups of people, shying away from contact as if the casual brush of shoulders might bruise her. Just as he'd noticed the marks of violence on her face that she tried to hide.

"I don't know anyone."

Wounded, Adam thought. He had always been drawn to the wounded. She was lovely, and injured. Dressed neatly in a quiet black suit and heels, she was only an inch or so shorter than his five ten and too thin for her height. Her hair was dark, with a sheen of red, and it fell in soft waves that reminded him of angel wings. He couldn't see her eyes behind the sunglasses, but he wondered about their color, and about what else he would read in them.

She had her father's chin, he noticed, but her mouth was soft and rather small, like a child's. There had been the faint hint of a dimple beside it when she'd tried to smile at him. Her skin was creamy, very pale—a fragile contrast to the marks on it.

She was alone, he thought, and afraid. It might take him some time to soften Willa's heart toward this woman, this sister.

"I have to check on a horse," he began.

"Oh." It surprised her that she was disappointed. She had wanted to be alone. She was better when she was alone. "I won't keep you."

"Would you like to walk down? See some of the stock?"

"The horses? I—" Don't be a coward, she ordered herself. He isn't going to hurt you. "Yes, I'd like that. If I wouldn't be in your way."

"You wouldn't." Knowing she'd shy away, he didn't offer a hand or take her arm, but merely led the way down the stairs and across the rough dirt road.

SEVERAL PEOPLE SAW THEM GO, AND TONGUES WAGGED as tongues do. Lily Mercy was one of Jack's daughters, after all, though, as was pointed out, she hardly had a word to say for herself. Something that had never been Willa's problem—no, indeed. That was a girl who said plenty, whatever and whenever she wanted.

As for the other one—well, that was a different kettle of fish altogether. Snooty, she was, parading around in her fancy suit and looking down her nose. Anybody with eyes could see the way she'd stood at the gravesite, cold as ice. She was a picture, to be sure. Jack had sired fine-looking daughters, and that one, the oldest one, had his eyes. Hard and sharp and blue.

It was obvious she thought she was better than the rest of them with her California polish and her expensive shoes, but there were plenty who remembered her ma had been a Las Vegas showgirl with a big, braying laugh and a bawdy turn of phrase. Those who did remember had already decided they much preferred the mother to the daughter.

Tess Mercy could have cared less. She was here in this godforsaken outback only until the will could be read. She'd

take what was hers, which was less than the old bastard
owed her, and shake the dust off her Ferragamos.

"I'll be back by Monday at the latest."

She carried the phone along as she paced about with
quick, jerky motions, nervous energy searing the air around
her. She'd closed the doors of what she supposed was a den,
hoping to have at least a few moments of privacy. She had
to work hard to ignore the mounted animal heads that pop-
ulated the walls.

"The script's finished." She smiled a little, tunneled her
fingers through the straightedge swing of dark hair that
curved at her jaw. "Damn right it's brilliant, and it'll be in
your hot little hands Monday. Don't hassle me, Ira," she
warned her agent. "I'll get you the script, then you get me
the deal. My cash flow's down to a dribble."

She shifted the phone and pursed her lips as she helped
herself to a snifter of brandy from the decanter. She was
still listening to the promises and pleas of Hollywood when
she saw Lily and Adam stroll by the window.

Interesting, she thought, and sipped. The little mouse and
the Noble Savage.

Tess had done some quick checking before she'd made
the trip to Montana. She knew Adam Wolfchild was the son
of Jack Mercy's third and final wife. That he'd been eight
when his mother had married Mercy. Wolfchild was Blackfoot, or mostly. His mother had been part Indian. The man
had spent twenty-five years on Mercy Ranch and had little
more to show for it than a tiny house and a job tending
horses.

Tess intended to have more.

As for Lily, all Tess had discovered was that she was
divorced, childless, and moved around quite a bit. Probably
because her husband had used her for a punching bag, Tess
thought, and made herself clamp down on a stir of pity. She
couldn't afford emotional attachments here. It was straight
business.

Lily's mother had been a photographer who'd come to
Montana to snap pictures of the real West. She'd snapped
Jack Mercy—for all the good it had done her, Tess thought.

Then there was Willa. Tess's mouth tightened as she thought of Willa. The one who had stayed, the one the old bastard had kept.

Well, she owned the place now, Tess assumed, shrugging her shoulders. And she was welcome to it. No doubt she'd earned it. But Tess Mercy wasn't walking away without a nice chunk of change.

Looking out the window, she could see the plains in the distance, rolling, rolling endlessly, as empty as the moon. With a shudder, she turned her back on the view. Christ, she wanted Rodeo Drive.

"Monday, Ira," she snapped, annoyed with his voice buzzing in her ear. "Your office, twelve sharp. Then you can take me to lunch." With that as a good-bye, she replaced the receiver.

Three days, tops, she promised herself, and toasted an elk head with her brandy. Then she'd get the hell out of Dodge and back to civilization.

"I SHOULDN'T HAVE TO REMIND YOU THAT YOU GOT guests downstairs, Will." Bess Pringle stood with her hands on her bony hips and used the same tone she'd used when Willa was ten.

Willa jerked her jeans on—Bess didn't believe in little niceties like privacy and had barely knocked before striding into the bedroom. Willa responded just as she might have at ten. "Then don't." She sat down to pull on her boots.

"Rude is a four-letter word."

"So's work, but it still has to be done."

"And you've got enough hands around this place to see to it for one blessed day. You're not going off somewhere today, of all days. It ain't fittin'."

What was or wasn't fitting constituted the bulk of Bess's moral and social codes. She was a bird of a woman, all bone and teeth, though she could plow through a mountain of hotcakes like a starving field hand and had the sweet tooth of an eight-year-old. She was fifty-eight—and had changed the date on her birth certificate to prove it—and had a head of flaming red hair she dyed in secret and kept pulled back in a don't-give-me-any-lip bun.

Her voice was as rough as pine bark and her face as smooth as a girl's, and surprisingly pretty with moss-green eyes and a pug Irish nose. Her hands were small and quick and able. And so was her temper.

With her fists still glued to her hips, she marched up to Willa and glared down. "You get your sassy self down those stairs and tend to your guests."

"I've got a ranch to run." Willa rose. It hardly mattered that in her boots she topped Bess by six inches. The balance of power had always tottered back and forth between them. "And they're not my guests. I'm not the one who wanted them here."

"They've come to pay respects. That's fittin'."

"They've come to gawk and prowl around the house. And it's time they left."

"Maybe some of them did." Bess jerked her head in a little nod. "But there's plenty more who are here for you."

"I don't want them." Willa turned away, picked up her hat, then simply stood staring out her window, crushing the brim in her hands. The window faced the mountains, the dark belt of trees, the peaks of the Big Belt that held all the beauty and mystery in the world. "I don't need them. I can't breathe with all these people hovering around."

Bess hesitated before laying a hand on Willa's shoulder. Jack Mercy hadn't wanted his daughter raised soft. No pampering, no spoiling, no cuddling. He'd made that clear while Willa had still been in diapers. So Bess had pampered and spoiled and cuddled only when she was certain she wouldn't be caught and sent away like one of Jack's wives.

"Honey, you got a right to grieve."

"He's dead and he's buried. Feeling sorry won't change it." But she lifted a hand, closed it over the small one on her shoulder. "He didn't even tell me he was sick, Bess. He couldn't even give me those last few weeks to try to take care of him, or to say good-bye."

"He was a proud man," Bess said, but she thought, Bastard. Selfish bastard. "It's better the cancer took him quick rather than letting him linger. He would've hated that and it would've been harder on you."

"One way or the other, it's done." She smoothed the wide, circling brim of her hat, settled it on her head. "I've got animals and people depending on me. The hands need to see, right now, that I'm in charge. That Mercy Ranch is still being run by a Mercy."

"You do what you have to do, then." Years of experience had taught Bess that what was fitting didn't hold much water when it came to ranch business. "But you be back by suppertime. You're going to sit down and eat decent."

"Clear these people out of the house, and I will."

She started out, turning left toward the back stairs. They wound down the east wing of the house and allowed her to slip into the mudroom. Even there she could hear the beehive buzz of conversations from the other rooms, the occasional roll of laughter. Resenting all of it, she slammed out the door, then pulled up short when she saw the two men smoking companionably on the side porch.

Her gaze narrowed on the older man and the bottle of beer dangling from his fingers. "Enjoying yourself, Ham?"

Sarcasm from Willa didn't ruffle Hamilton Dawson. He'd put her up on her first pony, had wrapped her head after her first spill. He'd taught her how to use a rope, shoot a rifle, and dress a deer. Now he merely fit his cigarette into the little hole surrounded by grizzled hair and blew out a smoke ring.

"It's"—another smoke ring formed—"a pretty afternoon."

"I want the fence checked along the northwest boundary."

"Been done," he said placidly, and continued to lean on the rail, a short, stocky man on legs curved like a wishbone. He was ranch foreman and figured he knew what needed to be done as well as Willa did. "Got a crew out making repairs. Sent Brewster and Pickles up the high country. We lost a couple head up there. Looks like cougar." Another drag, another stream of smoke. "Brewster'll take care of it. Likes to shoot things."

"I want to talk to him when he gets back."

"I expect you will." He straightened up from the rail, adjusted his mud-colored dishrag of a hat. "It's weaning time."

"Yes, I know."

He expected she did, and nodded again. "I'll go check on the fence crew. Sorry about your pa, Will."

She knew those simple words tacked onto ranch business were more sincere and personal than the acres of flowers sent by strangers. "I'll ride out later."

He nodded, to her, to the man beside him, then hitched his bowlegged way toward his rig.

"How are you holding up, Will?"

She shrugged a shoulder, frustrated that she didn't know what to do next. "I want it to be tomorrow," she said. "Tomorrow'll be easier, don't you think, Nate?"

Because he didn't want to tell her the answer was no, he tipped back his beer. He was there for her, as a friend, a fellow rancher, a neighbor. He was also there as Jack Mercy's lawyer, and he knew that before too much more time passed he was going to shatter the woman standing beside him.

"Let's take a walk." He set the beer down on the rail, took Willa's arm. "My legs need stretching."

He had a lot of them. Nathan Torrence was a tall one. He'd hit six two at seventeen and had kept growing. Now, at thirty-three, he was six six and lanky with it. Hair the color of wheat straw curled under his hat. His eyes were as blue as the Montana sky in a face handsomely scored by wind and sun. At the end of long arms were big hands. At the end of long legs were big feet. Despite them, he was surprisingly graceful.

He looked like a cowboy, walked like a cowboy. His heart, when it came to matters of his family, his horses, and the poetry of Keats, was as soft as a down pillow. His mind, when it came to matters of law, of justice, of simple right and wrong, was as hard as granite.

He had a deep and long-standing affection for Willa

Mercy. And he hated that he had no choice but to put her through hell.

"I've never lost anybody close to me," Nate began. "I can't say I know how you feel."

Willa kept walking, past the cookhouse, the bunkhouse, by the chicken house where the hens were going broody. "He never let anyone get close to him. I don't know how I feel."

"The ranch..." This was dicey territory, and Nate negotiated carefully. "It's a lot to deal with."

"We've got good people, good stock, good land." It wasn't hard to smile up at Nate. It never was. "Good friends."

"You can call on me anytime, Will. Me or anyone in the county."

"I know that." She looked beyond him, to the paddocks, the corrals, the outbuildings, the houses, and farther, to where the land went into its long, endless roll to the bottom of the sky. "A Mercy has run this place for more than a hundred years. Raised cattle, planted grain, run horses. I know what needs to be done and how to do it. Nothing really changes."

Everything changes, Nate thought. And the world she was speaking of was about to take a sharp turn, thanks to the hard heart of a dead man. It was better to do it now, straight off, before she climbed onto a horse or into a rig and rode off.

"We'd best get to the reading of the will," he decided.

TWO

Jack Mercy's office, on the second floor of the main house, was big as a ballroom. The walls were paneled in yellow pine lumbered from his own land and shellacked to a rich gloss that lent a golden light to the room. Huge windows provided views of the ranch, the land and sky. Jack had been fond of saying he could see all a man needed to see from those windows, which were undraped but ornately trimmed.

On the floor were layered the rugs he'd collected. The chairs were leather, as he'd preferred, in rich shades of teal and maroon.

His trophies hung on the walls—heads of elk and bighorn sheep, of bear and buck. Crouched in one corner as though poised to charge was a massive black grizzly, fangs exposed, glassy black eyes full of rage.

Some of his favored weapons were in a locked display case. His great-grandfather's Henry rifle and Colt Peacemaker, the Browning shotgun that had brought down the bear, the Mossberg 500 he'd called his dove duster, and the .44 Magnum he'd preferred for handgun hunting.

It was a man's room, with male scents of leather and wood and a whiff of tobacco from the Cubans he liked to smoke.

The desk, which he'd had custom-made, was a lake of glossy wood, a maze of drawers all hinged with polished brass. Nate sat behind it now, fiddling with papers to give everyone present time to settle.

Tess thought he looked as out of place as a beer keg at a church social. The cowboy lawyer, she thought with a quick twist of her lips, duded up in his Sunday best. Not that he wasn't appealing in a rough, country sort of fashion. A young Jimmy Stewart, she thought, all arms and legs and quiet sexuality. But big, gangling men who wore boots with their gabardine weren't her style.

And she just wanted to get this whole damn business over with and get back to LA. She rolled her eyes toward the snarling grizzly, the shaggy head of a mountain goat, the weapons that had hunted them down. What a place, she mused. And what people.

Besides the cowboy lawyer, there was the skinny, henna-haired housekeeper, who sat in a straight-backed chair with her knobby knees tight together and modestly covered with a perfectly horrible black skirt. Then the Noble Savage, with his heartbreakingly beautiful face, his enigmatic eyes, and the faint odor of horses that clung to him.

Nervous Lily, Tess thought, continuing her survey, with her hands pressed together like vises and her head lowered, as if that would hide the bruises on her face. Lovely and fragile as a lost bird set down among vultures.

When Tess's heart began to stir, she deliberately turned her attention to Willa.

Cowgirl Mercy, she thought with a sniff. Sullen, probably stupid, and silent. At least the woman looked better in jeans and flannel than she had in that baggy dress she'd worn to the funeral. In fact, Tess decided she made quite a picture, sitting in the big leather chair, her booted foot resting on her knee, her oddly exotic face set like stone.

And since she'd yet to see a single tear squeeze its way

out of the dark eyes, Tess assumed Willa had no more love
for Jack Mercy than she herself did.

Just business, she thought, tapping her fingers impatiently
on the arm of her chair. Let's get down to it.

Even as she had the thought, Nate lifted his eyes, met
hers. For one uncomfortable moment, she felt he knew exactly what was going through her mind. And his disapproval
of her, of everything about her, was as clear as the sky
spread in the window behind him.

Think what you want, she decided, and kept her eyes cool
on his. Just give me the cash.

"There's a couple ways we can do this," Nate began.
"There's formal. I can read Jack's will word for word, then
explain what the hell all that legal talk means. Or I can give
you the meaning, the terms, the options first." Deliberately
he looked at Willa. She was the one who mattered most, to
him. "Up to you."

"Do it the easy way, Nate."

"All right, then. Bess, he left you a thousand dollars for
every year you've been at Mercy. That's thirty-four thousand."

"Thirty-four thousand." Bess's eyes popped wide. "Good
Lord, Nate, what am I supposed to do with a fat lot of money
like that?"

He smiled. "Well, you spend it, Bess. If you want to
invest some, I can give you a hand with it."

"Goodness." Overwhelmed at the thought of it, she
looked at Willa, back at her hands, and at Nate again.
"Goodness."

And Tess thought: If the housekeeper gets thirty grand, I
ought to get double. She knew just what *she*'d do with a fat
lot of money.

"Adam, in accordance with an agreement Jack made with
your mother when they married, you're to receive a lump
sum of twenty thousand, or a two percent interest in Mercy
Ranch, whichever you prefer. I can tell you the percentage
is worth more than the cash, but the decision remains
yours."

"It's not enough." Willa's voice snapped out, making

Lily jump and Tess raise an eyebrow. "It's not right. Two
percent? Adam's worked this ranch since he was eight years
old. He's—"

"Willa." From his position behind her chair, Adam laid
a hand on her shoulder. "It's right enough."

"The hell it is." Fury for him, the injustice of it, had her
shoving the hand away. "We've got one of the finest strings
of horses in the state. That's Adam's doing. The horses
should be his now—and the house where he lives. He
should have been given land, and the money to work it."

"Willa." Patient, Adam put his hand on her again, held
it there. "It's what our mother asked for. It's what he gave."

She subsided because there were strangers' eyes watching. And because she would fix the wrongness of it. She'd
have Nate draw up papers before the end of the day.
"Sorry." She laid her hands calmly on the wide arms of
the chair. "Go on, Nate."

"The ranch and its holdings," Nate began again, "the
stock, the equipment, vehicles, the timber rights . . ." He
paused, and prepared himself for the unhappy job of de-
stroying hopes. "Mercy Ranch business is to continue as
usual, expenses drawn, salaries paid, profits banked or re-
invested with you as operator, Will, under the executor's
supervision for a period of one year."

"Wait." Willa held up a hand. "He wanted you to supervise the running of the ranch for a year?"

"Under certain conditions," Nate added, and his eyes
were already full of apology. "If those conditions are met
for the course of a year, beginning no later than fourteen
days from the reading of the will, the ranch and all its holdings will become the sole property and sole interest of the
beneficiaries."

"What conditions?" Willa demanded. "What beneficiaries? What the hell is going on, Nate?"

"He's left each one of his daughters a one-third interest
in the ranch." He watched the color drain from Willa's face
and, cursing Jack Mercy, continued with the rest. "In order
to inherit, the three of you must live on the ranch, leaving
the property for no longer than a one-week period, for one

full year. At the end of that time, if conditions are met, each beneficiary will have a one-third interest. This interest cannot be sold or transferred to anyone other than one of the other beneficiaries for a period of ten years.''

"Hold on a minute." Tess set her drink aside. "You're saying I've got a third interest in some cattle ranch in Nowhere, Montana, and to collect, I've got to move here? Live here? Give up a year of my life? No way in hell." She rose, gracefully unfolding her long legs. "I don't want your ranch, kid," she told Willa. "You're welcome to every dusty acre and cow. This'll never stick. Give me my share in cash, and I'm out of your way."

"Excuse me, Ms. Mercy." Nate sized her up from his seat behind the desk. Mad as a two-headed hen, he thought, and cool enough to hide it. "It will stick. His terms and wishes were very well thought out, very well presented. If you don't agree to the terms, the ranch will be donated, in its entirety, to the Nature Conservancy."

"Donated?" Staggered, Willa pressed her fingers to her temple. There was hurt and rage and a terrible dread curling and spreading inside her gut. Somehow she had to get beyond the feelings and think.

She understood the ten-year stipulation. That was to keep the land from being tax-assessed at the market price instead of the farm rate. Jack had hated the government like poison and wouldn't have wanted to give up a penny to it. But to threaten to take it all away and give it to the type of organization he liked to call tree huggers or whale kissers didn't make sense.

"If we don't do this," she continued, struggling for calm, "he can just give it away? Just give away what's been Mercy land for more than a century if these two don't do what it says on that paper? If I don't?"

Nate exhaled deeply, hating himself. "I'm sorry, Willa. There was no reasoning with him. This is the way he set it up. Any one of the three of you leaves, it breaks the conditions, and the ranch is forfeited. You'll each get one hundred dollars. That's it."

"A hundred dollars?" The absurdity of it struck Tess

straight in the heart, flopped her back into her chair laughing. "That son of a bitch."

"Shut up." Willa's voice whipped out as she got to her feet. "Just shut the hell up. Can we fight it, Nate? Is there any point in trying to fight it?"

"You want my legal opinion, no. It'd take years and a lot of money, and odds are you'd lose."

"I'll stay." Lily fought to regulate her breathing. Home, safety, security. It was all here, just at her fingertips, like a shiny gift. "I'm sorry." She got to her feet when Willa rounded on her. "It's not fair to you. It's not right. I don't know why he did this, but I'll stay. When the year's over, I'll sell you my share for whatever you say is fair and right. It's a beautiful ranch," she added, trying to smile as Willa only continued to stare at her. "Everyone here knows it's already yours. It's only a year, after all."

"That's very sweet," Tess spoke up. "But I'm damned if I'm staying here for a year. I'm going back to LA in the morning."

With her mind whirling, Willa sent her a considering look. However much she wanted both of them gone, she wanted the ranch more. Much more. "Nate, what happens if one of the three of us dies suddenly?"

"Funny." Tess picked up her brandy again. "Is that Montana humor?"

"In the event one of the beneficiaries dies within the transitory year, the remaining beneficiaries will be granted half shares of Mercy Ranch, under the same conditions."

"So what are you going to do, kill me in my sleep? Bury me on the prairie?" Tess flicked her fingers in dismissal. "You can't threaten me into staying here, living like this."

Maybe not, Willa thought, but money talked to certain types of people. "I don't want you here. I don't want either one of you, but I'll do what has to be done to keep this ranch. Miss Hollywood might be interested to know just how much her dusty acres are worth, Nate."

"At an estimate, current market value for the land and buildings alone, not including stock . . . between eighteen and twenty million."

Brandy slopped toward the rim of the snifter as Tess's hand jerked. "Jesus Christ."

The outburst earned Tess a hiss from Bess and a sneer from Willa. "I thought that would get through," Willa murmured. "When's the last time you earned six million in a year . . . sis?"

"Could I have some water?" Lily managed, and drew Willa's gaze.

"Sit down before you fall down." She gave Lily a careless nudge into a chair as she began to pace. "I'm going to want you to read the document word for word after all, Nate. I want to get this all straight in my head." She went to a lacquered liquor cabinet and did something she'd never done when her father had been alive. She opened his whiskey and drank it.

She drank quietly, letting the slow burn move down her throat as she listened to Nate's recital. And she forced herself not to think of all the years she had struggled so hard to earn her father's love, much less his respect. His trust.

In the end, he had lumped her in with the daughters he'd never known. Because in the end, she thought, none of them had really mattered to him.

A name Nate mumbled had her ears burning. "Hold it. Hold just a damn minute. Did you say Ben McKinnon?"

Nate shifted, cleared his throat. He'd been hoping to slide that one by her, for the time being. She'd had enough shocks for one day. "Your father designated myself and Ben to supervise the running of the ranch during the probationary year."

"That chicken hawk's going to be looking over my shoulder for a goddamn year?"

"Don't you swear in this house, Will," Bess piped up.

"I'll swear the damn house down if I want. Why the hell did he pick McKinnon?"

"Your father considered Three Rocks second only to Mercy. He wanted someone who knows the ins and outs of the business."

McKinnon can be mean as a snake, Nate remembered

Mercy saying. And he won't take any shit off a damn woman.

"Neither of us will be looking over your shoulder," Nate soothed. "We have our own ranches to run. This is just a minor detail."

"Bullshit." But Will reined it in. "Does McKinnon know about this? He wasn't at the funeral."

"He had business in Bozeman. He'll be back tonight or tomorrow. And yes, he knows."

"Had a hell of a laugh over it, didn't he?"

Had nearly choked with laughter, Nate remembered, but now he kept his own eyes sober. "This isn't a joke, Will. It's business, and temporary at that. All you have to do is get through four seasons." His lips curved. "That's what all of us have to do."

"I'll get through it. God knows if these two will." She studied her sisters, shook her head. "What are you trembling about?" she asked Lily. "You're facing millions of dollars, not a firing squad. For Christ's sake, drink this." She thrust the whiskey glass into Lily's hand.

"Stop picking on her." Incensed, instinctively moving to protect Lily, Tess stepped between them.

"I'm not picking on her, and get out of my face."

"I'm going to be in your face for a goddamn year. Get used to it."

"Then you better get used to how things run around here. You stay, you're not going to sit around on your plump little ass, you're going to work."

At the "plump little ass" remark, Tess sucked air through her nose. She'd sweated and starved off every excess pound she'd carried through high school, and she was damn proud of the results. "Remember this, you flat-chested, knock-kneed bitch, I walk, you lose. And if you think I'm going to take orders from some ignorant little pie-faced cowgirl, you're a hell of a lot more stupid than you look."

"You'll do exactly what I say," Willa corrected. "Or instead of having a nice cozy bed in this house you'll be pitching a tent in the hills for the next year."

"I've got as much right to be under this roof as you do.

Maybe more, since he married my mother first.''

"That just makes you older," Will tossed back, and had the pleasure of seeing that nice shaft strike home. "And your mother was a bottle-blonde showgirl with more tits than brains."

Whatever Tess would have done or said in retaliation was broken off when Lily burst into tears.

"Happy now?" Tess demanded, and gave Willa a hard shove.

"Stop." Tired of the sniping, Adam seared them both with a look. "You should both be ashamed of yourselves." He bent down, murmuring to Lily as he helped her to her feet. "You want fresh air," he said kindly. "And some food. You'll feel better then."

"Take her for a little walk," Bess told him, and got creakily to her own feet. Her head was hammering like a three-armed carpenter. "I'll put dinner on. I'm ashamed enough for both of you," she said to Tess and Willa. "I knew both of your mas. They'd expect better of you." She sniffed and, with dignity, turned to Nate. "You're welcome to stay for dinner, Nate. There's more than plenty."

"Thanks, Bess, but . . ." He was getting the hell out while he still had all of his skin. "I've got to get on home." He gathered his papers together, keeping a wary eye on the two women who remained in the room, scowling at each other. "I'm leaving three copies of all the documents. Any questions, you know where to reach me. If I don't hear from you I'll check back in a couple days, and see . . . And see," he ended. He picked up his hat and his briefcase and left the field.

In control again, Willa took a cleansing breath. "I've put sweat and I've put blood into this ranch from the day I was born. You don't give a damn about that, and I don't care. But I'm not losing what's mine. You figure that puts me over a barrel, but I know you're not walking away from more money than you've ever seen before, or hoped to. So that makes us even."

With a nod, Tess sat on the arm of a chair and crossed her silky legs. "So, we define terms of our own for living through the next year. You think it's a snap for me to give up my home, my friends, my life-style for a year. It's not."

Tess gave a quick, sentimental thought to her apartment, her club, Rodeo Drive. Then she set her jaw. "But no, I'm not walking away from what's mine, either."

"Yours, my ass."

Tess merely inclined her head. "Whether either one of us likes it, and I doubt either one of us does, I'm as much his daughter as you are. I didn't grow up here because he tossed me and my mother aside. That's fact, and after being here for a day, I'm beginning to be grateful for it. But I'll stick the year out."

Thoughtfully, Willa picked up the whiskey Lily hadn't touched. Ambition and greed were excellent motivators. She'd stick, all right. "And at the end of it?"

"You can buy me out." The image of all that money made her giddy. "Or failing that, you can send the checks for my share of profits to LA. Which is where I'll be one day after the year is up."

Will sampled the whiskey again and reminded herself to concentrate on now. "Can you ride?"

"Ride what?"

With a snort, Will drank. "Figures. Probably don't know a hen from a cock either."

"Oh, I know a cock when I see one," Tess drawled, and was surprised to hear Willa laugh.

"People live here, they work here. That's another fact. I've got enough to do handling the men and cattle without worrying with you, so you'll take your orders from Bess."

"You expect me to take orders from a housekeeper?"

Steel glittered in Willa's eyes. "You'll take orders from the woman who's going to feed you, tend your clothes, and clean the house where you'll be living. And the first time you treat her like a servant will be the last time. I promise you. You're not in LA now, Hollywood. Out here everybody pulls their weight."

"I happen to have a career."

"Yeah, writing movies." There were probably less useful enterprises, but Willa couldn't think of any. "Well, there're twenty-four hours in a day. You're going to figure that one out fast enough.'' Tired, Will wandered to the window behind the desk. ''What the hell am I going to do with the little lost bird?''

''More like a crushed flower.''

Surprised at the compassion in the tone, Willa glanced back, then shrugged. ''Did she say anything to you about the bruises?''

''I haven't talked to her any more than you have.'' Tess struggled to push away the guilt. Noninvolvement, she reminded herself. ''This isn't exactly a family reunion.''

''She'll tell Adam. Sooner or later everyone tells Adam what hurts. For now at least, we'll leave the wounded Lily to him.''

''Fine. I'm going back to LA in the morning. To pack.''

''One of the men will drive you to the airport.''

Dismissing Tess, Willa turned back to the window. ''Do yourself a favor, Hollywood, and buy some long underwear. You'll need it.''

WILL RODE OUT AT DUSK. THE SUN WAS BLEEDING AS IT fell behind the western peaks, turning the sky to a rich, ripe red. She needed to think, to calm herself. Beneath her, the Appaloosa mare pranced and pulled on the bit.

''Okay, Moon, let's both run it off.'' With a jerk of the reins, Will changed directions, then gave the eager mare her head. They streaked away from the lights, the buildings, the sounds of the ranch and into the open land where the river curved.

They followed its banks, riding east into the night where the first stars were already gleaming and the only sounds were the rush of water and the thunder of hooves. Cattle grazed and nighthawks circled. As they topped a rise, Will could see mile after mile of silhouette and shadow, trees spearing up, the waving grass of a meadow, the endless line of fence. And in the distance in the clear night air the faint glint of lights from a neighboring ranch.

McKinnon land.

The mare tossed her head, snorted, when Will reined in. "We didn't run it out, did we?"

No, the anger was still simmering inside her just as the energy simmered inside her mount. Willa wanted it gone, this tearing, bitter fury and the grief that boiled under it. It wouldn't help her get through the next year. It wouldn't help her get through the next hour, she thought, and squeezed her eyes tight.

Tears would not be shed, she promised herself. Not for Jack Mercy, or his youngest daughter.

She breathed deep, drew in the scent of grass and night and horse. It was control she needed now, calculated, unbending control. She would find a way to handle the two sisters who had been pushed on her, to keep them in line and on the ranch. Whatever it took, she would make certain that they saw this through.

She would find a way to deal with the overseers who had been pushed on her. Nate was an irritant but not a particular problem, she decided as she set Moon into an easy walk. He would do no more and no less than what he considered his legal duty. Which meant, in Willa's opinion, that he would stay out of the day-to-day business of Mercy Ranch and play his part in broad strokes.

She could even find it in her heart to feel sorry for him. She'd known him too long and too well to think even for an instant that he would enjoy the position he'd been put in. Nate was fair, honest, and content to mind his own business.

Ben McKinnon, Will thought, and that bitter anger began to stir again. That was a different matter. She had no doubt that he would enjoy every minute. He'd push his nose in at every opportunity, and she'd have to take it. But, she thought with a grim smile, she wouldn't have to take it well and she wouldn't have to make it easy for him.

Oh, she knew what Jack Mercy had been about, and it made her blood boil. She could feel the heat rise to her skin and all but steam off into the cool night air as she looked down at the lights and silhouettes of Three Rocks Ranch.

McKinnon and Mercy land had marched side by side for

generations. Some years after the Sioux had dealt with Custer, two men who'd hunted the mountains and taken their stake to Texas bought cattle on the cheap and drove them back north into Montana as partners. But the partnership had severed, and each had claimed his own land, his own cattle, and built his own ranch.

So there had been Mercy Ranch and Three Rocks Ranch, each expanding, prospering, struggling, surviving.

And Jack Mercy had lusted after McKinnon land. Land that couldn't be bought or stolen or finessed. But it could be merged, Willa thought now. If Mercy and McKinnon lands were joined, the result would be one of the largest, certainly the most important, ranches in the West.

All he had to do was sell his daughter. What else was a female good for? Willa thought now. Trade her, as you would a nice plump heifer. Put her in front of the bull often enough and nature would handle the rest.

So, since he'd had no son, he was doing the next best thing. He was putting his daughter in front of Ben McKinnon. And everyone would know it, Will thought as she forced her hands to relax on the reins. He hadn't been able to work the deal while he lived, so he was working the angles from the grave.

And if the daughter who had stood beside him her entire life, had worked beside him, had sweated and bled into the land wasn't lure enough—well, he had two more.

"Goddamn you, Pa." With unsteady hands, she settled her hat back onto her head. "The ranch is mine, and it's going to stay mine. Damned if I'll spread my legs for Ben McKinnon or anyone else."

She caught the flash of headlights, murmured to her mare to settle her. She couldn't make out the vehicle, but noted the direction. A thin smile spread as she watched the lights veer toward the main house at Three Rocks.

"Back from Bozeman, is he?" Instinctively she straightened in the saddle, brought her chin up. The air was clear enough that she heard the muffled slam of the truck's door, the yapping greeting of dogs. She wondered if he would look over and up on the rise. He would see the dark shadow of horse and rider. And she thought he would know who was watching from the border of his land.

"We'll see what happens next, McKinnon," she murmured. "We'll see who runs Mercy when it's done."

A coyote sang out, howling at the three-quarter moon that rode the sky. And she smiled again. There were all kinds of coyotes, she thought. No matter how pretty they sang, they were still scavengers.

She wasn't going to let any scavengers on her land.

Turning her mount, she rode home in the half-light.

THREE

"THE SON OF A BITCH." BEN LEANED ON HIS SADDLE horn, shaking his head at Nate. His eyes, shielded by the wide brim of a dark gray hat, glittered cold green. "I'm sorry I missed his funeral. My folks said it was quite the social event."

"It was that." Nate slapped a hand absently against the black gelding's flanks. He'd caught Ben minutes before his friend was taking off for the high country.

In Nate's opinion, Three Rocks was one of the prettiest spreads in Montana. The main house itself was a fine example of both efficiency and aesthetics. It wasn't a palace like Mercy, but an attractive timber-framed dwelling with a sandstone foundation and varying rooflines that added interest, with plenty of porches and decks for sitting and contemplating the hills.

The McKinnons ran a tidy place, busy but without clutter.

He could hear the bovine protests from a corral. Calves being separated from their mamas for weaning didn't go happily. The males'll be unhappier yet, Nate mused, when they're castrated and dehorned.

It was one of the reasons he preferred working horses.

"I know you've got work to see to," Nate continued. "I don't want to hold you up, but I figured I should come by and let you know where we stand."

"Yeah." Ben did have work on his mind. October bumped into November, and that shaky border before winter didn't last long. Right now the sun was shining over Three Rocks like an angel. Horses were cropping in the near pasture, and the men were going about their duties in shirt-sleeves. But drift fences needed to be checked, small grains harvested. The cattle that weren't to be wintered over had to be culled out and shipped.

But his gaze skimmed over paddocks and pastures to the rise, toward Mercy land. He imagined Willa Mercy had more than work on her mind this morning. "Nothing against your lawyering skills, Nate, but that legal bullshit isn't going to hold up, is it?"

"The terms of the will are clear, and very precise."

"It's still lawyer crap."

They'd known each other too long for Nate to take offense. "She can fight it, but it'll be uphill and rough all the way."

Ben looked southwest again, pictured Willa Mercy, shook his head. He sat as comfortably in the saddle as another man would in an easy chair. After thirty years of ranch life, it was more his natural milieu. He didn't have Nate's height, but stood a level six feet, his wiry build ropey with muscle. His hair was a golden brown, gilded by hours in the sun and left long enough to tease the collar of his chambray shirt. His eyes were as sharp as a hawk's and often just as cold in a face that had the weathered, craggy good looks of a man comfortable in the out-of-doors. A horizontal scar marred his chin, a souvenir of his youth and a slip of the hand when he'd been playing mumblety-peg with his brother.

Ben ran his hand over the scar now, an absentminded, habitual gesture. He'd been amused when Nate had first informed him of the will. Now that it was coming into effect, it didn't seem quite so funny.

"How's she taking it?"

"Hard."

"Shit. I'm sorry for that. She loved that old bastard, Christ knows why." He took off his hat, raked his fingers through his hair, adjusted it again. "And it's got to stick in her craw that it's me."

Nate grinned. "Well, yeah, but I think it'd sit about the same with anybody."

No. Ben mused, not quite. He wondered if Willa knew that her father had once offered him ten thousand acres of prime bottomland to marry his daughter. Like some sort of fucking king, Ben thought now, trying to merge kingdoms.

Mercy would give it away, he thought, squinting into the sun. He'd give it away rather than ease his hold on the reins.

"She doesn't need either one of us to run Mercy," Ben said. "But I'll do what it says to do. And hell . . ." His grin spread slow, arrogant, and shifted the planes on his face. "It'll be entertaining to have her butting heads with me every five minutes. What are the other two like?"

"Different." Thoughtful, Nate leaned back on the fender of his Range Rover. "The middle one—that's Lily—she spooks easy. Looks like she'd jump out of her skin if you made a quick move. Her face was all bruised up."

"She have an accident?"

"Looked like she'd accidentally run into somebody's fists. She's got an ex-husband. And she's got a restraining order on him. He's been yanked in a few times for wife battering."

"Fucker." If there was one thing worse than a man who abused his horse, it was a man who abused a woman.

"She jumped on staying," Nate continued, and in his quiet, methodical way began to roll a cigarette. "I have to figure she's looking at it as a good place to hide out. The older one, she's slicker. Hails out of LA, Italian suit, gold watch." He slipped the pouch of Drum back in his pocket, struck a match. "She writes movies and is royally pissed at the idea of being stuck out in the wilderness for a year. But she wants the money it'll bring her. She's on her way back to California to pack up."

"She and Will ought to get along like a couple of she-cats."

"They've already been at each other." Nate blew out smoke contemplatively. "Have to admit, it was entertaining to watch. Adam simmered them down."

"He's about the only one who can simmer Willa down." With a creak of leather, Ben shifted in the saddle. Spook was growing restless under him, signaling his wishes to be off with quick head tosses. "I'll be talking to her. I've got to check on a crew we sent up to the high country. We're getting some storms. Mom's got coffee on at the main house."

"Thanks, but I've got to get back. I've got work of my own. See you in a day or two."

"Yeah." Ben called to his dog, watching as Nate climbed into his Range Rover. "Nate—we're not going to let her lose that ranch."

Nate adjusted his hat, reached for his keys. "No, Ben. We're not going to let her lose it."

It was a good ride across the valley and up into the foothills. Ben took it at an easy pace, scanning the land as he went. The cattle were fat; they'd be cutting out some of the Angus for finishing in feedlots before winter. Others they would rotate from pasture to pasture, hold over for another year.

The choices, and the selling, had been his province for nearly five years, as his parents were gradually turning over the operation of Three Rocks to their sons.

The grass was high and still green, glowing against the paintbrush backdrop of trees. He heard the drone overhead and looked up with a grin. His brother, Zack, was doing a flyover. Ben lifted the hat off his head, waved it. Charlie, the long-haired Border collie, raced in barking circles. The little plane tilted its wings in a salute.

It was still hard for him to think of his baby brother as a husband and a father. But there you were. Zack had taken one look at Shelly Peterson and had fallen spurs over Stetson. Less than two years later, they'd made him an uncle.

And, Ben thought, made him feel incredibly old. It was beginning to feel as though there were thirty rather than three years separating him and Zack.

He adjusted his hat and guided his horse uphill through a stand of yellow pine. The air freshened and cooled. He saw signs of deer, and another time might have given in to the urge to follow the tracks, to bring fresh venison home to his mother. Charlie was sniffing hopefully at the ground, glancing back now and then for permission to flush game. But Ben wasn't in the mood for a hunt.

He could smell snow. He was still far below the snow line, but he could smell it teasing the air. Already he'd seen flocks of Canadian geese heading south. Winter was coming early, and he thought it would come hard. Even the rush of water from the creek spurting downhill sounded cold.

As the trees thickened, the ground roughened, he followed the water. The forest was as familiar to him as his own barnyard. There, the dead larch where he and Zack had once dug for buried treasure. And there, in that little clearing, he had brought down his first buck, with his father standing beside him. They'd fished here, plucking trout from the water as easily as plucking berries from a bush.

On those rocks he'd once written the name of his love in flint. The words had faded and washed away with the years. And pretty Susie Boline had run off to Helena with a guitar player, breaking Ben's eighteen-year-old heart.

The recollection still brought him a tug, though he'd have suffered torments of hell before admitting he was a sentimental man. He rode past the rocks, and the memories, and climbed, keeping to the beaten path through trees as lively with color as women at a Saturday night dance.

As the air thinned and chilled and the scent of snow grew stronger, he whistled between his teeth. His time in Bozeman had been productive, but it had made him yearn for this. The space, the solitude, the land. Though he'd told himself he'd brought a bedroll only as a precaution, he was already planning on camping for a night. Maybe two.

He could shoot himself a rabbit, fry up some fish, maybe hang with the crew for the night. Or camp apart. They'd drive the cattle down to the low country. This much snow in the air could mean an early blizzard, and disaster for a herd grazing in the high mountain meadows. But Ben thought they had time yet.

He paused a moment, just to look out over a pretty ridge-top meadow dotted with cows, bordered by a tumbling river, to enjoy the wave of autumn wildflowers, the call of birds. He wondered how anyone could prefer the choked streets of a city, the buildings crowded with people and problems, to this.

The crack of gunfire made his horse shy and cleared his own mind of dreamy thoughts. Though it was a country where the snap of a bullet usually meant game coming down, his eyes narrowed. At the next shot, he automatically turned his horse in the direction of the sound and kicked him into a trot.

He saw the horse first. Will's Appaloosa was still quivering, her reins looped over a branch. Blood had a high, sweet smell, and scenting it, Ben felt his stomach clutch. Then he saw her, holding the shotgun in her hands not ten feet away from a downed grizzly. A growl in his throat, the dog streaked ahead, coming to a quivering halt at Ben's sharp order.

Ben waited until she'd glanced over her shoulder at him before he slid out of the saddle. Her face was pale, he noted, her eyes dark. "Is he all the way dead?"

"Yeah." She swallowed hard. She hated to kill, hated to see blood spilled. Even seeing a hen plucked for dinner could cause her gorge to rise. "I didn't have any choice. He charged."

Ben merely nodded and, taking his rifle out of its sheath, approached. "Big bastard." He didn't want to think what would have happened if her aim had been off, what a bear that size could have done to a horse and rider. "She-bear," he said, keeping his voice mild. "Probably has cubs around here."

Willa slapped her shotgun back in its holder. "I figured that out for myself."

"Want me to dress her out?"

"I know how to dress game."

Ben merely nodded and went back for his knife. "I'll give you a hand anyway. It's a big bear. Sorry about your father, Willa."

She took out her own knife, the keen-edged Bowie a near mate to Ben's. "You hated him."

"You didn't, so I'm sorry." He went to work on the bear, avoiding the blood and gore when he could, accepting it when he couldn't. "Nate stopped by this morning."

"I bet he did."

Blood steamed in the chilly air. Charlie snacked delicately on entrails and thumped his tail. Ben looked over the carcass of the bear and into her eyes. "You want to be pissed at me, go ahead. I didn't write the damn will, but I'll do what has to be done. First thing is I'm going to ask you what you're doing riding up here alone."

"Same thing as you, I imagine. I've got men up in the high country and cattle that need to come down. I can run my business as well as you can run yours, Ben."

He waited a moment, hoping she'd say more. He'd always been fascinated by her voice. It was rusty, always sounding as though it needed the sleep cleared out of it. More than once Ben had thought it a damn shame that such a contrary woman had that straight sex voice in her.

"Well, we've got a year to find that out, don't we?" When that didn't jiggle a response out of her, he ran his tongue over his teeth. "You going to mount this head?"

"No. Men need trophies they can point to and brag on. I don't."

He grinned then. "We sure do like them. You might make a nice trophy yourself. You're a pretty thing, Willa. I believe that's the first time I've said that to a woman over bear guts."

She recognized his warped way of being charming and refused to be drawn in. Over the last couple of years, refusing to be drawn to Ben McKinnon had taken on the proportions of a second career. "I don't need your help with the bear or the ranch."

"You've got it, on both counts. We can do it peaceable,

or we can do it adversarial.'' He gave Charlie an absent pat when the dog sat down beside him. "Don't matter much to me either way.''

There were shadows under her eyes, he noted. Like smudged fingerprints against the golden skin. And her mouth, which he'd always found particularly appealing, was set in a hard, thin line. He preferred it snarling—and figured he knew how to bring that about.

"Are your sisters as pretty as you?'' When she didn't answer, his lips twitched. "Bet they're friendlier. I'll have to come calling, see for myself. Why don't you invite me to supper, Will, and we can sit ourselves down and discuss plans for the ranch.'' Now her eyes flashed up to his, and he grinned hugely. "Thought that would do it. Christ Almighty, you've got a face, and nothing suits it better than pure orneriness.''

She didn't want him to tell her she was pretty, if that's what he was doing. It always made her insides fumble around. "Why don't you save your breath for getting this carcass up to bleed out?''

Rocking back on his heels, he studied her. "We can get this whole thing over quick. Just get ourselves married and be done with it.''

Though her hand clenched on the bloody knife, she took three slow, easy breaths. Oh, he was riding her, and she knew he'd like nothing better than to watch her scream and shout and stomp her feet. Instead she angled her head, and her voice was as cool as the water in the nearby stream.

"There's about as much chance of that as there is of what's left of this bear rearing up and biting you on the ass.''

He rose as she did, circled her wrist with his fingers, and ignored her quick jolt of protest. "I don't want you any more than you want me. I just thought it would be easy on everybody if we got it out of the way. Life's long, Willa,'' he said more gently. "A year isn't much.''

"Sometimes a day's too much. Let go of me, Ben.'' Her gaze lifted slowly. "A man who hesitates to listen to a woman with a knife in her hand deserves whatever he gets.''

He could have had the knife out of her hand in three seconds flat, but he decided to leave it where it was. "You'd like to stick me, wouldn't you?" The fact that he knew it to be true both aroused and irritated him. But then, she usually managed to do both. "Get it through your head: I don't want what's yours. And I don't plan on being bartered for more land and more cattle any more than you do." She went pale at that, and he nodded. "We know where we stand, Will. Could be I'll find one of your sisters to my taste, but meanwhile, it's just business."

The humiliation of it was as raw as the blood on her hands. "You son of a bitch."

He shifted his grip to her knife hand, just in case. "I love you too, sweetheart. Now, I'll hang the bear. You go wash up."

"I shot it, I can—"

"A woman who hesitates to listen to a man with a knife in his hand deserves what she gets." He smiled again, slow and easy. "Why don't we try to make this business go down smooth for both of us?"

"It can't." All the passion and frustration that whirled inside her echoed in the two words. "You know it can't. How would you take it if you were standing where I am?"

"I'm not," he said simply. "Go wash the blood off. We've got a ways to ride yet today."

He let her go, crouched again, knowing she was standing over him fighting to regain control. He didn't fully relax until she'd stomped off toward the stream with his dog happily at her heels. Blowing out a breath, he looked down at the exposed fangs.

"She'd rather a bite from you than a kind word from me," he muttered. "Goddamn women."

While he finished the gruesome task, he admitted to himself that he'd lied. He did want her. The puzzle of it was, the less he wanted to, the more he did.

It was nearly an hour before she spoke again. They wore sheepskin jackets now against the cold and wind, and the horses were plodding through nearly a foot of snow, with Charlie happily blazing the trail.

"You take half the bear meat. It's only right," Willa said.

"I'm obliged."

"Being obliged is the problem, isn't it? Neither of us wants to be."

He understood her, he thought, better than she might like. "Sometimes you have to swallow what you can't spit out."

"And sometimes you choke." One of the wounds in her heart split open. "He left Adam next to nothing."

Ben studied her profile. "Jack drew a hard line." And Adam Wolfchild wasn't blood, Ben thought. That would have been uppermost in Jack's mind.

"Adam should have more." Will have more, she promised herself.

"I'm not going to disagree with you when it comes to Adam. But if I know anyone who can take care of himself and make his own, it's your brother."

He's all I've got left. She nearly said it before she caught herself, before she remembered it would be a mistake to open any part of her heart to Ben. "How's Zack? I saw his plane this morning."

"Checking fences. I'd have to say he's happy, the way he goes around grinning like a fool day and night. He and Shelly dote on that baby." They all did, Ben thought, but he wasn't going to mention the fact that he couldn't keep his hands off his infant niece.

"She's a pretty baby. It's still hard to see Zack McKinnon settling down to family life."

"Shelly knows when to yank his reins." Unable to resist, Ben grinned at her. "You're not still carrying a torch for my baby brother, are you, Will?"

Amused, she shifted and smiled sweetly. There had been a brief time when they were teenagers that she and Zack had made calf's eyes at each other. "Every time I think of him, my heart goes pitty-pat. Once a woman's been kissed by Zack McKinnon, she's spoiled for anyone else."

"Honey . . ." He reached over, flipped her braid behind her back. "That's because I've never kissed you."

"I'd sooner kiss a two-tailed skunk."

Laughing, he shifted his horse just enough so that his knee bumped Willa's. "Zack'd be the first to tell you, I taught him everything he knows."

"Maybe so, but I think I can live without either one of the McKinnon boys." She jerked a shoulder, then turned her head slightly. "Smoke." There was relief in that, in the sign of people and the near end of her solitary ride with Ben. "The crew's probably in the cabin. It's dinnertime."

With another woman, any other woman, Ben thought, he could have reached over, pulled her close, and kissed her breathless. Just on principle. Since it was Willa, he eased back in the saddle and kept his hands to himself.

"I could eat. I'm going to want to round up the herd, get them down. More snow's coming."

She only grunted. She could smell it. But there was something else in the air. At first she wondered if it was the sensory echo from the bear and the blood on her hands, but it lingered, seemed to grow stronger.

"Something's dead," she murmured.

"What?"

"Something's dead." She straightened in the saddle, scanned the ridges and trees. It was dead quiet, dead still. "Can't you smell it?"

"No." But he didn't doubt she could, and he turned his horse as she did. Already on the scent, Charlie was moving ahead. "It's the Indian in you. One of the hands probably shot dinner."

It made sense. They would have brought provisions, and the cabin was always stocked, but fresh game was hard to resist. Still, that didn't explain the dread in her stomach or the chill along her spine.

There was the scream of an eagle overhead, the wild, soul-stirring echo of it, then the utter silence of the mountains. The sun glittered off the snow, blinding. Following instinct, Willa left the rough path and walked her horse over broken, uneven ground.

"We don't have a lot of time for detours," Ben reminded her.

"Then go on."

He swore, reaching around to check that his rifle was within easy reach. There were bear here, too. And cougar. He thought of camp, hardly more than ten minutes away, and the hot coffee that would be boiling to mud on the stove.

Then he saw it. His nose might not have been as sharp as hers, but his eyes were. Blood was splattered and pooled over the snow, splashed against rock. The black hide of the steer was coated with it. The dog stopped circling the mangled steer and raced back to the horses.

"Well, shit." Ben was already dismounting. "Made a mess of it."

"Wolves?" It was more than the market price to Willa. It was the waste, the cruelty.

He started to agree, then stopped short. A wolf didn't kill, then leave the meat. A wolf didn't hack and slice. No predator but one did.

"A man."

Willa drew a sharp breath as she stepped closer, saw the damage. The throat had been slit, the belly disemboweled. Charlie pressed against her legs, shivering. "It's been butchered. Mutilated."

She crouched, and thought of the bear. No choice there but to kill, and the field dressing had been done efficiently with the tools at hand. But this—this was wild and vicious and without purpose.

"Almost within sight of the cabin," she said. "The blood's frozen. It was probably done hours ago, before sunup."

"It's one of yours," Ben told her after checking the brand.

"Doesn't matter whose." But she noted the number on the yellow ear tag. The death would have to be recorded. She rose and stared over at the stream of smoke rising. "It matters why. Have you lost any cattle this way?"

"No." He straightened to stand beside her. "Have you?"

"Not until now. I can't believe it's one of my men." She took a shallow breath. "Or yours. There must be someone else camping up here."

"Maybe." He was frowning down at the ground. They stood shoulder to shoulder now, linked by the waste at their feet. She didn't jerk away when he ran a hand down her braid, or when he laid that hand companionably on her arm. "We had more snow, a lot of wind. The ground's pretty trampled up, but it looks like some tracks heading north. I'll take some men and check it out."

"It's my cow."

He shifted his eyes to hers. "It doesn't matter whose," he repeated. "We have to get both herds rounded up and down the mountain, and we have to report this. I figure I can count on you for that."

She opened her mouth, closed it again. He was right. She was next to useless at tracking, but she could organize a drive. With a nod, she turned back to her horse. "I'll talk to my men."

"Will." Now he laid a hand over hers, leather against leather, before she could mount. "Watch yourself."

She vaulted into the saddle. "They're my men," she said simply, and rode toward the rising smoke.

SHE FOUND HER MEN ABOUT TO HAVE THEIR MIDDAY MEAL when she came into the cabin. Pickles was at the little stove, sturdy legs spread, ample belly spilling over the wide buckle of his belt. He was barely forty and balding fast, compensating for it with a ginger-colored moustache that grew longer every year. He'd earned his name from his obsessive love of dill pickles, and his personality was just as sour.

When he saw Willa, he grunted in greeting, sniffed, and turned back to the ham he was frying.

Jim Brewster sat with his booted feet on the table, enjoying the last of a Marlboro. He was just into his thirties with a face pretty enough for framing. Two dimples winked in his cheeks, and dark hair waved to his collar. He beamed at Willa and sent her a cocky wink that made his blue eyes twinkle.

"Got us company for dinner, Pickles."

Pickles gave another sour grunt, belched, and flipped his

ham. "Barely enough meat for two as it is. Get your lazy ass up and open some beans."

"Snow's coming." Willa tossed her coat over a hook and headed for the radio.

" 'Nother week easy."

She turned her head, met Pickles's sulky brown eyes. "I don't think so. We'll start rounding up today." She waited, holding his gaze. He hated taking his orders from a female, and they both knew it.

"Your cattle," he muttered, and turned the ham out onto a platter.

"Yes, they are. And one of them's been butchered a quarter mile east of here."

"Butchered?" Jim paused in the act of handing Pickles an open can of beans. "Cougar?"

"Not unless cats are carrying knives these days. Someone opened one up, hacked it to pieces, and left it."

"Bullshit." Eyes narrowed, Pickles took a step forward. "That's just shit, Will. We've lost a couple to cougar. Jim and me tracked a cat just yesterday. She musta circled around and got another cow, that's all."

"I know the difference between claws and a knife." She inclined her head. "Go look for yourself. Dead east, about a quarter mile."

"Damned if I won't." Pickles stomped over for his coat, muttering about women.

"Sure it couldn't have been a cat?" Jim asked the minute the door slammed.

"Yeah, I'm sure. Get me some coffee, would you, Jim? I'm going to radio the ranch. I want Ham to know we're heading down."

"McKinnon's men are up here, but—"

"No." She shook her head, pulled out a chair. "No cowboy I know does that."

She contacted the ranch, listening to static, waiting for it to clear. The coffee and the crackling fire chased the worst of the chill away as she made arrangements for the drive. She was on her second cup when she finished passing the information along to the McKinnon ranch.

Pickles slammed back in. "Son of a bitching bastard."

Accepting this as the only apology she'd get, Willa moved to the stove and filled her plate. "I rode up with Ben McKinnon. He's following some tracks. We're going to help get his herd down with our own. Has either of you seen anyone around here? Campers, hunters, eastern assholes?"

"Came across a campsite yesterday when we were tracking the cat." Jim sat again with his plate. "But it was cold. Two or three days cold."

"Left goddamn beer cans." Pickles ate standing up. "Like it was their own backyard. Oughta be shot for it."

"Sure that cow wasn't shot?" Jim looked to Pickles for confirmation, a fact that Willa struggled not to resent. "You know how some of those city boys are—shoot at anything that moves."

"Wasn't shot. Ain't no tourist done that." Pickles shoved beans into his mouth. "Fucking teenagers what it is. Fucking crazy teenagers all doped up."

"Maybe. If it was, Ben'll find them easy enough." But she didn't think it had been teenagers. It seemed to Willa it took a lot more years to work up that kind of rage.

Jim pushed the barely warm beans around on his plate. "Ah, we heard about how things are." He cleared his throat. "We radioed in last night, and Ham, he figured he should, you know, tell us how things are."

She pushed her plate away and stood. "Then I'll tell you just how things are." Her voice was very cool, very quiet. "Mercy Ranch runs the way it always has. The old man's in the ground, and now I'm operator. You take your orders from me."

Jim exchanged a quick look with Pickles, then scratched his cheek. "I didn't mean to say different, Will. We were just sorta wondering how you were going to keep the others, your sisters, on the ranch."

"They'll take their orders from me too." She jerked her coat off the hook. "Now, if you've finished your meal, let's get saddled up."

"Goddamn women," Pickles muttered as soon as the

door was safely closed behind her. "Don't know one that isn't a bossy bitch."

"That's 'cause you don't know enough women." Jim strolled over for his coat. "And that one *is* the boss."

"For the time being."

"She's the boss today." Jim shrugged into his coat, pulled out his gloves. "And today's what we've got."

FOUR

IN DEALINGS WITH HER MOTHER — AND TESS ALWAYS thought of contacts with Louella as dealings — Tess prepped herself with a dose of extra-strength Excedrin. There would be a headache, she knew, so why chase the pain?

She chose mid-morning, knowing it was the only time of day she would be likely to find Louella at home in her Bel Air condo. By noon she would be out and about, having her hair done, or her nails, indulging in a facial or a shopping spree.

By four, Louella would be at her club, Louella's, joking with the bartender or regaling the waitresses with tales of her life and loves as a Vegas showgirl.

Tess did her very best to avoid Louella's. Though the condo didn't make her much happier.

It was a lovely little stucco in California Spanish with a tiled roof, graceful shrubbery. It could, and should, have been a small showplace. But as Tess had said on more than one occasion, Louella Mercy could make Buckingham Palace tacky.

When she arrived, promptly at eleven, she tried to ignore

what Louella cheerfully called her lawn art. The lawn jockey with the big, stupid grin, the rearing plaster lions, the glowing blue moonball on its concrete pedestal, and the fountain of the serene-faced girl pouring water from the mouth of a rather startled-looking carp.

Flowers grew in profusion, in wild, clashing colors that seared the eyes. There was no rhyme or reason to the arrangement, no plot or plan. Whatever plants caught Louella's eye had been plunked down wherever Louella's whim had dictated. And, Tess mused, she had a lot of whims.

Standing amid a bed of scarlet and orange impatiens was the newest addition, the headless torso of the goddess Nike. Tess shook her head and rang the bell that played the first bump-and-grind bars of "The Stripper."

Louella opened the door herself and enfolded her daughter in draping silks, heavy perfume, and the candy scent of discount cosmetics. Louella never stepped beyond her own bedroom door in less than full makeup.

She was a tall woman, lushly built, with mile-long legs that still could—and did—execute a high kick. The natural color of her hair had been forgotten long ago. It had been blond for years, as brassy a tone as Louella's huge laugh, and worn big, in a teased and lacquered style admired by TV evangelists. She had a striking face despite the troweled-on layers of base and powder and blush, with strong bones and full lips, slicked now with high-gloss red. Her eyes were baby blue, as was the shadow that decorated their lids, with the brows above them mercilessly plucked and stenciled into dark, thin brackets.

As always, Tess was struck with conflicting waves of love and puzzlement. "Mom." Her lips curved as she returned the embrace, and her eyes rolled as the two yapping Pomeranians her mother adored set up an ear-piercing din in their excitement at having company.

"Back from the Wild West, are you?" Louella's East Texas twang had the resonance of plucked banjo strings. She kissed Tess on the cheek, then rubbed away the smear of lipstick with a spit-dampened finger. "Well, come tell

me all about it. They sent the old bastard off in proper style,
I hope.''

''It was . . . interesting.''

''I'll bet. Let's have us some coffee, honey. It's Carmine's morning off, so we'll have to fend for ourselves.''

''I'll make it.'' She preferred brewing the coffee herself
to facing her mother's studly houseboy. Tess tried not to
imagine what other services the man provided Louella.

She moved through the living area, decorated in scarlets
and golds, into a kitchen so white it was like being snow-
blinded. As usual, there wasn't a crumb out of place. Whatever else Carmine did during his daily duties, he was tidy
as a nun.

''Got some coffee cake around here, too. I'm hungry as
a bear.'' With her dogs scrambling around her feet, Louella
rummaged in cupboards, through the refrigerator. Within
minutes there was chaos.

Tess's lips twitched again. Chaos followed her mother
around as faithfully as the yapping Mimi and Maurice did.

''You meet your kin out there?''

''If you mean the half sisters, yes.'' With trepidation,
Tess eyed the coffee cake her mother had unearthed. Louella
was slicing it into huge slabs with a steak knife. Being transferred to a plate decorated with gargantuan roses were ap-
proximately ten billion calories.

''Well, what are they like?'' With the same generous
hand, Louella cut a piece for her dogs, setting the china plate
on the floor. The dogs bolted cake and snarled at each other.

''The one from wife number two is quiet, nervous.''

''That's the one with the ex who likes to use his fists.''
Clucking her tongue, Louella slid her ample hips onto the
counter stool. ''Poor thing. One of my girls had that kind
of trouble. Husband would as soon beat the shit out of her
as wink. We finally got her into a shelter. She's living up
in Seattle now. Sends me a card now and again.''

Tess made a small sound of interest. Her mother's girls
were anyone who worked for her, from the waitresses to the
bartenders, the strippers to the kitchen help. Louella embraced them all, lending money, giving advice. Tess had

always thought Louella's was part club, part halfway house for topless dancers.

"How about the other one?" Louella asked as she attacked her coffee cake. "The one that's part Indian."

"Oh, that one's a real cowgirl. Tough as leather, striding around in dirty boots. I imagine she can punch cattle, literally." Amused at the thought, Tess poured out coffee. "She didn't trouble to hide the fact that she didn't want either of us there." With a shrug, she sat down and began to pick at her cake. "She's got a half brother."

"Yeah, I knew about that. I knew Mary Wolfchild—at least I'd seen her around. She was one beautiful woman, and that little boy of hers, sweet face. Angel face."

"He's grown up now, and he's still got the angel face. He lives on the ranch, works with horses or something."

"His father was a wrangler, as I recall." Louella reached in the pocket of her scarlet robe, found a pack of Virginia Slims. "How about Bess?" She let out smoke and a big, lusty laugh. "Christ, that was a woman. Had to watch my p's and q's around her. Had to admire her—she ran that house like a top and didn't take any crap off Jack either."

"She's still running the house, as far as I could tell."

"Hell of a house. Hell of a ranch." Louella's bright-red lips curved at the memory. "Hell of a country. Though I can't say I'm sorry I only spent one winter there. Goddamn snow up to your armpits."

"Why did you marry him?" When Louella arched a brow, Tess shifted uncomfortably. "I know I never asked before, but I'm asking now. I'd like to know why."

"It's a simple question with a simple answer." Louella poured an avalanche of sugar into her coffee. "He was the sexiest son of a bitch I'd ever seen. Those eyes of his, the way they could look right through you. The way he'd cock his head and smile like he knew just what he'd be up to later and wanted to take you along."

She remembered it all perfectly. The smells of sweat and whiskey, the lights dazzling her eyes. And the way Jack Mercy had swaggered into the nightclub when she'd been onstage in little more than feathers and a twenty-pound headdress.

The way he'd puffed on a big cigar and watched her.

Somehow she'd expected that he'd be waiting for her after the last show. And she'd gone with him without a thought, from casino to casino, drinking, gambling, wearing his Stetson perched on her head.

Within forty-eight hours, she'd stood with him in one of those assembly-line chapels with canned music and plastic flowers. And she'd had a gold ring on her finger.

It was hardly a surprise that the ring had stayed put for less than two years.

"Trouble was, we didn't know each other. It was hot pants and gambling fever." Philosophically, Louella crushed out her cigarette on her empty plate. "I wasn't cut out for life on a goddamn cattle ranch in Montana. Maybe I could've made a go of it—who knows? I loved him."

Tess swallowed cake before it stuck in her throat. "You loved him?"

"For a while I did." With the ease of years and distance, Louella shrugged. "A woman couldn't love Jack for long unless she was missing brain cells. But for a while, I loved him. And I got you out of it. And a hundred large. I wouldn't have my girl, and I wouldn't have my club if Jack Mercy hadn't walked in that night and taken a shine to me. So I owe him."

"You owe the man who kicked you, and his own daughter, out of his life? Cut you off with a lousy hundred thousand dollars?"

"A hundred K went a lot farther thirty years ago than it does today." Louella had learned to be a mother and a businesswoman from the ground up. She was proud of both. "And from where I'm sitting, I got a pretty good deal."

"Mercy Ranch is worth twenty million. Do you still think you got a good deal?"

Louella pursed her lips. "It was his ranch, honey. I just visited there for a while."

"Long enough to make a baby and get the boot."

"I wanted the baby."

"Mom." Most of Tess's anger faded at the words, but the injustice of it remained hot in her heart. "You had a right to more. I had a right to more."

"Maybe, maybe not, but that was the deal at the time." Louella lit another cigarette, decided to be late for her afternoon session at the beauty parlor. There was more here, she thought. "Time goes on. Jack ended up making three daughters, and now he's dead. You want to tell me what he left you?"

"A problem." Tess took the cigarette from Louella's hand and indulged in a quick drag. Smoking was a habit she didn't approve of—what sensible person did? But it was either that or the several million calories still on her plate. "I get a third of the ranch."

"A third of the—Good Jesus and little fishes, Tess, honey, that's a fortune." Louella bounced up. She might have been five ten and a generous one-fifty, but she'd been trained as a dancer and could move when she had to. She moved now, skimming around the counter to crush her daughter's ribs in an enthusiastic hug. "What are we doing sitting here drinking coffee? We need ourselves some French champagne. Carmine's got some stashed somewhere."

"Wait. Mom, wait." As Louella tore into the fridge again, Tess tugged on her robe. "It's not that simple."

"My daughter the millionaire. The cattle baron." Louella popped the cork, spewing champagne. "Fucking A."

"I have to live there for a year." Tess blew out a breath as Louella cheerfully clamped her mouth over the lip of the bottle and sucked up bubbles. "All three of us have to live there for a year, together. Or we don't get zip."

Louella licked champagne from her lips. "You have to live in Montana for a year? On the ranch?" Her voice began to shake. "With the cows? You, with the cows."

"That's the deal. Me, and the other two. Together."

One hand still holding the bottle, the other braced on the counter, Louella began to laugh. She laughed so hard, so long that tears streamed down her face, running with Maybelline mascara and L'Oréal ivory base.

"Jesus H. Christ, the son of a bitch always could make me laugh."

"I'm glad you think it's so funny." Tess's voice cracked like ice. "You can chuckle over it nightly while I'm out in bumfuck watching the grass grow."

With a flourish, Louella poured champagne into the coffee cups. "Honey, you can always spit in his eye and go on just as you are."

"And give up several million in assets? I don't think so."

"No." Louella sobered as she studied her daughter, this mystery she had somehow given birth to. So pretty, she mused, so cool, so sure of herself. "No, you wouldn't. You're too much your father's daughter for that. You'll do the time, Tess."

And she wondered if her daughter would get more out of it than a third interest in a cattle ranch. Would the year soften the edges, Louella wondered, or hone them?

She lifted both cups, handed one to Tess. "When do you leave?"

"First thing in the morning." She sighed loud and long. "I've got to go buy some goddamn boots," she muttered, then with a small smile toasted herself. "What the hell. It's only a year."

W HILE TESS WAS DRINKING CHAMPAGNE IN HER mother's kitchen, Lily was standing at the edge of a pasture, watching horses graze. She'd never seen anything more beautiful than the way the wind blew through their manes, the way the mountains rose behind, all blue and white.

For the first time in months, she had slept through the night, without pills, without nightmares, lulled by the quiet.

It was quiet now. She could hear the grind of machinery in the distance. Just a hum in the air. She'd heard Willa talking to someone that morning about harvesting grain, but she had wanted to stay out of the way. She could be alone here with the horses, bothering no one, with no one bothering her.

For three days she'd been left to her own devices. No one said anything when she wandered the house, or went out to explore the ranch. The men would tip their hats to her if they passed by, and she imagined there were comments and murmurings. But she didn't care about that.

The air here was sweet to the taste. Wherever she stood, it seemed, she could see something beautiful—water rushing over rocks in a stream, the flash of a bird in the forest, deer bounding across the road.

She thought a year of this would be paradise.

Adam stood for a moment, the bucket in his hand, watching her. She came out here every day, he knew. He'd seen her wander away from the house, the barn, the paddocks, and head for this pasture. She would stand by the fence, very still, very quiet.

Very alone.

He'd waited, believing she needed to be alone. Healing was often a solitary matter. But he also believed she needed a friend. So now he walked toward her, careful to make enough noise so that she wouldn't be startled. When she turned, her smile came slow and hesitant, but it came.

"I'm sorry. I'm not in the way here, am I?"

"You're not in anyone's way."

Because she was already learning to be relaxed around him, she shifted her gaze back to the horses. "I love looking at them."

"You can have a closer look." He didn't need the bucket of grain to lure any of the horses to the fence. Any of them would come for him at a quiet call. He handed the bucket to Lily. "Just give it a shake."

She did, then watched, delighted, as several pairs of ears perked up. Horses trotted over to crowd at the fence. Without thinking, she dipped a hand into the grain and fed a pretty buckskin mare.

"You've been around horses before."

At Adam's comment, she pulled her hand back. "I'm sorry. I should have asked before I fed her."

"It's all right." He was sorry to have startled that smile away from her face. That quick light that had come into eyes that were somewhere between gray and blue. Like lake water, he thought, caught in the shadows of sunset. "Come along, Molly."

At her name, the roan mare pranced along the fence toward the gate. Adam led her into a corral and slipped a bridle over her head.

Self-conscious again, Lily wiped grain dust on her jeans, took one hesitant step closer. "Her name's Molly?"

"Yes." He kept his eyes on the horse, giving Lily a chance to settle again.

"She's pretty."

"She's a good saddle horse. Kind. Her gait's a bit rough, but she tries. Don't you, girl? Can you ride Western, Lily?"

"I—what?"

"You probably learned on English." Keeping it light, Adam spread the blanket he'd brought along over Molly's back. "Nate keeps some English tack if you'd rather. We can borrow a saddle from him."

Her hands reached for each other, as they did when her nerves jittered. "I don't understand."

"You want to ride, don't you?" He slid one of Willa's old saddles onto Molly's back. "I thought we'd go up in the hills a little way. Might see some elk."

She found herself caught between yearning and fear. "I haven't ridden in—It's been a long time."

"You don't forget how." Adam estimated the length of her legs and adjusted the stirrups accordingly. "You can go alone once you know your way around." He turned then, noting the way she kept glancing back toward the ranch house. As if gauging the distance. "You don't have to be afraid of me."

She believed him. That was what she was afraid of—that it was so easy to believe him. How often had she believed Jesse?

But that was done, she reminded herself. That was over. Her life could begin again, if she'd let it.

"I'd like to go, for a little while, if you're sure it's all right."

"Why wouldn't it be?" He moved toward her, stopping instinctively before she shied again. "You don't have to worry about Willa. She has a good heart, and a generous one. It's just hurting right now."

"I know she's upset. She has every right to be." Unable to resist, Lily lifted a hand to stroke Molly's cheek. "Even more upset since they found that poor cow. I don't understand who would do something like that. She's so angry. And she's so busy. She's always got something to do, and I'm, well, I'm just here."

"Do you want something to do?"

With the horse between them, it was easy to smile. "Not if it involves castrating cows. I could hear them this morning." She shuddered, then managed to laugh at herself. "I got out of the house before Bess could make me eat breakfast. I don't think I'd have held it down for long."

"It's just one of the things you get used to."

"I don't think so." Lily exhaled, barely noticing how close her hand was to Adam's on the mare's head. "Willa's natural with all of it. She's so sure and confident. I envy that, that knowing just who you are. To her I'm just a nuisance, which is why I haven't been able to work up the courage to talk to her, to ask if there's something I could do around here to help."

"You don't have to be afraid of her, either." He brushed his fingertips against hers, continuing to stroke the mare even when Lily's hand slid out of reach. "But meanwhile, you could ask me. I can use some help. With the horses," he added, when she only stared at him.

"You want me to help you with the horses?"

"It's a lot of work, more when winter gets here." Knowing he'd planted the seed, he stepped back. "Think about it." Then he cupped his hands, smiled again. "I'll give you a leg up. You can walk her around the corral, get acquainted, while I saddle up."

Her throat was closed so that she had to swallow hard to clear it. "You don't even know me."

"I figure we'll get acquainted too." He stood as he was, hands linked in a cup, his eyes patient on hers. "You just have to put your foot in my hands, Lily, not your life."

Feeling foolish, she grabbed the saddle horn and let him

boost her into the saddle. She looked down at him, her eyes solemn in her battered face. "Adam, my life is a mess."

He only nodded as he checked her stirrups. "You'll have to start tidying it up." He rested a hand on her ankle a moment, wanting her to grow easy to his touch. "But today, you just have to take a ride into the hills."

THE LITTLE BITCH, LETTING THAT HALF-BREED PAW HER. Sniveling little whore thought she could get rid of Jesse Cooke, figured she could run and he wouldn't catch her. Put the cops on his ass. She was going to pay for that.

Jesse stared through the field glasses while little bubbles of fury burst in his blood. He wondered if the half-breed horse wrangler had already gotten Lily on her back. Well, the bastard would pay too. Lily was Jesse Cooke's wife, and he was going to be reminding her of that soon enough.

Stupid little cunt thought she was real clever hightailing it to Montana. But the day Jesse Cooke couldn't outwit a woman was the day the sun didn't rise in the east.

He'd known she wouldn't make a move without contacting her dear old mama. So he'd just camped himself within sight of the pretty house in Virginia. And every morning he'd gotten to the mail and checked through it for a letter from Lily.

Persistence had paid off. The letter had come, as he'd known it would. He'd taken it back to the motel room, steamed it open. Oh, Jesse Cooke was nobody's fool. He'd read it, seen where she was going, what she was up to.

Going to cash in on an inheritance, he thought bitterly. And cut her own husband out of his share of the pie. Not in this lifetime, Jesse mused.

The minute the letter had been resealed and put back in the box, he'd headed for Montana. And had gotten there, he thought now, two full days before his idiot wife. Long enough for a man as smart as Jesse Cooke to get the lay of the land and get himself a job on Three Rocks.

A miserable fucking job, he thought now, keeping machines in repair. Well, he knew his way around engines, and there was always a rig that needed fine-tuning. When he wasn't doing that, they had him out checking fences day and night.

But that came in handy, damn handy, like now. A man out riding in a four-wheel to check fences could take a little detour and check out what else was going on.

And he saw plenty.

Jesse rubbed his fingers over the moustache he'd grown and dyed like his hair, medium brown. Just a precaution, he thought, just a temporary disguise, in case Lily blabbed about him. If she did, they'd have their eye out for a clean-shaven man with blond hair. He had let his hair grow too and would keep on letting it grow. Like a fucking pansy, he thought, resenting the necessity of giving up his severe Marine Corps crew cut.

It would all be worth it in the end. When he had Lily back, when he reminded her who was boss. Who was in charge.

Until that happy day he would stay close. And he would watch.

"You have a good time, bitch," Jesse muttered, his eyes narrowing behind the high-powered lenses as Lily walked her mount beside Adam's. "Payback time's coming."

MOST OF THE DAY HAD DIED OUT OF THE SKY BY THE time Willa got back to the ranch house. Dehorning and cas-trating cattle was a messy, miserable job, and a tedious one. She knew she was pushing herself, and knew she would continue to push. She wanted the men to see her at every angle, at every job. Shifting operators under the best of cir-cumstances could be a rough transition. And these were far from the best of circumstances.

Which is why she'd been on hand when a herd of elk had trampled through a fence, creating havoc. And why she'd personally headed the crew to chase them off again, to repair the fence.

Now with the work done for the day and the hands set-tling down for supper and cards in the bunkhouse, she wanted nothing more than a hot bath and a hot meal. She was halfway up the steps to get the first when the knock sounded on the door. Knowing that Bess was likely in the kitchen, Willa stomped back down to answer.

She greeted Ben with a scowl. "What do you want?"

"A cold beer would go down good."

"This isn't a saloon." But she swung away from the door and into the living room to the cold box behind the bar. "Make it fast, Ben. I haven't had my supper."

"Neither have I." He took the bottle she handed him. "But I don't expect I'm going to get an invitation."

"I'm not in the mood for company."

"I've never known you to be in the mood for company." He tipped back the beer and drank deep. "I haven't seen you since we were up in the high country. Thought I should let you know I didn't find anything. Trail died out on me. I'd have to say whoever was up there knew his way around tracking."

She took a beer for herself, and since her feet were aching, dropped down beside Ben on the sofa. "Pickles thinks it was kids. Doped up and crazy."

"And you?"

"I didn't." She moved a shoulder. "Now that sounds like the best explanation."

"Maybe. There's not much use going back up. We've got the cattle down. Is your sister back from LA?"

Willa stopped rolling her head to loosen her shoulders and frowned at him. "You're awfully interested in Mercy business, McKinnon."

"That's part of my job now." He liked reminding her of it, just as he liked looking at her, with her hair falling out of her braid and her boots propped beside his. "Have you heard from her?"

"She'll be here tomorrow, so if that concludes your prying into my business, you can—"

"Going to introduce me?" To please himself he reached out to toy with her hair. "Maybe I'll take a shine to her and keep her occupied and out of your way for a while."

She knocked his hand aside, but he only brought it back. "Do women always fall at your feet?"

"All but you, darling. And that's just because I haven't

found the right way to tip your balance." He skimmed a fingertip down her cheek, watched her eyes narrow. "But I'm working on it. What about the other one?"

"The other what?" Willa wanted to shift over a couple of inches, but she knew it would make her look like a fool.

"The other sister."

"She's around. Somewhere."

He smiled, slowly. "I'm making you nervous. Isn't that interesting?"

"Your ego needs pruning again." But she started to rise. He stopped her with a hand on her shoulder.

"Well, well," he murmured, feeling her vibrate under his hand. "It looks like I haven't been paying close enough attention. Come here."

She concentrated on evening her breathing, slowly changed her grip on the beer she held. Oh, he looks so arrogant, she thought. So cocky. So sure I'll melt if he bothers to push the right button.

"You want me to come there," she purred, watching his eyes widen slightly in surprise at the warm tone. "And what'll happen if I do?"

He might have called himself a fool—if there'd been any blood left in his head to allow him to think. But all he could do at that moment was feel the gradual simmer of lust set off by that husky voice.

"I'd say it's long past time we found out." He curled his fingers into her shirt, tightened his grip, and pulled her against him. If his gaze hadn't drifted down from hers to lock onto her mouth, he would have seen it coming. Instead he found himself an inch away from that mouth and soaked from the beer she dumped over his head.

"You're such a jerk, Ben." Pleased with herself, she leaned forward to set the empty bottle on the table. "You think I could live on a ranch surrounded by randy men all my life and not see a move like that a mile off?"

Slowly, he dragged a hand through his wet hair. "Guess not. But then again—"

He moved fast. When she found herself trapped under him, Willa thought, even a snake rattles before he strikes.

Now she could only be disgusted with herself for being pressed into the couch by a wiry male with blood in his eye.

"You didn't see that coming." He handcuffed her wrists, hauled her arms over her head. Her face was flushed, but he didn't think it was only temper. Temper didn't make her tremble, didn't put that sudden female awareness in her eyes. "Are you afraid to let me kiss you, Willa? Afraid you'll like it?"

Her heart was beating too fast, felt as though it would shatter through her ribs. Her lips were tingling, as if the nerves centered there were revving up for action. "If I want your mouth on me, I'll tell you."

He only smiled, leaned down closer to her face. "Why don't you tell me you don't? Go ahead, tell me." His voice thickened as he nipped lightly at her jaw. "Tell me you don't want me to taste you. Just once."

She couldn't. It would have been a lie, but lying didn't worry her. She simply couldn't get a word through her dry throat. So she took the other option, and brought her knee up, fast and hard.

She had the pleasure of seeing him go dead pale before he collapsed on her.

"Get off me. Get off, you goddamn idiot. You're crushing my lungs." Desperate for air, she arched, bucked, making him moan. She managed to gasp in a breath before she grabbed a handful of his hair and yanked.

They rolled off the couch and crashed to the floor. She saw stars as her elbow hit the edge of the table. It was pain and fury that had her tearing into him. Something shattered on the floor as they wrestled over it, grunting and cursing.

He was trying to defend himself, but she was obviously out for blood. And proved it by biting his arm just under the shoulder. Yelping, certain that she was going to take a chunk out of him, he managed to get a grip on her jaw and squeeze. Under the pressure the tear of her teeth loosened.

They rolled, boots clattering and digging for purchase, elbows jabbing, hands grappling. Willa didn't realize she was laughing until he had her pinned. She kept right on laughing, helpless even to stop for breath as he stared down at her.

"You think it's funny?" He had to squint, then huff out a breath to get the hair out of his eyes. But all in all, he was grateful she hadn't managed to tear it out of his head by the handful. "You bit me."

"I know." Her voice hitched as she ran a tongue over her teeth. "I think I've got some of your shirt in my mouth. Turn me loose, Ben."

"So you can bite me again, or try to kick my balls into my throat?" Since they were still aching—more than a little—he narrowed his eyes, sneered. "You fight like a girl."

"So what? It works."

His mood was shifting again. He could feel that hot, slick transition from temper to lust, from insult to interest. The way they'd ended up, her breasts were pressed nicely against his chest, and her legs were spread with his snugged between them.

"Yeah, it does. You being female seems to suit the situation."

She saw the change in his eyes, teetered between panic and longing. "Don't." His mouth was barely an inch from hers now, and her breath was gone again.

"Why not? It's not going to hurt anybody."

"I don't want your mouth on me."

He lifted a brow, and he smiled. "Liar."

And she shuddered. "Yeah."

His mouth was only a whisper from hers when she heard the first piercing screams.

FIVE

BEN ROLLED, GAINED HIS FEET. THIS TIME, AS WILLA RAN behind him she could admire the speed with which he could move. The screams were still echoing when he wrenched open the front door.

"Christ." He muttered it even as he stepped over the bloody mess on the porch and gathered Lily in his arms. "It's all right, honey." Automatically he shifted so that he blocked her view and, with his hands stroking easy down her back, looked over her head into Willa's eyes.

The shock was there, but it wasn't the quaking, glassy-eyed horror of the woman he held. This one was fragile, he thought, whereas Willa would always be sturdy.

"You ought to get her inside," he said to Willa.

But Willa was shaking her head, staring down now at the mangled and bloody mess at her feet. "Must be one of the barn cats." Or it had been, she thought grimly, before someone had decapitated it and cut its guts open and left it like a gory gift at her front door.

"Take her inside, Will," Ben repeated.

The screams had brought others running. Adam was the

first to reach the porch. The first thing he saw was Lily weeping in Ben's arms. The quick hitch in his gut had almost as much to do with that as what he saw spread on the porch.

Instinctively he stepped up, laid a hand on her arm, soothing when she jerked. "It's all right, Lily."

"Adam, I saw . . ." Nausea churned a storm in her stomach.

"I know. You go on inside now. Look at me," he murmured, carefully easing her away from Ben and leading her around and toward the door. "Willa's going to take you inside."

"Look, I've got—"

"Take care of your sister, Will," Adam interrupted, and taking her hand, placed it firmly over Lily's.

Willa lost the battle when Lily's hand trembled under hers. With a mumbled oath she tugged. "Come on. You need to sit down."

"I saw—"

"Yeah, I know what you saw. Forget it." Willa closed the door with a decisive click, leaving the men to ponder the headless corpse on the porch.

"Christ, Adam, is that a cat?" Jim Brewster swiped a hand over his mouth. "Somebody sure did a number on it."

Adam glanced back, studying each man in turn: Jim, face pale, Adam's apple bobbing; Ham tight-lipped; Pickles with a rifle over his shoulder. There was Billy Vincent, barely eighteen and all eager eyes, and Wood Book, stroking his silky black beard.

It was Wood who spoke, his voice calm. "Where's the head? Don't see it there." He stepped closer. It was Wood who oversaw the planting, tending, and harvesting of grain, and his wife, Nell, who cooked for the ranch hands. He smelled of Old Spice and peppermint candy. Adam knew him to be a steady man, as implacable as the Rock of Gibraltar.

"Whoever did this might like trophies." Adam's words stopped the murmurs. Only Billy continued to babble.

"Jee-sus Christ, you ever seen anything like that? Spread

the guts all over hell and back, didn't he? Now who'd do that to some stupid cat? What do you think—"

"Shut the hell up, Billy, you asshole." The weary order came from Ham. He sighed once, took out his pack of smokes. "Get on back to supper, all of you. Nothing for you to do here now but gawk like a bunch of old ladies at a fashion show."

"Don't have much appetite," Jim murmured, but he and the others drifted back.

"Sure is a sorry mess," Ham commented. "Guess a kid might do this. Wood's boys are a little wild, but they're not mean. You ask me, it takes mean to do this. But I'll talk to them."

"Ham, mind if I ask if you know what the men have been up to for the past hour?"

Ham studied Ben through a haze of smoke. "Been here and there, washing up for supper and the like. I haven't had my eye on them, if that's what you're asking. The men that work here don't go cutting up a cat for frolic."

Ben merely nodded. It wasn't his place to ask more, and they both knew it. "It had to have happened in the last hour. I've been here awhile, and this wasn't here before."

Ham sucked in more smoke, nodded. "I'll talk to Wood's boys." He gave one last look at what lay on the porch. "Sure is a sorry mess," he repeated, then walked away.

"You've had two animals torn up in a week, Adam."

Adam crouched down, laid his fingertip on the bloody fur. "His name was Mike. He was old, mostly blind in one eye, and should have died in his sleep."

"I'm sorry about that." Ben understood the affection, even the intimacy, with animals well and dropped a hand on Adam's shoulder. "I think you've got a real problem here."

"Yeah. Wood's boys didn't do this. They've got no harm in them. And they weren't up in the hills slaughtering a steer either."

"No, I wouldn't say they were. How well do you know your men?"

Adam lifted his gaze. Whatever the grief, it was hard,

direct. "The men aren't my territory. The horses are." Still warm, he thought as he stroked the matted fur. Cooling fast, but still warm. "I know them well enough. All but Billy have been here for years, and he signed on last summer. You'd have to ask Willa, she'd know more." He looked down again and grieved for an old half-blind tom who had still liked to hunt. "Lily shouldn't have seen this."

"No, she shouldn't have." Ben sighed and wondered how close she'd come to seeing who it was. "I'll help you bury him."

Inside, Willa paced the living room. How the hell was she supposed to take care of the woman? And why had Adam pushed such a useless task on her? All Lily did was cower in the corner of the sofa and shake.

She'd given Lily whiskey, hadn't she? She'd even patted her head for lack of anything better. She had a problem on her hands, for God's sake, and she didn't need some weak-stomached Easterner to add to it.

"I'm sorry." Those were the first words she'd managed since she'd come inside. Taking a deep breath, Lily tried them again. "I'm sorry. I shouldn't have screamed that way. I've never seen anything . . . I'd been with Adam, helping with the horses, and then I . . . I just—"

"Drink the damn whiskey, would you?" Willa snapped, then cursed herself as Lily cringed and obediently lifted the glass to her lips. Disgusted with herself, Willa rubbed her hands over her face. "I expect anybody would have screamed coming across something like that. I'm not mad at you."

Lily hated whiskey, the burn of it, the smell. Jesse had favored Seagram's. And as the level in the bottle dropped, his temper rose. Always. But now she pretended to drink. "Was it a cat? I thought it was a cat." Lily bit down hard on her lip to keep her voice steady. "Was it your cat?"

"The cats are Adam's. And the dogs. And the horses. But they did it to me. They didn't leave it on Adam's porch. They did it to me."

"Like—like the steer."

Willa stopped pacing, glanced over her shoulder. "Yes. Like the steer."

"Here's a nice pot of tea." Bess hurried in, carrying a tray. The minute she set it down, she began fussing. "Will, what are you thinking of, giving the poor thing whiskey? It's just going to upset her stomach is all." Gently, Bess took the glass from Lily and set it aside. "You drink some tea, honey, and rest yourself. You've had a bad shock. Will, stop that pacing and sit down."

"You take care of her. I'm going out."

Though she poured the tea with a steady hand, Bess gave Willa's retreating back a hard look. "That girl never listens."

"She's upset."

"Aren't we all."

Lily lifted the cup with both hands, felt the warmth spread at the first sip. "She takes it deeper. It's her ranch."

Bess cocked her head. "Yours too."

"No." Lily drank again, gradually grew calmer. "It'll always be hers."

The cat was gone, but there was still blood pooled over the wood. Willa went back for a bucket of soapy water, a scrub brush. Bess would have done it, she knew, but it wasn't something she would ask of another.

On her hands and knees, in the glow of the porch light she washed away the signs of violence. Death happened. She had believed she accepted and understood that. Cattle were raised for their meat, and a chicken who stopped laying ended up in the pot. Deer and elk were hunted and set on the table.

That was the way of things.

People lived, and died.

Even violence wasn't a stranger to her. She had sent a bullet into living flesh and dressed game with her own hands. Her father had insisted on that, had ordered her to learn to hunt, to watch a buck go down bleeding. That she could live with.

But this cruelty, this waste, this viciousness that had been laid at her door wasn't part of the cycle. She erased it, every drop. And with the bloody bucket beside her, she sat back on her heels and stared up into the sky.

A star died, even as she watched, blazing its white trail across the night and falling into oblivion.

From somewhere near an owl hooted, and she knew prey would be scrambling for cover. For tonight there was a hunter's moon, full and bright. Tonight there would be death—in the forest, in the hills, in the grass. There was no denying it.

It should not have made her want to weep.

She heard the footsteps and hastily composed herself. She was getting to her feet as Ben and Adam came around the side of the house.

"I would have done that, Will." Adam took the bucket from her. "There was no need for you to do this."

"It's done." She reached out, touched his face. "I'm sorry, Adam, about Mike."

"He used to like to sun himself on the rock behind the pole barn. We buried him there." He glanced toward the window. "Lily?"

"Bess is with her. She'll do her more good than I would."

"I'll get rid of this, then check on her."

"All right." But she kept her hand on his cheek another moment, murmured something in the language of their mother.

It made him smile, not the comforting words as much as the tongue. She rarely used it, and only when it mattered most. He stepped away and left her with Ben.

"You've got a problem on your hands, Will."

"I've got several of them."

"Whoever did that did it while we were inside." Wrestling, he thought, like a couple of idiot children. "Ham's going to talk to Wood's kids."

"Joe and Pete?" Will snorted, then rocked on her heels to comfort herself. "No way in hell and back, Ben. Those boys like to run wild around here and regularly beat the hell out of each other, but they aren't going to torture some old cat."

He rubbed the scar on his chin. "Saw that, did you?"

"I've got eyes, don't I?" She had to take a steadying breath as her stomach tipped again. "Cut little pieces off of him, and it looked like burns, probably from a cigarette on the fur. It wasn't Wood's boys. Adam gave them a couple of kittens last spring. They spoil those cats like babies."

"Adam piss anybody off lately?"

She didn't look down at him. "They didn't do it to Adam. They did it to me."

"Okay." Because he saw it the same way, he nodded. And he worried. "You piss anybody off lately?"

"Besides you?"

He smiled a little, climbed up a step until they were eye to eye. "You've been pissing me off all your life. Hardly counts. I mean it, Willa." He closed a hand over hers, linked fingers. "Is there anybody you can think of who'd want to hurt you?"

Baffled by the link, she stared down at their joined hands. "No. Pickles and Wood, they might have their noses a little out of joint now that I'm in charge. Pickles especially. It's the female thing. But they haven't got anything against me personally."

"Pickles was up in high country," Ben pointed out. "Would he do something like this to get at you? Scare the female?"

She sneered out her pride. "Do I look scared?"

"I'd feel better if you did." But he shrugged. "Would he do it?"

"A couple of hours ago I'd have said no. Now I can't be sure." That was the worst of it, she realized. Not being sure who to trust, or how much to trust them. "I wouldn't think so. He's got a temper and he likes to bitch and stew, but I can't see him killing things for no reason."

"I'd say there's a reason here. That's what we have to figure out."

She angled her chin. "Do we?"

"Your land marches with mine, Will. And for the next year you're part of my responsibilities." He only tightened his grip when she tugged at her hand. "That's a fact, and I imagine we'll both get used to it. I aim to keep my eye on you, and yours.''

"You keep it too close, Ben, it's liable to get blackened."

"I'll take that chance." But just in case, he took her other hand, held them both at her sides. "I have a feeling I'm going to find the next year interesting. All around interesting. I haven't wrestled with you in . . . must be twenty years. You filled out nice."

Knowing she was outweighed and outmuscled, she stood still. "You've got a real way with words, Ben. Like poetry. You should feel my heart thudding."

"Honey, I'd love to, but you'd just try to deck me."

She smiled and felt better for it. "No, Ben. I *would* deck you. Now go away. I'm tired and I want my supper."

"I'm going." But not quite yet, he thought. He slid his hands up to her wrists and was intrigued to find her pulse hammering there. You wouldn't have known it from her eyes, so cool and dark. You wouldn't know a lot, he decided from just a quick look at Willa Mercy. "Aren't you going to kiss me good night?"

"I'd just spoil you for all those other women you like to play with."

"I'd take my chances on that, too." But he backed off. It wasn't the time, or the place. Still, he had a feeling he'd be looking for both very soon. "I'll be back."

"Yeah." She dipped her hands into her pockets as he climbed into his rig. Her pulse was still drumming. "I know."

She waited until his taillights disappeared down the long dirt road. Then she glanced over her shoulder at the house, at the lights. She wanted that hot bath, that hot meal, and a long night's sleep. But all of that would have to wait. Mercy Ranch was hers, and she had to talk to her men.

As operator, she tried to stay away from the bunkhouse. She believed the men were entitled to their privacy, and this wood-framed building with its rocking chairs on the porch was their home. Here they slept and ate, read their books if reading was what pleased them. They played cards and argued over them, watched television and complained about the boss.

Nell would cook the meals in the bungalow she shared with Wood and their sons, then cart the food over. She didn't serve the men, and one of them was assigned cleanup duty every week. That way they could eat as they pleased. They might eat dusty from work, or in their underwear. They could lie about women or the size of their cocks.

It was, after all, their home.

So she knocked and waited to be hailed inside. They were all there but Wood, who was eating his supper at home with his family. The men ranged around the table, Ham at the head, his chair tipped back since he'd just finished his meal. Billy and Jim continued to shovel in chicken and dumplings like a pair of wolves vying for meat. Pickles washed his back with beer and scowled.

"I'm sorry to interrupt your meal."

"We're about done here," Ham told her. "Billy, get to the dishes. You eat any more, you'll bust. You want some coffee, Will?"

"I wouldn't mind." She walked to the stove herself, poured a cup, and left it black. She understood that this was a delicate matter and she'd have to be both tactful and direct. "I can't figure who would slice up that old cat." She sipped, let it stew. "Anybody have an idea?"

"I checked on Wood's boys." Ham rose to pour coffee for himself. "Nell says they were in the house with her most of the evening. Now they both have pocketknives, and Nell had them fetch them to show me. They were clean." He grimaced as he drank. "The younger one, Pete, he busted out crying when he heard about old Mike. Tall boy, Pete. You forget he's only eight."

"I heard about kids doing shit like that." Pickles sulked in his beer. "Grow up to be serial killers."

Willa spared him a glance. If anybody found a way to make things worse, it was Pickles. "I don't think Wood's boys are John Wayne Gacys in training."

"Coulda been McKinnon." Billy clattered dishes in the sink and hoped Willa would notice him. He was always

hoping she'd notice him; his crush on her was as wide as
Montana. "He was here." He jerked his head to flop his
straw-colored hair out of his eyes. Scrubbed harder than
necessary at dishes so the muscles on his arms would flex.
"And his men were up in the hills when the steer got laid
open."

"You ought to think before you start flapping your lips,
you asshole." Ham made the statement without heat. Anyone under thirty, in his mind, had the potential to be an
asshole. Billy, with his eager eyes and imagination, had
more potential than most. "McKinnon isn't a man who'd
cut up some damn cat."

"Well, he was here," Billy said stubbornly, and slanted
his eyes sideways to see if Willa was listening.

"He was here," she agreed. "And he was inside with
me. I let him into the house myself, and there wasn't anything on the porch then."

"Nothing like this happened when the old man was
around." Pickles tipped back his beer again and flicked a
glance at Willa.

"Come on, Pickles." Uncomfortable, Jim shifted in his
creaking chair. "You can't blame Will for something like
this."

"Just stating fact."

"That's right." Willa nodded equably. "Nothing like this
happened when the old man was around. But he's dead, and
I'm in charge now. And when I find out who did this, I'll
take care of them personally." She set her cup down. "I'd
like all of you to think about it, to see if you remember
anything, or saw anything, anyone. If something comes to
you, you know where to find me."

When the door closed behind her, Ham kicked at Pickles's chair and nearly sent it out from under him. "Why do
you have to be such a damn fool? That girl's never done
anything but her best."

"She's a female, ain't she?" And that, he thought, was
that. "You can't trust them, and you sure as hell can't depend on them. Who's to say whoever cut up a cow and a
cat won't try it on a man next?" He swigged his beer while

he let that little seed root. "Are you going to look to her to watch your back? I know I'm not."

Billy bobbled a dish. His eyes were huge and filled with glassy excitement. "You think somebody'd try to do that to one of us? Try to knife us?"

"Oh, shut the hell up." Ham slammed down his cup. "Pickles is just trying to get everybody worked up 'cause his pecker's in a twist at having a woman in charge. Killing cows and some old flea-bitten cat isn't like doing a man."

"Ham's right." But Jim had to swallow, and he wasn't interested in the rest of the dumpling on his plate. "But maybe it wouldn't hurt to be careful for a while. There are two more women on the ranch now." He pushed away his plate as he rose. "Maybe we should look after them."

"I'll look after Will," Billy said quickly, and earned a quick cuff on the ear from Ham.

"You'll do your work like always. I'm not having a bunch of pussies jumping at shadows over a cat." He topped off his coffee, picked up the cup again. "Pickles, if you haven't got anything intelligent to say, keep your mouth shut. That goes for the rest of you too." He took a moment to aim a beady eye at every man, then nodded, satisfied. "I'm going to watch *Jeopardy*."

"I tell you this," Pickles said under his breath. "I'm keeping my rifle close and a knife in my boot. If I see anybody acting funny around here, I'll take care of them. And I'll take care of myself." He took his beer and stalked outside.

Jim bypassed the coffeepot for a beer himself, glancing at Billy's pale face along the way. Poor kid, he thought, he'll be having nightmares for sure. "He's just blowing it out his ass, Billy. You know how he is."

"Yeah, but—" He wiped a hand over his mouth. It was just a cat, he reminded himself. Just an old, mangy cat. "Yeah, I know how he is."

W ILLA HAD NIGHTMARES. THEY WOKE HER IN A COLD sweat with her heart pounding against her ribs and a scream locked in her throat. She fought her way out of the tangle of sheets, struggling for air. Alone and shivering, she sat in the center of the bed as the moonlight streamed through her windows and a fitful little breeze tapped slyly on the glass.

She couldn't remember clearly what had haunted her sleep. Blood, fear, panic. Knives. A headless cat stalking her. She tried to laugh over it, dropped her head on her drawn-up knees, and tried hard to laugh at herself. It came perilously close to a sob.

Her legs threatened to buckle when she climbed out of bed, but she made herself walk into the bath, switched on the light, lowered her head over the sink, and ran the water icy cold into her cupped hands. It was better then, with the clammy sweat washed off. Lifting her head, she studied herself in the mirror.

It was still the same face. That hadn't changed. Nothing had changed, really. It had simply been a hellish night. Didn't she have the right to be shaken, just a little, by all that was going on? Worry was like lead on her shoulders, and she had to carry it alone. There was no passing it off, no sharing the load.

The sisters were hers, and the ranch, and whatever was plaguing it. She would handle it all.

And if there was a change inside her, something irksome, something she recognized as essentially female, she would handle that as well. She didn't have the time or the temperament to play mating games with Ben McKinnon.

Oh, he was just trying to rile her anyway. She brushed the hair away from her damp cheeks, poured cold water into a glass. He'd never been interested in her. If he was now, it was only for the hell of it. Which was just like Ben. She nearly smiled as she let the water cool her throat.

She thought she might kiss him after all. Just to get it out of the way. A kind of test. She might sleep better for it. That might chase him out of her dreams and nightmares. And once she stopped wondering, stopped thinking about what kept stirring inside her, she would be able to concentrate more fully on the ranch.

She looked toward the bed, shuddered. She needed to

sleep, but she didn't want to see the blood again, to see the mangled bodies. So she wouldn't.

She took a deep breath before climbing back into bed. She'd will them away, think of something else. Of spring that was so far off. Of flowers blooming in meadows and warm breezes floating down from the hills.

But when she dreamed, she dreamed of blood and death and terror.

SIX

*After two days of life on the ranch, I've decided I hate
Montana, I hate cows, horses, cowboys, and most particularly chickens. I've been assigned the chicken coop by Bess
Pringle, the scrawny despot who runs the house where I'm
being held prisoner. I learned of this new career move after
dinner last night. A dinner, I might add, of roast hunk of
bear. It seems Danielle Boone went up in the hills and shot
herself a grizzly. It was yummy.*

*Actually, it was quite good until I learned what I'd been
eating. I can report that grizzly does not, despite what may
have been stated by others, taste remotely like chicken.
Whatever else I could say about Bess—and I could say
plenty, given the way she eyeballs me—the woman can cook.
I'm going to have to watch myself or I'll be back to the
tubby stage I lived through in my youth.*

*There's been some excitement around the Ponderosa
while I was back in the real world. Apparently someone
butchered a cow up in what they call high country. When I*

said I thought that's what you did with cows, Annie Oakley did her best to wither me with a look. I have to admit she's got some good ones. If she wasn't such a tight-assed know-it-all, I might actually like her.

But I digress.

The cow butchering was more in the way of a mutilation and has caused some concern among the rank and file. The night before my return, one of the barn cats was decapitated and left on the front porch. Poor Lily found it.

I don't know whether to be concerned that this isn't a usual event around here or to pretend it is and make sure my door is locked every night. But the cowgirl queen looks worried. Under other circumstances, that would give me a small warm glow of satisfaction. She really gets under my skin. But with the way things stand, and thinking—or trying not to think—of the long months ahead of me, I find myself uncomfortable.

Lily spends a lot of her time with Adam and his horses. The bruises are fading, but her nerves are alive and well. I don't think she has a clue that the gorgeous Noble Savage is developing a case on her. It's kind of fun to watch. I can't help but like Lily, she's so harmless and lost. And after all, the two of us are in the same boat, so to speak.

The other characters in the cast include Ham; he's perfect, straight out of Central Casting. The bowlegged, grizzled cattleman with a beady eye and a callused hand. He tips his hat to me and says little.

Then there's Pickles. I have no idea if the man has another name. He's a sour-faced, surly character who looks like a bloated string in pointy-toed boots and is nearly hairless but for an enormous reddish moustache. He scowls a lot, but I did see him working with the cattle, and he seems to know his stuff.

There's the Book family. Nell cooks for the hands and has a sweet, homely face. She and Bess get together to gossip and do women-on-the-ranch things I don't want to know about. Her husband is Wood, which I've discovered is short for Woodrow. He has a lovely black beard, a very nice smile and manner. He calls me ma'am and suggested very politely that I should get myself a proper hat so as not to burn my face when I'm out in the sun. They have two boys, about ten and eight, I'd say, who love to run around whooping and pounding on each other. They're awfully pretty. I saw them practicing their spitting behind one of the outbuildings. They seemed to be quite skilled.

There's Jim Brewster, who seems to be one of the good ol' boy types. He's the lanky, I'm getting to it, boss sort. He's very attractive, looks appealing in jeans with that little round outline in the back pocket, which I'm sure is something revolting like chewing tobacco. He's given me a few cocky grins and winks. So far I have been able to resist.

Billy is the youngest. He looks barely old enough to drive and has his puppy eyes on our favorite cowgirl. He's a big talker and is constantly being told by anyone within hearing distance to shut up. He takes it well and rarely listens. I feel almost maternal toward him.

I haven't seen the cowboy lawyer since my return and have yet to meet the infamous Ben McKinnon of Three Rocks Ranch, who appears to be the bane of Willa's existence. I'm sure I'll like him enormously for that alone. I believe I'll have to find a way to soften Bess up in order to get all the dish on the McKinnons, but meanwhile I have a date in the chicken coop.

I'm going to try to think of it as an adventure.

TESS DIDN'T MIND RISING EARLY. SHE WAS INVARIABLY UP by six in any case. An hour at the gym, perhaps a breakfast meeting, then she would hunker over her work until two. Then she'd take a dip in the pool, or take another meeting, perhaps do a little shopping. Maybe she'd have a date or maybe she wouldn't, but her life was hers and ran just as she liked.

Rising early to deal with a bunch of chickens had an entirely different flavor.

The chicken house was big, and certainly looked clean. To Tess's untrained eye, the fifty hens Mercy boasted seemed a legion of beady-eyed, ominously humming predators.

She dumped the feed as Bess had instructed, dealt with the water, then dusted off her hands and eyed the first roosting hen.

"I'm supposed to get the eggs. I believe you may be sitting on one, so if you don't mind . . ." Gingerly she reached out, her eyes locked on the hens. It was immediately apparent who was in charge. Yelping as beak nipped flesh, Tess jumped back. "Look, sister, I've got my orders."

It was an ugly battle. Feathers flew, tempers snapped. The henhouse erupted with clucking and squawking as neighboring hens joined the fray. Tess managed to get her hand around a nice warm egg, wrenched it clear, then stepped back red-faced and panting.

"That's quite a technique you got there."

At the voice behind her, Tess let loose of the egg. It spurted out of her fingers and fell splat on the floor. "Goddamn it! After all that."

"I spooked you." The commotion inside the henhouse had lured Nate. Instead of heading on to see Willa, he'd detoured and found the California connection—in her designer jeans and shiny new boots—battling chickens. He could only think she made a picture. "Looking for breakfast?"

"More or less." She pushed her hair back from her face. "What are you looking for?"

"I've got some business with Will. Your hand's bleeding," he added.

"I know it." In a bad temper, she sucked on the wounds on the back of her hand. "That vicious birdbrain attacked me."

"You're just not going about it right." He offered her a bandanna to wrap around her hand, then stepped up to the next roost. And managed, Tess noted, to look graceful despite the necessity of stooping and bending to keep from bashing his head on the ceiling. "You've just got to go in like it's natural. Make it quick but not abrupt." He demonstrated, slipping a hand under the roosting hen and pulling it out with an egg. Not a feather stirred.

"It's my first day on the job." Pouting only a little, she

held up the bucket. "I like to find my chicken in the freezer section, wrapped in cellophane." As he walked along, gathering eggs, she followed behind. "I suppose you keep chickens."

"Used to. I don't bother with them now."

"Cattle?"

"Nope."

She raised an eyebrow. "Sheep? Isn't that a risk? I've seen all those western movies, the range wars."

"I don't raise sheep either." He settled an egg in the bucket. "Just horses. Quarter horses. You ride, Miz Mercy?"

"No." She tossed her hair back with a shrug. "Though I'm told I'd better learn. And I suppose it would give me something to do around here."

"Adam would teach you. Or I could."

"Really?" She smiled slowly with a flutter of lashes. "And why would you do that, Mr. Torrence?"

"Just being neighborly." She sure had a nice smell about her, he thought. Something just a little dark, just a little dangerous. And all female. He set another egg inside the bucket. "It's Nate."

"All right." Her voice warmed to a purr, and her eyes slanted up a sly look under thick, spiky lashes. "Are we neighbors, Nate?"

"In a manner of speaking. My place is east of here. You smell good, Miz Mercy, for someone who's been fighting with chickens."

"It's Tess. Are you flirting with me, Nate?"

"Just flirting back." His smile was slow and easy. "That's what you were doing, wasn't it?"

"In a manner of speaking. Habit."

"Well, if you want advice—"

"And lawyers are full of it," she interrupted.

"We are. My advice would be to tone down the power. The boys around here aren't used to women with as much style as you've got."

"Oh." She wasn't sure if she'd been complimented or insulted, but she decided to give him the benefit of the doubt. "And are you used to women with style?"

"Can't say I am." He gave her a long, thoughtful look out of quiet blue eyes. "But I recognize one. You'll have them crazy and thinking of killing each other within a week."

Now that, she decided, *was* a compliment. "That ought to liven things up."

"From what I hear, they've been lively enough."

"Dead cats and cows." She grimaced. "A nasty business. I'm glad I missed it."

"You're here now. That seems to be the lot," he added, and she looked down in the bucket.

"Plenty of them. And Christ, they're filthy." It was liable to put her off omelets for quite a while.

"They'll wash." He took the bucket from her and started out. "You settling in?"

"As best I can. It's not my milieu—my usual environment."

He tucked his tongue in his cheek. "Folks from your—what was it?—milieu come out here all the time. Not that they stay." Automatically he ducked down to avoid rapping his head on the low doorway of the henhouse. "Those Hollywooders come charging out, buying up land, plunking down houses that cost the earth and more. Think they're going to raise buffalo or save the mustangs or God knows what."

"You don't like Californians?"

"Californians don't belong in Montana. As a rule. They go running back to their restaurants and nightclubs soon enough." He turned, studied her. "That's what you'll do when your year's up."

"You bet your ass. You can keep your wide-open spaces, pal. I'll take Beverly Hills."

"And smog, mudslides, earthquakes."

She only smiled. "Please, you're making me homesick." She figured she had his number. Montana-born and -bred, a slow, thorough thinker who liked his beer cold and his women modest. The sort who would have kissed his horse at the end of the last reel in any B western.

But my, oh my, he was cute.

"Why the law, Nate? Somebody sue your horses?"

"Not lately." He continued to walk, shortening his stride to let her keep pace. "It interested me. The system. And it helps keep the ranch going. Takes time and money to build up a solid herd and a reputation."

"So you went to law school to supplement your ranch income. Where? University of Montana?" Her mouth was smug and amused. "There is a university in Montana, isn't there?"

"I've heard there is." Recognizing the sarcasm, he slid his gaze down to hers. "No, I went to Yale."

"To—" As she'd stopped dead, he was well ahead of her before she recovered. She had to scramble to catch up. "Yale? You went to Yale and came back here to play range lawyer for a bunch of cowboys and ranch hands?"

"I don't play at the law." He tipped his hat in good-bye and circled around to a corral beside the pole barn.

"Yale." She said it again, shook her head. Fascinated now, she shifted the bucket he'd handed back to her and scurried after him. "Hey, listen. Nate—"

She stopped. There was a great deal of activity in the corral. Two men and Willa were doing something to a small cow. Something the cow didn't appear to appreciate. Tess wondered if they were branding, and thought she'd like to see how that little trick was done. Besides, she wanted to talk to Nate again, and he was moving to the action.

She hefted her bucket, strode up to the gate and through it. No one bothered to look at her. They were focused on their work and the cow had all their attention. Lips pursed, Tess stepped closer, leaned forward to check out the activity over Willa's shoulder.

When she saw Jim Brewster quickly, neatly, and efficiently castrate the calf, her eyes rolled back in her head and she fainted dead away, with barely a sound. It was the crash of the bucket and breaking eggs that made Willa glance around.

"Well, Jesus Christ, will you look at that?"

"She's done passed out cold, Will," Jim informed her, and earned a bland scowl.

"I can see that. Deal with the calf." She straightened, but Nate was already lifting Tess into his arms. "Looks like a handful."

"She's not a featherweight." He grinned. "Your sister's built just fine, Will."

"You can enjoy that little benefit while you haul her into the house. Damn it." She scooped up the bucket. "She busted damn near every egg. Bess'll have a fit." Disgusted, she looked back at Jim and Pickles. "You two keep at it. I'm going to have to see to her first. As if I've got nothing better to do than find smelling salts for some brainless city girl."

"You shouldn't be so hard on her, Will," Nate began as he carried Tess across the road toward the ranch house. His lips twitched. "She's out of her milieu."

"I wish to hell she'd get back in it and out of mine. I've got this one fainting on me, and the other one tiptoeing around as if I'd shoot her between the eyes if she looked at me."

"You're a scary woman, Will." He glanced down as Tess stirred in his arms. "I think she's coming around."

"Dump her somewhere," Willa suggested, pulling open the door of the house. "I'll get some water."

He had to admit Tess was an interesting armful. Not one of the bony, pencil-thin California types but a soft, round woman who had her weight distributed just where it belonged. She groaned, and her lashes fluttered as he carried her toward a sofa. Her eyes, blue as cornflowers, stared blankly into his.

"What?" was the best she could manage.

"Take it easy, honey. You just had yourself a swoon, that's all."

"A swoon?" It took a moment for her brain to get around to the word and its meaning. "I fainted? That's ridiculous!"

"Went down real graceful too." She'd toppled like a tree, he remembered, but didn't think she'd appreciate the analogy. "Didn't hurt your head, did you?"

"My head?" Still dazed, she lifted a hand to it. "I don't think so. I . . ." And then she remembered. "Oh, God, that cow. What they were doing to that cow. What are you grinning at?"

"I'm imagining what it was like for you to see a bull turned into a steer for the first time. Guess you don't see much of that in Beverly Hills."

"We keep all our cattle in the guest house."

He nodded appreciatively. "There now, you're coming around."

She was, indeed. Enough to realize she was being cradled against his chest like a baby. "Why are you carrying me?"

"Well, it didn't seem neighborly to drag you by the hair. Your color's coming back."

"Haven't you put her down yet?" Willa demanded as she strode back into the room holding a glass of water.

"I like it this way. She smells pretty."

The exaggerated drawl made Willa chuckle and shake her head. "Stop playing with her, Nate, and dump her. I've got work to do."

"Can't I keep her, Will? I don't have me a female out on the ranch. Gets lonely."

"You two are a riot." Striving to restore some dignity, Tess swiped the hair out of her eyes. "Put me down, you idiot beanpole."

"Yes'm." From a considerable height, he dropped her onto the leather couch. She bounced once, scowled, and pushed herself up.

"Drink this." With little sympathy, Willa thrust the glass of water into Tess's hand. "And stay away from the corrals."

"You can be sure I will." Furious with herself, and the fact that she was still shaky, Tess drank. "What you were doing out there was revolting, barbaric, and cruel. If mutilating a helpless animal isn't illegal, it should be." She set her teeth when Nate beamed at her. "And stop grinning at me, you fool. I don't imagine you'd appreciate having your balls snipped off with pruning shears."

He felt them draw up, cleared his throat. "No, ma'am, I can't say I would."

"We don't castrate the men around here till we're through with them," Willa said dryly. "Look, Hollywood, weaning and castration are part of ranch life. Just what do you think would happen if we left every cow with his works? We'd have bulls humping everything."

"Cattle orgies every night," Nate put in, then backed off at the searing looks delivered by both women.

"I don't have time to explain the facts of life to you," Willa continued. "Just get over it and stay away from the corral for the next couple of days. Bess'll find work for you inside the house."

"Oh, joy."

"I don't see what else you're good for. You can't even gather eggs without breaking the lot of them." When Tess hissed at her, she turned to Nate. "You wanted to talk to me?"

"Yeah, I did." He hadn't expected quite so much entertainment. "First, I wanted to see if you were all right. I heard about the trouble you've been having."

"I'm all right enough." Willa took the glass of water out of Tess's hand and drank the rest of it down herself. "There doesn't seem to be a lot I can do about it. The men are a little spooked, and they're keeping their eyes out." She set the empty glass down, pushed her hat back. "You haven't heard about this sort of thing happening to anyone else?"

"No." And it worried him. "I don't know what I can do to help, but if there is anything, just ask."

"I appreciate it." Willa took his hand and squeezed it, a gesture that caused Tess to purse her lips thoughtfully. "Were you able to deal with that other business we talked about?"

Her will, he thought, naming Adam as beneficiary. And the papers transferring his house, the horses, and half of her interest in Mercy to him at the end of the year. "Yeah, I'll have a draft to you on all of it by the end of the week."

"Thanks." She released his hand, adjusted her hat. "You can talk to her if you've got time to waste on it." She sent

Tess a wicked smile. "I've got cows to castrate."

As Willa strode out, Tess folded her arms and tried to settle her temper. "I could learn to hate her. It wouldn't take any effort at all."

"You just don't know her."

"I know she's cold, rude, unfriendly, and riding on a power trip. That's more than enough for me." No, she realized as she got to her feet, the temper wasn't going to settle. "I haven't done a damn thing to deserve that attitude from her. I didn't ask to be stuck out here, and I sure as hell didn't ask to be related to that gnat-assed witch."

"She didn't ask for it either." Nate sat on the arm of a chair, methodically rolled a cigarette. He had a little time and thought there were things that needed to be said. "Let me ask you something. How would you feel if you suddenly found out your home could be taken away? Your home, your life, everything you've ever loved?"

His eyes were mild as he struck a match, held it to the tip of the cigarette. "To keep it, you have to rely on strangers, and even if you manage to hold on, you won't keep it all. Good chunks of it are going to belong to those strangers. People you don't know, never had the opportunity to know, are living in your house with as much legal right as you. There's nothing you can do about it. Added to that, you've got all the responsibility, because these strangers don't know squat about ranching. It's up to you to hold it together. All they have to do is wait, and if they wait, they'll get as much as you, even though you were the one to work, to sweat, to worry."

Tess opened her mouth, closed it again. Put that simply, it changed the hue. "I'm not to blame for it," she said quietly.

"No, you're not. But neither is she." He turned his head, studied the portrait of Jack Mercy above the fireplace. "And you didn't have to live with him."

"What was he—" She broke off, cursed herself. She didn't want to ask. Didn't want to know.

"What was he like?" Nate blew out smoke. "I'll tell you. He was hard, cold, selfish. He knew how to run a ranch, better than anyone I know. But he didn't know how to raise a child.'' Remembering that, thinking of that, fired him up. Now his voice was clipped. ''He never gave her an ounce of affection or, as far as I know, one single word of praise, no matter how she worked her skin off for him. She was never good enough, or fast enough, or smart enough to suit him.''

Guilt wasn't going to work, Tess told herself. He wasn't going to make her feel guilt or sympathy. ''She could have left.''

''Yeah, she could have left. But she loved this place. And she loved him. You don't have to grieve for your father, Tess. You lost him years ago. But Willa's grieving. It doesn't matter that he didn't deserve it. He didn't want her any more than he wanted you, or Lily, but she wasn't lucky enough to have a mother.''

All right, guilt was going to work. A little. ''I'm sorry about that. But it doesn't have anything to do with me.''

He took a slow drag on his cigarette, then crushed it out carefully as he rose. ''It has everything to do with you.'' He studied her, and his eyes were suddenly cool and detached and uncomfortably lawyerlike. ''If you don't understand that, you've got too much of Jack Mercy in you. I'll be going.'' He touched the brim of his hat in farewell and walked out.

For a long time, Tess stood where she was, staring up at the portrait of the man who'd been her father.

MILES AWAY ON THREE ROCKS LAND, JESSE COOKE WHIS-tled between his teeth as he changed the points and plugs in an old Ford pickup. He was feeling fine, pumped up from the conversation over breakfast about the animal mutilations at Mercy. What was more rewarding, what was so damn perfect, was that Lily had come across that headless cat.

He only wished he could have seen it.

But Legs Monroe had it straight from Wood Book over at Mercy that the little city woman with the black eye had screamed her head off.

Oh, that was sweet.

Jesse whistled a country tune as his clever fingers made adjustments. He'd always hated country music, the whiny women sobbing over their men, dickless men moaning over their women. But he was adjusting. Every damn one of his bunkhouse mates was a fan, and it was all anyone listened to. He could handle it. In fact, he was beginning to think Montana was the place for him.

It was a land for real men, he'd decided. Men who knew how to handle themselves and keep their women in line. After he'd taught Lily a proper lesson, they'd settle down here. She was going to be rich.

The thought of that had him chuckling and tapping his foot to his own tune. Imagine dumb-ass Lily inheriting a third of one of the top ranches in the state. Worth a fucking fortune, too. All it was going to take was a year.

Jesse pulled his head out from under the hood and looked around. The mountains, the land, the sky—they were all hard. Hard and strong, like him. So this was his place, and Lily was going to learn that her place was with him. Divorce didn't mean shit in Jesse Cooke's book. The woman belonged to him, and if he had to use his fists to remind her of that from time to time, well, that was his right.

All he had to do was be patient. That was the hard part, he admitted, wiping a greasy hand over his cheek. If she found out he was close, she'd run. He couldn't afford to let her run until the year was up.

That didn't mean he wasn't going to keep his eye on her, no, indeedy. He was going to keep watch over his useless stick of a wife.

It was easy enough to make friends with a couple of the asshole hands over at Mercy. Drink a few beers, play some cards, and pump them for information. He could wander over to the neighboring ranch at will, as long as he didn't let Lily see him.

And the day Jesse Cooke, ex-Marine, let a woman outwit him was the day they'd eat cherry Popsicles in hell.

Ducking under the hood again, he got back to work. And reviewed his plans for his next visit to Mercy.

SEVEN

SARAH MCKINNON FLIPPED FLAPJACKS ON THE GRIDDLE and enjoyed the fact that her older son was sitting at her kitchen table drinking her coffee. More often than not these days, he brewed his own in his quarters over the garage.

She missed him.

Fact was, she missed having both of her boys underfoot, squabbling and picking on each other. God knew there'd been times she'd thought they would set her crazy, that she would never have a moment's peace again.

Now that they were grown and she had that peace, she found herself yearning for the noise, the work, the tempers.

She'd wanted more children. With all her heart she'd wanted a little girl to fuss over in her houseful of men. But she and Stu had never had any luck making a third baby. She'd comforted herself that they'd made two healthy, beautiful boys, and that was that.

Now she had a daughter-in-law she loved, and a granddaughter to dote on. She would have more grandchildren, too. If she could ever push Ben toward the right woman.

The boy was damn particular, she mused, slanting a look

toward him as he frowned over the morning paper. He wasn't still single at thirty for lack of opportunity. Lord knew there'd been women in and out of his life—and his bed too, but she didn't care to dwell on that.

But he'd never stumbled over a woman, and Sarah supposed it was just as well. You had to stumble before you could fall, and falling in love was a serious business. When a man chose carefully, he usually chose well.

But, damn it, she wanted those grandchildren.

With a plate heaped with flapjacks in her hand, she paused a moment by the kitchen window. Dawn had broken through the eastern sky, and she watched it bloom, going rosy with light and low-lying clouds.

In the bunkhouse the men would be up and at their own breakfast. Within moments, she would hear her husband's feet hit the floor above her head. She'd always risen before him, hoarding these first cozy moments to herself in the core of the house. Then he would come down, all fresh-shaven and smelling of soap, his hair damp. He'd give her a big morning kiss, pat her bottom, and slurp up that first cup of coffee as if his life depended on it.

She loved him for his predictability.

And she loved the land for its lack of it.

She loved her son, this man who had somehow come from her, for his combination of both.

As she set the plate on the table, she ran her hand over the thick mop of Ben's hair. Remembered, with odd and sudden clarity, his first paid-for haircut, at the age of seven.

How proud he'd been. And how foolishly she'd wept at those gilded curls hitting the barbershop floor.

"What's on your mind, fella?"

"Hmm?" He set the paper aside. Reading at the table was allowed, until the food was on it. "Nothing much, beautiful. What's on yours?"

She sat, cradled her coffee cup. "I know you, Benjamin McKinnon. The gears are turning in there."

"Ranch business mostly." To buy time, he started on his breakfast. The flapjacks were so light they should have been floating an inch off his plate, and the bacon was crisp enough to crack. "Nobody cooks like my ma," he said, and grinned at her.

"Nobody eats like my Ben." She settled back and waited.

He said nothing for a while, enjoying the food, the smells, the light glowing through the window as morning spread. Enjoying her. She was as dependable as the sunrise, he thought. Sarah McKinnon, with her pretty green eyes and her shiny strawberry blond hair. She had the milky-white Irish complexion that defied the sun. There were lines on it, he mused, but they were so soft, so natural, you didn't even see them. Instead you saw that smile, warm and confident.

She was a slip of a woman, slim in her jeans and plaid shirt. But he knew the strength in her. Not just the physical, though she had lifted him off his feet with her hand on his rump many a time, could ride tirelessly on horse or tractor through the bitter cold or the merciless heat, and could heft a fifty-pound bag of feed on her shoulder like a woman lifting a cooing baby.

But what was inside, where it counted most, was iron. She never faltered. In all his life, he'd never seen her turn her back on a challenge, or a friend.

If he couldn't find a woman as strong, as kind, as generous, he'd live his life a bachelor.

The idea of that would have rocked Sarah's heart.

"I've been thinking about Willa Mercy."

Sarah's brows lifted, perked by a kernel of hope. "Oh? Have you?"

"Not that way, Ma." Though he had. He very much had. "She's in a bad spot."

The dancing light in her eyes faded. "I'm sorry for that. She's a good girl, doesn't deserve this heartache. I've been thinking of riding over, paying a call. But I know how busy she is just now." Sarah's lips curved. "And I'm dying of curiosity about the others. I didn't get much time to look them over at the funeral."

"I think Will would appreciate a visit." Biding his time, he forked up more flapjacks. "We've got things under control around here. I think I could spare a little extra time over at Mercy. Not that Will would like it, but having an extra man around there, now and again, might smooth things out some.''

"If you wouldn't poke at her so much, you'd get along better.''

"Maybe." He lifted a shoulder. "The fact is, I don't know how much of the managing she did before the old man died. You have to figure she can handle it, but with Mercy dead, they're a man short. I haven't heard anything about her hiring another hand.''

"There was some speculation she'd hire someone out of the university as foreman." That was how gossip ran from ranch to ranch—speculations over the phone wires. "A nice young man with experience in animal husbandry. Not that Ham doesn't know his business, but he's getting on in years.''

"She won't do it. She's got too much to prove, and too much fondness for Ham. I can give her a hand," he continued. "Not that she thinks much of my college degree. I thought I'd ride over later this morning, feel her out.''

"I think that's very kind of you, Ben.''

"I'm not doing it to be kind." He grinned over the rim of his cup, and it was the same wicked devil of a grin he'd had since childhood. "It'll give me the chance to poke at her again.''

She chuckled and rose to fetch the coffeepot. She'd heard her husband's feet hit the floor. "Well, that'll help keep her mind off her troubles.''

SHE COULD HAVE USED A DISTRACTION. WOOD'S BOYS HAD snuck into the bull pasture to play matador with their mother's red Christmas apron. They'd escaped with their lives, and only one sprained ankle between them. She'd rescued them herself, hauling a dazed and clammy-faced Pete over the fence and leaving an angry, fire-eyed bull behind.

The ensuing lecture she'd delivered to two hanging heads had given her no pleasure—nor had the bone-shaking fear that the incident had shot through her. She ended up playing accessory after the fact by taking the red apron and agreeing to launder it herself before Nell could notice it was missing.

This earned her undying and desperate admiration from the culprits. And, Willa hoped, instilled enough fear in them to keep them from shouting *"Toro"* at a snorting black Angus bull again anytime in the near future.

One of the tractors had thrown a rod, and she'd had to ship Billy off to town for parts. Elk had broken through a portion of the northwest fence again, and now there were cattle to round up.

Bess was down with a cold, Tess had broken most of the eggs for the third time this week, and Lily the mouse was in temporary charge of the kitchen.

To top it all off, her men were bickering.

"A man plays poker and has a run of luck, I say he sticks around to give the rest of the table a chance to even the score." Pickles adjusted the annoyed calf's horns in the squeeze shoot and popped them off to the tune of Tammy Wynette backed up by insulted moos.

"You can't afford to lose," Jim shot back, "you don't play."

"A man's got a right to get back his own."

"And a man's got a right to turn in when he wants. Ain't that right, Will?"

She medicated the cow, plunging the needle in swiftly and efficiently. It was cooler today, autumn coming in strong. But the jacket she'd started out with was now slung over a rail as she sweated through her shirt. "I'm not getting in the middle of your petty feuds."

Pickles's frown carved vertical lines between his brows and set his moustache quivering. "Between Jim and that cardsharp over to Three Rocks, they took me for two hundred."

"J C's not a cardsharp." More to spite Pickles than anything else, Jim flew to his new friend's defense. "He just played better than you. You couldn't bluff a blind man on a galloping horse. And you're just pissed off because he fixed Ham's rig and had it purring like a kitten."

Because it was true, down to the ground, Pickles's chin jutted like a lance. "I don't need some a-hole from over to Three Rocks coming 'round and fixing our rigs and taking my money at cards. I'da fixed the rig when I had the chance.''

"You've been saying that for a week.''

"I'da got to it.'' Grinding his teeth, Pickles got to his feet. "I don't need somebody coming around taking over. I don't need somebody changing the way things are. I've been working this ranch for eighteen years come next May. I don't need no Johnny-come-lately a-holes telling me what's what.''

"Who're you calling an a-hole?'' Eyes hot, Jim sprang to his feet, pushed his face into Pickles's. "You want to take me on, old man? Come ahead.''

"That's enough.'' Even as fists raised, white-knuckled, Willa stepped between them. "I said enough.'' Using both hands she shoved the men apart. One sweeping glance dared either one to take a punch. "As far as I can see, there are two assholes right here who don't have the sense to keep their minds on their work when they're hip-deep in it.''

"I can do my work.'' Pickles's jaw clenched as he glared down at her. "I don't need him, or you, to tell me what has to be done.''

"That's fine, then. And I don't need you to start a pissing contest when we're hip-deep in balls and horns. You go cool off. And when you've cooled off, you ride out and check on the fence crew.''

"Ham doesn't need anybody checking on him, and I've got work right here.''

Willa stepped closer, bumped her temper against his. "I said go cool off. Then get your butt in your rig and check fences. You do it, and do it now, or you pack up your gear and pick up your last paycheck.''

His color rose high, as much in anger as at the humiliation of being ordered around by a woman half his age. "You think you can fire me?''

"I know I can, and so do you.'' She jerked her head toward the gate. "Now get moving. You're in my way here.''

They stared at each other for ten humming seconds. Then he stepped aside, spat on the ground, and stalked toward the gate. Beside Willa, Jim blew out a breath between his teeth.

"You don't want to lose him, Will. He's ornery, Christ knows, but he's a hell of a cowboy."

"He's not going anywhere." If she had been alone, she could have pressed a hand against her jittery stomach. Instead, she crouched and prepared the next hypo. "Once he clears the mad out, he'll be all right. He didn't mean to swipe at you, Jim. He likes you as well as he likes anybody."

Grinning now, Jim hauled a cow toward the squeeze shoot. "That ain't saying much."

"I guess not." She smiled herself. "Prickly old bastard. How much you win off him last night?"

"About seventy. Got my eye on some pretty snakeskin boots."

"You're such a dude, Brewster."

"I like to look sharp for the ladies." He winked at her and the routine fell back into place. "Maybe you'll come dancing with me sometime, Will."

It was an old joke, and cleared more tension. Willa Mercy didn't dance. "And maybe you'll lose the seventy back to him tonight." She wiped sweat off her forehead and kept her voice causal. "This guy from Three Rocks?"

"J C. He's okay."

"Did he have any news from over there?"

"Not much." As Jim worked he recalled that J C had been more interested in the workings of Mercy. "He said how John Conner's girl broke things off, and John got himself shit-faced drunk and passed out in the toilet."

It was easier now, and again routine. Old gossip, familiar names. "Sissy breaks up with Conner every other week, and he always gets shit-faced."

"Just so you know things are as usual."

They grinned at each other, two people hunkered down in blood and manure with the cool breeze blowing the stink everywhere. "Twenty says he'll buy her a bauble and she'll take him back by Monday."

"No bet. I ain't no greenhorn."

They worked together for another twenty minutes, com-

municating with grunts and hand signals. When they paused
long enough to cool dry throats, Jim shifted his feet. "Will,
Pickles didn't mean to ride you, either. He's missing the old
man is all. Pickles had a powerful respect for him."

"I know." She ignored the nagging ache in her heart as
she squinted her eyes. The line of dust coming down the
road meant Billy was back. She thought she'd go hunt down
Pickles, soothe his ruffled feathers, and give him the tractor
to repair. "Go on and get your dinner, Jim."

"My favorite words."

She took her own meal with her, climbing into the cab
of her Land Rover and eating the roast beef sandwich one-
handed as she negotiated the dirt road, crisscrossed with tire
tracks and hoofprints. The path cut through pastures, toward
hillocks, then rose, and gave her a breathless view of autumn
color.

It was passing its peak, she mused, going soft as it faded
and leaves were stripped from the trees. But she could hear
a meadowlark's high, insistent call as she left the window
down to the play of the wind. It should have soothed her,
that familiar music. She wanted it to soothe her, and she
couldn't understand why it didn't.

With a careful eye she studied the fencing she passed,
satisfied that it was, for now, in good repair. Cattle grazed
placidly, a cow occasionally raised its head to stare with
marked disinterest at the passing rig and driver.

To the west the sky was growing dark and bad-tempered,
casting shadow and eerie light on the peaks. She imagined
there'd be snow in the mountains and rain here in the valley
before evening. God knew they could use the rain, she
thought, but she had little hope it would be the slow, serene
soaker that the land would absorb. Likely as not, it would
come in hard, brittle drops that would batter the crops and
bounce like bullets off the ground.

Already she yearned to hear it pound on the roof like
angry fists, to be alone with that violent sound and her own
thoughts for a few hours. And to look out her window, she
thought, at a wall of mean rain that masked everything and
everyone.

Maybe it was the coming storm that was making her so restless, so edgy, she thought, as she caught herself checking her rearview mirror for the fourth time. Or maybe she was just annoyed that she'd come across evidence of the fence crew and not the crew themselves.

No rig, no sound of hammer, no men walking the fence line in the distance. Nothing but road and land and hills rising into a bruised sky.

She felt too alone. And that made no sense to her. She liked being alone on her own land. Even now she was longing for time by herself with no one asking her questions, demanding answers, or listing complaints.

But the nerves remained, jumping like trout in her stomach, crawling over the back of her neck like busy ants. She found herself reaching behind her, laying her fingers on the stock of the shotgun in her gun rack. Then, very deliberately, stopping the rig and stepping out to scan the land for signs of life.

It was risky. He knew it was risky. But he had a taste for it now and couldn't stop himself. He thought he'd chosen his time and place well enough. There was a storm brewing, and the fence crew had finished in this section. He imagined they were back at the ranch yard by now, hunting up their dinner.

It didn't give him much of a window, but he knew how to make the best of it. He'd chosen a prime steer out of the pasture, one that was fat and sleek and would have brought top money at market.

He'd chosen his spot carefully. Once he was finished, he could ride fast and soon be back at the ranch yard, or on a far point of Mercy land. One edge of the road butted the rising hills that went rocky under a cloak of trees.

No one would come upon him from that direction.

The first time he'd done it, his stomach had revolted at the first spurt of blood. He'd never cut into anything so alive, so big before. But then—well, then it had been so . . . interesting. Cutting into such a weighty living thing, feeling the pulse beat, then slow, then fade like a clock run down.

Watching the life drain.

Blood was warm, and it pulsed. At least it pulsed at first, then it just pooled, red and wet, like a lake.

The steer didn't fight him. He lured it with grain, then led it with a rope. He wanted to do it dead center of the ranch road. Sooner or later someone would come along, and my, oh, my, what a surprise. The birds would circle overhead, drawn by the smell of death.

The wolves might come down, lured by it.

He'd had no idea how seductive death could smell. Until he'd caused it.

He smiled at the steer munching from the bucket of grain, ran a hand over the coarse black hide. Then tugging at the plastic raincoat to be sure it covered him well, he raked the knife over the throat in one smooth move—he really thought he was getting better at it—and laughed delightedly as blood flew.

"Get along, little dogie," he sang as the steer crumpled to the ground.

Then he got to the interesting work.

PICKLES WAS HAVING A FINE TIME SULKING. AS HE DROVE along the fence line, he played several conversations in his head. He and Jim. He and Willa. Then he tried out the words he'd use when he complained to Ham about how Willa had gotten in his face and threatened to fire him.

As if she could.

Jack Mercy had hired him, and as far as Pickles was concerned nobody but Jack Mercy could fire him. As Jack was dead—God rest his soul—that was that.

Could be he'd just up and quit. He had a stake laid by, growing interest in the bank down at Bozeman. He could buy his own ranch, start out slow and easy and build it into something fine.

He'd like to see what that bossy female would do if she lost him. Never make it through the winter, he thought sourly, much less through a whole damn year.

And maybe he'd just take Jim Brewster along with him, Pickles thought, conveniently forgetting he was mighty put out at Jim. The boy was a good hand, a hard worker, even if he was an a-hole most of the time.

He might just do it, buy him some land up north, raise some Herefords. He could take Billy along, too, just for the hell of it. And he'd keep the ranch pure, he thought, adding to his fantasy. No damn chickens or small grains, no pigs, no horses but what a man needed as a tool. This diversifying shit was just that. Shit. As far as he was concerned, it was the only wrong turn Jack Mercy had ever made.

Letting that Indian boy breed horses on cattle land.

Not that he had anything against Adam Wolfchild. The man minded his business, kept to himself, and he trained some fine saddle horses. But it was the principle. The girl had her way, she and the Indian would be running Mercy shoulder to shoulder.

And in Pickles's opinion, they'd run it straight into the ground.

Women, he told himself, belonged in the goddamn kitchen, not out on the land ordering men around. Fire him, his ass, he thought with a sniff, and turned onto the left fork to see if Ham and Wood had finished up.

Storm brewing, he thought absently, then spotted the rig stopped in the road. It made him smile.

If a rig had broken down, he had his toolbox in the back. He'd show anybody in southwest Montana with sense enough to scratch their butt that he knew more about engines than anybody within a hundred miles.

He stopped his rig and, tucking his thumbs in the front pockets of his jeans, sauntered over. "Got yourself some trouble here?" he began, then stopped short.

The steer was laid wide open, and there was enough blood to bathe in. The stink of it had his nostrils flaring as he stepped closer, barely glancing at the man crouched beside the body.

"We got us another one? Jesus fucking Christ, what's going on around here?" He bent closer. "It's fresh," he began, then he saw—the knife, the blood running off the blade. And the eyes of the man who held it. "God Almighty, you? Why'd you do it?"

"Because I can." He watched knowledge come into the man's eyes and saw them dart quickly toward the rig. "Because I like it," he said softly. With some regret, he jerked the knife up and plunged it into Pickles's soft belly. "Never killed a man before," he said, and yanked the knife upward with a steady, nerveless hand. "It's interesting."

Interesting, he thought again, studying the way Pickles's eyes went from shocked, to pained, to dull. He kept the knife moving up, toward the heart, leaning with the body as it fell, then straddling it.

All his fascination with the steer was forgotten. This, he realized, was far bigger game. A man had brains, he mused, pulling his knife free with a wet, sucking sound. A cow was just stupid. And a cat, while clever, was just a small thing.

Considering, he leaned back, wondering how to make this moment, this new step, something special. Something people would talk about everywhere, and for a long, long time.

Then he smiled, giggled until he had to press his bloody hand to his mouth. He knew just how to make his mark.

He turned the knife in his hand and went cheerfully to work.

WHEN WILLA SAW THE RIDER GALLOPING OVER HER PASture, she stopped the rig. She recognized the big black that Ben rode, and the dog Charlie, who was bounding along beside Spook like a shadow. Relief was the first reaction, and one she didn't welcome. But there was something eerie in the air, and she'd have been grateful to see the devil himself riding up.

Though it was an impressive sight, she sniffed, the way he and the black gelding sailed over the fence with a careless bunch and flow of muscle.

"You make a wrong turn, McKinnon?"

"Nope." He reined in his horse beside the rig. Charlie, in happy welcome, lifted a leg and peed on Willa's front tire. "You get that fence fixed?" He smiled when she stared at him. "Zack saw you had one down when he went up this morning. The elk have been a real pain in the ass this year."

"They always are. I expect Ham's dealt with it by now.
I was going to ride by and check."

He swung off the horse, then leaned in the window. "Is
that a sandwich over there?"

She glanced at the second half of her dinner. "Yeah.
So?"

"You going to eat it?"

With a sigh, she picked it up and handed it to him. "Did
you hunt me down for a free meal?"

"That's just a side benefit. I'm going to be shipping some
cattle down to the feedlot in Colorado, but I thought you
might want to take a couple hundred head off my hands to
finish." Companionably, he broke off a corner of the sandwich, tossed it to the hopeful dog.

She watched the dog gulp down bread and beef, then grin.
The grin, she mused, wasn't so far off from his master's
arrogant, self-satisfied smirk. "You want to dicker over
price here?"

"I thought we could do it friendlier. Over a drink later."
He reached a hand through the window to toy with the hair
that had come loose from her braid. "I still haven't met
your oldest sister."

Will shoved the jeep in gear. "She's not your type, Slick,
but you come ahead by if you want." She watched him
mow through the last bite of sandwich. "*After* supper."

"Want me to bring my own bottle too?"

She only smiled and eased on the gas. After a moment's
thought, Ben remounted and trotted after her. They both
knew she was keeping her speed slow enough so that he
could.

"Adam going to be around?" Ben raised his voice so she
could hear it clearly over the engine. "I'm interested in a
couple new saddle ponies."

"Ask him. I'm too busy to socialize, Ben." To irritate
him, she accelerated, spewing dust in his face. Still, she was
disappointed when she took the left fork and he turned and
rode off in the opposite direction.

She wished she could have fought with him about something, made him mad enough to grab hold of her again.

She'd been thinking quite a bit about the way he'd grabbed hold of her.

She didn't do a lot of thinking about men—not that way. But it was certainly diverting to think—that way—about Ben. Even if she didn't intend to do anything about it.

Unless she changed her mind.

She grinned to herself. She might just change her mind, too, just to see what it was all about. She had a feeling that Ben could show her more clearly and more thoroughly than most just what a man could do with a woman.

Maybe she'd irritate him into kissing her tonight. Unless he got distracted by big-busted Tess and her fancy French perfume. At that idea she gunned the engine, then braked hard as she spotted Pickles's rig on the curve of the road.

"Well, shit, found him." And now, she thought, she'd have to placate him. She climbed out, scanning the fence line and the pasture on either side. She didn't see any sign of him, or any reason why he would have left his rig across the road.

"Gone off somewhere to sulk," she muttered, and moved toward the cab of the rig to sound the horn.

Then she saw him, him and the steer stretched out in front of the rig, side by side in a river of blood. She didn't know why she hadn't smelled it, not with the way the air was thick and raw with death. But the smell reared up and slammed into her gut now, and she stumbled toward the side of the road and violently threw up her dinner.

Her stomach continued to heave painfully as she staggered toward her own rig and lay hard on the horn. She kept her hand pressed down, her head against the window frame as she fought to get her breath.

Turning her head, she tried to spit out the taste of sickness clawing in her throat, then rubbed her hands over her clammy face. When her vision grayed and wavered, she bit down hard on her lip. But she couldn't make herself walk back down the road, couldn't make herself look again. Giving in, she folded her arms and laid her head down. She didn't lift it even when she heard the thunder of hoofbeats and Charlie's high barks.

"Hey." Ben slid off his horse, the rifle slung by its strap over his shoulder. "Willa."

A springing wildcat wouldn't have surprised him as much as her turning, burying her face in his chest. "Ben. Oh, God." Her arms came around him, clung. "Oh, God."

"It's all right, darling. It's all right now."

"No." She squeezed her eyes tight. "No. In front of the rig. The other rig. There's . . . God, the blood."

"Okay, baby, sit down. I'll see to it." Grim-faced, he eased her down on the running board of the rig, frowning when she put her head between her knees and shuddered. "Just sit there, Will."

By the look on her face, and the din his dog was sounding, Ben thought it must be another steer, or one of the ranch dogs. He was already furious before he stepped up to the abandoned rig. Before he saw it was more, much more, than a steer.

"Sweet Jesus."

He might not have recognized the man, not after what had been done to him. But he recognized the rig, the boots, the hat covered with blood lying near the body. His stomach twisted with both sickness and fury. One thought broke through both as he gave Charlie a sharp order to silence: Whoever did this wasn't simply mad, he was evil.

He turned quickly at the sound behind him, then spread out an arm to block Willa's path. "Don't." His voice was rough, and the hand on her arm firm. "There's nothing you can do, and no need for you to see that again."

"I'm all right now." She put a hand on Ben's and stepped closer. "He was mine, and I'll look at him." She rubbed the heels of her hands under her eyes. "They scalped him, Ben. For God's sake. For God's sweet sake. They cut him to pieces and scalped him."

"That's enough." His hands weren't gentle as he turned her around, forced her head back until their eyes met. "That's enough, Willa. Go back to your rig, radio the police."

She nodded, but when she didn't move, he wrapped his arms around her again, cradled her head on his chest. "Just hold on a minute,'' he murmured. ''Just hold on to me.''

''I sent him out here, Ben.'' She didn't just hold, she burrowed. ''He pissed me off and I told him to ride out here or pack up and pick up his check. I sent him out here.''

''Stop it.'' Alarmed by the way her voice fractured on each word, he pressed his lips to her hair. ''You know you're not to blame for this.''

''He was mine,'' she repeated, then shuddering once, drew away. ''Cover him up, Ben. Please. He needs to be covered up.''

''I'll take care of it.'' He touched her cheek, wishing he could rub color back into it. ''Stay in the rig, Will.''

He waited until she was back in the vehicle, then pulled the grease-stained tarp out of the bed of Pickles's truck. It would have to do.

EIGHT

From the kitchen window Lily could see the forest and the climb of mountains into the sky. Night was coming more quickly as October gave way to November. From the window, she could watch the sun drop toward the peaks. It had hardly been two weeks since she'd come to Montana, but already she knew that once the sun fell behind those shadowy hills night would come swiftly and the air would quickly chill.

The dark still frightened her.

She looked forward to the dawns. To the days. There was so much to do, she could spend hours on the chores. She was grateful to be useful again, to feel a part of something. In so short a time she had come to depend on seeing that wide spread of sky, the rise of mountains, the sea of land. She'd come to count on hearing the sounds of horses, cattle, and men. And the smell of them.

She loved her room, the privacy of it, and the grace, and the house with all its space and polished wood. The library was stuffed with books, and she could read every night if she chose to, or listen to music, or leave the TV murmuring.

No one cared what she did with her evenings. No one criticized her small mistakes, or raised a hand to her.

Not yet.

Adam was so patient. And he was gentle as a mother with the horses. With her as well, she admitted. When he guided her hands down a horse's leg to show her how to check for strains, he didn't squeeze. He'd shown her how to use a dandy brush, how to medicate a split hoof, how to mix supplements for a pregnant mare.

And when he'd caught her feeding an apple to a yearling on the sly, he hadn't lectured. He'd just smiled.

The hours they worked together were the best of her life. This new world that had opened up for her had given her hope, a chance for a future.

Now that could be over.

A man was dead.

She shuddered to think of it, to be forced to admit that murder had slunk into her bright new world. In one vicious stroke, a man's life was over, and she was once again helpless to control what happened next.

It shamed her that she thought more of herself and what would happen to her than of the man who had been killed. It was true that she hadn't known him. With the skill of the hunted, Lily had easily avoided the men of Mercy Ranch. But he had been part of her new world, and it was selfish not to think of him first.

"Christ, what a mess."

Lily jumped as Tess swung into the kitchen, and her hand tensed on the dishrag she'd forgotten she was holding. "I made coffee. Fresh. Are they . . . is everyone still here?"

"Will's still talking to the cowboy cops, if that's what you mean." Tess wandered to the stove, wrinkled her nose at the coffeepot. "I stayed out of the way, so I don't know what's going on, exactly." She walked to the pantry, opening and closing the door in jerks. "Anything stronger than coffee around here?"

Lily twisted the dishrag in her hands. "I think there's wine, but I don't think we should disturb Willa to ask."

Tess just rolled her eyes and wrenched open the refrigerator. "This adequate, if slightly inferior, bottle of Chardonnay is as much ours as hers." Taking it out, Tess asked, "Got a corkscrew?"

"I saw one earlier." She made herself put down the cloth. She'd already wiped the counters clean twice. Opening a drawer, she took out a corkscrew and handed it to Tess. "I, ah, made some soup." She gestured toward the pot on the stove. "Bess is still running a fever, but she managed to eat a bowl of it. I think—I hope she'll be feeling better by tomorrow."

"Uh-huh." Tess searched out wineglasses herself, poured. "Sit down, Lily. I think we should talk."

"Maybe I should take out some coffee."

"Sit down. Please." Tess slipped onto the wooden bench of the breakfast nook and waited.

"All right." Lily sat down across the polished table and folded her hands in her lap.

Tess slid the wineglass over, lifted her own. "I suppose eventually we should get into the story of our lives, but this doesn't seem to be the right time." From her pocket she took the single cigarette she'd slipped out of her secret emergency pack, twirling it in her fingers before reaching for the book of matches. "This is a pretty ugly business."

"Yes." Automatically Lily rose, fetched an ashtray, and brought it back to the table. "That poor man. I don't know which one he was, but—"

"The balding one, with the big moustache and bigger belly," Tess told her, and with a shrug for willpower, lit the cigarette.

"Oh." Now that she had a face to focus on, Lily felt the shame grow. "Yes, I've seen him. He was stabbed, wasn't he?"

"I think it was worse than that, but I don't have a lot of the details other than Will found him on one of those roads that go all over the ranch."

"It must have been horrible for her."

"Yeah." Tess grimaced, picked up her wine. She might not have been fond of her youngest half sister, but she wouldn't have wished this particular experience on anyone.

"She'll handle it. They breed them tough out here. Anyway . . ." She sipped, found the wine not quite as inferior as she'd thought. "What about you? Are you staying or going?"

More out of a need to do something with her hands than a desire for wine, Lily reached for her glass. "I don't really have anyplace else to go. I suppose you'll be going back to California."

"I've thought about it." Tess leaned back, studied the woman across from her. Keeps her eyes down, Tess mused, and her hands busy. She'd been certain that shy Lily would already have booked a flight to anywhere. "I figure it this way. People are murdered every day in LA. Kids regularly whack each other for painting graffiti in the wrong territory. There are drug hits every time you blink. Shootings, knifings, muggings, bludgeonings." She smiled. "God, I love that town."

Catching Lily's appalled expression, Tess threw back her head and laughed. "Sorry," she managed after a moment, pressing a hand to her heart. "My point is that as bad as this is, as close as it is, it's only one murder. Comparatively, it just isn't that big a deal, certainly not big enough to chase me away from collecting what's mine."

Lily drank again, struggled to gather her thoughts. "You're staying. You're going to stay."

"Yeah, I'm going to stay. Nothing's changed."

"I thought—" Closing her eyes, Lily let the relief run through her and twine with the shame. "I was sure you wouldn't, and then I'd have to leave." She opened her eyes again, soft, quiet blue with hints of haunted gray. "That's horrible. That poor man's dead, and all I've been able to think about is how it affects me."

"That's just honest. You didn't know him. Hey." Because there was something about Lily that tugged at her, Tess reached for her sister's hand. "Don't beat yourself up over it. We've all got a lot at stake here. We're entitled to think about what's ours."

Lily looked down at the joined hands. Tess's were so pretty, she thought, with the glitter of rings and the enviable strength and confidence in the fingers. She lifted her gaze. "I didn't do anything to deserve this place. Neither did you."

Tess merely nodded and, withdrawing her hand, lifted her glass again. "I didn't do anything to deserve being ignored my entire life. And neither did you."

Willa came into the kitchen, stopped short when she saw the women at the table. Her face was still pale, her movements still jerky. After all the questions, the going over and over her discovery of the body, she'd been more than happy to see the police on their way.

"Well, this is cozy." She slipped her hands into her pockets as she stepped toward the table. Her fingers still tended to shake. "I figured the two of you would be packing, not sitting around having a chat."

"We've been talking about that." Tess lifted an eyebrow but made no comment when Will picked up her wineglass and drank. "We're not going anywhere."

"Is that so?" Because wine seemed like a fine idea, Willa crossed to the cupboards and took out a tumbler. Then she just stood there, unable to move, barely able to think.

She hadn't been able to fully consider the loss of the ranch. It had been there, in the back of her mind, the certainty that the two women who had been pushed on her would run. And with them would go her life. But it wasn't until now, until she knew they would stay, that it hit her. And it hit hard.

Giving in, she rested her head against the cupboard door and closed her eyes.

Pickles. Dear God, would she see him for the rest of her life, what had been done to him, what had been left of him? And all that blood, baking in the sun. The way his eyes had stared up at her, the horror frozen in them.

But the ranch, for now, was safe.

"Oh God, oh God, oh God."

She didn't realize she'd moaned it out loud until Lily laid a tentative hand on her shoulder. Shrinking from the touch, Willa straightened quickly.

"I made soup." Lily felt foolish saying it but could think

of nothing else. "You should eat something."

"I don't think I could handle food right now." Willa stepped back, afraid that too much comfort would break her. She walked back to the table and, under Tess's fascinated eye, filled the tumbler full of wine.

"That's good," Tess murmured, watching in admiration as Willa gulped wine like water. "That's damn good. How long can you do that and still stand up?"

"We'll have to find out." She turned when the kitchen door opened, drew a steadying breath when Ben came in.

She didn't want to berate herself for leaning on him, for collapsing in his arms, for letting him do the dirty work while she had sat by, too ill to function. But it was hard to swallow.

"Ladies." In a gesture that mimicked Willa's habit, he took the glass from her hand and sipped. "Here's to the end of a lousy day."

"I'll drink to that." Tess did, as she studied him. The gilded cowboy, she mused. And a mouthwaterer. "I'm Tess. You must be Ben McKinnon."

"Nice to meet you. Sorry it isn't under more pleasant circumstances." He lifted a hand to Willa's chin, turned her face to his. "Go lie down."

"I have to talk to the men."

"No, you don't. What you have to do is go lie down and turn this off for a while."

"I'm not going to pull the covers over my head because—"

"There's nothing you can do," he interrupted. She was trembling. He could feel just how hard she was fighting it, but the tremors came through and into his fingertips. "You're sick and you're tired, and you've just had to relive an ugly experience half a dozen times. Adam is taking the cops down to talk to the men in the bunkhouse, and there's nothing for you to do but try to get some sleep."

"My men are—"

"Who's going to pull them together tomorrow—and the day after—if you break down?" He inclined his head when she shut her mouth. "Now you can go up and lie down under your own steam, Will, or I'll take you myself. Either way, that's what you're going to do. Right now.''

Tears burned the back of her eyes, bubbled hot in her throat. Too proud to shed them in front of him, she shoved his hand aside, swiveled on her heel, and stalked out.

"I'm impressed," Tess murmured when the kitchen door slammed. "I didn't think anyone could push her around."

"She'd have pushed back, but she knew she'd break. Will won't let herself break." He frowned into his wine, wishing he'd been able to gentle her into it instead of browbeating her. "I don't know many who could have gotten through what she did today without breaking."

"Should she be alone?" Lily pressed her fingers to her lips. "I could go up with her, but . . . I don't know if she'd want that."

"No, she's better off alone." But Ben smiled, pleased that she'd offered. "This hasn't exactly been a weekend at a dude ranch resort for either of you, but I'll say welcome to Montana anyway."

"I love it here." The minute she'd said it, Lily flushed and scrambled to her feet as Tess chuckled. "Would you like something to eat? I made soup, and there's plenty of fixings for sandwiches."

"Angel, if that's your soup I'm smelling, I'd be grateful to have a bowl."

"Good. Tess?"

"Sure, why the hell not?" Since Lily seemed eager to serve, Tess stayed where she was, tapping her fingers on the table. "Do the police think it was someone from the ranch who did it?"

Ben slid in across from her. "I imagine they'll concentrate here, first anyway. There's no public access to the ranch, but that doesn't mean someone from outside couldn't have found the way out there. A horse, a jeep." He moved his shoulders, skimmed a hand through his hair. "It's easy enough access from Three Rocks to Mercy land. Hell, I was there myself."

He lifted an eyebrow at Tess's speculative look. "Of course, I can tell you I didn't do it, but you don't know me.

It's also possible to get there through the Rocking R Ranch, or Nate's place, or the high country.''

"Well''—Tess poured herself more wine—"that certainly narrows things down, doesn't it?''

"I'll tell you this—anyone who knows the mountains, the land around here, could hide out for months, go pretty much wherever the hell he pleased. And be damn hard to find.''

"We appreciate your easing our minds.'' She flicked a glance at Lily as she set steaming bowls on the table. "Don't we, Lily?''

"I'd rather know.'' Lily sat on the edge of the bench next to Tess and folded her hands again. "You can take precautions better if you know.''

"That's exactly right. I'd say a good precaution would be for neither of you to wander far from the house here alone, for the time being.''

"I'm not much of a wanderer.'' Though her stomach suddenly felt uneasy, Tess spooned up soup. "And Lily sticks pretty close to Adam.'' She looked at Ben. "Is he a suspect?''

"I don't know what the police think, but I can tell you that Adam Wolfchild would no more gut and scalp a man than he'd sprout wings and fly to Idaho.'' He glanced over when Tess's spoon crashed onto the table. He'd have cursed himself if it would have done any good. "I'm sorry. I thought you knew the details.''

"No.'' Tess went for the wine rather than the soup. "We didn't.''

"She saw that?'' Lily twisted her hands in her lap. "She found that?''

"And she'll live with that.'' They both would, Ben thought, for it was an image he knew would never completely fade from his memory. "I don't want to scare you, I just want you to be careful.''

"You can count on it,'' Tess promised him. "But what about her?'' She jerked a thumb toward the ceiling. "You're not going to keep her close to the house without shackles.''

"Adam will keep an eye on her. And so will I.'' Hoping to ease the tension, he spooned up more soup. "And hanging around here isn't going to be much of a hardship if this is the kind of cooking I'm in for.''

Both women jumped when the outside door opened. Adam came in, along with the night chill. ''They're done with me for now.''

''Join the party,'' Tess invited. ''Soup and wine is our menu tonight.''

He gave her a solemn look before studying Lily. ''I think I'd go for coffee. No, sit,'' he added when Lily started to get up. ''I can get it myself. I just came by to check on Willa.''

''Ben made her go up and lie down.'' Nerves and relief had words bubbling out before Lily could stop them. ''She needed to rest. I can fix you some soup. You should eat something, and there's plenty.''

''I can get it. Sit down.''

''There's bread. I forgot to put the bread out. I should—''

''You should sit.'' He spoke very quietly as he ladled up soup. ''And try to relax.'' He filled a second bowl, brought both to the table. ''And you should eat. I'll get the bread.''

She stared at him, baffled, while he moved competently around the kitchen. None of the men in her life had so much as picked up a dish unless it was to ask for seconds. She flicked a glance at Ben, looking for the sneer, but he continued to eat as though there was nothing unusual at all about having a man serve food.

''Do you want me to stay over, Adam, give you a hand with things for a day or two?''

''No. Thanks anyway. We'll have to take it a step at a time.'' He sat down across from Lily and looked her in the eye. ''Are you all right?''

She nodded, picked up her spoon, and tried to eat.

''Pickles didn't have any family,'' Adam continued. ''I think there was a sister maybe, down in Wyoming. I guess we'll try to find her, if she's still around, but I'd say we'll handle the arrangements once they release the body.''

''You ought to have Nate do that.'' Ben broke off a hunk of bread. ''Willa will pass that to him if you suggest it.''

''All right, I'll do that. I don't think she'd have gotten

through this without you. I want you to know that.''

"I just happened to be there.'' It still unnerved him, the way she'd all but crawled into his arms. And the way she'd fit when she had. "Once she's over the shock, she'll likely be sorry it was me who was.''

"You're wrong. She'll be grateful, and so am I.'' He turned his hand over, palm up, where there was a long, thin scar between the lines of heart and head. "Brother.''

Ben's lips twitched as he looked at the similar mark on his own hand. And he remembered when two young boys had stood on the banks of a river in the half-light of a canyon and solemnly mixed their blood in brotherhood.

"Uh-oh, male ritual time.'' Absurdly touched, Tess nudged Lily so that she could slide out. "That's my cue to leave you gentlemen to your port and cigars while I go up and do something exciting like paint my toenails.''

Appreciating her, Ben grinned. "I bet they're real pretty, too.''

"Sweetheart, they are awesome.'' It was simple to decide she liked him. And not a very large step from there to decide to trust him. "I guess I'll range myself with Adam and say I'm grateful you were here. Good night.''

"I'll go too.'' Lily reached down for Tess's half-eaten bowl of soup.

"Don't go.'' Adam laid a hand over hers. "You haven't eaten.''

"You'll want to talk. I can take it up with me.''

"Don't run off on my account.'' Pretty sure that he saw how the wind blew here, Ben slid off the bench. "I've got to get home. I appreciate the meal, Lily.'' He reached up to touch her cheek, felt her instinctive wince of defense. Smoothly, he dropped his hand, as if the moment hadn't happened. "You eat while it's hot,'' he advised. "I'll be around tomorrow, Adam.''

"Good night, Ben.'' Adam kept his hand over Lily's, giving it a coaxing tug until she sat again. Then he took her other hand, linked his fingers in hers, and waited until she lifted her eyes to his. "Don't be afraid. I won't let anything happen to you.''

"I'm always afraid."

Her hands flexed under his, but he judged it was time to take the chance, so he continued to hold them. "You came to a strange place, with only strangers around you. And you stayed. There's courage there."

"I only came to hide. You don't know me, Adam."

"I will when you let me." He released one of her hands, lifted his own, and brushed his thumb over the faded bruise beneath her eye. She went very still, watched him warily as he traced his thumb down to the marks on her jaw. "I want to know you, Lily, when you're ready."

"Why?"

His eyes smiled and stirred her heart. "Because you understand horses, and you sneak kitchen scraps to my dogs." The smile moved to his mouth when she flushed. "And because you make good soup. Now, eat," he said, and released her hand. "Before it's cold."

Watching him from under her lashes, she picked up her spoon and ate.

Upstairs, armed with a book she'd chosen from the library and a bottle of mineral water she'd taken from behind the bar, Tess walked toward her room. She had decided to read until her eyes crossed, hoping that it would bring her undisturbed and dreamless sleep.

Her imagination was much too vivid, she thought. It was the very reason she was beginning to make her mark as a screenwriter. And the very reason that the details Ben had provided were going to shift and stir until they formed many ugly visions in her head.

She had great hope that the thick paperback romance whose cover promised plenty of passion and adventure would steer her mind to other venues.

Then she passed Willa's door and heard the bitter, broken weeping. She hesitated, wished to hell she'd thought to come up the other stairs. More, wished the helpless sobbing didn't touch a chord in her. When a strong woman wept, she thought, the tears came from the deepest and darkest corners of the heart.

She lifted a hand to knock, then on an oath just laid her

palm on the wood. Perhaps if they had known each other, or if they had been complete strangers, she could have gone in. If they had had no ghosts between them, no harbored resentments, she could have opened that door and offered . . . something.

But she knew she wouldn't be welcomed. There could be no woman-to-woman comfort here, much less sister to sister. And realizing she was sorry for that, very sorry, she continued to her own room, carefully closed, carefully locked the door behind her.

But she no longer thought her dreams would be undisturbed.

IN THE DARK, IN THE MIDDLE OF THE NIGHT WHEN THE wind kicked up and threatened and the rain came hard and vicious, he lay smiling. Reliving every moment of the kill, second by second, brought a curious thrill.

It had been like being someone else while it was happening, he realized. Someone with vision so clear, with nerves so steady, he was barely human.

He hadn't known he'd had that inside him.

He hadn't known he would like it so much.

Poor old Pickles. To keep from laughing aloud, he pressed both hands to his mouth like a child giggling in church. He hadn't had anything against the old fart, but he'd come along at the wrong time, and needs must.

Needs must, he thought again, snorting into his hands. That's what his dear old ma had always said. Even when she'd been stoned, she'd been happy to dispense such homilies. Needs must. A stitch in time. Early to bed and a penny saved. Blood's thicker than water.

Recovered, he let out a breath and dropped his hands on his belly.

He remembered how the knife had slid into Pickles's belly. All those layers of fat, he mused, patting himself. It had been like stabbing a pillow. Then there had been that sucking sound, the kind you could make giving a woman a nice fat hickey to brand her.

But the best, the very best, had been lifting what was left

of Pickles's hair. Not that it made much of a trophy, all thin and straggly, but the way the knife had made that wicked flap had been so fascinating.

And the blood.

Good Jesus, did he bleed.

He wished he could have taken more time with it, maybe done a little victory dance. Now the next time . . .

He had to stifle another chuckle. For there would be a next time. He was through with cattle and pets. Humans were much more challenging. He'd have to be careful, and he'd have to wait. If he took another one too quick, it would spoil the anticipation.

And he wanted to choose the next one, not just stumble over someone.

Maybe he should do a woman. He could take her into the trees, where he had hidden his trophies. He could cut her clothes away while she was begging him not to hurt her. Then he could rape the shit out of her.

He grew hard thinking of it, idly stroked himself while he planned. It would certainly add a new thrill to be able to take his time over it, to watch his prey, watch the eyes bulge with fear as he explained every little thing he was going to do.

It had to be even better that way. When they knew.

But he would need to practice. A woman would be the next stage, and he hadn't perfected this one yet.

No rush, he thought dreamily, and began to masturbate in earnest. No rush at all.

PART TWO

WINTER

*They that know the winters of that country
know them to be sharp and violent....*

—*William Bradford*

NINE

Even murder couldn't stop work. The men were jumpy, but they took orders. Now that they were another hand short, Willa pushed herself to take up the slack. She rode fences, drove out to the fields to check on the harvest, manned the squeeze shoot herself, and huddled over the record books at night.

The weather turned, and turned fast. The chill in the air threatened winter, and there was frost on the pastures every morning. What cattle wouldn't be wintered over had to be shipped to feed pens for finishing—Mercy's own outside of Ennis or down to Colorado.

If she wasn't on horseback or driving a four-wheeler, she went up with Jim in the plane. She'd considered getting her pilot's license, but had quickly discovered that air travel didn't suit her. She didn't care for the noise of the engine or how the quick dips and turns affected her stomach.

Her father had loved to buzz the land in the little Cessna. The first time she'd flown with him, she'd been miserably ill. It had been the last time he had taken her up.

Now that there was only Jim qualified to pilot—and he had a tendency to hotdog—she wondered if she'd have to reconsider. An operation like Mercy needed a backup pilot, and maybe if she was at the controls she wouldn't get light-headed or nauseous.

"Pretty as a picture from up here." Grinning, Jim dipped the wings, and Willa felt her breakfast slide greasily toward her throat. "Looks like we got another fence down." Cheerfully he dropped altitude to get a closer look.

Willa gritted her teeth and made a mental note of their position. She forced herself to scan the cattle, take a broad head count. "We need to rotate those cows before they take the grass down." She hissed between her teeth when the plane angled sharply. "Can't you fly this damn thing straight?"

"Sorry." He tucked his tongue in his cheek to hold back a chuckle. But when he got a look at her face, he leveled off gently. She was a pale shade of green. "You oughtn't to come up, Will, leastwise without taking some of those airsick pills first."

"I took the damn things." She concentrated on her breathing, wished she could appreciate the beauty of the land, the pastures green and glinting with frost, the hills thick with trees, the peaks white with snow.

"Want me to take us down?"

"I'm handling it." Barely. "We'll finish."

But when she looked down again, she saw the road where she had found the body. The police had taken the body away, had even taken the mutilated carcass of the steer. They'd combed the area looking for and gathering evidence. And the rain had washed away most of the blood.

Still, she thought she could see darker patches on the dirt that had soaked in deep. She couldn't tear her eyes away, and even when they flew past and over pasture, she could still see the road, the dark patches.

Jim kept his eyes trained on the horizon. "The police came by again last night."

"I know."

"They haven't found anything. It's been damn near a week, Will. They don't have squat."

The anger in his voice cleared her vision, helped her turn her eyes away and toward his face. "I guess it's not like the TV shows, Jim. Sometimes they just don't get the bad guy.''

"I keep thinking how I won that money off him the night before it happened. I wish I hadn't won that money off him, Will. I know it doesn't mean a damn, but I wish I hadn't.''

She reached over, gave his shoulder a quick squeeze. "And I wish I hadn't had words with him. That doesn't mean a damn either, but I wish I hadn't.''

"Goddamn bitchy old fart. That's what he was. Just a goddamn bitchy old fart.'' His voice hitched, and Jim cleared his throat. "I—we heard you were maybe going to bury him in Mercy cemetery.''

"Nate hasn't been able to locate his sister, or anyone. We'll bury him on Mercy land. I guess Bess would say that was fittin'.''

"It is. It's good of you, Will, to put him where there's only family.'' He cleared his throat again. "The boys and me were talking. We thought maybe we could be like the pallbearers and we'd pay for his stone.'' His color rose when he caught Willa staring at him. "It was Ham's idea, but we all agreed to it. If you do.''

"Then that's the way we'll do it.'' She turned her head, stared out the window. "Let's go down, Jim. I've seen enough for now.''

WHEN WILLA DROVE BACK INTO THE RANCH YARD, SHE spotted Nate's rig, and Ben's. Deliberately, she stopped in front of Adam's little white house. She needed time before she faced anyone. Her legs weren't much steadier than her stomach. There was a headache, brought on, she supposed, by the incessant humming of the plane, kicking behind her eyes.

She climbed out, stepped through the gate of the picket fence, and indulged herself by squatting down to pet Beans. He was fat as a sausage, with floppy ears and huge mop paws. Elated to see her, he rolled over to offer his belly for a rub.

"You fat old thing. You going to lie here and sleep all

day?'' He thumped his tail in agreement and made her smile. ''Your back end's wide as a barn.''

Her voice brought Adam's spotted hound, Nosey, racing around the side of the house. With his ears perked up and his tail waving like a flag, he trotted over and pushed himself under Willa's arm.

''Been up to no good again, haven't you, Nosey? Don't think I don't know you've had your eye on my chickens.''

He grinned at her, and in his attempt to lick her hands, her face, stepped on his buddy. When the two dogs began to wrestle and dance, Willa got to her feet. She felt better. Maybe it was just being in Adam's yard, where the fall flowers were still stubbornly blooming and dogs had nothing better to do than play.

''You finished fooling with those useless dogs?''

She looked over her shoulder. Ham stood on the other side of the gate, a cigarette dangling from his mouth. His jacket was buttoned and he wore leather gloves, making her think perhaps he felt the cold more these days.

''I reckon I am.''

''And you're finished flying around in that death trap?''

She ran her tongue over her teeth as she walked toward him. In his sixty-five years, Ham had never been inside a plane of any kind. And he was damn proud of it. ''Seems like. We need to rotate cattle, Ham. And we've got another fence down. I want those cows moved from the southmost pasture today.''

''I'll put Billy on it. Only take him twice as long to do it as anybody with half a brain. Jim can handle the fencing. Wood's got his hands full down at the fields, and I've gotta get the shipment down to the feedlot.''

''Is this your not-so-subtle way of telling me we're running thin?''

''I'm going to talk to you about that.'' He waited until she came through the gate, took his time enjoying his smoke. ''We could use another hand, two would be best. But it's my thinking you should wait, till spring at least, to hire on.''

He flicked the miserly butt of his cigarette away, watched

it fly. Behind them, Beans and Nosey whined at the gate, hoping for more attention. "Pickles was a pain in the ass. The man would bitch if the sun was shining or if a cloud covered it up. He just liked to complain. But he was a good cowboy and a halfway good mechanic."

"Jim told me that you and the men want to buy his stone."

"Only seems right. Worked with the picky old bastard damn near twenty years." He continued to stare out at middle distance. He'd already looked into her face, seen what was there. "You ain't helping anybody, blaming yourself for what happened to him."

"I sent him out."

"That's crap, and you know it. You may be a stiff-necked temperamental female, but you ain't stupid."

She nearly smiled. "I can't get past it, Ham. I just can't."

He knew that, understood that because he knew her. Understood her. "Finding him the way you did, that's going to prey on you. Nothing much to do about that but wait it out." He looked back at her again, shifted his disreputable hat against the angle of the sun. "Working yourself into the ground isn't going to make it go away any quicker."

"We're two hands short," she began, but he only shook his head.

"Will, you ain't sleeping much and you're eating less." Beneath the grizzled beard, his lips curved slightly. "Bess being back on her feet, I get plenty of the news from inside the main house. That woman can talk the ears off a rabbit. And even if she wasn't rattling away at me every chance she gets, I could see it for myself."

"I've got a lot on my mind."

"I know that." His voice roughened with his own brand of affection. "I'm just saying you don't have to have your hand in every inch of this ranch. I've been here since before you were born, and if you don't trust me to do my job, well, maybe you should be looking for three new hands come spring."

"You know I trust you, it's not—" She broke off, sucked in a breath. "That's low, Ham."

Pleased with himself, he nodded. Yeah, he knew her all right. He understood her.

And he loved her.

"As long as it makes you stop and think. We can get through the winter the way things are. That oldest boy of Wood's is coming along fine. He'll be twelve before long, and he can pull his weight. The younger one's a goddamn farmer." Baffled by it, Ham took out another cigarette, rolled fresh that morning. "Rather bale hay than sit a horse, but he's a good worker, so Wood claims. We'll do well enough through winter with what we've got."

"All right. Anything else?"

Again, he took his time. But since he had her attention, he figured he might as well finish up. "Them sisters of yours. You might tell the short-haired one to buy her some jeans that don't fit like skin. Every time she walks by, that fool Billy drops his tongue on his boots. He's going to hurt himself."

It was the first laugh she'd had in days. "And I don't suppose you look, do you, Ham?"

"I look plenty." He blew out smoke. "But I'm old enough not to hurt myself. The other one sits a horse real pretty." He squinted, gestured with his cigarette. "Well, you can see that for yourself."

Willa looked down the road, saw the riders heading east. Adam sat on his favored pinto, hatless and flanked by two riders. Willa had to admit that Lily handled the roan mare well, moving as smooth as silk with the mare's gait. On the other hand, Tess was jogging in the saddle atop a pretty chestnut. Her heels were up rather than down, her butt bouncing against leather in quick, jerky slaps that had to hurt, and she appeared to be gripping the saddle horn for dear life.

"Christ, will she be sore tonight." Amused, Willa leaned on the gate. "How long has that been going on?"

"Last couple days. Seems she took it in her mind to learn to ride. Adam's been working with her." He shook his head as Tess nearly slid out of the saddle. "Don't know if even that boy can do anything with her. You could saddle Moon and catch up with them.''

''They don't need me.''

''That's not what I said. You should take yourself a nice long ride, Will. It's always what worked best for you.''

''Maybe.'' She thought about it, a nice long gallop with the wind slapping her face and clearing her mind. ''Maybe later.'' For another moment she watched the three riders and envied them the easy camaraderie. ''Maybe later,'' she repeated, and climbed back in her rig.

WILLA WASN'T SURPRISED TO FIND BOTH NATE AND BEN in the kitchen, enjoying Bess's barbecued beef. To keep Bess from scolding her for not eating, she took a plate herself, pulled up a chair.

''About time you got back.'' A bit disappointed that she hadn't been able to order the girl to eat, Bess fell onto the next best thing. ''Past dinnertime.''

''Food's still warm,'' Willa commented, and made herself take the first bite. ''Since you're busy feeding half the county, you shouldn't have missed me.''

''Got worse manners than a field hand.'' Bess plopped a mug of coffee at Willa's elbow, sniffed. ''I've got too much work to do to stand around here trying to teach you better.'' She flounced out, wiping her hands on a dish towel.

''She's been watching for you for the past half hour.'' Nate pushed his empty plate away, picked up his own coffee. ''She worries.''

''She doesn't need to.''

''She will as long as you keep riding out alone.''

Willa spared Ben a look. ''Then she'll have to get over it. Pass the salt.''

He did so, slapping it in front of her. On the opposite end of the table, Nate rubbed the back of his neck. ''I'm glad you got back, Will. I've got some papers for you.''

''Fine. I'll look at them later.'' She drizzled salt over her beef. ''That explains why you're here.'' She looked pointedly at Ben.

''I had business with Adam. Horse business. And I stuck

around in my supervisory capacity. And for the free meal.''

"I asked Ben to stay," Nate put in before Willa could snarl. "I talked to the police this morning. They'll be releasing the body tomorrow.'' He waited a moment for Willa to nod, to accept. "Some of the papers I have for you deal with the funeral arrangements. There's also some financial business. Pickles had a small passbook savings account and a standard checking. Combined, we're only talking about maybe thirty-five hundred. He owed nearly that on his rig.''

"I'm not worried about the money.'' She couldn't have eaten now if there'd been a gun to her head. "I'd appreciate it if you'd just handle the details and bill the ranch. Please, Nate.''

"All right.'' He took a legal pad out of the briefcase at his feet, scribbled some notes. "As to his personal effects. There's no family, no heirs, and he never had a will made.''

"There wouldn't be much anyway.'' Misery settled over her, heavy and thick. "His clothes, his saddle, tools. I'll leave that to the men, if that's all right.''

"I think that's the way it should be. I'll handle the legal points.'' He touched a hand to hers, let it linger briefly. "If you think of anything, or you have any questions, just give me a call.''

"I'm obliged.''

"No need to be.'' He unfolded himself and stood. "If you don't mind, I'm going to borrow a horse, ride out after Adam to ah . . .''

"You're going to have to think faster than that,'' Ben told him, "if you're going to lie about sniffing after a woman.''

Nate only grinned and took his hat from the hook by the back door. "Thank Bess for the meal. I'll be around.''

Willa frowned at the door Nate closed behind him. "Sniffing after what woman?''

"Your big sister wears some mighty pretty perfume.''

She snorted, picked up her plate, and took it to the counter beside the sink. "Hollywood? Nate's got more sense than that.''

"The right perfume can kick the sense right out of a man. You didn't eat your dinner."

"Lost my appetite." Curious, she turned back, leaned on the counter. "Is that what yanks your chain, Ben? Fancy perfume?"

"It doesn't hurt." He leaned back in his chair. "Of course, soap and leather on the right kind of skin can do the same damn thing. Being female's a powerful and mysterious thing." He picked up his coffee, watching her over the rim of the cup. "But I guess you'd know that."

"Doesn't matter around a ranch which way your skin stretches."

"Like hell. Every time you go within five feet of young Billy, his eyes cross."

She smiled a little because it was pure truth. "He's eighteen and randy as they come. Saying the word 'breast' around him drains all the blood out of his head into his lap. He'll get over it."

"Not if he's lucky."

Feeling friendlier, she crossed her feet at the ankles. "I don't know how you men tolerate it. Having your ego, your personality, and your idea of romance all dangling between your legs."

"It's a trial. Are you going to sit down and finish your coffee?"

"I've got work."

"That's what you've said every time I've come within five feet of you the last couple of days." He picked up her mug, rose, and carried it to her. "You keep working and not eating, Willa, you're going to end up flat on your face." He took her chin in his hand and gave her a long, long look. "And the face isn't half bad."

"You're grabbing onto it enough lately." She jerked her head, struggling to remain cool when his fingers stayed put. "What's your problem, McKinnon?"

"I don't have one." To test them both, he skimmed a finger up and over her mouth. It had a shape to it, he mused, even in a snarl, that made a man want a bite. "But you seem to have one. I've been noticing you're jumpy around me lately. Used to be you were just mean."

"Maybe you can't tell the difference."

"Yeah, I can." He shifted, boxing her neatly between the counter and his body. "You know what I think, Will?"

He had broad shoulders, long legs. Lately she'd been entirely too aware of the size and shape of him. "I'm not interested in what you think."

Being a cautious man with a good memory, he pressed against her to block a well-aimed knee. "I'll tell you anyway." He took his hand off her chin and gathered up the hair she'd left loose that morning. "You do smell of soap and leather, now that I'm close enough to tell."

"Any closer, you'd be on the other side of me."

"Then there's all this hair, a good yard of it. Straight as a pin and soft as silk." He kept his eyes on hers, drew her head back a fraction more. "Your heart's pounding. And there's this little pulse right here in your throat." He used his free hand to trace it, feel it skitter. "Jumping so hard it's a wonder it doesn't come right through the skin and bounce into my hand."

She wasn't entirely sure it wouldn't happen if he didn't give her room to breathe. "You're irritating me, Ben." It took every ounce of effort to keep her voice even.

"I'm seducing you, Willa." He all but purred it, in words like honey. And his smile came slow and potent when she trembled. "That's what you're afraid of, to my way of thinking. That I could, and I will, and you won't be able to do a damn thing about it."

"Back off." Her voice wasn't steady now, nor were the hands she lifted to his chest.

"No." He tugged her hair again. "Not this time."

"You said yourself not long ago that you don't want me any more than I want you." What was happening inside her? she wondered in panic. The shivering and shakes, the long, liquid pulls. "There's no point in playing like you do just to annoy me."

"I was wrong. What I should have said was that I want

you every bit as much as you want me. I was irritated over it. You're just scared of it.''

"I'm not scared of you." What was happening inside her was frightening. But not because of him. She promised herself it wasn't because of him.

"Prove it." Those eyes of his, sharp green and close, lit with challenge. "Right here. Right now."

"Fine." Accepting the dare, afraid not to, she grabbed a handful of his hair and dragged his mouth down to hers.

He had the McKinnon mouth, she realized. Like Zack's, it was full and firm. But there the similarity ended. None of the dreamy kisses she'd shared with Zack years before compared to this burst, this shock of having a man's skillful lips devouring hers. Or the hot, impatient way he used tongue and teeth to simply overpower, to focus every thought, every feeling, every need into that point where mouth met mouth.

The edge of the counter bit into her back. The fingers she'd twined through his hair curled into a hard, taut fist. And the primal male taste of him coursed through her body and left it in ruins. He hadn't given her even a moment to defend herself.

He didn't intend to.

He felt her body jerk, stiffen against the onslaught. And wondered if what was battling through her was even close to what was battling through him. He'd expected heat, or cold. She had both in her. He'd expected power, for she was anything but weak. He'd hoped to find pleasure, as her mouth seemed to have been created to give and to take it.

He hadn't known he'd find them all, a rage of all that would slam into him like bare-knuckled fists and leave him reeling.

"Goddamn it." He dragged his mouth away, stared into her eyes, so big and dark and shocked. "Goddamn it all to hell."

And his mouth came down on hers again to feed.

She moaned, a sound trapped in her throat, a sound he could feel when he closed his hand over that smooth column and squeezed lightly. He wanted to taste there, just there where that pulse jumped and that moan sounded, but for the life of him he couldn't get enough of her mouth. And she was holding him now, holding hard, moving against him, hips grinding.

He closed a hand over her breast, so firm through the flannel. When it wasn't enough, not nearly enough, he yanked her shirt free of her jeans and streaked under to flesh.

The feel of his hand, hard and callused and strong on her, had the muscles in her thighs going loose, the tension in her stomach pushing toward pain. His thumb flicked over her nipple, ricocheting bullets of heat from point to point through her overtaxed system.

She went limp, might have slid through his arms like vapor if he hadn't changed his grip. That sudden and utter surrender aroused him more than all the flash and fire.

"We need to finish this." He cupped her breast, fingers skimming, stroking as he waited for her eyes to open and meet his. "And though it's tempting to go right on with it here, Bess might be miffed if she came in and found us waxing her floor the way I have in mind."

"Back off." She fought to suck in air. "I can't breathe, back off."

"I'm having some trouble with that myself. We'll breathe later." He lowered his head, nipped at her jaw. "Come home with me, Willa, let me have you."

"I'm not going to do that." She struggled free, stumbled to the table, and braced her palms on it for balance. She had to think, had to. But she could only feel. "Keep away," she snapped when he moved toward her. "Keep away and let me breathe."

It was the lick of real panic in her voice that had him leaning back against the counter. "All right, breathe. It isn't going to change anything." He reached for the mug of coffee beside him and, when he noted his hands weren't steady, left it where it sat. "I don't know if I'm too pleased about this either."

"Fine. That's just fine." Steadier, she straightened, faced him. "You think because you've talked a dozen women onto their backs you can just come in here and talk me onto mine. Easy pickings, too, since I've never done it before.''

"Can't be more than ten women by my count,'' he said easily. "And I didn't have to—'' He broke off, eyes going wide, jaw dropping. "Never done what, exactly?''

"You know damn well what, exactly.''

"Ever?'' He pushed his hands into his pockets. "At all ever?''

She merely stared, waiting for him to laugh. Then she'd have the perfect excuse to kill him.

"But I figured you and Zack . . .'' He trailed off again, realizing that might not have sat too well with him under the circumstances.

"Did he say I did?'' Her eyes narrowed to slits as she poised, ready to spring.

"No, he never—no.'' At a loss, Ben dragged a hand out of his pocket and raked it through his hair. "I just figured, that's all. I just figured you . . . at some time or other. Well, hell, Willa, you're a grown woman. Of course I figured you'd—''

"Slept around?''

"No, not exactly.'' Hand me a shovel, he thought. I'm getting tired of digging this hole for myself with my bare hands. "You're a good-looking woman,'' he began, and winced, knowing he could have done better than that. Would have, too, if his tongue wasn't so tangled up. "I just assumed that you'd had some experience in the area.''

"Well, I haven't.'' Temper was clearing just enough to let in flickers of embarrassment. "And it's up to me when and if I want to change that, and who I want to change it with.''

"Absolutely. I wouldn't have pushed if I'd realized . . .'' He couldn't take his eyes off her, the way she stood there all flushed and rumpled, with that sexy mouth swollen from his. "Or maybe I'd have pushed different. I've been thinking about you, that way, for a while.''

Suspicion flickered in her eyes. "Why?''

"Damned if I know. It just is. Now that I've had my hands on you, I'd have to say I'm going to be thinking more. You've got a nice feel to you, Willa.'' The humor came back, curving his lips. "And you were doing a damn fine job of kissing me back, for an amateur."

"You're not the first man I've kissed, and you won't be the last."

"That doesn't mean you can't practice on me—when you get the urge." He walked over to take his hat and jacket from the pegs by the door. If either of them noticed that he gave her a wide berth, neither commented. "What are friends for?"

"I don't have any trouble controlling my urges."

"You're telling me," he said, with feeling, and fit his hat on his head. "But I have a notion I'm about to have a hell of a time controlling mine where you're concerned."

He opened the door, gave her one long last look. "You've got one hell of a mouth, Willa. One hell of a mouth."

He shut the door, shrugged into his jacket. As he circled around the house toward his rig, he let out a whistling breath. He'd thought a little nuzzling in the kitchen would take both of their minds off the trouble hanging over Mercy. It had done a hell of a lot more than that.

He rubbed a hand over his belly, knowing the knots twisting inside would be there for quite a while yet. She'd gotten to him, and gotten to him hard. And the fact that she had no idea what they could do to each other in the dark only made it more terrifying.

And arousing.

He'd always chosen women who knew the ropes, who understood the pleasures, the rules and the responsibilities. Women, he admitted, who didn't expect more than a good, healthy ride where nobody got hurt, nobody got hobbled.

He glanced back at the house as he climbed behind the wheel, turned the key in the ignition. It wouldn't be so simple with Willa, not when he'd be her first.

He drove away from Mercy without a clue to what he would do about her. All he knew for certain was that Willa was going to have to accept that Ben McKinnon was going to be the one she'd change things with.

He glanced toward the bunkhouse as he drove past and thought of everything she'd been through in the past few weeks. Enough, he thought, to break anyone to bits. Anyone but Willa.

Letting out a long sigh, he headed for his own land. He'd be there for her, whether she liked it or not. And he'd take it slow in that certain area. He'd even try his hand at being gentle.

But he'd be there.

TEN

SNOW CAME HARD AND FAST AND EARLY. IT BURIED THE pastures and had the drift fences groaning. Men worked day and night to see that the cattle—too stupid to dig through the snow to grass—were fed and tended.

November proved to be a poor boundary against winter, and before the end of it, the valley was socked in.

Skiers came, flocking to Big Sky and other resorts to schuss down slopes and drink brandy by roaring fires. Tess gave some thought to joining them for a day or two. Not that she'd ever been much on skiing, but the brandy sounded fine. In any case there would be people, conversations, perhaps flirtations, certainly civilization.

It might be worth strapping herself to a couple of slats of wood and tumbling down a mountain.

She talked to her agent constantly, using Ira more as a bridge to her life than a representative of her work. She wrote, making progress with a new screenplay and detailing daily life in her journal.

Not that she considered the routine on the ranch much of a life.

She continued to take charge of the chickens and was actually rather pleased that she had a handle on the job now and could slip an egg from under a broody hen without so much as a peck.

She had a bad moment, very bad, one day when she strolled behind the coop and walked into Bess, quickly, competently, ruthlessly wringing the neck of one of Tess's flock.

There'd been a lot of squawking then—though not from the chickens. Two of them lay dead as Judas on the ground while the women shouted at each other over the corpses.

Tess had skipped dinner that night—chicken pot pie— but it had taught her the error of assigning names to her beaked and feathered friends.

Every evening she made use of the indoor pool with its curved-glass wall and southern exposure. And she'd decided there was something to be said for looking at snow while she lounged in her personal lake with steam rising around her.

Yet every morning she rose, crossed her eyes at the view of snow out her window, and dreamed of palm trees and lunching at Morton's.

She kept up her horseback riding out of sheer stubbornness. It was true that she didn't climb whimpering out of the saddle with muscles screaming now. And she'd developed a certain wary affection for Mazie, the mare Adam had assigned her. Still, riding out into the wind and the cold wasn't her idea of high entertainment.

"Jesus. Jesus Christ." Tess stepped outside, hunched inside the thick wool jacket, and wished she'd pulled on two pairs of long underwear. "It's like breathing broken glass. How does anyone stand this?"

"Adam says it makes you appreciate spring more."

To ward off the wind, Lily wrapped her scarf more securely around her neck. Yet she appreciated the winter—the majestic, powerful sweep of it, the way the snow seemed to freeze the peaks into sharp relief against the sheer wall of sky. The dark belt of trees that clung to the rising foothills was so prettily draped with snow, and the silver of rock and ridge formed shadows and contrasts, like folds in a stunning blanket.

"It's so beautiful. Miles and miles of white. And the pines. The sky's so blue it almost hurts your eyes." She smiled at Tess. "It's nothing like a city snow."

"I don't have much experience with snow, but I'd say this is nothing like anything." She flexed her fingers in her gloves as they walked toward the horse barn.

At least the ranch yard was negotiable, Tess thought. Paths to and from paddocks and corrals had been plowed. And the roads had been scraped off as well with a blade attached to one of the four-wheelers. Young Billy had done that, she remembered. He'd appeared to be having the time of his life.

She watched her breath plume out in front of her and was tempted to complain again. But it was beautiful, coldly beautiful. The sky was such a hard, brittle blue she expected it to crack at any moment, and the mountains that speared into it were so well defined in the clear air that they seemed to have been painted. Sunlight danced off the fields of snow in glittering sparks, and when the wind rushed, it lifted that snow and those dancing lights into the air in thin drifts.

Palm trees, warm beaches, and mai tais seemed light-years away.

"What's she up to today?" Tess pulled out sunglasses and put them on.

"Willa? She went out early in one of the pickups."

Tess's mouth thinned. "Alone?"

"She almost always goes alone."

"Asking for trouble," Tess muttered, and stuck her hands in her pockets. "She must think she's invincible. If whoever killed that man is still around . . ."

"You don't think that, do you?" Alarmed, Lily began to scan the fields as if a madman might rise up out of one of the drifts like a grinning gnome. "The police haven't come up with anything. I thought it had to be someone camped in the hills. With this weather, he couldn't still be here. And it's been weeks since—since it happened."

"Sure, that's right." Though she was far from convinced,

Tess saw no reason to set Lily's nerves more on edge. "Nobody'd camp out in this cold, especially some itinerant maniac. I guess she just gets under my skin." She narrowed her eyes at the rig heading toward the ranch from the west road. "Speak of the devil."

"Maybe if you—" Lily broke off, shook her head.

"No, go ahead. Maybe if I what?"

"Maybe if you didn't try so hard to irritate her."

"Oh, it's not so hard." Tess's lips curved in anticipation. "In fact, it's effortless." She changed directions as the rig pulled up. "Been out surveying the lower forty?" Tess asked, as Willa rolled down her window.

"Are you still here? I thought you were going to Big Sky to soak in a Jacuzzi and hustle men."

"I'm thinking about it."

Willa shifted her attention to Lily. "If Adam's taking you out, go soon and don't stay long. Snow's coming in." She flicked her eyes toward the sky, the telltale clouds piling together in thick layers. "You may want to tell him I spotted a herd of mule deer northwest of here. About a mile and a half. You might like to see them."

"I would." She patted her pocket. "I have my camera. Can you come with us? Bess sent plenty of coffee along."

"No, I've got things to do. And Nate's coming by later."

"Oh?" Tess lifted an eyebrow, struggled to sound casual. "When?"

Willa slid the gearshift into first. "Later," she repeated, and drove away toward the house.

She knew very well that Tess had her eye on Nate, and she didn't intend to encourage it. As far as she was concerned, Nate would be completely out of his depth with a slick Hollywood piranha.

And maybe he had his eye focused right back, but that was only because men always got dopey around beautiful, stacked women. Grabbing her thermos of coffee from the seat beside her, Willa climbed out of the rig. Tess was beautiful and stacked, she admitted, with just a quick twinge of envy. And confident and quick-tongued. So sure of herself and her control over her own femininity. And her power over men.

Willa wondered if she'd be more like that if she'd had a mother to teach her the ropes. If she'd been raised in a different environment, where there were females giggling over hairdos and hemlines, over lipstick shades and perfume.

Not that she wanted that, she assured herself, as she stepped inside and pulled off her gloves. She wasn't interested in all that fussing and foolishness, but she was beginning to think those very things could add to a woman's confidence around men.

And she wasn't feeling as confident as she wanted to. At least not around one man.

She shucked her coat and hat, then carried the thermos with her to the office upstairs. She'd changed nothing inside it yet. It was still Jack Mercy's domain with its trophy heads and whiskey decanters. And entering, walking over, seating herself at his desk always brought a quick twist to her gut.

Grief? she wondered. Or fear. She just wasn't sure any longer. But the office itself brought on a swarm of unpleasant and unhappy emotions, and memories.

She had rarely come in there when he was alive. If he sent for her, ordered her to take a chair across from that desk, it was to criticize or to shuffle her duties.

She could see him perfectly, sitting where she sat now. A cigar clamped between his fingers, and if it was evening and the workday finished, a glass of whiskey on the blotter.

Girl, he'd called her. He'd rarely used her name. Girl, you fucked up good this time.

Girl, you better start pulling weight around here.

You'd better get yourself a husband, girl, and start having babies. You're no use otherwise.

Had there ever been kindness in this room? she asked herself, and rubbed hard at her temples. She wanted badly to remember even one moment, one incident when she came in here and found him sitting behind this desk and smiling. One time, only one time when he'd told her he was proud of what she'd done. Of anything she'd done.

But she couldn't. Smiles and kind words hadn't been Jack Mercy's style.

And what would he say now? she wondered. If he walked in here and saw her, if he knew what had happened on the land, to one of his men, while she'd been in charge.

You fucked up, girl.

She rested her head in her hands a moment, wishing she had an answer for that. In her mind she knew she'd done nothing to cause a vicious murder. But in her heart, the responsibility weighed heavy.

"Done and over," she murmured. She opened a drawer, took out record books. She wanted to check them over, the careful detailing of number of head, of weight. The pasture rotations, the additives and grain. She'd make sure there was not one figure out of place before Nate came later today to look over her accounts.

Burying her resentment that he, or anyone, had power over Mercy, she got to work.

NEARLY TWO MILES FROM THE RANCH HOUSE, LILY HAPpily snapped pictures of mule deer. It made her laugh to look at them with their shaggy winter coats and bored eyes. The prints would likely be out of focus—she knew she hadn't inherited her mother's skill with a camera—but they would please her.

"I'm sorry." She let the camera dangle from the strap around her neck. "I'm taking too long. I get caught up."

"We've got some time yet." After a brief study of the clouds, Adam shifted in the saddle and turned to Tess. "You're riding well. You learn."

"Self-defense," she claimed, but felt a warm spurt of pride. "I never want to hurt the way I did those first couple of days. And I need the exercise."

"No, you're enjoying it."

"All right, I'm enjoying it. But if it gets much colder than this, I won't be enjoying it till spring."

"It'll get colder than this. But your blood'll be thicker. Your mind tougher." He leaned down to stroke the neck of his mount. "And you'll be hooked. Every day you don't ride, you'll feel deprived."

"Every day I can't stroll down Sunset Boulevard I feel deprived. I manage."

He laughed. "When you get back to Sunset Boulevard, you'll think of the sky here, and the hills. Then you'll come back."

Intrigued, she tipped down her sunglasses, peered at him over the tops. "What is this? Indian mysticism and fortune-telling?"

"Nope. Psychology one-oh-one. Can I use the camera, Lily? I'll take a picture of you and Tess."

"All right. You don't mind, do you?" she asked Tess.

"I never turn away from a camera." She walked her horse around Adam's, turned her—rather smoothly, she thought—and came close to Lily's right. "How's this?"

"It's good." He lifted the camera, focused. "Two beautiful women in one frame." And snapped, twice. "When you look at these, you'll see how much you share. The shape of the face, the coloring, even the way you sit in the saddle."

Automatically, Tess straightened her shoulders. She felt what she considered a mild affection for Lily, but she was far from ready for sisterhood. "Let's have the camera, Adam. I'll take the two of you. The Virginia Magnolia and the Noble Savage."

The minute it was out of her mouth, she winced. "Sorry. I tend to think of people as characters. No offense."

"None taken." Adam passed her the camera. He liked her, the way she went after what she wanted, said what was on her mind. He doubted very much she'd appreciate being told those were two of his favorite qualities about Willa. "How do you think of yourself?"

"Shallow Gal. That's why my screenplays sell. Smile."

"I like your movies," Lily said when Tess lowered the camera. "They're exciting and entertaining."

"And play to the least common denominator. Nothing wrong with that." She handed the camera back to Lily.

"You write for the masses, you take off your brain and keep it simple."

"You're not giving yourself or your audience enough credit." Adam flicked his gaze toward the trees, scanned.

"Maybe not, but..." Tess trailed off as a movement caught her eye. "There's something back there in the trees. Something moved."

"Yes, I know. It's upwind. I can't smell it." Casually, he laid his hand on the butt of his rifle.

"Bears are hibernating now, right?" Tess moistened her lips and tried not to think of a man and a knife. "It wouldn't be a bear."

"Sometimes they wake up. Why don't you start heading home? I'll take a look."

"You can't go up there alone." Instinct made Lily reach over, grab his reins. At the abrupt movement his horse shied and kicked up snow. "You can't. It could be anything. It could be—"

"Nothing," he said calmly, and soothed his horse. A few innocent flakes danced into the air. He didn't think they'd stay innocent for long. "But it's best to see."

"Lily's right." Shivering, Tess kept her eyes trained on the tree line. "And it's starting to snow. Let's just go. Right now."

"I can't do that." Adam locked his dark, quiet eyes on Lily's. "It's probably nothing." He knew better by the way his horse was beginning to quiver beneath him, but kept his voice easy. "But a man was killed barely a mile from here. I have to see. Now head back, and I'll catch up with you. You know the way."

"Yes, but—"

"Please, do this for me. I'll be right behind you."

Knowing she was useless in an argument, Lily turned her horse.

"Stay together," Adam told Tess, then rode toward the tree line.

"He'll be all right." Her teeth threatened to chatter as Tess made the reassurance. "Hell, Lily, it's probably a squirrel." Too much movement for a squirrel, she thought.

"Or a moose or something. We'll have to tease him about saving the womenfolk from a marauding moose."

"And what if it's not?" Lily's quiet southern voice fractured like glass. "What if the police and everyone are wrong and whoever killed that man is still here?" She stopped her horse. "We can't leave Adam alone."

"He's the one with the gun," Tess began.

"I can't leave him alone." Quaking at the prospect of defying an order, Lily nonetheless turned and started back.

"Hey, don't—oh, hell. This'll make a dandy scene in a script," Tess muttered, and trotted after her. "You know, if he shoots us by mistake, we're going to be really sorry."

Lily only shook her head and, veering off the road, started into the hills, following Adam's tracks. "You know how to get back if you had to ride quickly?"

"Yeah, I think, but—Christ, this is insane. Let's just—"

The gunshot split the air and echoed like thunder. Before Tess could do more than cling to her skittish horse, Lily was galloping headlong into the trees.

NATE DIDN'T COME ALONE. BEN DROVE UP BEHIND HIM, with his sister-in-law and his niece. Shelly came into the house chattering and immediately began unwrapping the baby.

"I should have called, I know, but when Ben said he was coming by I just grabbed Abigail and jumped into the rig. We've been dying for company. I know you've got business to tend to, but Abby and I can visit with Bess while you're talking. I hope you don't mind."

"Of course I don't. It's good to see you."

It was always good to see Shelly, with her happy chatter and sunny smile. She was, Willa had always thought, perfect for Zack. They meshed like butter on popcorn, both lively and entertaining.

With the baby happily kicking on the sofa, Shelly peeled off her hat and fluffed her sunny blond hair. The short, sassy cut suited her pixie face and petite build, and her eyes were the color of fog in the mountains.

"Well, I didn't give Ben much choice, but I swear I'll stay out of your way until you've finished."

"Don't be silly. I haven't been able to play with the baby in weeks. And she's grown so. Haven't you, sweetheart?" Indulging herself, Willa lifted Abby and hefted her high over her head. "Her eyes are turning green."

"She's going to have McKinnon eyes," Shelly agreed. "You'd think she'd have the gratitude to take after me a bit, since I'm the one who carried her around for nine months, but she looks just like her pa."

"I don't know, I think she's got your ears." Willa brought Abby close to kiss the tip of her nose.

"Do you?" Shelly perked up immediately. "You know she's sleeping right through the night already. Only five months old. After all the horror stories I heard about teething and walking the floor, I figured I'd—" She held up both hands as if to signal herself to stop. "There I go, and I promised I'd stay out of the way. Zack says I could talk the bark off a tree."

"Zack'll talk you blind," Ben put in. "Surprises me that with the two of you as parents, Abby didn't pop out talking." He reached out to tweak the baby's cheek and grinned at Willa. "She's a pretty handful, isn't she?"

"And sweet-natured, which proves she isn't all Mc-Kinnon." With some regret, Willa passed the cooing baby back to her mother. "Bess is back in the kitchen, Shelly. I know she'd love to see you and Abby."

"I hope you have time for a little visit when you're done, Will." Shelly laid a hand on Willa's arm. "Sarah wanted to come by, too, but she couldn't get away. We've been thinking about you."

"I'll be down soon. Maybe you can talk Bess into parting with some of the pie she's been making for supper. Everything's up in the office," she added to the others, and started upstairs.

"You understand this is just for form's sake, Will," Nate began. "Just so there's no question about adhering to the terms of the will."

"Yeah, no problem." But her back was stiff as she led the way into the office.

"Didn't see your sisters around."

"They're out riding with Adam," Willa told him, moving behind the desk. "I don't imagine they'll be out too much longer. Hollywood's blood's too thin for her to handle the cold for more than an hour or so."

Nate sat, stretched out his legs. "So, I see you two are still getting along beautifully."

"We stay out of each other's way." She handed him a record book. "It works well enough."

"It's going to be a long winter." Ben eased a hip onto the edge of the desk. "You two ought to think about making peace, or just shooting each other to get it done."

"The second part doesn't seem quite fair. She wouldn't know the difference between a Winchester and a posthole digger."

"I'll have to teach her," was Nate's comment as he scanned figures. "Things all right around here otherwise?"

"Well enough." Unable to sit, Will pushed away from the desk. "From what I can tell, the men are convinced that whoever killed Pickles is long gone. The police haven't been able to prove any different. No signs, no weapon, no motive."

"Is that what you think?" Ben asked her.

She met his eyes. "That's what I want to think. And that's what I'll have to think. It's been three weeks."

"That doesn't mean you should let your guard down," Ben murmured, and she inclined her head.

"I've no intention of letting my guard down. In any area."

"Everything here looks in perfect order to me." Nate passed the record book to Ben. "All things considered, you've had a good year."

"I expect the next will be even better." She paused. She didn't clear her throat, but she wanted to. "I'm going to be sowing natural grasses come spring. That was something Pa and I disagreed on, but I figure there's a reason for what grows native to this area, so we're going back to it."

Intrigued, Ben flicked a glance at her. He'd never known her to talk about change when it came to Mercy. "We did that at Three Rocks more than five years ago, with good results."

She looked at Ben again. "I know it. And once we're reseeding, we'll be rotating more often. No more than three weeks per pasture." Pacing now, she didn't notice that Ben set the book aside to study her. "I'm not as concerned as Pa was with producing the biggest cattle. Just the best. Past few years we've had a lot of trouble at birthing time with oversized calves. It might change the profit ratio at first, but I'm thinking long term."

She opened the thermos she'd left on the desk and poured coffee, though it was no more than lukewarm by now. "I've talked to Wood about the cropland. He's had some ideas about it that Pa wasn't keen on. But I think it's worth some experimenting. We've got a little more than six hundred acres cultivated for small grains, and I'm going to give Wood control of them. If it doesn't work, it doesn't, but Mercy can carry some experimentation for a year or two. He wants to build a silo. We'll ferment our own alfalfa."

She shrugged. She knew what some would say about the changes, and her interest in crops and silos and her other plans to ask Adam to increase the string of horses: She was forgetting the cattle, forgetting that Mercy had been pure for generations.

But she wasn't forgetting anything. She was looking ahead.

She set her cup down. "Do either of you, in your supervisory capacity, have a problem with my plans?"

"Can't say that I do." Nate rose. "But then, I'm not a cattleman. I think I'll go on down and see if there's pie, leave you two to discuss this."

"Well?" Willa demanded when she faced Ben alone.

"Well," he echoed, and picked up her cup. "Damn, Will, that's cold." He winced as he swallowed it down. "And stale."

"I didn't ask your opinion on the coffee."

He stayed where he was, sitting on the edge of the desk,

and leveled his eyes to hers. "Where'd all these ideas come from?"

"I've got a brain, don't I? And an opinion."

"True enough. I've never heard you talk about changing so much as a blade of grass around here. It's curious."

"There wasn't any point talking about it. He wasn't interested in what I thought or had to say. I've done some studying up," she added, and stuck her hands in her pockets. "Maybe I didn't go to college like you, but I'm not stupid."

"I never thought you were. And I never knew you wanted to go to college."

"It doesn't matter." With a sigh, she walked to the window and stared out. Storm's coming, she thought. Those first pretty flecks of white were only the beginning. "What matters is now, and tomorrow and next year. Winter's planning time. Figuring-things-out time. I'm starting to plan, that's all." She went stiff when his hands came down on her shoulders.

"Easy. I'm not going to jump you." He turned her to face him. "If it matters, I think you're on the mark."

It did matter, and that was a surprise in itself. "I hope you're right. I've been getting calls from the vultures."

He smiled a little. "Developers?"

"Bastards jumped right in. They'd give me the moon and the sun to sell the land so they can break it up, make a fancy resort or fucking vanity ranches for Hollywood cowboys." If she'd had fangs, they would have been gleaming. "They'll never get their fat fingers on a single acre of Mercy land while I'm standing on it."

Automatically he began to knead her shoulders. "Sent them off scalded, did you, darling?"

"One called just last week. Told me to just call him Arnie. I told him I'd see him skinned and staked out for the coyotes if he set a foot on my property." The corner of her lip quirked. "I don't think he'll be coming by."

"That's the way."

"Yeah. But the other two." She turned, looked out again at the snow and the hills and the land. "I don't think they understand yet just how much money's involved, what those jackasses'll pay to get hold of a ranch like this. Hollywood, she'll figure it out sooner or later. And then . . . they've got me two to one, Ben.''

"The will holds the land for ten years.''

"I know what it said. But things change. With enough money and enough pressure they could change quicker.'' And ten years was nothing, she thought, in the grand scheme of things. Her grand scheme to turn Mercy into not *one* of the best but *the* best. "I can't buy them out after the year's up. I've figured it every way it can be figured, and I just can't. There's money, sure, but most of it's in the land and on the hoof. When the year's up, they'll own two-thirds to my one.''

"No point worrying over what can't be changed, or what may or may not happen.'' He stroked a hand down her hair once, then a second time. "Maybe what you need is a distraction. Just a little one.''

He turned her again, then shook his head. "Don't go shying off. I've been thinking a lot about this since the first time.'' He touched his lips to hers, a teasing brush. "See? That didn't hurt anything.''

Her lips were vibrating, but she couldn't claim it was painful. "I don't want to get all started up again. There's too much going on for distractions.''

"Darling.'' He leaned down, toyed with her lips again. "That's just when you need them most. And I'm willing to bet this makes us both feel a lot better.''

His eyes stayed open and on hers as he gathered her close, as he lowered his head, rubbed lip to lip. "It's working for me already,'' he murmured, then quick as lightning, deepened the kiss.

The jolt, the heat, the yearning all melded together to swim in her head, through her whole body. And she forgot, when the sensations seized her, to be worried or tired or afraid. It was easy to move into him, to press close and let everything else fall away.

And harder, much harder than she'd anticipated, to pull back and remember.

"Maybe I've been thinking about it, too.'' She raised a

hand to keep the distance between them. "But I haven't finished thinking about it."

"As long as I'm the first to know when you do." He twined her hair around his finger, released it. "We'd better go downstairs before I give you too much to think about."

The riders coming in fast caught his eye. With one hand resting on Willa's shoulder, he stepped closer to the window. "Adam's back with your sisters."

She saw them, and more. "Something's wrong. Something's happened."

He could see for himself the way Adam helped Lily out of the saddle, and held on to her. "Something's happened," he agreed. "Let's go find out."

They were halfway down the stairs when the front door swung open. Tess strode in first. The cold had whipped strong color into her cheeks, but her eyes were huge, her lips white.

"It was a deer," she said. "Just a deer. Bambi's mom," she managed, and a tear slipped out of her eye as Nate came down the hall from the kitchen. "Oh, God, why would anybody do that to Bambi's mom?"

"Ssh." Nate draped an arm over her shoulders. "Let's go sit down, honey."

"Lily, let's go in with Tess."

She shook her head and kept her hand gripped tight in Adam's. "No, I'm all right. Really. I'm going to make some tea. It would be better if we had some tea. Excuse me."

"Adam." Willa watched Lily hurry toward the kitchen. "What the hell happened? Did you shoot a doe while you were out?"

"No, but someone had." Revolted, he peeled off his coat, tossed it over the newel post. "They'd left it there, torn to pieces. Not for the game, not even for the trophy, just to kill. The wolves were at it." He rubbed his hands over his face. "I fired to scatter them and get a better look, but Lily and Tess rode up. I wanted to get them back here."

"I'll get my coat."

Before Willa could turn, Adam stopped her. "There's no point. There won't be much left by now, and I saw enough.

She'd been shot clean, in the head. Then she'd been gutted, hacked, left there. He cut off her tail. I guess that was enough trophy this time around.''

''Like the others, then.''

''Like the others.''

''Can we track him?'' Ben demanded.

''Snow's come in since it was done, a day ago at least. More's coming in now. Maybe if I could have set off right then, I'd have had some luck.'' Adam moved his shoulder, a gesture that communicated both frustration and acceptance. ''I couldn't go off and leave them to get back here alone.''

''We'd better have a look anyway.'' Ben was already reaching for his hat. ''Ask Nate to drive Shelly home, Willa.''

''I'm coming with you.''

''There's no point, and you know it.'' Ben took her shoulders. ''No point.''

''I'm coming anyway. I'll get my coat.''

ELEVEN

The snow came down in sheets, white and wild and wicked. By nightfall, there was nothing to see from the windows but a constant fall of thick flakes that built a wall between the glass and the rest of the world.

Lily stared at it, tried to stare through it, while the heat from the blazing logs in the fire licked at her back and worry ate at her nerves.

"Will you sit down?" Tess snapped, and hated the edge in her voice. "There's nothing you can do."

"They've been gone a long time."

Tess knew how long they'd been gone. Exactly ninety-eight minutes. "Like I said, there's nothing you can do."

"You could use some more tea. This is cold." Even as Lily turned to gather the tray, Tess leaped to her feet.

"Will you *stop?* Just stop waiting on me—on everyone. You're not a servant around here. Just sit the hell down, for Christ's sake."

She shuddered once, pressed her fingers to her eyes, and took a long, deep breath. "I'm sorry," she murmured, as Lily stood where she was, hands locked together, eyes blank. "I've got no business yelling at you. I've never seen anything like that. Never seen anything like that."

"It's all right." Empathy eased the tension in her fingers. "It was horrible. I know. Horrible."

They sat, on either end of the long leather couch, silent for a full thirty seconds while the wind beat at the windows with vicious gusts. Tess found herself holding back a sickly laugh.

"Oh, hell." She blew out a breath and repeated, "Oh, hell. What have we got ourselves into here, Lily?"

"I don't know." The wind sent a demon howl down the chimney. "Are you scared?"

"Damn right I'm scared. Aren't you?"

Eyes sober and steady, Lily pursed her lips in consideration. She lifted a fingertip, rubbed it lightly over her bottom lip. It tended to quiver, she knew, when fear had a grip on her.

"I don't think I am. I don't understand it, not really, but I'm not scared, not the way I expect to be. Just sorry and sad. And worried," she added, as her eyes were pulled back to the window and her mind drew a picture of three riders, lost in whirling white. "About Adam and Willa and Ben."

"They'll be all right. They live here."

Nerves bouncing, Tess rose to pace. The sharp snap of a flame in the fireplace made her jump. Swear. "They know what they're doing." If they didn't, she thought, who the hell did? "Maybe that's why I'm so scared right now. I don't know what the hell I'm doing. And I always do, you know. It's one of my best things. Set the goal, form the plan, take the steps. But this time I don't know what I'm doing."

Turning, she sent Lily a thoughtful look. "You do. You know what you're doing with your tea trays and soup simmering and fire building."

Lily shook her head, forced herself to keep her eyes away from the windows. "Those aren't important things."

"Maybe they are," Tess said softly, then stiffened when she saw the glare of lights through the curtain of snow. "Someone's here."

Because she once again didn't know what to do—run? hide?—Tess turned deliberately and walked into the foyer, to the front door to open it. Moments later, Nate appeared, coated with white.

"Get back inside," he ordered, nudging her out of the way as he closed the door behind him. "Are they back yet?"

"No. Lily and I . . ." She gestured toward the living area. "What are you doing here?"

"It's a bad one," he said. "I got Shelly and the baby home all right, but barely made it back." He took off his hat, shook off snow. "It's been two hours now. I'll give them a few more minutes before I head out after them."

"You're going out again. In that?" She'd never experienced a blizzard, but was certain she was living through one now. And blizzards killed. "Are you insane?"

He merely gave her shoulder an absent pat—a man with his mind obviously elsewhere. "Got any coffee hot? I could use a cup. And a thermos to go."

"You're not going out in that." In a gesture she knew to be foolish even as she made it, she stepped between Nate and the door. "No one's going out in that."

He smiled, traced a fingertip down her cheek. He didn't see her gesture as foolish, but as sweet. "Worried about me?"

Terrified was closer to it, but she'd think about that later. "Frostbite, hypothermia. Death." She snapped off the words like frozen twigs. "I'd be worried about anyone who didn't have the good sense to stay inside during a storm like this."

"Three of my friends are out in it." His voice was quiet, the purpose behind them unshakable. "Coffee would help, Tess. Black and hot." Before she could speak, he held up a hand, cocked his head. "There. That should be them."

"I didn't hear anything."

"They're back," Nate said simply, and settling his hat again, went out to meet them.

•   •   •

HE WAS RIGHT, WHICH MADE TESS DECIDE NATE HAD THE ears of a cat. They came in out of the howling wind layered with snow. Gathered in the living room, drinking coffee Bess had delivered within minutes, they thawed out.

"Too much snow to see anything." Ben sank into a deep chair as Adam sat cross-legged in front of the fire. "We got out all right, but there was already a couple new inches down. No way to track."

"But you saw." Tess perched on the arm of the sofa. "You saw what was there."

"Yeah." With a quick glance at Adam, Willa moved her shoulders. She didn't see any point in adding that the wolves had come back. "I'll talk to the men about it in the morning. There's enough to do now."

"To do now?" Tess echoed.

"They're already out rounding up the herd, getting them into shelter. I'll find Ham."

"Wait." Certain that she was the only sane person left, Tess held up a hand. "You're going back out in this. For cows?"

"They'd die in this," Willa said briskly.

As Tess watched in amazement, everyone but her and Lily shrugged back into outdoor gear and headed out. With a shake of her head, she reached for the brandy. "For cows," she muttered. "For a bunch of stupid cows."

"They'll be hungry when they get back." Lily didn't look out the window this time, nor did she listen for the engine of the four-wheeler. "I'll go help Bess with supper."

She could be irritated, Tess thought, or resigned. She decided that being resigned was easier on the system. "I'm not going to sit here alone." But she took the brandy with her as she caught up with Lily. "Do you get storms like this back east?"

Distracted, Lily shook her head. "We get our share of snow in Virginia, but I haven't seen anything quite like this. It comes in so quickly, with so much wind. I can't imagine having to be out in it, to work in it. I expect Nate will stay the night, don't you? I'll have to ask Bess if there's a room ready for him."

She pushed open the kitchen door and found Bess already at the stove nursing an enormous pot steaming fragrantly. "Stew," Bess announced, sampling from a wooden spoon. "Enough for an army. Needs an hour or two yet to simmer."

"They've gone out again." Automatically, Lily went to the pantry to take an apron from a peg. Tess raised an eyebrow at the ease of the gesture. Already routine, she realized.

"Figured as much," said Bess. "I'm going to put together an apple cobbler here." She glanced at Tess, sniffed at the brandy in her hand. "You looking to be useful?"

"Not particularly."

"The woodboxes are half empty," Bess told her, and hauled a basket of apples out of the pantry. "The men don't have time to bring in fuel."

Tess swirled the brandy in her hand. "You expect me to go outside and bring in wood?"

"The power goes out, girl, you'll want to keep your butt warm just like the rest of us."

"The power." At the idea of losing power, of being stuck in the cold, in the dark through the night, her color drained.

"We got a generator." Bess moved her shoulders as she began briskly paring apples. "But we can't waste it on heating bedrooms when we got plenty of fuel. You want to sleep warm, you bring in wood. You give her a hand, Lily. She needs it more than I do. There's a rope leading from that door there to the woodpile. You follow that, and bring it in by hand. You won't be able to push the wheelbarrow through the snow, and there's no use shoveling the path out until it's done falling. Get bundled up good, take a flashlight."

"All right." Lily took one look at Tess's annoyed face. "I can bring it in. Why don't you stay inside, and you can carry wood up to the bedrooms?"

It was tempting. Very. Even now Tess could hear the frigid howl of the wind threatening the kitchen windows. But the smirk on Bess's face caused her to set her snifter aside. "We'll both bring it in."

"Not with those fancy lady's gloves," Bess called out as they started out. "Get yourself some work gloves from the mudroom after you've got the rest of your gear on."

"Hauling in wood," Tess muttered on her way to the foyer closet. "There's probably enough inside already to last a week. She's just doing this to get to me."

"She wouldn't ask us to go out if it wasn't necessary."

Tess dragged on her coat, then shrugged. "She wouldn't ask you," she agreed, then plopped down at the base of the steps to tug on her boots. "The two of you seem to be pretty chummy."

"I think she's great." Lily wound the knit scarf around her neck twice before buttoning her coat over it. "She's been nice to me. She'd be nice to you too, if you'd . . ."

Squashing a ski cap onto her head, Tess nodded. "No, don't spare my feelings. If I'd what—?"

"Well, it's just that you're a little abrasive with her. Abrupt."

"Well, maybe I wouldn't be if she wasn't always finding some idiotic chore for me to do, then complaining that I don't do it to her specifications. I'll get frostbite bringing in this damn wood, and she'll say I didn't stack it right. You wait and see."

Miffed, she headed back down the hall again, went through the kitchen without a word and into the mudroom to hunt up a pair of thick, oversized work gloves.

"Ready?" Lily grabbed a flashlight and prepared to follow Tess.

The minute Tess opened the door, the wind slapped ice-edged snow into their faces. Wide-eyed, they stared at each other; it was Lily who took the first step into the wolf bite of the wind.

They grabbed the leading rope, pulling themselves along as the wind shoved them rudely back a step for every three they took. Boots sank knee-deep into snow, and the flashlight bobbled along through the dark like a drunken moonbeam. They all but stumbled over the tarp-covered woodpile.

Tess kept a grip on the flashlight and held her arms out

while Lily filled them with wood. Legs spread to hold her balance, the tip of her nose tingling, Tess gritted her teeth. "Hell has nothing to do with fire," she shouted. "Hell is winter in Montana."

Lily smiled a little and began to fill her own arms. "Once we're inside and warm, with the fires going, we'll look out and think it's pretty."

"Bullshit," Tess muttered as they fought their way back to the house to dump the first load. "How bad do you want a warm bed?"

Lily looked toward the toasty kitchen, then back out into the thundering storm. "Pretty bad."

"Yeah." Tess sighed, rolled her shoulders. "Me too. Once more into the breach."

They repeated the routine three times, and Tess began to get into the swing of it. Until she lost her footing and fell headlong and face first into a three-foot drift. The flashlight buried itself like a mole in topsoil.

"Are you all right? Did you hurt yourself?" In her rush to help, Lily leaned over, lost her balance, overcompensated, and sat down hard on her butt. With her breath gone, she stayed where she was, sunk to the waist, while Tess rolled over and spat out snow.

"Fuck, fuck, fuck." Struggling to sit up, Tess narrowed her eyes at Lily's giggles. "What's so goddamn funny? We'll be buried any minute, and they won't find us until the spring thaw." But she felt her own laughter bubbling up as she studied Lily, sitting in a deep throne of snow like some miniature ice queen. "And you look like an idiot."

"So do you." Breath hitching, Lily pressed a snow-coated glove to her heart. "And you're the one with a beard."

Philosophically, Tess swiped the snow off her chin and tossed it into Lily's face. It was all they needed. Despite the mule kick of the wind, they scooped snow into lopsided balls and pummeled each other. Shrieking now, scrambling to their knees, they heaved and tossed and dodged. They were no more than a foot apart, so aim wasn't a factor in the battle. Speed was all that mattered. As snow slapped her face and snuck down the collar of her coat, Tess had to admit that Lily had her there. She might appear delicate, but she had an arm like a bullet.

There was only one way to even the odds.

Tess tackled her and sent them both rolling. Laughing like hyenas, white as snowmen, they plopped on their backs to catch their breath. Flakes drifted down on them, huge and heavy, with the iced edges smoothed out.

"We used to make snow angels when I was a kid," Lily said, and lazily demonstrated by skimming her arms and legs over the snow. "And once it snowed enough for us to be out of school for two days. We built a snow fort and an army of snow people. My mother came out and took pictures of it."

Tess blinked up, trying to see the black sky through the curtain of white. "The one and only time I went skiing, I decided snow and I weren't compatible." She mimicked Lily's moves. "I guess it's not so bad, really."

"It's beautiful." Then she laughed. "I'm freezing."

"I'll buy you a huge mug of coffee laced with brandy."

"I'll take it." Still smiling, Lily sat up. Then her heart leaped into her throat, blocking the scream. Her hand clamped over Tess's as the shadow moved, became a man. Came closer.

"Did you all take a tumble?"

Tess's head jerked around, her pulse roaring in her ears. They were alone, she thought in panic, too far from the house for a shout to carry over the wind. The image of the butchered deer reared up in her mind, turning her to helpless mush.

The flashlight, she thought, as her eyes darted right and left. He had one, the beam strong enough to blind her while keeping him in silhouette. She wanted to run, ordered herself to run, to drag Lily with her, but she couldn't seem to move.

"You shouldn't be out here in the dark," he said, and stepped closer.

Now she moved, survival instincts springing free like a cat out of a cage. She bounded up, snatched a log from the woodpile, and prepared to swing. "Stay back," she ordered, and despite her shaking hands the order was strong and firm. "Lily, get up. Get up, goddamn it."

"Hey, I didn't mean to spook you." He angled the light so that it played along the snow. "It's Wood, Miss Tess. Billy and me just got in, and the wife thought you might need some help up here."

His voice was easy, nonthreatening—even, Tess thought, slightly amused. But they were alone, basically helpless, and he was a strong man with his face still in shadow. Trust no one, she decided, and took a firmer grip on the log.

"We're fine. Lily, go inside and tell Bess that Wood's here. Tell her," she hissed, and Lily finally snapped into action and moved.

"No need to put Bess to any trouble." Wood angled the flashlight toward the woodpile, skimmed the beam over the trampled path to the house. "The wife's got supper on for me, but I can haul some logs in for you. Power's bound to go before long."

Completely alone with Wood now, Tess prayed that Lily was inside and alerting Bess. Fear licked along her spine with a sharp-edged tongue. She took one step back, then two. "We've already taken some in."

"Can't have too much in this kinda storm." He held the flashlight out to her, and she jerked back, visualizing a knife. "You want to take this," he said gently, "I'll load up."

Still poised to run, Tess reached out, took the light. Wood bent to the pile as Lily came flying back. "Bess has coffee on." Her voice rose and fell like an arpeggio. "She said there was plenty if Wood wanted a cup."

"Well, now, I appreciate that." He continued to stack logs competently in the crook of one arm. "But I'll get one back to home. The wife's waiting on me. You all go back in, use that light now. I can find my way well enough."

"Yes, let's go in. Let's go inside, Tess." Shivering, Lily tugged on Tess's arm. "Thank you, Wood."

"Don't mention it," he murmured, shaking his head as they backed down the path. "Women," he said to himself.

"I was so scared," Lily managed. The moment they were inside the mudroom she threw her arms around Tess. "You were so brave."

"I wasn't brave. I was terrified." As fresh realization set in, she clutched Lily and shook violently. "How could we have forgotten? How could we be playing out there like a couple of idiots after everything that's happened? God! God, it could be anyone. Why did it take so long for that to sink in?" She drew back, met Lily's eyes. "It could be anyone."

"Not Adam." After tearing her gloves off, Lily rubbed her chilled hands together. "He couldn't hurt anyone, or anything. And he was with us when we—when we found it today."

Tess opened her mouth, closed it again. What point was there in speculating that Adam could have gone out before dawn, done what had been done, then led them to it, taken them to see what he'd wanted them to see?

"I don't know, Lily. I just don't know. But if we're going to stay here, get through this winter, we'd better start thinking, and we'd better start watching our backs." She pulled off her hat, her coat. "I can't imagine Adam doing that. Or Ben, or Nate. Hell, I can't imagine anyone doing it, and that's the problem. We have to start imagining it."

"We're safe here." Lily turned her back, carefully hung her coat. "We're safe. I haven't felt safe in a long time, and I'm not going to let anything spoil it."

"Lily." Tess laid a hand on her shoulder. "Staying safe means staying careful. And staying smart. We both want something here," she continued as Lily turned back. "And we want it badly enough to risk being here. The way I see it, we have to look out for each other. And we have to trust each other. If I see anything odd, I'm going to tell you, and you're going to do the same. Anything that doesn't feel right, anyone who doesn't act right. Agreed?"

"Yes, I'll tell you. And Willa." She shook her head before Tess could protest. "She deserves that, Tess. She has every bit as much at stake. She has more at stake."

Exactly, Tess thought, then shrugged. "Okay, we'll play it that way. For now, anyway. Now I want that coffee."

•　　•　　•

THEY HAD COFFEE. AND WAITED. THEY ATE STEW. AND waited.

The wind screamed at the windows, the fire snapped in the grate, and the grandfather clock in the study bonged the hours away.

It was past midnight when Willa came in, and she came in alone.

Tess stopped pacing the living room and studied her. Willa's face was sheet-white with exhaustion, those dark, exotic eyes bruised with it. She walked directly to the fire, trailing snow and wet behind her over the exquisite rugs and gleaming floors.

"Where are the others?" Tess asked her.

"They had to get back. They've got their own worries."

With a nod, Tess went to the whiskey decanter and poured a generous glass. She'd have preferred having Nate and Ben in the house, but she was learning that Montana was filled with little disappointments. She handed the glass to Willa.

"Cows all tucked in for the night?"

Without bothering to answer, Will tossed back half the whiskey, shuddered hard.

"I'll run you a bath."

With her mind too weary to focus, Willa blinked at Lily. "What?"

"I'm going to run you a hot bath. You're frozen and exhausted. You must be starving. There's stew on the stove. Tess, you fix Willa a bowl."

Willa had just enough energy left to be amused. Her baffled smile followed Lily out of the room. "She's going to run me a bath. Can you beat that?"

"Our resident domestic expert. Anyway, you could use one. You smell."

Willa sniffed, winced. "Guess I do." Because the first blast of whiskey had her head reeling, she set the glass aside. "I'm too tired to eat."

"You need something. You can eat in the tub."

"In the tub. Eat in the tub?"

"Why the hell not?"

Willa spared Tess one smirking glance. "Why the hell not?" she agreed, and stumbled her way upstairs to strip.

Lily had the water steaming and frothy with bubbles. Naked, Willa stared down at it for a full ten seconds. A bubble bath, she thought. She couldn't remember the last time she'd had a bubble bath. The big scarlet tub had been one of her father's indulgences, and she'd rarely used it. And then only when he'd been away.

He was away now, she reminded herself. Dead away.

She swung a leg over the side, hissed as hot water met chilled skin. Then with an enormous sigh, she lowered herself to the chin.

She emptied her mind of snow, of wind, of the raging dark, the brutal fight to round up cattle. They would have missed some, and they would lose some. That was inevitable. The blizzard had come in too fast and too mean to prevent that. But they had done their best.

Her muscles wept as she laid her head back, closed her eyes. Can't think, she realized as her mind clicked on and off. Had to think. What to do. Every movement, every chore, every decision made come morning would be instinctive. She knew what to do there. It wasn't her first blizzard, nor would it be her last.

But murder—murder and butchery.

What to do.

"Fall asleep in there and you'll drown," Tess said from the doorway.

Willa sat up, scowling. She wasn't particularly modest. The scowl was for the intrusion, even if it did include the heavenly scent of stew. "You ever try knocking?"

"You left the door open, champ." Rather amused at her role of server, Tess settled the tray across the tub. "I want to talk to you."

Willa only sighed. She scooted up enough to manage the meal, dipped a spoon into the stew while bubbles melted off her breasts. "So talk."

Tess sat on the wide ledge of the tub. Quite a bathroom, she mused. It was as plush as any movie star's fantasy with its ruby, sapphire, and white tiles, its forest of ferns in brass and copper pots. The separate shower was walled in clear glass, boasted half a dozen showerheads at different angles and heights. And the tub where Willa was lounging was easily big enough for a small, tasteful orgy.

Idly she dipped a finger into the bubbles, sniffed at them. "Violets," she commented. "Must be Lily's."

"You want to talk about bubble baths?" Willa scooted up higher as she gained more enthusiasm for the meal. She could have eaten a truckload of stew.

"We'll leave the girl stuff for later." She glanced over as Lily came to the doorway, her gaze politely fixed inches above Willa's head. "I've got your robe, for when you're finished. I'll just hang it on the back of the door."

"Come on in, have a seat," Willa invited with a wave of her hand. "Tess wants to talk." When Lily hesitated, Willa rolled her eyes. "We've all got tits here, Lily."

"And hers are barely noticeable, anyway," Tess added with a smug smile. "Have a seat," she ordered. "You're the one who wanted to bring her in on all of this."

"All of what?" Willa demanded with her mouth full.

"Let's just say Lily and I are a little nervous. Wouldn't you agree with that, Lily?"

Flushing, Lily lowered the lid on the toilet and sat. "Yes."

Despite the heat of the water, Willa's skin chilled. "You two planning to bolt?"

"We're not cowards." Tess inclined her head. "Or fools. The three of us have equal interest in getting through this year. I assume we all have equal interest in getting through it in one piece. Somebody, very possibly somebody on this ranch, is—let's say knife happy. How do we deal with it?"

Willa's mouth went stubborn. "I know my men."

"We don't," Tess pointed out. "Maybe we should start by you filling us in. Telling us what you know about each one of them. As appealing as it sounds, the three of us can't travel in a pack twenty-four hours a day for the next nine or ten months."

"You're right."

The careless agreement caused Tess's mouth to drop open. "Well, well, I must mark this day on my calendar. Willa Mercy agrees with me."

"I still can't stand you." Scraping her bowl, Willa continued. "But I do agree. The three of us need to cooperate if we're going to get through this. Until the police, or we, find out who killed Pickles, I don't think either of you should wander around alone."

"I can defend myself. I've taken classes."

Tess's announcement made Willa snort.

"I could take you down," Tess tossed out. "In ten seconds I'd have you on your back seeing stars. But that's beside the point." She had a low-grade urge for a cigarette, and promised herself she'd indulge it soon. "Lily and I can't very well attach ourselves to each other at the hip."

"I'm with Adam most of the day. With the horses."

Willa nodded at Lily and slid back into the water. "You can depend on Adam. And Bess. And Ham."

"Why Ham?" Tess wanted to know.

"He raised me," Willa said shortly. "The weather's going to keep the two of you close to the house for the next little while anyway."

"What about you?" Lily asked.

"I'll worry about me." Willa submerged, holding her breath under the water, then came up feeling nearly human again. "I haven't had the benefit of Hollywood's self-defense courses, but I know the men, I know the land. If either one of you is nervous, you can saddle up and go to work with me. Now, unless one of you wants to scrub my back, I'd like some privacy."

Tess rose, and as an afterthought reached down for the tray. "Being cocky isn't much protection against a knife."

"A Winchester is." And satisfied with that, Willa reached for the soap.

SHE SLEPT POORLY. EXHAUSTION, AS POWERFUL AS IT WAS, couldn't beat back the nightmares. Willa tossed and turned, fighting for sleep as images of blood and gore raced through her head.

When that thin winter light crept through the wall of steadily falling snow, she shivered and wished there was something, someone, to hold on to. For just a little while.

SOMEONE ELSE WOKE IN THAT SAME STINGY LIGHT WITH those same images running like a river through his head.

But they made him smile.

TWELVE

I'm beginning to like snow. Or I'm going slowly insane. Each morning when I look out my bedroom window, there it is, white and shiny. Miles of it. I can't say I care for the cold. Or the fucking wind. But the snow, particularly when I'm inside looking out, has a certain appeal. Or maybe I'm beginning to feel safe again.

It's a week before Christmas, and nothing has happened to interrupt the routine. No murdered men, no slaughtered wildlife. Just the eerie quiet of snow-smothered days. Maybe the cops were right after all, and whoever killed that poor bald guy was a psychotic hiker. We can only hope.

Lily is big into the holiday spirit. Funny, sweet woman. She's like a child about it, hustling bags into her bedroom, wrapping presents, baking cookies with Bess. Great cookies, which means I've been adding an extra fifteen minutes to my morning workouts.

We took a trip into Billings, for what it's worth, to do some Christmas shopping. Lily was easy enough. I found a pretty brooch of a rearing horse, very delicate and feminine. Figured I had to come up with something for sour-face Bess, and settled on a cookbook. Lily approved it, so I suppose I'm safe. The cowgirl's another matter. I still haven't pinned her down.

Is this woman fearless or stupid?

She goes out every day, more often than not alone. She works her ass off, swaggers down to the old bunkhouse every evening to talk to her men. When she's in the house, she's often buried up to her eyeballs with ledgers and cow reports.

I'm afraid I'm starting to admire her, and I'm not sure I like it. I got her a cashmere sweater, I don't know why. She never wears anything but flannel. But it's screaming siren red, very soft and female. She'll probably end up tossing it on over her long underwear and castrating cows in it. Hell with it.

For Adam, because he appeals to me on a surprisingly fraternal level, I found a lovely little watercolor of the mountains. It reminded me of him.

After much debate with myself, I decided to spring for a token gift for both Ben and Nate, since they spend so much time around here. I picked up a video of Red River *for Ben, kind of a gag that I hope will be taken in the proper spirit.*

And after some subtle probing, I learned that Nate has a weakness for poetry. He's getting a volume of Keats. We'll see.

Between the shopping, the smells from the kitchen, and the decorating, I'm getting in the holiday mood myself. Just shipped off a ton of presents for Mom. With her, it's not the quality but the quantity, and I know she'll be happily ripping off shiny paper for hours.

The damnedest thing, I miss her.

Despite all the Santa Clausing, I'm antsy. Too many hours indoors, I think. I'm using this extra time—winter is chock-full of time around here since it's dark before five in the evening—to play with an idea for a book. Just for fun, just to pass the time during these incredibly long nights.

And speaking of long nights . . . Since all seems quiet

again, I'm taking one of the jeeps—I mean rigs—and driving over to Nate's to deliver my gift. Ham gave me directions to Nate's—what would I call it—spread, I suppose. I've been waiting weeks for an invitation to his house, and for him to make a move. I guess it's up to me to start the ball rolling.

I can't decide how subtle I should be about getting him into bed, and so will play it by ear. At the rate he's going, it could be spring before I get laid.

The hell with that, too.

"GOING SOMEWHERE?" WILLA DEMANDED AS TESS GLIDED downstairs.

"As a matter of fact." She tilted her head, took in Willa's usual uniform of flannel and denim. "You?"

"I just got in. Some of us don't have time to primp in front of a mirror for an hour." Willa's brow furrowed. "You're wearing a dress."

"Am I?" Feigning surprise, Tess looked down at the simple, form-fitting blue wool that skimmed above her knees. "Well, how did that happen?" With a snicker, she came down the rest of the way and walked to the closet for her coat. "I have a Christmas present to deliver. You remember Christmas, don't you? Even with your busy schedule you must have heard of it."

"There was a rumor." Sexy dress, heels, fuck-me perfume, Willa mused, and narrowed her eyes. "Who's the present for?"

"I'm dropping in on Nate." Tess swirled on her coat. "I hope he has some wassail handy."

"Should have figured it," Willa muttered. "You're going to break your neck getting to the rig in those ice picks."

"I've got excellent balance." With a careless wave, Tess glided out. "Don't wait up, Sis."

"Yeah. Good balance," Willa repeated, watching as Tess made her way gracefully to the rig. "I hope Nate's got good balance."

She turned away, walked into the living room, and stretched out on the sofa. After one long look at the tall, elaborately decorated tree framed in the front window, she buried her face in the leather.

Christmas had always been a miserable time of year for her. Her mother had died in December. Not that she remembered, but she knew it, and it had always put a cloud over the holidays. Bess had tried, God knew, to make up for it with decorations and cookies, with silly presents and carols. But there had never been family gathered around the piano, or family huddled under the tree opening gifts on Christmas morning.

She and Adam had exchanged theirs on Christmas Eve, always. After her father was rip-roaring drunk and snoring in his bed.

There had been presents under the tree with her name on them. Bess had seen to that, and for years had put Jack's name on them. But when Willa had turned sixteen, she'd stopped opening those. They were a lie after all, and after a couple of further attempts, Bess had given up the pretense.

Christmas morning had meant hangovers and bad temper, and on the one occasion she'd been brave enough to complain, a stinging backhand.

She'd stopped looking forward to the holidays a long time ago.

And now she was tired, so damn tired. The winter had come so soon, and so brutally. They'd lost more cows than she'd expected, and Wood was worried they hadn't gotten the winter wheat in soon enough. The market price per head had dipped—not enough for panic, but enough for worry.

And she found herself waiting, every day waiting, to find something, or someone, slaughtered on her doorstep again.

No one to talk to, she thought. So she kept her worries to herself. She didn't want Lily and Tess terrified every minute of the day, but neither could she relax and ignore it. She made certain that either she or Adam or Ham kept an eye on both of them when they were out of the house.

Now Tess was gone, driving off, and Willa hadn't had the energy or the wisdom to stop her.

Call Nate, she told herself. Get up and call Nate to tell him she's coming. He'll look out for her. But she didn't move, just couldn't seem to swing her legs down and sit up. To sit up and face that brightly, pitifully cheerful tree with the pretty presents under it.

"If you're going to sleep, you should go to bed."

She heard Ben's voice, resigned herself to it. "I'm not sleeping. I'm just resting a minute. Go away."

"I don't know; when I come over here you don't tell me to leave again." So he sat down, settling in the middle of the sofa. "You're wearing yourself out, Will." Reaching down, he turned her face away from the back of the sofa. The tears on it made him drop his hand as if she'd burned him. "You're crying."

"I am not." Humiliated, she pressed her face into leather again. "I'm just tired. That's all." Then her voice hitched, broke, and disgraced her. "Leave me alone. Leave me alone. I'm tired."

"Come here, darling." Though he had little experience with weeping females, he figured he could handle this one. As easily as if she'd been a child, he lifted her up, cradled her on his lap. "What's the matter?"

"Nothing. I'm just . . . Everything," she managed, and let her head rest on his shoulder. "I don't know what's wrong with me. I'm not crying."

"Okay." Deciding they were both better off pretending she wasn't, he gathered her closer. "Let's just sit here awhile anyway. You're a comfortable armful for a bony woman."

"I hate Christmas."

"No, you don't." He pressed his lips to the top of her head. "You're just worn out. You know what you should do, Will? You and your sisters should take a few days off and go to one of those fancy spas. Get yourself pampered and pummeled, take mud baths."

She snorted, felt better. "Yeah, right. Me and the girls swapping gossip in the mud. That's my style, all right."

"Better yet, you could go with me. We could get a room with one of those big bubble tubs, a heart-shaped bed with a mirror over it. That way you can see what's going on when we make love. You'll learn faster that way."

It had a certain decadent, dizzying appeal, but she shrugged. "I'm not in any hurry."

"I'm getting to be in one," he muttered, then tilted her head back. "Haven't done this in a while." And closed his mouth over hers.

She didn't pretend to resist or protest, not when it was exactly what she needed. The warmth, the steady hand, the skilled mouth. Instead, she slid her arms around his neck, turned into him, and let all those worries and doubts and bad memories fade away.

Here was comfort and, regardless of anything, someone who would listen, and perhaps even care. She sank into that, into the wanting of that as much as the wanting of him.

He felt the need he'd kept carefully reined strain at its tether. The unexpected sweetness of her, the surprising and arousing pliancy, the little licks of heat that hinted of passion simmering beneath innocence.

The combination came close to snapping that straining tether.

So it was he who drew back, she who protested. Struggling to temper instinct with sense, he shifted her again, settled her head once more in the curve of his shoulder. "Let's just sit here awhile."

She felt his heart beat, fast, under her hand. Heard her own pound in her head. "You get me stirred up. I don't know why it's you who gets me stirred up, Ben. I just can't figure it."

"Well, I feel heaps better now." He sighed once, then rested his head against hers. "This isn't so bad."

"No, I guess it isn't." So she sat in his lap while her feelings settled again. She watched the twinkle of the lights on the tree, and the fall of light snow, just a whisper of white, through the window beyond. "Tess went over to Nate's," she said at length.

He heard the tone, knew her well enough to interpret it. "You're worried about that?"

"Nate can handle himself. Probably." She made a restless movement, then gave up and let her eyes drift closed.

"It's Tess you're worried about."

"Maybe. Some. Yes. Nothing's happened for weeks now, but . . ." She exhaled. "I can't watch her every minute of the day and night."

"No, you can't."

"She thinks she knows all the answers. Miss Big City Girl with her self-defense courses and her snappy clothes. Shit. She's as lost out here as a mouse in a roomful of hungry she-cats. What if the rig breaks down, or she runs off the road?" She drew a deep breath and said what was most on her mind. "What if whoever killed Pickles is still around, watching?"

"Like you said, nothing's happened in weeks. Odds are he's long gone."

"If you believe that, why are you here most every day, using every lame excuse in the book to drop by?"

"They aren't so lame," he muttered, then shrugged. "There's you." He didn't bother to scowl when she snorted. "There is you," he repeated. "And there's the ranch. And yeah, I think about it." He tilted her head up again and kissed her hard and quick. "Tell you what, I'll just ride by Nate's and make sure she got there."

"Nobody's asking you to check up on my problems."

"Nope, nobody is." He lifted her, set her aside, then rose. "One day you might just ask me for something, Willa. You might just break down and ask. Meanwhile I'll do things my own way. Go on to bed," he told her. "You need a decent night's sleep. I'll see to your sister."

She frowned after him as he walked out, and wondered what he was waiting for her to ask.

TESS GOT THERE. SHE CONSIDERED IT A FINE ADVENTURE to drive through the light snowfall in the deep country dark. She had the radio turned up to blast, and by some minor miracle she found a station that played downright rock. She wailed along with Rod Stewart as she approached the lights of Nate's ranch.

Tidy as a Currier and Ives painting, she decided. The well-plowed dirt road with its fresh sprinkle of white, the neat outbuildings and rectangles of fence, the rising shadows of trees.

Her headlights must have stirred the horses, as three trotted out of the barn and into the corral to watch her drive by.

Pretty as a painting themselves, she thought, with their flowing tails and dancing hooves. One of them loped over to the fence, luring her into slowing down to study its trim lines and glossy color.

She drove on, taking the gentle curve in the road that led to the main house. It, too, was pretty and neat. Unpretentious, she decided, a boxy two stories with a generous covered porch, white shutters against dark wood, double chimneys with smoke pumping into the snowy sky. Simple, she mused, hold the pretenses and fancywork. Just like the man who lived there.

She was smiling as she gathered up her bag, the gift, and climbed out of the rig. And managed, barely, to hold back the scream when she spotted the wildcat.

She took three stumbling steps back, rapped up hard against the rig. The cat's eyes stared into hers. It was dead, stone cold dead and draped over the hitching rail. But it gave her a very bad moment.

The fangs and claws were lethally sharp and told her exactly what would happen to a woman careless enough to stumble onto a live one. It hadn't been mutilated, and the lack of blood settled her thundering heart. It was simply draped, like a rug, she thought in wonder, over the rail. With a shudder, she gave it a wide berth and climbed the steps to the front door.

What kind of people, she wondered, draped the carcass of a wildcat over their front entrance? With a nervous laugh, she looked down at the gift in her hand. Then read Keats?

Jesus, what a country.

Even as she lifted her hand to knock, the door opened. In the mood she was in, Tess was pleased she didn't add a shriek to her jolt.

The short, dark woman studied her solemnly. She was nearly as wide as she was tall, wrapped now in a thick black coat and many scarves. Her black hair was bundled under yet another scarf, but Tess could see it was salted with gray.

"Señorita," she said in a gorgeous, fluid voice. "May I help you?"

The liquid, sexy voice coming out of the tiny, wrinkled face fascinated Tess, and she immediately started casting character. Her smile spread and brightened. "Hello, I'm Tess Mercy."

"Yes, Señorita Mercy." At the Mercy name, the woman opened the door wider, stepping back in invitation.

"I'd like to see Nate, if he's free."

"He's in his office. Just down the hall. I will show you."

"You're on your way out." And Tess didn't want her arrival announced. "I can find it. Señora . . . ?"

"Cruz." She blinked a moment at Tess's offered hand, then took it in a brisk grip. "Mister Nate will be pleased to see you."

Will he? Tess thought, but she continued to smile. "I have a little gift for him," she said, and held up the brightly wrapped book. "A surprise."

"That is very generous. It is the third door on the left." The ghost of a smile around the woman's mouth told Tess that the underlying reason for her visit was all too obvious. At least to another female. "Good night, Señorita Mercy."

"Good night, Señora Cruz." And Tess chuckled to herself as the door closed between them and she was left alone in the quiet hall.

Bright geometric-patterned rugs over dark wood floors, clever pen-and-ink sketches on ivory-toned walls. Lovely dried-flower arrangements in brass urns—that would be the señora's touch, Tess assumed as she wandered.

A fire was burning nicely in the living room, simmering in a stone hearth beneath a stone mantel on which stood pewter candlesticks and a collection of intriguing paperweights. The furniture was wide and deeply cushioned and masculine. Dark colors to contrast with light walls and the bright rugs.

An interesting mix, Tess decided. Simple, male, yet pleasing to the eye.

She caught the low strains of a Mozart concerto as she walked closer to the open office door.

And there he was, all gangling and sexy and Jimmy Stewart-ish in a high-backed leather chair behind a big oak desk. The desk lamp slanted light over his hands as he made notations on a yellow legal pad. His brow was knotted, his tie loose, his hair, all that thick gold of it, mussed. From his own hands, she noted, as he raked his fingers through it.

Well, well, she thought, just feel my heart go pitty-pat. Amused at herself, she watched him another minute, pleased to be able to study him when he was working and unaware of her.

The room was filled with books, and a single mug of coffee sat at his elbow while the lovely music murmured in the background.

Nate, she decided, giving her hair a brief stroke, you're a goner.

"Well, good evening, Lawyer Torrence." Well aware that she was posed in the doorway, she smiled slowly as his head jerked up, as his eyes cleared of business, then surprise, and focused.

"Well, hello, Miz Mercy." Tension whipped into him as he saw her there, snow still lightly dusted over her hair and the shoulders of her coat. That tension increased when he saw the secret female smile on her lips, but he leaned back in his chair like a man perfectly at ease. "This is a pleasant surprise."

"I hope so. And I hope I'm not interrupting something vitally important."

"Not vital." The notes he'd been taking had already gone completely out of his mind.

"Señora Cruz let me in." She started toward the desk, thinking of the wildcat. She would take a page from the feline book and toy with her prey before moving in for the kill. "Your housekeeper."

"My keeper." He was quite simply baffled. Should he get up, offer her a drink, stay where he was? Why the hell was she looking at him as though she was already licking the remains of him from her lips? "Maria and her husband,

Miguel, keep things running around here. Is this a social visit, Tess, or do you need a lawyer?''

"Social, for the moment. Completely social." She slipped off her coat and watched his eyes flicker. Yes, she concluded, the dress was definitely a success. "To be honest, I needed to get out of the house." She draped her coat over the back of a chair, then eased a hip onto the corner of his desk, letting the skirt slide sneakily up her thigh. "A little cabin fever."

"It happens." He hadn't forgotten her legs, but it had been a while since he'd seen them in anything but jeans or thick wool pants. Displayed in sheer hose to well above the knee, they made his mouth go dry. "Can I get you a drink?"

"That would be lovely." She crossed her legs, slowly. Another sneaky slide. "What have you got?"

"Ah . . ." He couldn't remember, and felt like an idiot.

Better and better, she decided, and slithered off the desk. "I'll just see for myself, shall I?" She walked to the decanters on a cabinet across the room and chose vermouth. "Would you like one?"

"Sure, thanks." He nudged the coffee aside. Caffeine sure as hell wasn't going to get him through this. "I haven't been able to get over for a couple of days. How are things?"

"Quiet." She poured two glasses, brought them to the desk. After handing Nate his, she slipped onto the desk again, on his side. "Though festive." She leaned down, just a bit, tapped her glass to his. "Happy holidays. In fact . . ." She took a small sip. "That's one of the reasons I came by." Reaching over, she picked up the package she'd put on the desk. "Merry Christmas, Nate."

"You got me a present?" He narrowed his eyes at the package, expecting a slam.

"Just a little one. You've been a good friend, and counselor." She smiled over the last word. "Do you want to open it now, or wait till Christmas morning?" She touched her tongue to her top lip, and all the blood drained out of his brain into his lap. "I can come back."

"I'm a sucker for presents," he told her, and ripped the paper off. When he saw the book he teetered between being faintly embarrassed and gently moved. "I'm a sucker for Keats, too," he murmured.

"So I hear. I thought when you read it, you might think of me."

He lifted his eyes to hers. "I manage to think of you without visual aids."

"Do you?" She inched closer, leaning down so that she could take hold of his loosened tie. "And what do you think?"

"I think, at the moment, you're trying to seduce me."

"You're so quick, so smart." She laughed and slid into his lap. "And so right." One quick tug on the tie and she had his mouth on hers.

Like the house, like the man, the hunger was simple and without pretense. His hands closed over her breasts, the warm, full weight of them. And when she shifted to straddle him, his hands moved around to cup her bottom.

She had already tossed his tie aside and was working on his shirt before he'd taken the first breath.

"If I'd had to go another week without your hands on me, I'd have screamed." She fastened her teeth low on his neck. "I'd rather scream with them on me."

He still hadn't managed to breathe, but his hands were busy enough, pushing that short, snug skirt of the dress up her hips, finding the delight of firm bare skin over the lacy tops of stockings. "We can't—here." He went back to her breasts, unable to decide where he needed to touch first. "Upstairs," he managed as he savaged her mouth. "I'll take you upstairs."

"Here." She threw back her head as his lips ran down her throat. He had a wonderful mouth. She'd been sure of it. "Right here, right now." On the verge of exploding already, she dragged at his belt. "Hurry. The first time fast. We'll worry about finesse later."

He was with her there. Hard as steel, aching, desperate. He struggled with the zipper in the back of her dress as she struggled with his. "I haven't got any . . . Christ, you're built." He dragged the dress down far enough to find those lovely, full breasts spilling over the top of a low-cut black bra. He nipped the bra down with his teeth, then used them on her.

It was a shock. She'd always considered herself healthily sexual. But when that busy mouth on her flesh shot her over the edge without a net, her body bucked, her mind spun. "God. Oh, my God." Letting her head fall back, she absorbed that first, delightful orgasm. "More. Now."

She'd exploded over him—wildly, gorgeously—and dazed him. With his hands full of her, he pressed his lips to hers and tried to think. "We have to go upstairs, Tess. I don't generally have sex at my desk. I'm not prepared for it."

"That's okay." She let her brow rest against his, drew three deep breaths. Lord, she was quaking like a schoolgirl. "I am."

Reaching back, she fumbled over the surface of the desk, knocking a number of things to the floor as he took advantage of the thrust of her breast and suckled. She heard her breath wheeze, swore she could feel her eyes cross as she groped behind her for her bag. She opened it, tossed it aside, and let a trail of condoms spill out.

He blinked. A quick guess told him there were at least a dozen. So Nate cleared his throat. "I don't know whether to be afraid or flattered."

It made her laugh. Sitting there, half naked and aroused to hell and back, she let loose a low, rocking laugh. "Consider it a challenge."

"Good call." But when he reached for them, she drew them teasingly out of reach.

"Oh, no. Allow me."

With her eyes on his, she ripped a packet off, tore it open. Mozart continued to play with grace and dignity as she freed Nate from his slacks, gave a feline hum of anticipation, and slowly, torturously protected them both.

His lungs clogged, his fingers dug into the arms of the chair. Her hands were clever, delicate as a rose. And he was suddenly terrified that he would disgrace himself like a teenage virgin. "Goddamn, you're good."

She smiled, shifted. "I've been thinking about this since the first time I saw you."

He gripped her hips as she rose over him, held her there while both of them quivered. "Yeah? Well, that makes two of us."

She braced her hands on his shoulders, let her fingers dig in for purchase. "Why'd we wait so long?"

"Damned if I know." Slowly, his eyes locked on hers, he lowered her, pierced her, filled her. She shuddered once, moaned low and long in her throat, and didn't move a muscle. Her eyes closed, then opened.

"Yes," she said, and smiled again.

"Yes." His hands stayed fastened on her hips as she rode him, hard and fast and well.

LATER, WHEN SHE WAS LIMP IN HIS ARMS, HE MANAGED to reach the phone. She moaned a little as he shifted her, dialed.

"Will? It's Nate. Tess is here . . . Yeah. She'll be staying here tonight." He turned his head, nipped at her bare shoulder, and realized he'd never gotten that dress completely off. Plenty of time for that, he thought, and tuned back in to Willa's voice. "No, she's fine. She's great. She'll be back in the morning. 'Bye."

"That was considerate of you," Tess murmured. She'd popped a few of the buttons off his shirt somewhere along the line, and now enjoyed the smooth bare skin of his chest under her lazy fingertips.

"She'd worry." He worked the bunched-up dress from around her waist and pulled it over her head. Now she wore nothing but lace-topped stockings, sexy high heels, and a satisfied smirk. The smirk was the only thing he wanted to see slip off her. "How do you feel?"

"I feel wonderful." Tossing back her hair, she linked her hands behind his neck. "And you?"

He slipped his hands under her bottom, lifting her as he rose. "Lucky," he told her, and laid her back on his desk. He took a moment to toss the legal pad that rested beside her head over his shoulder. "And about to get luckier."

Surprised, interested, she grinned. "My, my, round two already?"

"Just hold on, honey." He ran his hands up and over her, pleased when she trembled. "And hold on tight."

It didn't take long for her to take the warning seriously.

THIRTEEN

The temperature rose on New Year's eve. One of El Niño's wild weather patterns that make sense only to God brought bright blue skies, sunlight, and warm air. Though it would mean mud and slop—and ice when the wind blew capriciously again—it was a moment to be enjoyed.

Willa rode fences in a light denim jacket, whistling as she made repairs. The mountains were snowcapped, the white lacing deep in the folds and waves. The chinook had teased patches of ground and grass through the white in pastures, while the snowpack along the ranch roads was still higher than a rig. But the cottonwoods had lost their ermine trim and stood bare and black with wet while the pines rose sassily green.

She thought it was Lily's simple happiness that was influencing her mood. The woman's holiday mood was still in high gear, and only a true grinch could have resisted it.

Why else, Willa thought, had she agreed to Lily's hesitant request for a New Year's Eve party? All those people in the house, Willa mused, having to dress up, make conversation. With everything else on her mind, it should have been a misery.

But she could admit, at least to herself, that she was looking forward to it.

Even now, Lily and Bess and Nell were huddled in the kitchen creating the feast. The house had been scrubbed raw and polished blind, and Willa had orders to be bathed and dressed by eight sharp. She would do it, Willa realized, for Lily.

Somehow over the months she'd fallen in love with the stranger who had become her sister.

Who wouldn't? she asked herself as she mounted Moon and rode on. Lily was sweet and kind and patient. And vulnerable. No matter how hard she'd tried to maintain a distance between them, they had grown closer and closer until now she couldn't imagine Mercy without Lily's touch.

Lily liked to gather twigs, stick them in old bottles. And somehow she made them look cheerful and charming. She hunted up old bowls out of cupboards, filled them with fruit, or dumped pinecones into straw baskets. She snuck plants out of the pool house and scattered them through the rooms.

When no one complained, she'd foraged for more, digging candlesticks out of closets, buying scented candles and lighting them in the evening so that the house smelled of vanilla and cinnamon and lord knew what else.

But it was pleasant. It was, Willa decided, homey.

And anyone with eyes could see that Adam was in love with her. A little afraid of that vulnerability Lily carried around, Willa mused, but quietly in love. It could work, she supposed, with time and care. She doubted that Lily realized just how deep Adam's feelings went. As far as Willa could see, Lily thought he was being kind.

Dismounting, she began to repair more broken wire.

Then there was Tess. Willa couldn't claim to be in love with Miss Hollywood, but she might have become slightly less resentful. For the most part, Tess stayed out of her way, closeting herself for several hours a day with her writing or phone calls to her agent. She did the chores assigned to her. Not cheerfully, and not often well, but she did them.

Willa was fully aware of what was going on between Tess and Nate. She just didn't choose to dwell on it. That, she concluded, would never work. The minute the time was up, Tess would be on a flight back to LA and would never give Nate another thought.

She only hoped he was prepared for it.

And what about you, Will? she wondered. Leaning on a fence post, she looked up into the mountains, wished for a moment that she could mount Moon and ride off, up and up until she lost herself in snow and trees and sky. The quiet that was there. The utter peace of it, the music of water thawing and forcing its way through ice, over rocks, the sweep of wind through pine, and that glorious scent that was the land just breathing.

No responsibilities, just for a day. No men to order, no fence to ride, no cattle to feed. Just a day to do nothing but stare at the sky and dream.

Of what? she asked herself, and shook her head. With all the love and longing, the sex and snapping air around her, would she dream of that? Would she indulge herself in a little fantasy about what it would be like to let Ben show her what a man could do to a woman? And for her?

Or would she dream of blood and death, of failure and guilt? Would she ride into those hills and find something, or someone else, slaughtered because she'd let down her guard?

She couldn't take the chance.

Turning back to Moon, she laid a hand over her rifle, sighed once, then mounted.

She saw the rider and hoped it was Ben galloping toward her, with Charlie running by his side. And it shamed her that she was disappointed, even for an instant, that it was Adam.

How beautiful he is, she thought. And how sturdy.

"Don't see you riding alone much these days," she called out.

He grinned, reining in. "God, what a day!" He drew a deep breath of it, lifting his face to the sky. "Lily's party planning, and she's rooked Tess into it."

"So you settled for me." She watched his face, laughed at his stunned and guilty expression. "I'm only teasing,

Adam. And even though I know it's no hardship on you, I'm grateful you're keeping an eye on them."

"Lily's put it out of her mind. All of it." He turned his mount to ride alongside Willa. "I imagine it's how she dealt with her marriage. I don't know if it's healthy, but it seems to give her peace of mind."

"She's happy here. You make her happy."

He understood that Willa would know his deepest feelings. She always did. "She needs time yet, to feel safe. To trust that I can want her and not hurt her because of it."

"Has she told you anything about her ex-husband?"

"Bits and pieces." Adam shrugged his shoulders restlessly. He wanted more, he wanted all of it. And it was difficult to wait. "She was teaching when she met him, and they got married very quickly. It was a mistake. She says little more than that. But inside, she's still afraid. If I move too quickly, turn abruptly, she jumps. It breaks my heart."

It would, she thought. The wounded always broke his heart. "I've seen her change in the short time she's been here. Been with you. She smiles more. Talks more."

He angled his head. "You've grown fond of her."

"Some."

He smiled. "And the other one. Tess?"

" 'Fond' isn't the word I'd use," she said dryly. "I'm working on 'tolerate.' "

"She's a strong woman, smart, focused. More like you than Lily."

"Please, don't insult me."

"She is. She confronts things, makes them work for her. She hasn't your sense of duty, and perhaps her heart isn't as soft, but she has both duty and heart. I like her very much."

Her brow knit as she turned to look at him. "Do you really?"

"Yes. When I was teaching her to ride, she fell off, several times. She would get up, brush off her jeans, and climb right back on." With a look on her face, he remembered, that was the mirror of the one Willa wore when she was fighting to conquer a new problem. "That takes courage and determination. And pride. She makes Lily laugh. She makes me laugh. And I'll tell you something she doesn't know.''

"Secrets?'' Grinning, Willa nudged her horse closer to his, dropping her voice, though there was no one for miles. The sun was easing down toward the western peaks, softening the light. ''Tell all.''

"She's fallen for the horses. She doesn't know it, or isn't ready to admit it, but I see it. The way she touches them, talks to them, sneaks them sugar when she thinks I don't see.''

Willa pursed her lips. ''We'll be into foaling season soon. Let's see how well she likes birthing.''

"I think she'll do well. And she admires you.''

"Bullshit.''

"You aren't ready to see that, but I do.'' He squinted, gauged the distance back home. ''Race you to the barn.''

"You're on.'' With a whoop, she kicked Moon into action and hustled back at a dead run.

SHE WALKED INTO THE HOUSE WITH COLOR IN HER cheeks and a gleam in her eye. No one beat Adam on horseback, but she'd come close. Damn close, and it had lifted her mood—which plummeted immediately when Tess came down the stairs.

"There you are. Upstairs, Annie Oakley. Party time, and your eau de sweat won't do for tonight.''

"I've got two hours.''

"Which may be barely enough time to transform you into something resembling a female. Hit the showers.''

She'd intended to do just that, but now her back was up. "I've got some paperwork.''

"Oh, you can't.'' Lily came up behind her, hands fluttering. ''It's already six.''

"So? Nobody's coming that I need to impress.''

"Nobody's coming you need to offend either.'' With a sigh, Tess took her arm and began to haul her up the stairs.

"Hey!''

"Come on, Lily. This is going to take both of us.''

Biting her lip, Lily took Willa's other arm. ''It's going to be so nice, really it is, to see people. You've been working so hard. Tess and I want you to enjoy yourself.''

"Then take your damn hands off me." She dislodged Lily easily enough, but Tess tightened her grip and steered Willa into the bedroom. "Five more seconds, and I deck you if you don't—" She broke off, staring at the dress laid out on the bed.

"What the hell is that?"

"I went through your closet, and as there's nothing in it remotely resembling party wear—"

"Hold on." This time Willa jerked free, spun around. "You went through my clothes?"

"I didn't see anything in there to be proprietary about. In fact, I thought I'd stumbled into the rag bin, but Bess assured me it was indeed your wardrobe."

Though her palms had gone damp, Lily stepped between them. "We altered one of Tess's dresses for you."

"Hers?" With a sneer, Willa looked Tess up and down. "You'd have had to lose half the material to make that work."

"True enough," Tess shot back. "And all in the bust. But it turns out that Bess is very clever with a needle. It's possible that even with your toothpick legs and flat chest you might look oddly attractive in it."

"Tess." Lily hissed the word and nudged her older sister aside. "It's a beautiful color, don't you think? You'd look so dramatic in jewel tones, and this shade of blue is just made for you. It was so generous of Tess to let it be altered for you."

"I never really cared for it," Tess said carelessly. "One of those little fashion mistakes."

Lily closed her eyes briefly and prayed for peace. "I know I'm putting you to a lot of trouble with this party, Will. I appreciate so much that you'd let me plan it, and all but take over the house the last couple of days. I know it's an inconvenience for you."

Done in, Willa dragged a hand through her hair. "I don't know who's better at getting to me, but the hell with it. Just get out, both of you. I can manage to shower and put on some stupid hand-me-down dress all by myself.''

Accepting victory, Tess took Lily's arm and urged her toward the door. "Wash your hair, champ."

"Go to hell." Willa kicked the door shut behind them.

SHE FELT LIKE A FOOL. A FOOL WHO WOULD UNDOUBT-edly freeze her ass off in this excuse for a dress before the evening was over. As she stood in front of her mirror, Willa tugged at the hem. That little action had the effect of moving it down close to an inch, while the low-cut neckline dipped distressingly in reaction, toward her navel.

Tits or ass, she thought, scratching her head—which did she want to cover more?

The dress did have sleeves, which was something. But they began at mid-shoulder, and nothing she tried seemed to convince them to settle a bit closer to her neck. Whatever the dress was made of was thin and soft and clung like a second skin.

Grudgingly she stepped into her heels and got a quick lesson in physics. As she went up, so did the hemline.

"Oh, screw it." Stepping closer to the mirror, she decided she might as well go all out and use her miserly hoard of cosmetics. It was, after all, New Year's Eve.

And the dress, what there was of it, was a pretty color. Electric blue, she supposed. Maybe she didn't have much cleavage, despite the best efforts of that dipping, clinging V neck, but her shoulders weren't half bad. And damned if her legs were toothpicks. They were long, sure, but they were muscled, and the dark-toned panty hose she struggled into hid the couple of new bruises she'd discovered after her shower.

She refused to fuss with her hair. She wasn't any good with curls or complicated styles in any case, so she left it straight, spilling down her back. Which would at least keep the flesh warm that the plunge back bared.

She remembered earrings only because Adam had given them to her for Christmas, and she fixed the pretty dangling stars on her lobes.

Now if she could manage to stay on her feet all night—

since sitting down in that dress wasn't an option—she'd be fine.

"Oh, you look wonderful" were the first words out of Lily's mouth when Willa came downstairs. "Just wonderful," she repeated, dancing to the landing in something floaty and winter white. "Tess, come see. Willa looks fabulous."

Tess's comment was a grunt as she stepped out of the room looking dangerous in basic black. "Not half bad," she decided, secretly thrilled with the results as she tapped her pearl choker and circled Willa. "A little makeup and you'll do."

"I have makeup on."

"Christ, the woman has eyes like a goddess and doesn't know how to use them. Come on."

"I'm not going back up there and glopping gunk on my face," Willa protested as Tess dragged her back up the stairs.

"Honey, for what I pay, it's first-class gunk. Hold the fort, Lily."

"All right. Don't be long, though." And she beamed after them, flushed with the warmth of sisterhood.

She wished they could see how much fun they were together, from her point of view. Squabbling, just as she imagined sisters would. And now sharing clothes, makeup, dressing for a party together.

She was so grateful to be a part of it all. Giving in to the thrill, she spun in a circle, then stopped short when she saw Adam standing in the hall behind her.

"I didn't hear you come in."

"I came in the back." He could have looked at her endlessly, the dark-haired fairy in a floating white dress. "You look beautiful, Lily."

"Thank you."

She felt very nearly beautiful. But he, he was so outrageous, so perfect in every detail, she could barely believe he was real. A thousand times over the past months she'd longed to touch him. Not just a hand, a brush of shoulders, but to touch him. Part of her was certain he would be offended or amused, and that she wouldn't risk.

"I'm glad you're here," she said, speaking too quickly now. "Tess took Will back up for some last-minute touches, and people will start coming any minute. I don't do very well playing hostess. I never know what to say."

She stepped back as he stepped forward, then made herself stop. Her heart turned over when he brushed his fingers down her cheek. "You'll be fine. They won't know what to say either, once they look at you. I don't."

"I—" Oh, she would make a fool of herself now, she was certain, with this need to fling herself into his arms and be held close. Just to be held. "I should help Bess. In the kitchen."

"She's got everything under control." He kept his eyes on hers and his moves slow as he reached for her hand. "Why don't we pick out some music? We might even squeeze in a dance before anyone comes."

"I haven't danced in a long time."

"You'll dance tonight," he promised, and led her into the great room.

They'd no more than made their initial selections and filled the CD player when the first headlights glanced off the window.

"Promise me the midnight dance," he said, twining their fingers together again.

"Of course. I'm nervous," she admitted with a quick smile. "Stay close, won't you?"

"As long as you need me." He glanced over as Tess and Willa came down, sniping at each other. Because it was expected, and warranted, Adam let out a heartfelt whistle. Tess winked. Willa scowled.

"I'm going to want a drink, as soon as possible." Hissing through her teeth, Willa strode to the door and greeted the first guests.

WITHIN AN HOUR, THE HOUSE WAS FILLED WITH PEOPLE and voices and clashing scents. Apparently no one was too weary to attend another holiday party, too jaded to drink another glass of champagne, or too restrained to refrain from discussing politics and religion. Or their neighbors and friends.

Willa remembered why she didn't care for socializing when Bethanne Mosebly sidled up to her and began to pump her for details of the murder.

"We were all shocked to hear about what happened to John Barker." Bethanne inhaled champagne between sentences with such fervor that Willa was tempted to offer her a straw. "Must have been a terrible shock for you."

Though Willa didn't immediately snap to John Barker and Pickles being one and the same, Bethanne's greedily excited eyes tipped her off. "It's not an experience I'm looking to repeat. Excuse me, I'm just going to—"

That was as far as she got before Bethanne's hand clamped down on her arm. "They said he was cut to pieces." She toasted the fact with another gulp of champagne, leaving her small bird's mouth wet and gleaming. "Just hacked to ribbons." The long needle fingers pinched harder. "And scalped."

It was the glee that sickened her, even more than the image that burst full-blown into her brain. Even knowing that Bethanne had no harm in her other than an overly well-developed affection for chatter and gossip, Willa had to fight off a shudder.

"He was dead, Bethanne, and it was brutal. Too bad I didn't have my video camera for pictures at eleven."

The disgust and sarcasm couldn't puncture the avid interest. Bethanne inched closer, giving Willa an unwelcome whiff of wine, Scope, and Obsession. "They say it could have been anyone, anyone at all who did it. Why, you could be murdered in your own bed any night of the week. Why, I was just telling Bob on the drive here how much it's been on my mind."

Willa forced her lips into a thin smile. "I'll sleep easier knowing you're so worried about it. You're out of champagne, Bethanne. The bar's that way."

Willa ducked away, then kept moving. Her one thought was to find air. How could anyone breathe with so many people gulping up the oxygen? she wondered. She pushed her way into the hall and didn't stop until she reached the front door, wrenched it open, and found herself face-to-face with Ben.

He gawked at her, and she fumbled. Recovering before he did, she shoved past him and strode over to lean on the porch rail. It was cold enough now to send her breath steaming in clouds, to make the chill bumps rise on her skin. But the air was fresh as a wish, and that was exactly what she needed.

When his hands came to her shoulders and turned her around, she ground her teeth. "The party's inside."

"I wanted to make sure I wasn't hallucinating."

No, he thought, she was real enough. Cool, bare skin shivered a bit under his hands. Those big doe eyes seemed even darker, even larger. The bold blue of the dress gleamed in the starlight and clung intimately to every curve and angle before it stopped dead, teasingly high on long, firm thighs.

"God Almighty, Will, you look good enough to eat in three quick bites. And you're going to freeze your pretty butt off standing out here."

His coat was already open. He made use of it by stepping forward and wrapping it around her, enjoying the added benefit of having that tight little body pressed up hard to his.

"Turn me loose." She squirmed, but he had her caught, arms pinned, body trapped. "I came out here to be alone for five damn minutes."

"Well, you should've put on a coat." Pleased with the situation, he sniffed at her—more like a dog than a lover— and heard her muffling a chuckle. "Smell good."

"That idiot Tess, spraying stuff on me." But she was beginning to relax again in the warmth. "Gunking up my face."

"It looks good gunked." He grinned when she tipped it back to his, eyeing him pityingly.

"What's wrong with men, anyway, that they fall for this kind of stuff? What's so hot about looks that come out of pots and tubes?"

"We're weak, Will. Weak and foolish and easy. Wanna

neck?'' He rooted at her throat and made her laugh.

"Cut it out, McKinnon. You ass.'' But her arms were around his waist now, comfortable, and she'd forgotten what had put her in such a foul mood. "You're late,'' she added. "Your parents are already here, and Zack and Shelly. I thought you weren't coming.''

"I got hung up.'' He kissed her before she could duck, drew the kiss out when she forgot to protest. "Miss me?''

"No.''

"Liar.''

"So?'' Because he was grinning just a bit too smugly, she looked over his shoulder, through the brightly lit window at the crowd of people. "I hate parties. Everybody just stands around and yaks. What's the point?''

"Social and cultural interaction. A chance to dress up, drink for free, and ogle each other. I'm planning on ogling you once we're back inside. Unless you'd rather go off to the horse barn and let me get you out of that pretty dress.''

More intrigued with the prospect than she wanted to be, she lifted a brow. "Are those my only choices?''

"We could use my rig, but it wouldn't be as cozy.''

"Why do men think about sex day and night?''

"Because thinking's the closest thing to doing. You got anything on under this?''

"Sure. I had to slick myself down with oil to get it on.''

He winced, tried not to moan. "I deserved that. Let's go inside and stand around and yak.''

When he stepped back, the cold hit her like a slap. She shivered her way to the door. Still, she stopped with her hand on the knob, turned to him. "Ben, why have you suddenly developed this thing about getting my clothes off?''

"There's nothing sudden about it.''

He opened the door himself, nudged her inside. Very much at home, he shrugged out of his coat and tossed it over the newel post. Unlike Willa, he liked parties just fine, the noise and fuss and smells of them. People deep in conversation were sitting on the staircase with plates of food. Others jammed into the hall, spilled back through the open doors of other rooms. Most had a greeting for him, or a few words to exchange as he kept one hand firmly on Willa's arm to prevent her escape.

Escape was what she had in mind, he knew, but he had a point to make. He was going to make it to her, and to everyone—including several duded-up cowhands who had their eye on her. The end of the old year, the beginning of the new with all its mysteries and possibilities seemed like the perfect time.

"If you'd turn loose of me a minute," she muttered close to his ear, "I could—"

"I know what you could. I'm hanging on. Get used to it."

"What the hell's that supposed to mean?" She could only swear under her breath as he tugged her into the great room.

Guests had moved back, making room for dancing. Ben grabbed a beer on his way and watched with pleasure as his parents executed a quick, intricate two-step.

"You can tell something about people who dance together that way," he said.

Willa looked up at him. "What?"

"They know each other inside and out. And like what they see on both sides. Now, take them." He inclined his head toward Nate and Tess, who were swaying—you couldn't call it dancing—on the edge of the crowd and grinning at each other. "They don't know each other yet, not all the way, but they're having a hell of a good time finding out."

"She's just using him for sex."

"And he looks all broken up about it, doesn't he?" With a chuckle, Ben set his beer aside. "Come on."

Horrified, she pulled back, trying to dig in those unfamiliar heels as he towed her to the dance floor. "I can't. I don't want to. I don't know how."

"So learn." He put a firm hand on her waist, positioned hers on his shoulder.

"I don't dance. Everybody knows I don't dance."

He merely propped the hand she'd taken away back on his shoulder again. "Sometimes you can go a long way following someone who knows where he's going."

He swung her around so it was either move her feet or fall on her butt. She felt miserably clumsy, embarrassingly spotlighted. And held herself rigid as a board.

"Relax," he murmured in her ear. "It doesn't have to hurt. Look at Lily there. Pretty as a picture with her face all flushed and her hair mussed. Brewster's having the time of his life teaching her to two-step."

"She looks happy."

"She is. And Jim Brewster'll be half in love with her before the dance is over. Then he'll partner up with another woman and fall half in love with her." Because she was thinking about that and forgetting to pull back, he eased her a little closer. "That's the beauty of dancing. You get your hands on a woman, get the feel of her, the scent of her."

"And move on to the next."

"Sometimes you do. Sometimes you don't. Look here a minute, Willa."

She did, saw the flicker in his eye, and barely had time to blink in shock before his mouth was on hers. He kissed her slow and deep, a stunning contrast to the quick moves of the dance. Her heart circled giddily in her chest, then seemed to plop over and thud to bursting.

She was moving with him when he lifted his head. "Why did you do that?"

The answer was simple, and he planned to be honest. "So all the men eyeing you know whose brand you're wearing these days." And he wasn't disappointed in her reaction. Her eyes went wide with shock, then narrowed with fury. Her skin went rosy with it. Even as she hissed, he clamped his lips to hers again. "You might as well get used to that, too," he told her. Then he stepped back. "I'll get you a drink."

He figured by the time he got back with it, she wouldn't be tempted to throw it in his face.

Willa was thinking more about shredding his face, layer by layer, when Shelly bustled up to her. "You and Ben. I didn't have a clue. That man can keep secrets from God." As she spoke, she steered Willa toward a corner. "When did all this start? What's going on?"

"It hasn't. Nothing." Temper percolated dangerously. She could feel it, physically feel it, bubble under her skin. "That son of a bitch. Branding me. He said he was branding me."

"He did?" A romantic through and through, Shelly patted a hand to her heart. "Oh, my. Zack never said anything like that to me."

"Which is why he's still breathing."

"Are you kidding? I'd love it." She burst out laughing at Willa's stunned gape. "Come on, Will, macho arrogance is sexy in small doses. I get all gooey inside when Zack flexes his muscles."

Willa shifted, looked hard into Shelly's eyes. "How much have you had to drink?"

"I'm not drunk, and I'm not kidding. And sometimes he just scoops me up and tosses me over his shoulder. With the baby it's not quite as spontaneous, but boy, does it work."

"For you, maybe. I don't like pushy men."

"I know. It was horrible the way everyone just stood around while you were beating Ben off." Shelly drawled it out, dipped a finger in her wine, licked it off. "Anyone could see how much you detested being kissed brainless."

Willa searched for an intelligent, pithy response. "Shut up, Shelly" was the best she could do before she stalked off.

"THE COWGIRL'S GOT A BUR UP HER BUTT," TESS commented.

"Ben likes to irritate her."

Tess raised an eyebrow at Nate. "I think he'd like to do more than that."

"Looks like. Speaking of doing more than that." He leaned down and whispered a suggestion in her ear that made her blood pressure spike. "Lawyer Torrence, you do have a way with words."

"We could slip out, go to my place, and see the new year in more . . . privately. Nobody'd miss us."

"Um." She turned so that her breasts nestled against his

chest. "Too far. Upstairs. My room. Five minutes."

His eyes widened. "With all these people in the house?"

"And a nice sturdy lock on the door. Top of the stairs turn left, make the first right, three doors down on the right." She skimmed her fingertips over his jaw. "I'll be waiting."

"Tess, I think—"

But she was already gliding away, with one smoldering look back over her shoulder. He could have sworn he heard his brain cells die. He took two steps after her, stopped, and tried to be sensible.

The hell with it. He hadn't been sensible since she'd swaggered into his office with sex on her mind. It didn't even matter that he was falling headlong in love and she wasn't even close to tripping. They fit. Whether she saw it or not, it had clicked for him.

Hoping to be discreet, he snagged a bottle of champagne and two glasses. And made it as far as the base of the stairs.

"Private party?" Ben asked, then chuckled at the flush that spread up Nate's throat. "Give Tess a Happy New Year's kiss from me."

"Get your own woman."

"I aim to."

But he took his time seeking her out and pinning her down again. His goal was to have her firmly planted in his arms at midnight. He gave her plenty of rope, and as the countdown began, firmly reeled her in.

"Don't you start on me again."

"Only a minute to go," he said easily. "I always think of that last minute between years as untime." When her brow furrowed, he knew he had her attention and slid his arms around her. "Not now, not then. Not anything. If we were alone, I could do what I want with you for those sixty seconds. But it wouldn't be real. So I'm going to wait till it is. Put your arms around me. It doesn't count yet. Not for seconds yet."

She couldn't hear anything but his voice, none of the noise, the laughter, the excited countdown of time penetrated. As if in a dream, she lifted her arms, wound them around his neck.

"Tell me you want me," he murmured. "It doesn't count. Not yet."

"I do. But I don't—"

"No buts. It doesn't matter." He slid a hand up, over her bare back, under her hair. "Kiss me. It's not real, not yet. You kiss me, Willa. Just once, you kiss me."

She angled in, kept her eyes open and her mind blank as she fit her lips to his. So warm, so welcoming, so unexpectedly gentle that she shuddered in reaction. And time ran out on her.

Cheers echoed somewhere in the back of her head. People jostled her in their hurry to exchange New Year's greetings. And as the seconds slid away from the end to the beginning, her heart ached with it.

"It is real." It was as much accusation as statement when she drew away. Her eyes glittered with the fresh awareness, and the fear of it. "It is."

"Yeah." He stunned her by taking her hand, bringing it to his lips. "Starting now." He slid an arm around her waist, kept her close to his side. "Look there, darling." He shifted her just a little. "That's a pretty sight."

Even through her own confusion, she had to admit it was. Adam, with his hands cupped on Lily's face, and Lily's fingers holding his wrists.

See how their eyes meet and hold, she thought. How her lips tremble just a little, how gently he brushes them with his. And how they stay there, just so, fixed in that bare whisper of a kiss.

"He's in love with her," Willa murmured. Emotions churned inside her. Too much to feel, she thought with a hand pressed to her stomach. Too much to think, too much to wonder. "What's going on? I wish I could understand what's going on. Nothing's the same anymore. Nothing's simple anymore."

"They can make each other happy. That's simple."

"No." She shook her head. "No, it won't be. Can't you

feel it? There's something . . ." She shuddered again, because she could feel it. And it was cold, and vicious and close. "Ben, there's something—"

That was when the screaming started.

FOURTEEN

THERE WASN'T MUCH BLOOD. THE POLICE WOULD CON-
clude that she had been killed elsewhere, then brought to
the ranch. No one recognized her. Her face was largely un-
marred. Just a bruise under the right eye.

Her hair was gone.

Her skin was faintly blue. That Willa had seen for herself
when she rushed outside and found young Billy struggling
to calm Mary Anne Walker after they'd stumbled over the
body. She was naked, and her skin had crisscrossing slashes
in it like hatch marks on a drawing.

Very little blood, and what there was had dried on that
pale blue skin.

Mary Anne had been sick right there on the front steps.
And Billy had soon followed suit, chucking up his share of
the beer he'd guzzled in the rig while he was busy getting
Mary Anne's panties down to her ankles.

Willa had gotten them both back inside and ordered
everyone who was crowding out on the porch, gawking and
talking at once, to come back inside. She told herself she
would think about the woman later, the woman with the blue

skin and no hair who was dead at the foot of the steps.

She would think about that later.

"Bess has already called the police." Adam laid a hand on her arm, waiting until her eyes shifted to his. The voices around them were too loud, too frightened. "I should go out there with Ben, stay with—stay with her until the police come. Can you handle this?"

"Yes." She looked up in relief as Nate came rushing down the stairs. "Yes, go on. Outside," she said, reaching for Nate's hand. "Please, go out with Ben and Adam. There's . . . there's another."

She turned and started into the great room. Stu McKinnon had already shut off the music, was using his strong, soothing voice to calm the guests. Willa let him take charge for the moment, while she just stood there staring at her father's portrait over the fireplace. Those cold blue eyes stared back at her. She could almost see him sneering at her, blaming her.

Barefoot, her dress not quite zipped, Tess barreled down the steps just as Lily came rushing down the hall. "What happened? Someone was screaming."

"There's been another murder." Lily gripped Tess's hand hard. "I didn't see. Adam wouldn't let me go out, but it's a woman. No one seems to know who she is. She was just there. Just there in front of the house."

"Oh, my God." Tess pressed her free hand to her mouth, forced herself to stay in control. "Happy fucking New Year. Okay." She took a deep breath. "Let's do whatever comes next."

They stepped up to Willa, instinctively flanking her. None of them was fully aware that they had linked hands.

"I don't know her," Willa managed. "I don't even know her."

"Don't think about it now." Tess tightened her grip on Willa's hand. "Don't think about it. Let's just get through this."

Hours LATER, JUST AS DAWN BROKE, SHE FELT A HAND on her shoulder. She'd fallen asleep, God knew how, in front of the living room fire. She jerked away, struggled away as Ben tried to lift her.

"I'm taking you upstairs. You're going to bed."

"No." She got to her feet. Her head was eerily light, her body numb, but her heart was pounding again. "No, I can't." Dazed, she stared around the room. The remnants of the party were all there. Glasses and plates, food going stale, ashtrays overflowing. "Where—"

"Everyone's gone. The last of the police left ten minutes ago."

"They said they wanted to talk to me again."

Take me into the library again, she thought, question me again. Take me through the steps again. And again. All leading to that moment when she had rushed outside to see two terrified teenagers and a dead woman with pale blue skin.

"What?" She pressed a hand to her head. Ben's. voice was like a buzz in the front of her brain.

"I said I told them they could talk to you later."

"Oh. Coffee? Is there any coffee left?"

He'd already had a good look at her, curled in the chair, her white face a hard contrast to the dark shadows under her eyes. She might be standing at the moment, but he knew it was only sheer will that kept her on her feet. And that was simple enough to deal with. He lifted her off them and into his arms.

"You're going to bed. Now."

"I can't. I have . . . things to do." She knew there were dozens of things to do but couldn't seem to think of even one. "Where . . . my sisters?"

His eyebrows lifted as he carried her up the steps. He figured she was too punchy to realize it was the first time she'd called Lily and Tess her sisters. "Tess went up an hour ago. Lily's with Adam. Ham can handle whatever needs to be done today. Go to sleep, Will. That's all you need to do."

"They asked so many questions." She didn't protest, couldn't, when he laid her on her bed. "Everybody asking questions. And the police, taking people into the library, one at a time."

She looked at him then, into his eyes—cold green now, she thought. Cold and hard and unreadable. "I didn't know her, Ben."

"No." He slipped off her shoes, debated with himself briefly, then gritted his teeth and turned her over to unzip her dress. "They'll check missing persons reports, check her prints."

"Hardly any blood," she murmured, quiet as a child as he slid the dress down. "Not like before. She didn't seem real, not like a person at all. Do you think he knew her? Did he know her when he did that to her?"

"I don't know, darling." And as tenderly as if she'd been a child, he tucked her under the blankets. "Put it away for now." Sitting on the edge of the bed, he stroked her hair. "Just let it go and sleep."

"He blames me." Her voice was thick and drunk with exhaustion.

"Who blames you?"

"Pa. He always did." And she sighed. "He always will."

Ben left his hand on her cheek a moment. "And he was always wrong."

When he rose and turned, he saw Nate in the doorway.

"She out?" Nate asked.

"For now." Ben laid the dress over a chair. "Knowing Will, she won't sleep long."

"I talked Tess into taking a pill." He smiled wanly. "Didn't take much talking." He gestured down the hall. Together they walked to Willa's office, shut the door. "It's early," Nate said, "but I'm having whiskey."

"Hate to see you drink alone. Three fingers," he added when Nate poured. "Don't think she was from around here."

"No?" Neither did he, but Nate wanted Ben's take. "Why?"

"Well." Ben sipped, hissed through his teeth at the lightning bolt of liquor. "Fingernails and toenails painted up with some shiny purple polish. Tattoos on her butt and her shoulder. Looked like three earrings in each ear. That says city to me."

"Didn't look more than sixteen. That says runaway to me." Nate drank, and drank deep. "Poor kid. Could have been riding her thumb, or working the streets in Billings or Ennis. Wherever this bastard found her, he kept her awhile."

Ben's attention sharpened. "Oh?"

"I got a little out of the cops. Abrasions around the wrists and ankles. She'd been tied up. They couldn't say for sure until they run the tests, but they seemed fairly sure she'd been raped, and that she'd been dead at least twenty-four hours before he left her here. That adds up to being kept somewhere."

Ben paced it off for a moment, the frustration and disgust. "Why here? Why dump her here?"

"Someone's focused on Mercy."

"Or on someone at Mercy," Ben added, and saw by the look in Nate's eyes that they agreed. "All this started after the old man died, after Tess and Lily came here. Maybe we should start looking closer at them and who'd want to hurt them."

"I'm going to talk to Tess when she wakes up. We know there's an ex-husband in Lily's past. One who liked to knock her around."

Ben nodded and absently rubbed the scar across his chin. "It's a long jump from wife abuse to slicing up strangers."

"Maybe not that long a jump. I'd feel better knowing where the ex is, and what he's up to."

"We feed his name to the cops, hire a detective."

"We're on the same beam there. You know his name?"

"No, but Adam will." Ben downed the rest of the whiskey, set the glass aside. "Might as well get started."

THEY FOUND HIM IN THE STABLES, EXAMINING A PREGnant mare. "She's going to foal early," Adam said, as he straightened up. "Another day or two." After a last stroke, he stepped out of the foaling stall, slid the door closed. "Will?"

"Sleeping," Ben told him. "For the moment."

He nodded, moved down the concrete aisle to the grain

bin. "Lily's in on my couch. She wanted to help with the morning feeding, but she dropped off while she was waiting for me to change. I'm glad she didn't see it. Tess either." His usual fluid movements were jerky with tension and fatigue. "I'm sorry Will did."

"She'll get through it." Ben moved to a hay net, filled it with fresh. "How much do you know about Lily's ex-husband?"

"Not a lot." Adam continued to work, as unsurprised by the assistance as the question. "His name's Jesse Cooke. They met when she was teaching, got married a couple months later. She left him about a year after that. The first time. She hasn't told me much more, and I haven't been pushing."

"Does she know where he is?" Ignoring his best suit, Nate filled a feeding trough.

"She thinks back East. That's what she wants to think."

For the next few minutes they worked in silence, three men accustomed to the routine, the smells, the work. The stables were lit with the morning sun trailing through the open corral door with hay motes dancing cheerfully in every slanting beam. Horses shifted on fresh bedding, munched on feed, blew an occasional greeting.

From the chicken house a rooster called, and there was the jangle of boots on hard-packed dirt as men went about their chores in the ranch yard. No radio played tinny country this morning, nor was the winter silence broken by the voices of men at work. If glances were tossed toward the main house, the porch, the space beneath, no one commented.

An engine gunned; a rig headed out. And the silence came back, a lingering guest at a party gone wrong.

"You may have to push her a bit now," Ben said at length. "It's an angle we can't afford to ignore. Not after this."

"I've already thought of that. I want her to get some rest first. Goddamn it." The grain scoop Adam held snapped at the handle with the quick flex of his hands. "She should be safe here."

The temper he rarely acknowledged swirled up so fast, so huge it choked his words. He wanted to pound something, rip something to shreds. But he had nothing. Even his hands were empty now.

"That was a child out there. How could someone do that to a child?"

He whirled on them, his hands in fists, his eyes dark and burning with rage. "How close was he? Was he out there, looking through the windows? Or was he inside with us? Did the son of a bitch touch her, dance with her? If she'd walked outside to get a breath of air, would he have been there?"

He looked down at his hands, opened them to stare at the palms. "I could kill him myself, and it would be easy." His gaze shifted, skimmed both men. "It would be so easy."

"Adam." Lily's voice was hardly a whisper, quiet fear at the edge of his black rage. With her arms crossed, her fingers digging hard into her shoulders, she stepped closer.

"You should be sleeping." His muscles quivered with the effort to hold back the fury. "We're nearly done here. Go on home to bed."

"I need to talk to you." She'd heard enough, seen enough to know the time had come. "Alone, please." She turned to Ben and Nate. "I'm sorry. I need to speak with Adam alone."

"Take her inside," Nate suggested. "Ben and I can finish this. Take her in," he repeated. "She's cold."

"You shouldn't have come out here." Adam moved to her, careful not to touch. "Let's go in, have some coffee."

"I put some on before I came out." She noted that he stayed an arm's length away, and it made her ashamed. "It should be ready now."

He walked her out the back, across the corral fence and to his rear door. From habit, he scraped his boots before going inside.

The kitchen smelled cozily of coffee just brewed, but the light was thin and stingy, and it prompted him to flip the switch and fill the room with hard artificial light.

"Sit down," she began. "I'll get it."

"No." He stepped in front of her as she reached for the cupboard door. Still he didn't touch her. "You sit."

"You're angry." She hated the tremor in her voice, hated the fact that anger from a man, even this man, could turn her knees to water. "I'm sorry."

"For what?" It snapped out of him before he could stop it. Even when she backed up a step, he couldn't block it all. "What the hell have you got to apologize to me for?"

"For everything I haven't told you."

"You don't owe me explanations." The cupboard door slammed against the wall as he wrenched it open. And out of the corner of his eye he saw her jerk in reaction. "Don't flinch from me." He leveled his breathing, kept his eyes on the cups set neatly in rows on the shelves. "Don't do that, Lily. I'd cut off my hands before I'd use them on you that way."

"I know." Tears swam into her eyes and were blinked brutally back. "I know that, in my heart. It's my head, Adam. And I do owe you." She walked to the round kitchen table with its simple white bowl of glossy red apples. "More than explanations. You've been my friend. My anchor. You've been everything I've needed since I came here."

"You don't pay someone back for friendship," he said wearily.

"You wanted me." Her breath hitched once as he turned slowly to face her. "I thought it was just . . . just the usual." Her nervous hands brushed at her hair, at the thighs of the jeans she'd pulled on before leaving the main house that morning. "But you never touched me that way, or pressured me, or made me feel obliged. You can't know what it's like to feel obliged to let someone have you just to keep peace. How degrading that is. I have things to tell you."

She couldn't look at him, turned her face away. "I'll start with Jesse. Could I cook breakfast?"

He held a cup in his hand as he stared at her. "What?"

"It will be easier for me if I have something to do while I talk. I don't know if I can get it out just sitting here."

Since it was what she wanted, he set the cup down,

walked to the table, and sat. "There's bacon in the refrigerator. And eggs."

She let out a long, unsteady breath. "Good." She went to the coffee first, poured him a cup. But her gaze avoided his. "I told you a little," she began as she went to the refrigerator. "About how I was teaching. I was never as smart or as creative as my mother. She's amazing, Adam. So strong and vital. I didn't know until I was twelve how much he'd hurt her. My father. I heard her talking to a friend once, crying. She'd just met my stepfather, and she was, I realize now, afraid of her feelings for him. She was talking about preferring to be alone, about never wanting to be vulnerable to a man again. About how my father had turned her out, and she'd been so much in love with him. He'd turned her out, she said, because she hadn't given him a son."

Adam said nothing as she arranged bacon in a black iron frying pan and set it to sizzle. "So it was because of me that she was alone and afraid."

"You know better than that, Lily. It was because of Jack Mercy."

"My heart knows it." She smiled a little. "It's my head again. In any case, I never forgot that. She did marry my stepfather two years later. And they're very happy. He's a wonderful man. He was strict with me. Never harsh, but strict, and a bit remote. It was my mother he wanted, and I came with the package. He wanted the best for me, gave me all he could, but he could never give me the kind of easy affection there might have been between a father and daughter. It was, I guess, too late in starting for us."

"And you were hungry for that easy affection."

"Oh, starved." She whipped eggs in a bowl. "I got a lot of this out of therapy and counseling much later. It's so easy to see it now. I'd never had a warm, loving relationship with a male figure. I'd never had a man focused on me. And I was shy, crushingly shy in school, with boys. I didn't date much, and I was very serious about my studies."

Her smile was a bit more natural as she grated cheese into the eggs. "Terribly serious. I couldn't see things the way my mother could, so I rooted myself in facts and figures. And I was good with children, so teaching seemed a natural course. I was twenty-two and teaching fifth grade when I met Jesse. In a coffee shop near my apartment. My first apartment, the first month I was out on my own. He was so charming, so handsome, so interested in me. I was dazzled.''

Automatically she sprinkled dill in the beaten eggs, ground a hint of pepper over them. ''I suppose he picked me up. That was a new experience for me. We went to the movies that same evening. And he called me every day after school. Brought me flowers and little gifts. He was a mechanic, and he tuned up this pitiful car I had.''

''You fell in love with him,'' Adam concluded.

''Oh, yes, completely, blindly in love. I never looked past the surface with Jesse, didn't know I should. Later I could pick out the lies he'd told me. About his family, his past, his work. His mother, I found out later, was in an institution. She'd beaten him as a child, she drank and used drugs. So did he, but I never knew until we were married. The first time he hit me . . .''

She trailed off, cleared her throat. For a moment there was only the sound of grease crackling as she took bacon out of the pan.

''It was about a month after we were married. One of my friends at school was having a birthday, and we were going to go to one of those clubs. Silly. Where the men dance and women tuck dollar bills into their jockstraps. Just foolishness. Jesse seemed to think of it that way too, until I was dressing to go. Then he started on what I was wearing, the dress, the hair, the makeup. I laughed, sure that he was teasing me. Suddenly he grabbed my purse, emptied it out, tore up my driver's license. I was so shocked, so angry, I grabbed it back from him. And he knocked me down. He was slapping me, shouting, calling me names. He tore my clothes and he raped me.''

With surprisingly steady hands, she poured eggs into the pan. ''He cried afterward, like a baby. Huge, racking sobs.'' She let out a little breath because it was too easy to remember, to see it all again. ''Jesse had been in the Marines—he was so proud of that, of his discipline and strength. You can't imagine what it was like to see someone I'd thought was so strong cry that way. It was shocking, and devastating, and in a terrible way empowering.''

Strength, Adam thought, had nothing to do with uniforms or biceps. He hoped she'd learned that as well.

''He begged me to forgive him,'' Lily went on. ''Said he'd gone crazy with jealousy, thinking about other men being near me. He said that his mother had left his father when he was a child. Ran off with another man. Before, he had told me she'd died. Both were lies, but I believed him, and I forgave him.''

It wasn't easy to be honest, all the way honest, but she wanted to be. ''I forgave him, Adam, because it made me feel strong, in that moment. And because I thought if he'd lost control that way it had to be because he loved me. That's part of the trap—the cycle. He didn't hit me again for eight weeks.''

Slowly, and with great concentration, she stirred the bubbling eggs. ''Doesn't matter what it was over. It was a pattern that I refused to see, that I was just as much responsible for as he was. He started to drink, and he lost his job, and he beat me. I forgot the toast,'' she said matter-of-factly, and walked over to the bread box.

''Lily—''

She shook her head. ''I let him convince me it was my fault. Every time my fault. I wasn't smart enough, sexy enough, quiet enough, loose enough. Whatever the situation called for. It went on for over a year. Twice he put me in the hospital and I lied and said I'd fallen. Then one day I looked at myself in the mirror. I saw what my friends had been seeing all those months, what they saw when they tried to talk to me about it, to help me. The bruises, that animal look in the eye, the bones sharp in my face because I couldn't keep weight on.''

She went back to the eggs, turning them gently as they set. ''I walked out. I don't remember exactly. I know I didn't take anything, and that I went home to my mother, just like the cliché. I know I was afraid, because he'd told me he would never let me go. That if I ever left, he'd come after me. But I knew I'd kill myself if I stayed even another day. I had thought about it, planned how I would do it. With pills, because I'm a coward.''

She arranged the eggs, the toast, the bacon on a plate and brought it to the table. ''He came after me,'' she said, and for the first time looked into Adam's face. ''He was waiting for me one day when I went out, and he dragged me to his car. He choked me, screaming at me. He drove off with me half unconscious beside him. He was calmer then, explaining things to me the way he'd always done. Why I was wrong, why I needed to be taught how a wife was supposed to behave. I was more terrified then than I'd ever been before. When he was calm, I was more afraid of what he would do—could do to me.''

She steadied herself, because the fear could sneak back at any time, peck away at her faltering courage. ''He had to slow down for traffic, and I jumped out. The car was still moving, but I didn't fall. I always thought it was a miracle. I went to the police and got a restraining order. I started to move around. He always found me. The last time, the time before I came here, he found me again, and I think he would've killed me that time, but a neighbor heard me screaming and beat at the door. Started breaking in the door. And Jesse ran.''

She sat, folded her hands on the table. ''So did I. I didn't think he could find me here. I've barely contacted my mother because I was afraid he'd get to me through her. But I spoke with her this morning, before I came out to the stables. She hasn't seen him or heard from him.'' She drew a deep breath. ''I know that you and Ben and Nate are going to talk to the police about this. I'll answer any questions about him. But he never hurt anyone but me that I know of. And he only ever used his hands. It seems that if he had found me, he would have come after me.''

''He'll never hurt you again.'' He nudged the plate aside so he could cover her hands with his. ''Whatever the answers are, Lily, he'll never touch you again. I swear it.''

''If it is him . . .'' She squeezed her eyes tight. ''If it is,

Adam, then I'm responsible. I'm responsible for two people's lives.''

"No, you're not.''

"If it is him,'' she continued calmly, "I have to face that, and live with it. I've been hiding here, Adam, using you and Will and this place to keep all the bad things away. It doesn't work.'' She sighed, turned her hands over in his. "I have to face it. I learned that in therapy too. I don't have courage, not the natural kind like Will and Tess have. What I have has been learned, practiced. I was afraid to tell you all this, and now I wish I had told you right from the start. It would make the rest of this easier.''

"There's more?''

"Not about Jesse, and not about the horrible things, but it's hard.''

"You can tell me anything.''

"With all that happened last night, my mind keeps coming back and rerunning this one moment.'' With a nervous laugh, she drew her hands out from under his. "I wish you'd eat. It's going cold.''

"Lily.'' Baffled, he pressed his fingers to his eyes, then obediently shifted his plate, lifted his fork. "What one moment?''

"It's just that I thought, as I was saying before, that you wanted me, that it was the usual. I didn't see how it could be anything but, well, that knee-jerk sort of response men have. Pheromones.'' She glanced up, wary as he choked. "It seemed that way,'' she said, defensive now. "And you never said or did anything to indicate otherwise. Until last night. And that moment when you took my face in your hands, and you looked at me. And everything went away but you when you kissed me. Everything went away except you, then it all went wrong, but for that moment, just that one moment, it was so lovely.''

She rose quickly, hurried to the stove. "I know it was New Year's. People kiss at midnight, and it doesn't mean—''

"I love you, Lily.''

The words slid through her like hope. She caught them, held them to her, and turned. He stood now, only a step behind her, the thin winter sunlight on his hair, and his eyes only for her.

"I fell in love the minute I saw you. But then, I'd been waiting for you all my life. Just for you." He held out a hand. "Only for you."

Joy broke through the hope, a hot, bubbling geyser through a calm pool. "It's so simple really." She took his hand. "When it's right, it's so simple." And went into his arms. "I don't want to be anywhere but with you."

"We're home here." He buried his face in her hair. "Stay with me."

"Yes." She turned her lips to his throat, caught the first sharp flavor of him. "I've wanted you to touch me. Adam, touch me now."

He cupped her face, as he had before. Kissed her, as he had before. But this time her arms came around him, and her response was soft and sweet and shy. When he drew her away, he didn't have to ask, but led her out of the kitchen into the bedroom with its tidily made bed and simple window shades.

Then he touched her hair, stepped back to give her room to decide. "Is it too soon?"

The wanting trembled inside her. "No, it's perfect. You're perfect."

Turning, he pulled the shades so that the sun pulsed gold behind them and turned morning into dusk inside the small room. She took the first step, and it was easier than she could have imagined. She sat on the side of the bed, the color high in her cheeks as she removed her boots. He sat beside her, did the same, then kissed her, quietly.

"Are you afraid?"

It was a wonder to her that she wasn't. Nervous, yes, but without real fear. She knew the flavor of real fear, and its bitter aftertaste, well. Shaking her head, she rose and lifted her hands to the buttons of her shirt.

"I just don't want you to be disappointed."

"The woman I love is going to lie with me. How could I be disappointed?"

Watching him, alert for every response, she slipped the

shirt off her shoulders. For a moment, she held it bunched in front of her breasts. She would remember this, Lily thought, every moment of this. Every word, every movement, every breath.

He stood, walked to her. A hand on her shoulder first, a light stroke along the curve, his eyes on hers. Gently, he took the shirt from her, let it fall. His gaze lowered, as did his hands, both skimming softly over the tops of her breasts.

She let her eyes close as his fingers trailed, dipped, traced. Then she opened them slowly to unfasten the buttons of his shirt, draw the flannel aside, then watch the pale skin of her hands glide over the smooth copper of his chest.

"I want to feel you against me." He murmured it as he unhooked her bra, slid the straps down, let it slip to the floor between them. Gathering her close, he held her. A tremor rippled through him, a calm lake disturbed by a lazy finger. "I won't hurt you, Lily."

"No." Of that she could be certain. Of that she could be sure, as his lips lowered to test the skin of her shoulders, her throat. There would be no pain here, not even that of embarrassment. Here there was trust, and desire could be kind.

She didn't jump when his fingers tugged at the snap of her jeans. She shuddered, but not with fear, as he slid the denim down over her hips, murmuring to her as he helped her step free.

Her heart quaked when he stripped off his own jeans, but it quaked in delight and wonder and keen anticipation.

He was so beautiful, that golden skin taut over lean muscles, that sleek, shiny hair skimming strong shoulders. And he wanted her, wanted to belong to her. It was, to Lily, a fine, glittering miracle.

"Adam." She sighed out his name as they lowered themselves to the bed. "Adam Wolfchild." With the good, solid weight of him pressing her into the mattress, she wrapped her arms tight around his neck, drew his mouth down to hers. "Love me."

"I do. I will."

• • •

WHILE THEY CELEBRATED LIFE IN A SHADOWY ROOM, AN-other celebrated death in the daylight. Deep in the forest, alone and gleeful, he studied the trophies he'd so carefully arranged in a metal box. Prizes of the kill, he thought, stroking the long golden hair of a young girl who'd taken a wrong turn.

Her name was Traci; she'd told him when he'd offered her a ride. Traci with an *I*. She claimed to be eighteen, but he'd seen the lie in that. Her face was pudgy still with baby fat, but her body, when he took her into the hills later and stripped her, was female enough.

It had been so easy. A young girl with her thumb out along the side of the road. A purple knapsack slung over her shoulders, tight jeans showing off her short legs. And that bright gold hair, out of a bottle, of course, but it had gotten his attention, gleaming like gilded fire in the sun. Her fingernails had been painted to match the knapsack, a bright, unnatural purple.

Later, he'd seen that her toes were accented with the same color.

He'd let her ramble awhile, he remembered as he stroked the hair. Getting out of Dodge, she said, and laughed. That's where she was from—Dodge City, Kansas.

"You're not in Kansas anymore," he told her, and nearly fell over laughing at his own wit.

He'd let her ramble awhile, he thought again, about how she was going to work her way up to Canada, and see some of the world. She took gum out of her sack, offered him some. He found four neatly rolled joints in it later, but had she offered him any of that? No, indeedy.

He knocked her unconscious, one quick fist to the cheek that had rolled her eyes back white. And he took her up into the hills, to where it was quiet, and private, and he could do whatever he liked.

He liked to do quite a lot.

He raped her first. A man had his priorities. Tied her up good and tight so she couldn't use those purple nails to scratch. She screamed herself hoarse, bucking and squiggling on that narrow cot while he did things to her, used things on her.

Smoked her pot and did it all again.

She begged and pleaded with him to let her go. Then she begged and pleaded some more when she saw he was going to leave her there, tied up and naked.

But a man had responsibilities, and he wasn't able to stay.

When he came back, twenty-four hours later, he could have sworn she was happy to see him, the way she cried. So he did her again, and when he told her to say how much she liked it, she agreed that she had. She told him everything he wanted to hear.

Until she saw the knife.

It had taken him more than an hour to clean up the blood, but it had been worth it. Well worth it. And the best part, the very best part, had been the inspiration of dumping what was left of Traci with an *I* from Dodge City, Kansas, right at the doorstep of Mercy Ranch.

Oh, that had been sweet.

Tenderly, he kissed the bloodied hair, placed it carefully in the box.

They were all running scared now, he thought as he put the box back in its hole, rebuilt the small cairn over it. All of them trembling in their shoes. Afraid of him.

When he rose, lifted his face to the cold winter sun, he knew he was the biggest man in Montana.

FIFTEEN

IF ANYONE HAD TOLD TESS SHE WOULD SPEND A FRIGID January night in a horse stall kneeling in blood and birth fluid and enjoy every minute of it, she would have given them the name of her agent's psychiatrist.

But that's exactly what she had done. For the second night running. She had seen two foals born, even had a small part in it. And it thrilled her.

"Sure as hell gets your mind off your problems, doesn't it?" She stood back with Adam and Lily as the newborn struggled to gain its feet for the first time.

"You've got a nice touch with horses, Tess," Adam told her.

"I don't know about that, but it's keeping me sane. Everybody's so jumpy. I came out of the chicken house yesterday and walked right into Billy. I don't know which of us jumped higher."

"It's been ten days." Lily rubbed her hands together to warm them. "It's starting to seem unreal. I know Will has talked to the police several times, but there's still nothing."

"Look." Adam slid an arm around her shoulders, drew

her to his side as the foal began to nurse. "That's real."

"And so's the ache in my back." Tess pushed a hand to it. It was as good an excuse as any to leave them alone. And she thought a hot bath and a few hours' sleep would set her up for a visit to Nate's. "I'm going in."

"You were a big help, Tess. I appreciate it."

Grinning, she picked up her hat, settled it on her head. "Christ. If my friends could see me now." She chuckled over the idea as she walked out of the stables and into the wild cold of the morning.

What would they say at her favorite beauty salon if she walked in like this, with God knew what under her nails, jeans and flannel smeared with afterbirth, her hair . . . well, that didn't bear thinking of, and not a lick of makeup.

She imagined that Mr. William, her stylist, would topple over in a dead faint on his pink carpet.

Well, she thought, the entire experience was going to make for some fascinating cocktail conversation once she was back in LA. She visualized herself at some tony party in Beverly Hills, regaling her hostess with tales of shoveling manure, gathering eggs, castrating cows—that part she would embellish—and riding the range.

A far cry, Tess mused, from the fancy vanity ranches some of the Hollywood set indulged in. Then she would add that there'd also been some psychopath on the loose.

She shuddered and drew her coat closer. Put it out of your mind, she told herself. Doesn't help to think about it.

Then she saw Willa on the porch, just standing on the second step staring out at the hills. Frozen, Tess thought, like Midas's daughter at his touch. Not a clue, Tess realized, what a picture she made. Willa was the only woman in Tess's acquaintance who had no real concept of her own power as a female. For Willa it was all work, the land, the animals, the men.

She was working at perfecting a sarcastic comment when she drew up close enough to see Willa's face. Devastated. Her hat dangled at her back over that black waterfall of loose hair. Her back was straight as an arrow, her chin angled. She should have appeared confident, even arrogant.

But her eyes were haunted and blind with what might have been guilt or grief.

"What is it?"

Willa blinked, the only movement she made. She didn't turn her head, didn't shift her feet. "The police were just here."

"Now?"

"Just a little while ago." She'd lost track of the time already, couldn't have said how long she'd been standing there in the cold.

"You look like you need to sit down." Tess came up one step, then two. "Let's go in."

"They found out who she was." Willa still didn't move, but her gaze shifted until it rested on the space at the bottom of the steps. "Her name was Traci Mannerly. She was sixteen. She lived in Dodge City with her parents and her two younger brothers. She'd run away from home, this was the second time, about six weeks ago."

Tess shut her eyes. She hadn't wanted a name, she hadn't wanted details. It was easier to get through the day without them. "Let's go in."

"They told me she'd been dead at least twelve hours before we found her here. She'd been tied up, at the wrists and the ankles. There were rope burns and abrasions where she'd tried to get free."

"That's enough."

"And she'd been raped. They said repeatedly, and sodomized. And she was . . . she was two months pregnant. She was pregnant and she was sixteen and she was from Kansas."

"That's enough," Tess said again. There were tears spilling out of her eyes as she wrapped her arms around Willa.

They swayed there, on the step, weeping and holding tight and hardly aware of it. A hawk screamed overhead. The clouds bundled up to block the sun and threaten snow. They stood together, clutched by the fear and grief only women fully understand.

"What are we going to do?" Tess shuddered out a breath. "Oh, God, what are we going to do?"

"I don't know. I just don't know anymore." Willa didn't pull away. Even as she realized they were holding tight to each other in the rising wind, she stayed where she was. "I can run this place. Even with all this I can do it. But I don't know if I can stand thinking about that girl."

"It doesn't do any good to think about it. We can think about why, why he brought her here. We can think about that. But not about her. And we can think about us." She eased back, scrubbed the tears from her face. "We'd better start thinking about us. I think Lily and I need lessons in how to handle a gun."

Willa stared at her a moment, began to see more than the glossy Hollywood façade. "I'll teach you." She took a steadying breath, slipped her hat back into place. "We'll get started now."

"IT'S A WORRISOME THING," HAM COMMENTED OVER HIS midday bowl of chili.

Jim helped himself to a second bowl and winked at Billy. "What's that, Ham?"

The answer waited, and the sound of gunfire echoed. "A woman with a gun," Ham said in his slow, dry voice. "More worrisome is three women with three guns."

"Tell you the truth"—Jim dumped a biscuit into his bowl and took a hefty bite—"that Tess looks mighty sexy with a rifle on her shoulder."

Ham eyed him pityingly. "Boy, you ain't got enough work to occupy you."

"No amount of work ought to keep a man from looking at a pretty woman. Right, Billy?"

"Right."

Though, for himself, Billy hadn't given women much thought since the night of the New Year's party. Bouncing on Mary Anne in the rig had been just fine and dandy. But the awful experience of finding the body with her had put a pall over the entire event.

"Scary, though," he said with his mouth full. "They've been at it better than a week, and I ain't seen Tess hit a target yet. Makes a man leery of going out of doors while the shooting's going on.''

"Tell you what I think.'' Jim thumped a burp out of his chest and rose. "I think what they need is a man to show them how it's done. I got a few minutes.''

"Nobody needs to show Will what to do with a gun.'' Quick pride peppered Ham's voice. After all, he'd been the one to teach her how to shoot. "She can outshoot you or anybody else in Montana with one eye closed. Why don't you leave those women alone?''

"I ain't going to touch.'' Jim shrugged into his coat. "Unless I get the chance.''

He stepped outside, and spotted Jesse climbing out of a rig. "Hey, J C.'' Grinning, he threw up a hand. "Haven't seen you for a couple weeks.''

"Been busy.'' He knew he was taking a chance, a big one, coming over to Mercy in the daylight hours. He visited there as often as he could at night, in the shadows. Often enough to know that his whore-bitch of a wife was spreading her legs for Wolfchild.

But that could wait.

"I was down at Ennis picking up some parts. You had an order come in.'' He tossed a package at Jim, then skimmed a finger over his moustache. He was beginning to like the feel of it. "Brought it by for you.''

"Appreciate it.'' Jim set the package on the rail. " 'Bout time for poker, I'd say.''

"I'm up for it. Why don't you and your boys come around to Three Rocks tonight?'' He grinned charmingly. "I'll send you back lighter in the pocket.''

"Might just do that.'' He glanced over at the sound of gunshots, chuckled. "We got us three females at target practice. I was about to give them some pointers.''

"Women ought to stay away from guns.'' Jesse took out a pack of cigarettes, shook one out, offered it.

"They're spooked. You'd have heard about the trouble here.''

"Sure.'' Jesse blew out smoke, wondered if he could risk

a glimpse of Lily in the daytime. "Bad business. Kid, wasn't it? From Nebraska?"

"Kansas, I hear. Runaway. Got the shit killed out of her."

"Young girls ought to stay home where they belong." Eyes narrowing, Jesse studied the flame of his cigarette. "Learn how to be wives. Women want to be men these days, you ask me." This time his grin was just a little mean. " 'Course, maybe that don't bother you, seeing as you got a woman for a boss."

Jim's back went up, but he nodded easily enough. "Can't say I care for it much, generally. But Will knows what's what."

"Maybe. The way I hear it, by next fall you'll have three women bosses."

"We'll see." His pleasant anticipation of showing off in front of the women faded. He picked up the package. "Appreciate you dropping this off."

"No problem." Jesse turned back to the rig. "You come on by tonight, and bring money. I'm feeling lucky."

"Yeah." Soured, Jim adjusted his hat, watched the rig drive off. "Asshole," he muttered, and went back in the bunkhouse.

ON THE MAKESHIFT TARGET RANGE, WELL BEHIND THE pole barn, Lily shuddered.

"Getting cold?" Tess asked.

"No. Just a chill." But she caught herself looking over her shoulder, peering against the sun at the glint of it on the chrome of a departing rig. "Someone walked over my grave," she murmured.

"Well, that's cheery." Resuming her stance, Tess drew a bead on the tin can with the little Smith & Wesson Ladysmith—what Willa called a pocket pistol—and fired. Missed by a mile. "Shit."

"You can always beat him over the head with it." Will stepped behind her again, steadied Tess's arm. "Concentrate."

"I was concentrating. It's just a little bullet. If I had a bigger gun, like yours—"

"You'd fall on your ass every time you fired it. You'll use a girl gun until you know what you're doing. Come on, even Lily hits the mark five times out of ten."

"I just haven't found my groove." She fired again, scowled. "That was closer. I know that was closer."

"Yeah, at this rate, you'll be able to hit the side of a barn in a year." Willa drew the single-action Army Colt out of the holster riding low on her hip. The .45 was a lot of gun— weighty and mean—but she preferred it. Showing off only a little, she picked off six cans with six shots.

"Annie Fucking Oakley." Tess sniffed and hated the surge of admiration and envy she felt. "How the hell do you do that?"

"Concentration, a steady hand, and a clear eye." Smiling, she slid the gun back into its sheath. "Maybe you need something more. Hate anybody?"

"Besides you?"

Willa merely raised an eyebrow. "Who was the first guy to dump you and break your heart?"

"No one dumps me, champ." Then her lips pouted. "There was Joey Columbo in sixth grade. Little son of a bitch led me on, then two-timed me with my best friend."

"Put his face over that can standing on the fence rail there and plug one between his eyes."

Teeth set, Tess shifted, aimed. Her finger trembled on the trigger. Then she lowered the gun with a laugh. "Christ, I can't shoot a ten-year-old."

"He's all grown up now, living in Bel Air, and still laughing about the chubby dork he dumped in junior high."

"Bastard." Now her teeth bared as she took her shot. "I nipped it." She shouted it, dancing a bit, and Willa cautiously removed the gun from her hand before Tess could shoot herself in the foot. "It moved."

"Probably the wind."

"Hell it was. I killed Joey Columbo."

"Just a flesh wound."

"He's lying on the ground, watching his life pass in front of his eyes."

"You're starting to enjoy this too much," Lily decided.

"I just pretend I'm in one of those arcades at the carnival and I'm trying to win the big stuffed teddy bear." Her cheeks flushed when her sisters both turned and stared at her. "Well, it works for me."

"What color?" Willa asked after a moment. "What color teddy bear?" she elaborated.

"Pink." Lily slanted her eyes left at Tess's chortle of laughter. "I like pink teddy bears. And I've won a good dozen of them while you've been shooting thin air."

"Oh, now she's getting nasty. I think we should have a contest. Not you, killer," Tess said, nudging Willa aside. "Just me and the teddy bear lover." She leaned closer to Lily. "Let's see if you can handle the pressure, sister."

"Then I suggest you reload." Willa bent down for the ammo. "You're both going to be shooting empty."

"What's the winner get?" Carefully reloading, Tess hunkered down. "Besides satisfaction. We need a prize. I do best with clear, set goals."

"Loser does the laundry for a week," Willa decided. "Bess could use a break."

"Oh." Lily rose. "I'd be happy to—"

"Shut up, Lily." With a shake of her head, Willa looked at Tess. "Agreed?"

"Everyone's laundry. Including delicates?"

"Including your fancy French panties."

"By hand. No silks in the washing machine." Satisfied with the deal, Tess stepped back. "You go first," she told Lily.

"Twelve shots each, in two rounds of six. When you're ready, Lily."

"Okay." She took a breath, replayed everything Willa had taught her about stance, breathing. It had taken her days to stop slamming her eyes shut as she squeezed the trigger, and she was proud of her progress. She fired slowly, steadily, and watched four cans fly.

"Four out of six. Not too shabby. Guns down, ladies," Willa ordered as she walked over to reset the targets.

"I can do that." Tess straightened her shoulders. "I can hit all of them. They're all that freckle-faced bastard Joey

Columbo. I bet he's on his second divorce by now. Two-timing Kool-Aid swiller.''

She shocked everyone, including herself, by knocking three cans from their perch. "I hit that other one. I heard it ping."

"It did," Lily agreed, generously. "We're tied."

"Reload." Enjoying herself, Willa strolled over to reset. When she turned and spotted Nate heading their way, she lifted an arm in salute.

"Hold your fire." He stopped short and threw his hands up when Lily and Tess turned. "I'm unarmed."

"Want to put an apple on your head?" Fluttering her lashes, Tess stepped closer and met him with a kiss.

"Not even for you, Dead Eye."

"We're in the middle of a shoot-off," Willa informed him. "Lily, you're up. I see a giant pink teddy bear in your future." She laughed and set her hands on her hips. "You had to be here," she told Nate, then whooped when Lily hit five out of six. "Sign her up for the Wild West Show. Beat that, Hollywood."

"I can do it."

But her palms were sweaty. She caught a whiff of horses and cologne that was Nate and rolled her tensed shoulders. She took aim, squeezed the trigger, and missed all six shots.

"I was distracted," she claimed as Willa cheered and pulled Lily's hand up over her head. "You distracted me," she told Nate.

"Honey, you're a wonder. Not everybody can hit thin air six times out of six." Nate cautiously took the gun, unloaded or not, out of her hand and gave her a hard kiss in consolation.

Willa smirked. "Don't forget to separate the whites, laundry girl. And pick up your spent shells."

Lily moved close as she and Tess gathered up shells. "I'll help you," she whispered.

"The hell you will. A bet's a bet." Tess cocked her head. "But next time, we arm-wrestle."

"I'm heading into Ennis for some supplies." Nate rocked back on his heels and tried, too obviously, not to stare at the denim straining over Tess's butt as she picked up spent shells from the ground. "Thought I'd stop by and see if you needed anything."

Like hell, Willa thought, noting just where his eyes kept wandering. "Thanks, but Bess went in a couple days ago and stocked up."

Tess straightened. "Want some company on the ride?"

"That'd be good."

Her eyes stayed on his as she dumped her handful of shells into Willa's open palm. "I'll just get my purse." She tucked her arm through Nate's and shot a sly look over her shoulder. "Tell Bess I won't be back for dinner."

"Just be back for wash day," Willa shouted after her. "She's got a clamp on his balls all right."

"I think they're nice together," Lily said. "Handsome and easy. His smile just breaks out whenever he sees her."

"That's because he knows his pants are going to end up around his ankles." She laughed at Lily's disapproving look. "Good for them. I just don't get the sex thing, that's all."

"Are you afraid of it?"

The question was so unexpected, considering the source, Willa could only gape. "Huh?"

"I was. Before Jesse, with him. After." Automatically Lily walked over to stack the target cans. "I think it's natural, before, you know. When you just can't know how things will be, whether you'll do something wrong or make a fool of yourself."

"It's pretty basic stuff. What could you do wrong?"

"A lot of things. I did a lot of things wrong. Or thought I did. But I wasn't afraid with Adam. Not when I realized he cared for me. I wasn't afraid at all with Adam."

"Who could be?"

A smile played around Lily's mouth, then she sobered. "You haven't said anything about . . . I know that you know that I'm—with him." She let out a breath, watched it fog in the chilly air, then disappear. "That I'm sleeping with him."

"Really?" Willa tucked her tongue in her cheek. "I

thought he waited for you at the side door every night, then walked you back at dawn because you were holding a secret canasta tournament. You mean you're having sex? I'm shocked.''

The smile came back. ''Adam said we wouldn't fool anyone.''

''Why would you want to?''

''He . . . he asked me to move into his house, but I didn't know how you'd feel about it. He's your brother.''

''You make him happy.''

''I want to.'' She hesitated, then slipped a chain from under her shirt, keeping her fingers closed around something that dangled from it. ''He wants . . . He gave me this.''

Stepping closer, Willa looked at what rested in Lily's open palm. It was a simple ring, Black Hills gold etched with a diamond pattern. ''It was my mother's,'' Willa whispered as her throat closed. ''Adam's father gave it to her when they were married.'' She lifted her eyes to Lily. ''Adam asked you to marry him.''

''Yes.'' He'd done so beautifully, Lily remembered, with simple words and quiet promises. ''I couldn't give him an answer yet. It didn't feel right. I made such a mess of things before—'' She broke off, cursed herself. ''I was in such a mess before,'' she corrected. ''And I've only been here a few months. I felt I had to speak with you first.''

''It has nothing to do with me. It doesn't,'' Willa insisted when Lily began to protest. ''This is between you and Adam, completely. I only have the benefit of being tremendously happy. Take it off the chain, Lily, put it on, and go find him. No, don't cry.'' She leaned forward and kissed Lily's cheek. ''He'll think something's wrong.''

''I love him.'' Lily slipped the chain over her head, slid the ring off. ''With everything I have, I love him. It fits,'' she managed as she put the ring on her finger. ''He said it would.''

''It fits,'' Willa agreed, ''beautifully. Go on and tell him. I'll finish up here.''

•   •   •   •

As THEY BUMPED ALONG THE ACCESS ROAD, TESS stretched luxuriously.

"You're looking awfully smug for someone who just lost a shoot-out."

"I'm feeling smug. I don't know why." Lowering her arms, she scanned the scenery, the snow-covered mountains, the long lay of the land. "Life's a mess. There's a mad killer still at large and I haven't had a manicure in two months. I'm actually thrilled with the prospect of going into some little bumfuck town and window-shopping. God help me."

"You like your sisters." Nate shrugged at her arch look. "You've gone ahead and bonded despite yourselves. I watched the three of you out there, and I'm telling you, Tess, I saw a unit."

"A common goal, that's all. We're protecting ourselves, and our inheritance."

"Bull."

She scowled, folded her arms. "You're going to wreck my fine mood, Nate."

"I saw the Mercy women. Teamwork, affection."

"The Mercy women." She laughed carelessly, then pursed her lips. It has a ring, doesn't it? she mused. "Maybe I don't think Will's quite as big a pain in the butt as I did. But that's because she's adjusting."

"And you're not?"

"Why would I have to? There was nothing wrong with me." She trailed a finger up his thigh. "Was there?"

"Other than being stuck-up, ornery, and hardheaded, not a thing." He hissed through his teeth when her fingers streaked up, found his weakness, and pinched.

"And you love it." Inspired, she struggled out of her coat.

"Too warm?" Automatically he reached down to adjust the heater.

"It's going to be," she promised, and tugged her sweater over her head.

"What are you doing?" Shock made him nearly run off the road. "Put that back on."

"Uh-uh. Pull over." And she flicked the front hook of

her bra so that her breasts spilled out like glory.

"It's a public road. It's broad daylight."

She reached over, tugged down his zipper, and found him hard and ready. "And your point is?"

"You're out of your mind. Anybody could come along and . . . Christ Jesus, Tess," he managed as she slid her head under his arm and clamped her mouth on him. "I'll kill us."

"Pull over," she repeated, but the teasing note had fled. Now there was hoarse and husky need as she tore open his shirt. "Oh, God, I want you inside me. All the way in. Hard, fast. Now."

The rig rocked, the wheels spun, but he managed to get to the shoulder of the road without flipping them over. He jerked on the brake, fought himself free of the seat belt. In one rough move he had her on her back, all but folded on the seat while he struggled with her jeans.

"We'll be arrested," he panted.

"I'll risk it. Hurry."

"We—oh, God." There was nothing under the denim but her. "You should have frozen." Even as he said it he was dragging her hips free. "Why aren't you wearing long johns?"

"I must be psychic." Right now she was simply desperate, and she arched up. Her moan was deep and throaty and melded with his as he rammed himself into her.

Then there were only gasps and groans and pants. The windows steamed, the seat squeaked, and they came almost in unison in less than a dozen thrusts.

"Good God." He would have collapsed on her if there'd been room. "I must be crazy."

She opened her eyes, then started to laugh. Her ribs were aching before she could control it. "Nate, the respected attorney and salt of the earth, how the hell are you going to explain my bootprints on the ceiling of your truck?"

He looked up, studied them, and sighed. "Pretty much the same way I'm going to explain the fact that I no longer have a single button on this shirt."

"I'll buy you a new one." She sat up, managed to locate her bra and snap it on. Giving her hair a quick shake, she boosted her hips to get her sweater. "Let's go shopping."

SIXTEEN

"You got a minute, Will?"

Willa looked up from the papers spread over the desk, pulled herself out of the figures. Christ, grass seed was dear, but if they were going to rebroadcast she wanted to start now. Birth and wean weights circled in her head as she closed a ledger.

"Sorry. Sure, Ham. Problem?"

"Not exactly."

He held his hat in his hands and eased himself into a chair. The winter had been hard on his bones. Age was hard on the bones, he corrected, and he was starting to feel the years more with every passing wind.

"I went down to the feedlot like you wanted. Looks good. Ran into Beau Radley from over High Springs Ranch?"

"Yes, I remember Beau." She rose to put another log on the fire. She knew Ham's bones as well as he did. "Lord, Ham, he must be eighty."

"Eighty-three this spring, so he tells me. When you can get a word in." Ham set his hat on his lap, tapped his fingers on the arms of the chair.

It was odd sitting there, where he'd sat so many times. Seeing Willa behind the desk, with coffee at her elbow, instead of the old man with a glass of whiskey in his hand.

Jumping up Jesus, that man could drink.

Willa struggled with impatience. Ham took his time, and everyone else's, when he had a point to make. She often thought conversations with him were like watching a glacier move. Generations were born and died before you got to the end of it.

"Beau Radley, Ham?"

"Uh-huh. You know his young'un moved on down to Scottsdale, Arizona. Must be twenty, twenty-five years ago. That'd be Beau Junior."

Who would be, by Willa's estimation, about sixty. "And?"

"Well, Beau's missus, that's Heddy Radley. She makes those watermelon pickles that always take first prize at the county fair? Seems she's got the arthritis pretty bad."

"I'm sorry to hear that." If they got a break in the weather early, Willa thought as her mind wandered, she would see if Lily wanted to start a kitchen garden. A real one.

"Winter's been hard," Ham commented. "Don't seem to be letting up, and it's coming to calf-pulling time."

"I know. I'm thinking about adding another pole barn."

"Might be an idea," Ham said noncommittally, then took out his tobacco and began to meticulously roll a cigarette. "Beau's selling out and moving down with his boy to Scottsdale."

"Is he?" Willa's attention snapped back. High Springs had excellent pastureland.

"Done made him a deal with one of those developers." Ham laid his tongue over the paper, spat lightly. Whether it was a comment on developers or tobacco in his mouth, Willa couldn't have said. "Going to break it up, put in some cussed dude ranch resort and raise frigging buffalo."

"The deal's already made?"

"Said it was, paid him three times what the land's worth for ranching. Goddamn city jackals."

''Well, that's that. We'd never match the price.'' She blew out a breath, rubbed her hands over her face, then lowered them as another idea came to her. ''What about his equipment, his cattle, horses?''

''I'm getting to it.''

Ham blew out smoke, watched it drift to the ceiling. Willa imagined cities being built, leveled, new stars being born, novas.

''He's got a new baler. Barely three seasons old. Wood sure would like to have it. Don't think much of his string of horses, but he's a good cattleman, Beau is.'' He paused, smoked some more. Oaks grew from acorns. ''Told him I thought you'd pay two-fifty a head for what he had on the feedlot. He didn't seem insulted by it.''

''How many head?''

''About two hundred, good Hereford beef.''

''All right. Make the deal.''

''All right. There's more.'' Ham tapped his cigarette out, settled back. The fire was warm, the chair soft. ''Beau's got two hands. One's a college boy he just signed on last year out of Bozeman. One of those animal husbandry fellas. Beau says he's got highfalutin ideas but he's smart as a whip. Knows to beat all about crossbreeding and embryo transplants. The other's Ned Tucker, known him ten years easy. Good cowboy, steady worker.''

''Hire them,'' Willa said into the next pause. ''At whatever wage they were getting at High Springs.''

''Told Beau I figured that. He liked the idea. Feels warm toward Ned. Wants him to be settled at a good spread.'' He started to rise, then settled back again. ''I got something else to say.''

Her brow raised. ''So say it.''

''Maybe you think I can't handle my job no more.''

Now it was shock, plain and simple, on her face. ''Why would I think that? Why would you think that?''

''Seems to me you're doing your work and half of mine besides, with a little of everybody else's tossed in. If you ain't in here going over your papers, then you're out riding fence, checking pasture, looking at the equipment, doctoring cows.''

"I'm operator now, and you know damn well I couldn't run this place without you.''

"Maybe I do.'' But it had been an opening and had gotten her full attention. "And maybe I been asking myself what the hell you're trying to prove to a dead man.''

She opened her mouth, closed it, swallowed. "I don't know what you're talking about.''

"Hell you don't.'' Anger hastened his words and brought him out of the chair. "You think I don't see, I don't know. You think somebody who tanned your hide when you needed it and bandaged your hurts don't know what's inside your head? You listen to me, girl, 'cause you're too big and mean for me to turn over my knee like I used to. You can beat yourself into the ground from here to the Second Coming and it don't mean a damn to Jack Mercy.''

"It's my ranch now,'' she said evenly. "Or a third of it is.''

He nodded, pleased to hear the echo of resentment in her tone. "Yeah, and he slapped you with that too, just like he slapped you all your life. He didn't do what was right for you, what was fitting. Now, maybe I think more of those two girls than I did when they first came around, but that ain't the point. He did what he did to you 'cause he could, that's all. And he brought in overseers from outside Mercy.''

Even as her temper simmered to the surface, she realized something she'd overlooked. "It should have been you,'' she said quietly. "I'm sorry, Ham. It never even occurred to me. It should have been you supervising the ranch through this year. I should have thought of that before, and realized how insulting it was.''

Insulting it was, but insults—some insults—he could live with. "I ain't asking you to think of it. And I ain't particularly insulted. It was just like him.''

"Yeah.'' She sighed once. "It was just like him.''

"I don't have anything against Ben and Nate, they're good men. Fair. And it would take a brainless moose not to see what Jack was up to, bringing Ben around here. Around you. But I ain't talking about that." He waved a hand at her as she scowled. "You got nothing to prove to Jack Mercy, and it's time somebody said so to your face." He nodded briskly. "So I am."

"I can't just push it away. He was my father."

"We pump sperm out of a bull and stick it in a cow, that don't make that bull a father."

Stunned, she got to her feet. "I never heard you talk about him like this. I thought you were friends."

"I had respect for him as a cattleman. Never said I respected the man."

"Then why did you stay on, all these years?"

He looked at her, shook his head slowly from side to side. "That's a damn fool question."

For me, she thought, and felt both foolish and humbled. Unable to face him, she turned, stared out the window. "You taught me to ride."

"Somebody had to." His voice went rusty, so he cleared it. "Before you broke your fool neck climbing on when nobody was looking."

"When I fell and broke my arm when I was eight, you and Bess took me to the hospital."

"The woman was too flustered to be driving you herself. Likely have wrecked the rig." Uneasy, he shifted in his chair, drummed his stubby fingers.

If his wife had lived past their first two years of marriage, he might have had kids of his own. He'd stopped thinking of that, and the lack, because there'd been Willa to tend to.

"And I ain't talking about all that. I'm talking now. You gotta back off a little, Will."

"There's so much going on. Ham, I keep seeing that girl, and Pickles. If I let my mind go clear, I see them."

"Nothing you can do to change what happened, is there? And nothing you did to make it happen. This bastard, he's doing what he's doing 'cause he can."

It was too close to what he'd said about her father—it made her shudder. "I don't want another death on my hands, Ham. I don't think I could stand it."

"Goddamn it, why don't you listen?" The furious shout

made her turn, stare at him. "It's not on your hands, and you're a big-headed fool if you think so. What happened happened, and that's that. This ranch don't need you to be fussing over every acre of it twenty hours a day, either. It's about time you tried being a female for a while."

Her mouth fell open. Shouting wasn't his way unless he was riled past patience. And never could she recall him referring to her gender. "Just what does that mean?"

"When's the last time you put on a dress and went out to kick up your heels?" he demanded, even though it made him flush to say it. "I'm not counting New Year's and whatever that thing was you were almost wearing that had the boys spilling drool out their mouths."

She laughed at that and, intrigued, slid a hip onto the corner of the desk. "Is that so?"

"If I'd been your pa, I'd have sent you back upstairs for a proper dress, with your ears ringing, too." Embarrassed by his outburst, he crushed his hat onto his head. "But that's done, too. Now I'm saying why don't you get that McKinnon boy to take you out to a sit-down dinner or a picture show or some such thing instead of you spending every waking hour in a pair of muddy boots? That's what I'm saying."

"And you've certainly had a lot to say this afternoon." Which meant, she reflected, that he'd been storing it up. "Just what makes you think I'd be interested in a sit-down dinner with Ben McKinnon?"

"A blind man coulda seen the way you two were plastered together pretending to be dancing." He decided not to mention the fact that at the poker game at Three Rocks the week before, Ben had pumped him dry for information on her. Conversation over five-card stud was as sacrosanct as that in a confessional. "That's all I have to say about it."

"Sure?" she asked sweetly. "No observations on my diet, my hygiene, my social skills?"

Oh, she's a sassy one, he thought, and bit back a smile. "You ain't eating enough to fill a rabbit, but you clean up good enough. Far as I can see, you ain't got any social skills." He was pleased to have worked a fresh scowl out of her. "I got work to do." He started out, then paused. "I hear Stu McKinnon is feeling poorly."

"Mr. McKinnon's ill? What's wrong with him?"

"Just a flu bug, but he ain't feeling up to snuff. Bess made a sweet potato pie. Be nice if you took it over. He's got a partiality for sweet potato pie, and for you. Be neighborly."

"And I could work on my lack of social skills." She glanced at the desk, the papers, the work. Then looked back at the man who'd taught her everything worth knowing. "All right, Ham. I'll run over and see him."

"You're a good girl, Will," he said, and sauntered out.

HE'D GIVEN HER PLENTY TO THINK ABOUT ON THE DRIVE over. two new men, another two hundred head of cattle. Her own stubborn need to prove herself worthy to a man who had never cared.

And, perhaps, her lack of sensitivity to a man who had always cared, and had always been there for her.

Had she been infringing on Ham's territory the last few months? Probably. That, at least, she could fix. But his words on the murder, however steady and sensible, couldn't wipe out her sense of responsibility.

Or her fear.

She shivered, bumped up the heater in the rig. The road was well plowed, easily navigated. Snow was heaped on the sides so that it was like driving through a white tunnel with white peaks spearing up into a hard blue sky.

There'd been an avalanche to the northwest that had buried three skiers. And some hunters camped in the high country had gotten caught in a blizzard and had to be brought out by copter and treated for frostbite. A neighboring ranch had lost some of its range cattle to wildcat looking for food. And two hikers climbing in the Bitterroots had been lost.

And somewhere, despite the brutal nature of winter, was a killer.

The Big Sky ski area was doing record business. More fortunate hunters claimed game was so plentiful this year that they hardly needed a weapon. Foals were already being dropped, and cattle were growing fat in feedlots and basin pastures.

Regardless of life and prosperity, death was lurking much too close.

Lily was flushed with love and planning a spring wedding. Tess had nudged Nate into a weekend away at one of the tony resorts. And Ham wanted her to put on her dancing shoes.

She was terrified.

And hit the brakes, hard, to avoid running into an eight-point buck. She swerved, skidded, ended up sideways across the road, as the buck simply lifted his head and watched the show with bored eyes.

"Oh, you're a beauty, aren't you?" Laughing at herself, she rested her head on the steering wheel while her heart made its way slowly out of her throat and back to her chest. It took a fast leap back up when someone tapped on her window.

She didn't recognize the face. It was a good one, angelically handsome, framed with curly golden-brown hair under a dung-brown hat. As his lips, accented with a glossy moustache, tipped up in smile, she slid a hand under her seat toward the .38 Ruger.

"You okay?" he asked when she rolled down the window an inch. "I was behind you, saw you skid. Did you hit your head or anything?"

"No. I'm fine. Just startled me. I should have been paying more attention."

"Big bastard, isn't he?" Jesse turned his head to watch as the buck walked regally to the side of the road, then leaped over the mound of snow. "Wish I had my thirty-thirty. A rack like that'd go fine on the bunkhouse wall." He looked back at her, amused to see fear and suspicion in her eyes. "Sure you're okay, Miz Mercy?"

"Yes." She slid her fingers closer to the gun. "Do I know you?"

"Don't think so. I've seen you around here and there. I'm J C, been working at Three Rocks the past few months."

She relaxed a little, but kept the window up. "Oh, the poker ace."

He flashed a grin, and it was as formidable a weapon as the Ruger. "Got me a rep, do I? Gotta say it's a pure pleasure taking your money, indirectly, that is, through your boys. You're a little pale yet."

He wondered what her skin would feel like. She was part Indian, he remembered, and had the look of it. He'd never had a half-breed before. And wouldn't that just fix Lily's butt if he went and fucked her sister?

"You ought to take a minute to get your breath back. If you hadn't had good reflexes, I'd be digging you out of the drifts now."

"I'm fine, really." He had gorgeous eyes, she mused. Cold, but beautiful. They shouldn't have made her insides curl up in defense. "I'm on my way to Three Rocks, as it happens," she continued, determined to work on those social skills. "I'm told Mr. McKinnon's under the weather."

"Flu. Put him down hard the last couple days, but he's feeling some better. You've had your own problems over to Mercy."

"Yes." She drew back instinctively. "You'd better get back in your rig. It's too cold to be standing out there."

"Wind's got a bite, all right. Like a healthy woman." He winked, stepped back. "I'll follow you in. You be sure to tell old Jim I'm up for a game anytime."

"I'll do that. Thanks for stopping."

"My pleasure." Chuckling to himself, he tipped his hat. "Ma'am."

He chuckled out loud when he climbed back into his rig. So that was Lily's half-breed half sister. He'd bet she would give a man a hard ride. He might have to find out. He hummed all the way into Three Rocks, and when Willa took the turn toward the main house, tooted his horn cheerfully and waved her on.

Shelly opened the door, with the baby on her shoulder. "Will, what a surprise. Pie!" Her eyes went huge and just a little greedy. "Come in, grab a fork."

"It's for your father-in-law." Willa held it out of reach. "How's he feeling?"

"Better. Driving Sarah crazy. That's why I'm here instead of home. Trying to give her a hand. Take off your coat, come on back to the kitchen." She patted the gurgling baby on the back. "Truth is, Will, I'm spooked staying home alone. I know it's stupid, but I keep thinking someone's watching me. Watching the house, looking through the windows. I've had Zack up three times this week to check locks. We never locked up before."

"I know. It's the same at Mercy."

"You haven't heard any more from the police."

"No, nothing helpful."

"We won't talk about it now." Shelly lowered her voice as they approached the kitchen. "No use getting Sarah upset. Look who I found," she announced as she swung through the door.

"Willa." Sarah put down the potatoes she was peeling for stew, wiped her hands. "How wonderful to see you. Sit down. There's coffee on."

"Pie." Though she was never quite sure how to respond to the spontaneous affection, Willa smiled when Sarah kissed her cheek. "For the invalid. Bess's sweet potato."

"Maybe that'll keep him busy and out of my hair. You tell Bess how much I appreciate it. You sit down now, have some cake with that coffee and talk to us. Shelly and I have about talked each other out. I swear winter gets longer and meaner every year."

"Beau Radley's selling out and moving to Arizona."

"No." Sarah pounced on the nibble of gossip like a starving mouse on cheese. "I hadn't heard that."

"Sold to developers. They're going to put in a resort. Dude ranch. Buffalo."

"Oh, my." Sarah whistled through her teeth as she poured coffee into her company cups. "Won't Stu have six fits when he hears."

"Hears what?" Silver hair flowing, bathrobe comfortably ratty, Stu strolled in. "We got company and nobody calls me?" He winked at Willa, gave her a quick pat on the head.

"And pie? We got pie and you leave me up there moldering in bed?"

"You won't stay in it long enough to molder. Well, sit then. We'll have pie instead of cake with coffee."

He pulled up a chair, eyed his daughter-in-law. "Going to let me hold my baby yet?"

"Nope." Shelly swiveled Abby around. "Not until you're germ-free. Look but don't touch."

"I'm being run into the ground by women," he told Willa. "Sneeze a couple of times and you find yourself strapped in bed having pills forced down your throat."

"He was running a fever. One-oh-one." Clucking, Sarah slid pie under his nose. "Eat that and stop complaining. Babies are less trouble when they're ailing than any grown man I know. I can't count the number of times I've been up and down those stairs in the past three days."

Even as she said it, she was cupping his chin, studying his face. "Color's better," she murmured, letting her hand linger. "You can have your pie and a visit, but then you go back and take a nap."

"See?" Stu gestured with his fork. "She can't wait until I'm feeling off to start bossing me around." He brightened considerably when the door opened and Zack came in. "Now we'll even the odds a bit. Come on in, boy, but don't think you're getting any of my pie."

"What kind? Hey, Will." Zack McKinnon was a slimly built man who stopped just shy of lanky. He'd inherited his mother's wavy hair and his father's squared-off jaw. His eyes were green, like Ben's, but dreamier. He was a man who liked to spend his days in the clouds. The minute he was out of coat and hat, he kissed his wife and picked up his daughter.

"Did you wipe your feet?" his mother demanded.

"Yes'm. Is that sweet potato?"

"It's mine," Stu said darkly, then nudged the pie closer possessively as the door opened again.

"The piebald mare's looking ready to—" Ben spotted Willa and his smile came slow. "Hey, Will."

"She brought pie," Zack said, eyeing it avariciously. "Dad won't share."

"What kind?" Ben dropped into a chair beside Willa and began to play with her hair.

"Your father's kind," she said, and brushed his hand away.

"Thata girl." Stu scooped up another forkful, then looked crushed when his wife sliced two more pieces. "I thought I was sick."

"You'll be sick if you eat all this yourself. Give Shelly the baby, Zack, and pour the coffee. Ben, stop fussing with Will and let the girl eat."

"Nag, nag, nag," Stu muttered, then beamed when Willa winked and slid her piece of pie from her plate to his.

"Stuart McKinnon, shame on you." Sarah put her hands on her hips as her husband dug in to the second piece.

"She gave it to me, didn't she? How are those pretty sisters of yours, Will?"

"They're fine. Ah . . ." Neither Lily nor Adam had asked that it be kept secret. In any case, Willa imagined tongues were already starting to wag. "Adam and Lily are engaged. They're going to be married in June."

"A wedding." Shelly bounced as happily as the baby. "Oh, that's wonderful."

"Adam's getting married." Sarah let out a sigh as her eyes went sentimentally moist. "Why, I can remember when he and Ben used to tramp off to the stream with fishing poles." She sniffed, dabbed her eyes. "We'll help you with the shower, Willa."

"Shower?"

"The bridal shower," Shelly said, gearing up. "I can't wait. They'll live in that adorable little house of his, won't they? I wonder what kind of dress she's looking for. I'll have to tell her about this wonderful shop in Billings where I found mine. And they have gorgeous bridesmaids' dresses too. I hope she wants vivid colors for you."

Willa set her cup down before she choked. "For me?"

"I'm sure you and Tess will be her attendants. Both of you want strong colors. Rich blue, dark pink."

"Pink?"

At the desperate look in her eyes, Ben howled. "You're scaring her bloodless, Shelly. Don't worry, Will. I'll look after you. I'm going to be best man." He toasted her with his coffee. "I just talked to Adam this morning. You beat me to the announcement."

With his plate scraped clean, Zack came up for air. "Better let me talk to him. I've still got the scars from our wedding." As Shelly's eyes narrowed, he grinned. "Remember those monkey suits we had to wear, Ben? Thought I'd strangle before I could say 'I do.' " He bent to his coffee when Shelly smacked the back of his head. "Of course, I had a lump in my throat when I looked down the aisle and saw this vision coming toward me. The most beautiful sight any man sees in his life."

"Good save, son," Stu commented. "I don't mind weddings myself, though your mom and I did it the easy way and eloped."

"That was only because my father wanted to shoot you. You tell Lily to let us know if there's anything we can do to help, Will. Just thinking about a wedding makes spring seem closer."

"I will. I know she'll appreciate it. I have to get back."

"Oh, don't go yet." Shelly reached out to grab her hand. "You've hardly been here at all. I can have Zack go down to the house and get my stack of *Bride's* magazines and the photo album. It might give Lily some ideas."

"I'm sure she'd like to come over herself and huddle with you." Now the idea of a wedding was making her shoulder blades itch. "I'd stay if I could, but the light's already going."

"She's right," Sarah murmured, shooting an uneasy glance out the window. "It's no time for a woman to be out on the road alone at night. Ben—"

"I'll ride over with her." Ignoring Willa's protests, he rose and fetched his hat and coat. "One of your men can drive me back, or I'll borrow a rig."

"I'd rest easier," Sarah put in before Willa could refuse

again. "It's a shameful thing what's happened here. We'd all rest easier knowing Ben's with you."

"All right, then."

Once the good-byes were said, with the rest of the McKinnons walking them to the door, Will climbed behind the wheel of the rig. "You're a lucky man, McKinnon."

"Why is that?"

She shook her head and stayed silent until they'd left the ranch house behind. "You can't know, you can't possibly understand how lucky you are because it just is for you. It's just the way it is and always has been."

Baffled, he shifted in his seat to study her profile. "What are you talking about?"

"Family. Your family. I sat there in that kitchen. I've sat there before, but I don't know if it all sank in. It did today. The ease and affection, the history, the bond. You wouldn't know what it's like not to have any of that. It's just yours."

It was true enough, and he didn't know if he'd ever thought it through. "You've got sisters now, Willa. There's a bond there, and it's easy to see."

"Maybe there's the beginnings of something, but there's no history. No memories. I've seen you start a story and Zack finish it. I've heard your mother laugh over something stupid the two of you did as boys. I never heard my mother laugh. I'm not being maudlin," she said quickly. "It just hit me, sitting there today, watching you and your family. That's the way it's supposed to be, isn't it?"

"Yeah, I'd say it is."

"He stole that from us. I'm just beginning to realize how much he stole from all three of us. Not just me. I'm going to make a detour."

When they came to the boundary of Mercy land, she shifted into four-wheel drive and swung onto a winter-rutted access road. He didn't ask where she was heading. He'd already figured it out.

Snow was mounded over the graves, burying the head-stones, smothering the wild grass and tender flowers. She thought it looked like a postcard, so perfect, so undisturbed, with only Jack Mercy's stone, higher, brighter than all the rest, thrusting up out of the snow toward the darkening sky.

"Do you want me to go with you?"

"No, I'd rather you didn't. If you could just wait here. I won't be long."

"Take your time," he murmured as she climbed out.

She sank knee-deep in snow, trudged her way through it. It was cold, bitterly, with the wind slapping the air, sending snow swirling from its bed. She saw deer, a small herd of doe on the rise of a hill, like sentinels for the dead.

There was no sound but the wind, and the wind was like the first stars groaning as she made her way to her father's grave.

The headstone was carved as he'd ordered, carved as he'd lived his life. Without a thought to anyone but himself. What did it matter? she wondered, for he was as dead as her mother, who was said to have lived kind, and gentle.

She had come from that, Willa thought, from the kind and the cruel. What it made her she couldn't say. Selfish on some levels. Generous on others, she hoped. Proud and filled with self-doubt. Impatient, but not without compassion.

Neither kind, she decided, nor cruel, and that wasn't so bad, all in all.

What she did understand, standing there in the rough wind, in the rougher silence, was that she had loved them both. The mother she had never known, and the father she had never touched.

"I wanted you to be proud of me," she said aloud. "Even if you couldn't love me. To be . . . satisfied with me. But it never happened. Ham was right today. You slapped me all my life. Not just the physical slaps—there wasn't much punch behind those because you didn't really give a damn. Emotionally. You hit me emotionally more times than I can count. And I just came back, my head lowered like a kicked dog, so you could do it again. I guess I'm here to tell you I'm done with that. Or I'm going to try to be."

She was going to try, very hard.

"You thought you'd pit the three of us against each other. I see that now. Doesn't look like we're going to oblige you.

We're keeping the ranch, you selfish son of a bitch. And I think we may just keep each other too. We're going to make it work. To spite you. We may not be much of a family now, but we're not done yet.''

She walked away the way she'd come.

He hadn't taken his eyes off her, and was grateful for the lack of tears. Still, he hadn't expected the smile, even the grim one that firmed her lips as she got back into the rig.

"You okay?"

"I'm fine." She drew a deep breath, pleased that it didn't hitch. "I'm just fine. Beau Radley's selling off," she said as she maneuvered the rig around. "I'm buying some of his equipment, a couple hundred head from the feedlot, and taking on two of his men."

The lack of segue left him a little muddled, but he nodded slowly. "Okay."

"I didn't tell you that for your approval, but so you can note it in your supervisory capacity." She swung onto another access road to shortcut it to the ranch. Quick gusts of wind that would drag the temperature down to unbearable rattled gleefully at the windows.

"I'll have the monthly report up to date by tomorrow so you can go over it."

He scratched his ear, wary of the trap. "That's fine."

"That's business." Her smile relaxed a bit as she saw the lights of the ranch house peek through the distance. "On a personal level, why haven't you ever asked me out for a sit-down dinner or a picture show instead of just trying to get my pants down?"

His mouth fell open so far he nearly had to use his hand to shove his jaw up again. "Excuse me?"

"You come sniffing around, get your hands on me when I let you, ask me to bed often enough, but you never once asked me out on a date."

"You want me to take you to dinner?" He'd never thought of it. He would have with another woman, but this was Willa. "To a movie?"

"Are you ashamed to be seen in public with me?" She stopped the rig again, left the engine running as she swiveled in the seat to face him. His face was in shadows now, but it was still light enough for her to read the stunned look in his eyes. "I'm all right to go rolling around in the horse barn with, but not good enough for you to put on a clean shirt and invest fifty bucks in a meal?"

"Where'd you get a damn fool idea like that? In the first place, I haven't rolled around in the horse barn with you because you're not ready, and in the second place, I never figured you were interested in sitting down in a restaurant and eating with me. Like a date," he finished lamely.

Maybe feminine power was fiercer than she'd imagined, Willa mused, if wielding just a hint of it caused a man like Ben McKinnon to flop like a trout on the hook. "Well, maybe you're wrong."

It was a trick, he thought, as she drove on. There was a trap here somewhere, and it would snap its teeth on his ankle as soon as he took a wrong step. He watched her narrowly, ready for signs as she pulled up in front of the main house, turned off the engine.

"Go on and drive this back," she said easily. "I can send someone over to get it tomorrow. Thanks for the company."

Damn it, he could almost hear the snap of the spring as he stepped a toe into the trap. "Saturday night. Six o'clock. Dinner and a movie."

Her stomach muscles quivered with laughter, but she nodded soberly. "Fine. See you then." And stepped out, shut the door in his face.

SEVENTEEN

Winter clung like a bur to the back of Montana. Temperatures remained brutal, and when they rose to tolerable, snow tumbled from the sky in frosty sheets. Twice, access roads at Mercy were blocked by ten-foot drifts, piled into glossy white mountains by the unforgiving wind.

Cows went into labor despite the weather. In the pole barn, Willa sweated through her shirt with the muscle-straining effort of pulling calves. An expectant mother mooed bitterly as Willa reached into the birth canal, grabbed hold. Still in the birth sac, the calf was slippery and stubborn. Willa dug in, hissing as the next contraction vised painfully on her hands.

Her arms would carry bruises to the elbow before it was done.

She waited it out, timed her pull, and dragged the first half of the cow out.

"Coming on the next," she called out as blood and amniotic fluid soaked her arms. "Let's go, baby, let's go." Like a diver going under, she took a quick breath to fill her lungs with air, then dragged hard with the next contraction. The calf popped out like an oiled cork.

Her boots were slimy, her thick cord pants stained. Her back was screaming. "Billy, stand by with the injections," she ordered. "Keep an eye on them."

If things went well, mother would clean baby up. If not, that task would also fall to Billy. In any case, she had trained him carefully over the past few weeks, with a hypo and an orange, until she was confident that he could inject the newborns with the necessary medication.

"I'm going on to the next one," she told him as she wiped an arm over her sweaty forehead. "Ham?"

"Coming along." He watched eagle-eyed as Jim pulled another calf.

It was always a worry that even with human assistance a calf would prove too large, or be turned wrong, and make the birthing process lethal for both baby and mother. Willa still remembered the first time she'd lost this battle, the blood and the pain and the helplessness. The vet could be called, if they knew in time. But for the most part, the calf-pulling season of February and March was the province of the cattleman.

Steroids and growth hormones, she thought as she examined the next laboring cow. The price per pound had seduced ranchers into producing bigger calves, turning what should have been a natural process into an unnatural one that required human hands and muscle.

Well, she would be cutting back on that, she thought as she sucked in a breath and plunged her cramping hands into the cow. And they would see. If her attempt to return to more natural ranching proved a failure in the long run, she would have only herself to blame.

"Ladies and gentlemen, coffee is served." Tess's entrance was spoiled when she went white and gagged. The air in the pole barn was thick with the mingling smells of sweat and blood and soiled straw. Visions of a slaughterhouse danced in her head as she turned straight around and gulped in the icy air.

"Jesus, Jesus, Jesus." No good deed goes unpunished, she thought, and waited for the dizziness to pass.

Bess had known, certainly Bess had known exactly what

she would walk in on when she'd casually asked Tess to take the thermoses of coffee out to the pole barn. With a shudder Tess made herself turn back around.

That little deed would require punishment as well, she decided. Later.

"Coffee," she repeated, staring, fascinated despite herself as Willa wrenched a calf partially out of a cow's vagina. "How can you do that?"

"Upper-body strength," Will said easily. "Go ahead and pour some." She spared her sister an arch look. "My hands are full."

"Yeah." Tess wrinkled her nose as the calf squirted out. It wasn't a pretty sight, she mused. At one time she would have said that no birth could be. But the horses . . . she'd been charmed and humbled by the sight of a foaling mare.

But this was nasty, she thought, and messy and almost assembly-line cold. Pull 'em out, clean 'em up. Maybe it was because they were destined to be steaks on a platter, she considered. Then she shook her head and handed a cup of coffee to Billy. Or maybe she just didn't like cows.

They were, in her opinion, too big, too homely, and too desperately uninteresting.

"Wouldn't mind a cup of that," Jim said, and his eyes twinkled at her. "We could switch places a minute. It's not as hard as it looks."

"I'll pass, thanks." And she smiled back at him, giving him a steaming cup so he could take a breather. It no longer insulted her to be considered an ignorant greenhorn. In fact, at the moment Tess thought it was a distinct advantage.

"How come they can't just push the calves out them-selves?" she asked him.

"Too big." Grateful, he gulped down the coffee. Even the burning of his tongue was welcome.

"Well, horses have pretty big foals, and when we're in the foaling stall we mostly just stand by and watch."

"Too big," he reiterated. "With the growth hormones we give them, cows can't throw off calves by themselves. So we pull 'em."

"But what if it happens when nobody's around to . . . pull?"

"Bad luck." He handed back an empty cup. She didn't want to think about what was smeared on the outside.

"Bad luck," she repeated. Because that didn't bear thinking about either, she left the thermoses and cups and went outside again.

"Your sister's all right, Will."

Willa shot a half smile at Jim and took a moment to pour herself coffee. "She's not all bad."

"Wanted to puke when she walked in," he pointed out. "I figured she'd haul ass back to the house, but she didn't."

"Maybe she could help out in here." Billy grinned. "I can't see her sticking her hands in a cow's hole, but she might could use a needle."

Willa rolled her shoulders. "I think we'll leave her to play with the chickens. For now, anyway." And now was what mattered, she decided, as she watched a newborn calf begin to nurse for the first time.

"And she was up to her elbows inside a cow." Tess shuddered over her brandy. Evening had come in cold and clear, there was a fire roaring in the grate, and Nate had come to dinner. The combination made her brave enough to recount the experience. "Inside, dragging out another cow."

"I thought it was fascinating." Lily enjoyed her tea, and the warmth of Adam's hand over hers. "I'd have stayed longer, but I was in the way."

"You could have stayed." Willa had a combo of coffee laced with brandy. "We'd have put you to work."

"Really?" Though Tess moaned at Lily's simple enthusiasm, Lily just smiled. "I'd love to help tomorrow."

"You haven't got enough brawn to pull, but you could medicate. Now you," Willa continued, giving Tess a long, considering look, "you're a big, strapping woman. Bet you could pull a calf without losing your breath."

"Just her lunch," Nate put in, and earned chuckles from everyone but Tess.

"I could handle it." Gracefully, she skimmed back her

hair, making the rings glitter on her pretty manicured fingers. "If I wanted to handle it."

"Twenty says you'd chicken before you were in to the wrists."

Damn it, Tess realized. Cornered. "Make it fifty, and you're on."

"Done. Tomorrow. And Mercy Ranch adds another ten for every calf you pull."

"Ten." Tess sniffed. "Big deal."

"Pull enough and you'd be able to pay for your next fancy haircut in Billings."

Tess flipped her hair again. She was about due for another trim. "All right, then. I say you're going to be springing for a facial as well." She raised an eyebrow. "You could use one of those yourself. And a paraffin wax on those hands. Unless, of course, you like skin that resembles leather."

"I don't have time to waste in some silly salon."

Tess swirled her brandy. "Chicken." She hurried on before Willa could hiss out a response. "I say I'll pull as many as you, and if so, Mercy Ranch treats all three of us—you, me, and Lily—to the works. A weekend at a spa in Big Sky. You'd like that, wouldn't you, Lily?"

Torn between loyalties, Lily fumbled. "Well, I—"

"And we could do some shopping for the wedding. Check out a couple shops Shelly talked about."

"Oh." The thrill of that had her looking dreamily at Adam. "That would be lovely."

"Bitch," Willa murmured at Tess without rancor. "You're on. But if you lose, you're back on laundry detail."

"Oops." Nate took the coward's way out and studied his brandy when Tess snarled at him.

"Meanwhile, I've got to finish recording the birth information from today." Willa rose, stretched. Then froze. Had that been a shadow at the window? Or a face? Slowly she lowered her arms, struggled to keep her features composed. "I wouldn't stay up too late," she said to Tess as she started out of the room. "You're going to need your strength tomorrow."

"I'm really going to love hearing you scream during your

bikini wax," Tess called out, and had the satisfaction of seeing Willa's head jerk around and her face register sheer horror. "I love having the last word," she murmured.

"Excuse me a minute." Adam rose and followed Willa. He found her in the library, loading a rifle. "What is it?"

So much for the poker face, she thought, snapping the chamber closed. "I thought I saw something outside."

"So you're going out alone." As he spoke he chose a shotgun, loaded it.

"No use spooking everyone. It might have been my imagination."

"You don't have a well-developed imagination."

She shook her head at that and decided it was hard to be insulted by the truth. "Well, it won't hurt to do a quick walk around. We'll go out the back."

They bundled into their outdoor gear in the mudroom. Though it was Willa's instinct to go out first, Adam beat her to it, gently easing her aside.

SOMEONE WATCHED THEM. IT WAS COLD, AND BITTER, BUT Jesse stood in the shadows, watching while his hand flexed eagerly on the weapon he carried. He dreamed of using it, on the man, taking out the man, leaving him bleeding.

And just taking the woman, dragging her away, using her until he was done with her. Then killing her, of course. What other choice would he have?

He wondered if he dared risk it, here, now. They were armed, and he'd seen how many people were in the house. He'd seen exactly. He'd seen Lily laughing, cozying up to that half-breed.

Maybe it was best to wait—wait, and watch for the right moment. It could come anytime.

It could come if they walked over to the pole barn. He knew what they would find there. He'd already been there.

"AROUND BY THE FRONT WINDOWS." IF SHE COULDN'T lead the way, at least she could move side by side. "It was just a flash, after I stood up to go. I thought it might have been a face, someone looking in at us, but it was too dark to be sure. And it was gone fast.''

Adam only nodded. He knew Willa too well to believe she would jump at shadows. There were prints in the snow alongside the walkway, but that was to be expected. With all the activity in the pole barn over the last couple of days, the snow on the lawn would hardly be undisturbed. There had been melt and refreezing, so the surface was brittle and gave way with a crackle under their boots.

"Might have been one of the men," Willa said while she studied the ground. "But it's unlikely. They would just have knocked."

"Don't see why they'd have gone through the flower beds to peek in the window either." Adam gestured toward tracks close to the house between evergreen shrubs where flowers would bloom late in the spring.

"So I did see something."

"I never doubted it." From where he stood, Adam could see clearly through the window into the lights of the front room. He watched Lily laugh, sip her tea, then rise to offer Nate more brandy. "Someone was watching us. Or one of us."

Willa shifted her gaze away from the lights in the window, toward the dark. "One of us?"

"Lily's ex-husband, Jesse Cooke. He's not in Virginia."

Instinctively Willa looked back to the window, shifted her grip on her rifle. "How do you know?"

"Nate did some checking for me. He hasn't shown up at his job or paid his rent since October."

"You think he's come after her? How would he know where to look?"

"I don't know." He moved back, away from the house. "Just speculating. That's why I don't see any point in bringing it up to her."

"I won't say anything to her. But I think we should tell Tess. That way one of us can keep our eye out for him. And for Lily. Do we know what he looks like?"

"No, but I'll see what I can find out."

"All right. Meanwhile, we'd better look around. I'll go this way, and—"

"We'll stick together, Will." He laid a hand on her arm. "Two people are dead. Maybe this was just a pissed-off ex-husband wanting to get back at his wife. Or maybe it was something else. We stick together."

In silence they moved through the wind, circling the house. Overhead the sky was clear as glass, with diamond-chip stars wheeling and a three-quarter moon casting pale blue light on the snow at their feet. Cottonwood trees loomed and seemed to shiver under their coating of ice.

In the frigid quiet, Willa heard the call of cattle. A mournful sound, she thought while her breath fumed out in front of her and was whisked away by the wind. Odd—such a sound had always seemed comforting to her before; now it was eerie.

"They're awfully stirred up for this late at night." She looked in the direction of the pole barn, the corral beyond. "Maybe we've got some cows in labor. I'd better check."

Adam thought uncomfortably of his horses, unattended in the stables. It wasn't easy to turn his back on them and go with Willa to the cattle.

"Hear that?" She stopped, ears straining. "Hear that?" she repeated in a whisper.

"No." But he turned so they were guarding each other's backs. "I don't hear anything."

"I don't hear it now either. It sounded like someone whistling 'Sweet Betsy from Pike.' " She shook it off, tried to laugh at herself. "Just the wind, and the creeps. Hell, it has to be twenty below with the windchill. Anybody out here whistling tunes would have to be . . . ."

"Crazy?" Adam finished, and fought to see through the shadows.

"Yeah." Willa shivered inside her sheepskin. "Let's go."

She'd intended to go straight into the pole barn, but the thick huddle of cattle at the far end of the corral drew her attention. "That's not right," she said half to herself. "Something's off here."

She walked to the gate, shoved it open.

At first she didn't believe it, thought her eyes were dazzled by moonlight on snow. But the smell—she recognized the smell of death too well by now.

"Oh, God, Adam." With her free hand she covered her mouth, fought back the gorge that rose like a fountain in her throat. "Oh, sweet God."

Calves had been slaughtered. It was impossible at first to tell how many, but she knew she'd brought some of them into the world herself, only hours before. Now, instead of huddling against their mamas for warmth, they lay tossed into the snow, throats and bellies slit.

Blood glittered on the ground, rich and red, in a hideous pool already crusting in the cold.

It was weak, but she turned away from the carnage, lowered her rifle, and leaned on the fence until her insides settled into place.

"Why? Why in God's name would anyone do something like this?"

"I don't know." He rubbed her back, but he didn't turn away. He counted eight infant calves, mutilated. "Let's get you back to the house. I'll deal with this."

"No, I can deal with it. I can." She wiped a gloved hand over her mouth. "The ground's too hard to bury them. We'll have to burn them. We'll have to get them out of here, away from the other calves and the females, and burn them."

"Nate and I can do that." He struggled not to sigh at her set expression. "All right, we'll all do it. But I want to get you back inside for a few minutes. Will, I have to check on the horses. If—"

"Jesus." Her own misery faded in fear for him, and his. "I didn't even think. Let's go. Hurry."

She didn't head back to the house, but half ran toward the horse barn. The fear raced giddily in her head that she would fling open the door and be met again with that hideous smell of death.

They hit the door together, wrenched it open. She was already prepared to grieve, prepared to rage. But all that met her was the scents of hay and horse and leather.

Nonetheless, by tacit agreement they checked every stall, then the corral beyond. They left lights burning behind them.

Adam moved to his house next, to look in on his dogs. He'd started locking them in at night right after the incident with the barn cat. They greeted him happily, tails thumping. He suspected, with a mixture of amusement and worry, that they would have greeted an armed madman with the same friendly enthusiasm.

"We can call the main house from here, ask Nate to meet us at the pole barn. You want Ham, too."

Willa bent down to scratch an eager Beans between the ears. "Everyone. I want everyone out there. I want them to see what we're up against." Her eyes hardened. "And I want to know what everyone's been doing for the last couple hours."

THE TASK WASN'T PHYSICALLY ARDUOUS, BUT IT WAS PAIN-ful. Dragging butchered newborns into a pile on the snow-covered ground. There were plenty of hands to help, and there was no conversation.

Once Willa caught Billy surreptitiously wiping a hand over his eyes. She didn't hold the tears against him. She would have wept herself if it would have done any good.

When it was done, she took the can of gasoline from Ham. "I'll do it," she said grimly. "It's for me to do this."

"Will—" He cut off his own protest, then nodded before gesturing the men to move back.

"How can she stand it?" Lily murmured, shivering with Tess beyond the corral fence. "How can she stand it?"

"Because she has to." Tess shuddered as Willa sloshed gas on the small heap. "We all have to," she added, draping an arm over Lily's shoulders. "Do you want to go inside?"

More than anything in the world, Lily thought, but she shook her head fiercely. "No, we'll stay till it's finished. Until she's finished."

Willa adjusted the bandanna she'd tied over her nose and mouth and took the box of matches from Ham. It took her three attempts to get a flame to hold in her cupped hand,

and with the teeth of the wind snapping against her, she had to crouch low and close to start the fire.

It burned high and fast, spewing heat. In only seconds, the odor of roasting meat was thick, and sickening. Smoke whipped out toward her, making her eyes water and her throat clog. She stepped back, one step, then two before she could hold her ground.

"I'll call Ben." Nate shifted to her side.

She kept her eyes on the flames. "For what?"

"He'll want to know. You're not alone in this, Willa."

But she felt alone, and helpless. "All right. I appreciate your help, Nate."

"I'll be staying the night."

She nodded. "No sense in me asking Bess to make up a guest room, is there?"

"No. I'll do a shift on guard, and use Tess's room."

"Take whatever gun you want." Turning, she moved to Ham. "I want a twenty-four-hour watch, Ham. Two men at a time. Nate's staying, so that makes six of us tonight. I want Wood to stay home with his family. They shouldn't be alone. Billy and I'll take the first, you and Jim relieve us at midnight. Nate and Adam will take over at four."

"I'll see to it."

"Tomorrow I want you to find out how soon we can sign on the two hands from High Springs. I need men. Offer them a cash bonus if you have to, but get them here."

"I'll see they're on within the week." In a rare show of public affection, he squeezed her arm. "I'm gonna tell Bess to make coffee, plenty of it. And you be careful, Will. You be careful."

"No one's killing any more of mine." Her face set, Willa turned, studied the women huddled together at the corral fence. "You get them inside for me, will you, Ham? Tell them to stay inside."

"I'll do that."

"And tell Billy to get a rifle."

She shifted again and watched the flames shoot into the black winter sky.

PART THREE

SPRING

A little Madness in the Spring . . .
—Emily Dickinson

EIGHTEEN

Ben looked over the operation at Mercy. The steady activity in the pole barn, so like the activity he'd left back at Three Rocks, the piled and tattered snow in the corrals, the gray puffs of smoke from chimneys.

Except for the blackened circle well beyond the paddock, there were no signs of the recent slaughter.

Unless you looked closely at the men. Faces were grim, eyes were spooked. He'd seen the same looks in the faces and in the eyes of his own hands. And like Willa, he had ordered a twenty-four-hour guard.

There was little he could do to help her, and the frustration of that made his own mouth tight as he gestured her away from the group.

"Don't have much time for chatting." Her voice was brisk. He didn't see fear in her eyes, but fatigue. Gone was the woman who had flirted him into a date, who had laughed with him over a white tablecloth and wine, shared popcorn at the movies. He wanted to take her away again, just for an evening, but knew better.

"You hired on the two men from High Springs."

"They came on last night."

Turning, she studied Matt Bodine, the younger of the two new hands, already dubbed College Boy. His carrot-colored hair was covered by a light gray Stetson. He had a baby face, which he'd tried to age with a straight line of red hair over his top lip. It didn't quite do the job, Willa thought.

Though they were nearly the same age, Matt seemed outrageously young to her, more like Billy than herself. But he was smart, had a strong back and a well of fresh ideas.

Then there was Ned Tucker, a lanky, taciturn cowboy of indeterminate age. His face was scored with lines from time and sun and wind. His eyes were an eerily colorless blue. He chewed on the stubs of cigars, said little, and worked like a mule.

"They'll do," she said after a moment.

"I know Tucker well enough," Ben began, then wondered if he knew anyone well enough. "Got a hell of a hand with a lasso, wins at the festival every year. Bodine, he's new." He shifted so that his eyes as well as the tone of his voice indicated his thought. "Too new."

"I need the help. If it's one of them who's been fucking with me, I'd just as soon have him close by. Easier to watch." She let out a little breath. They should have been talking about the weather, the calf pulling, not about murder. "We lost eight calves, Ben. I'm not losing any more."

"Willa." He laid a hand on her arm before she could walk away. "I don't know what I can do to help you."

"Nothing." Sorry for the snap in her voice, she slipped her hands into her pockets and softened her tone. "There's nothing anyone can do. We've got to get through it, that's all, and things have been quiet the last couple days. Maybe he's finished, maybe he's moved on."

She didn't believe it, but it helped to pretend she did.

"How're your sisters handling it?"

"Better than I could have expected." The tightness around her mouth eased as she smiled. "Tess was out here pulling calves. After the first couple, and a lot of squealing, she did okay."

"I'd have paid money to see that."

For an instant the smile spread into a grin. "It was worth the price of a ticket, especially when her jeans split."

"No shit? You didn't take pictures, did you?"

"Wish I'd thought of it. She cussed a lot, and the men—well, I got to say they appreciated the moment. We got her a pair of Wood's cords." Willa glanced over as Tess approached, in the cords, a borrowed hat, and one of Adam's cast-off coats. "They fit her a sight better than that sprayed-on denim she was wearing."

"Depends on your viewpoint," Ben said.

"Morning, Rancher McKinnon."

"Morning, Rancher Mercy."

Tess grinned at him, adjusted her hat to a rakish angle. "Lily's brewing up a few gallons of coffee," she told Willa. "Then she'll be out to help stick needles into cow butts."

"You gonna pull some more calves?"

Tess eyed Ben, then Willa. From the expressions on their faces, she could see that her reputation had preceded her. "I figured I could give it another day, seeing as I'm going to be spending the weekend at the spa in Big Sky."

Willa's grin fell off her face. "What the hell are you talking about?"

"Our little bet." Gotcha, Tess thought, and smiled sweetly. "I pulled two more calves than you the other day. Ham was doing the counting for me."

"What bet?" Ben wanted to know, and was ignored as Willa stepped into Tess's face.

"That's bull."

"No, it was calves. Of course, some of them might have been bulls, but you'll fix that in a few months—and that's something I won't lend a hand with. Mercy Ranch owes us a weekend at the resort. I've already made the reservations. We leave first thing Friday morning."

"The hell with that. I'm not leaving the ranch for two days to go sit in some stupid mud bath."

"Welsher."

Willa's eyes slitted dangerously, causing Ben to clear his throat and move, subtly he hoped, out of range. "It has nothing to do with welshing. After the trouble around here, I was hardly thinking about some lame bet. I had calls to make, the cops came out. I didn't pull calves for more than a couple hours all day."

"I did. And I won." Tess shifted forward until the toes of their boots bumped. "And we're going. You try to back out, I'll make sure everyone within a hundred miles knows your word isn't worth diddly."

"My word's solid, and anybody who says different is a liar."

"Ah, ladies . . ."

Willa's head whipped around, and her eyes seared Ben where he stood. "Back off, McKinnon."

"Backing off," he murmured, spreading his hands as he did so. "Backing way off."

"You want to go when we're hip-deep in this mess," Willa continued, and poked Tess hard in the shoulder, "you go. I've got a ranch to run."

"You're going." Tess poked her right back. "Because that was the deal. Because you lost the bet, and because Lily's counting on it. And because it's time you started thinking of the people around here with as much respect as you give the goddamn cows. I busted my ass to fix this. I've been stuck on this godforsaken ranch for nearly six months because some selfish son of a bitch wanted to play games beyond the grave."

"And in another six months you'll be gone." Why that— simply that—should infuriate her, Willa couldn't have said.

"Damn straight," Tess tossed back. "The minute my sentence is up, I'm gone. But meanwhile I've been playing the game, sticking to the rules. You're, by Christ, going to stick to them too. We're going if I have to beat you senseless, tie you up, and toss you in the nearest jeep."

"Rig." Willa angled her chin up as if inviting a fist. "It's a rig, Hollywood, and you couldn't whip a blind three-legged dog."

"Fuck your rigs." Fed up, Tess gave her a hard shove. "And fuck you."

That snapped it. The temper was there and full-blown before Willa could suck it in. Her fist was there, in full swing before she could pull it. It snapped Tess's head back, left an ugly red mark on the side of her jaw, and sent her butt first onto the slushy ground.

Even as Ben swore and stepped forward, Willa was apologizing. "I'm sorry. I shouldn't have done that. I—"

Then her breath pushed out of her lungs in a whoosh as Tess bulleted up and rammed her, full body. They tumbled to the ground in a flurry of arms and legs and shrieks.

It took Ben about five seconds to decide to keep his own skin whole and stay out of it.

They wrestled into the piled snow, back onto the wet ground, grunting and punching. He expected hair pulling, and he wasn't disappointed. Tipping his hat back on his head, he held up a hand as men came out of the pole barn to see what the excitement was about.

"Well, goddamn my ass," Ham said wearily. "What finally set them off?"

"Something about a bet, a mud bath, and a rig."

Ham took out his tobacco while the men formed an informal circle. "Will's outweighed, but she's mean." He winced when a fist connected with an eye. "Taught her better than that," he said with a shake of his head. "Will shoulda seen that coming."

"Think they'll start scratching?" Billy wondered. "Jeez."

"I think they'd both turn on anyone who got in the middle." Ben stuck his hands in his pockets. "That Tess has mighty long nails. I don't want them raking over my face."

"I say Will takes her." Jim nipped back as the two women rolled dangerously close to his boots. "I'll put ten on her."

Ben considered, shook his head. "Some things you're better off not betting on."

It was the fury that made Tess forget all her self-defense courses, her two years of karate training, made her just fight like a girl in a playground brawl. The red haze over her eyes darkened every time Willa landed a blow. Here there was no defensive padding, no rules, no instructor calling time.

She had her face pushed into wet, muddy snow and spat it out of her mouth on an oath.

Willa saw stars explode in glorious color as Tess yanked her hair. Tears of pain and rage burned her eyes as she wriggled around and fought for leverage. She heard something rip and had time to pray it was cloth and not her hair coming out at the roots.

It was only pride that prevented her from using her teeth. She regretted the pride when she found herself flipped headlong into the snow.

Tess had remembered her training and decided to combine it with inspiration—she sat on her sister.

"Give it up," Tess shouted, fighting to stay aboard as Willa bucked. "I'm bigger than you."

"Get your—fat—ass—off!" With one concentrated effort, Willa managed to shove Tess backward. She pushed herself away, swiveled, and struggled to sit up.

As the men stayed respectfully silent, the two women panted, gasped, and stared at each other. It was some satisfaction to Willa, as she wiped blood from her chin, to see the sleek, sophisticated Tess covered with dirt, her hair mashed and dripping into her eyes, and her mouth swollen and bleeding.

Now that she had time to breathe, Tess began to feel. Everything hurt, every bone, every muscle, every cell. She gritted her teeth, her gaze on Willa's face. "I say it's a draw."

However huge her relief, Willa nodded slowly, then flicked a glance at the fascinated, grinning men. She saw money changing hands and swore under her breath. "Am I paying you worthless cowboys to stand around scratching your butts?"

"No, ma'am." Judging it to be safe, Jim stepped forward. He started to offer a hand before he saw by the glint in Willa's eyes that it was premature. "I guess break's over, boys."

At the jerk of Ham's head, the men wandered back into the pole barn. The conversation and laughter came rolling out within seconds.

"You finished now?" Ham demanded.

Shrinking a little at the tone, Willa scrubbed at the dirt on her knee and nodded.

"That's fine, then." Ham tossed down his cigarette,

ground it out with his heel. "Next time you want to get into a catfight, try to do it where you won't distract the men. Ben," he added, with a flip of a finger on the brim of his hat.

A wise man, Ben suppressed the grin as Ham strode off. "Ladies," he said, with what he hoped was appropriate sobriety, "can I help you up?"

"I can get up myself." Willa didn't quite swallow the groan as she struggled to her feet. She was wet, freezing, filthy, her shirt was torn, and her left eye was throbbing like a bad tooth.

Thinking of teeth, she ran her tongue over them and was relieved to find them all in place.

"I'll take a hand." Like a princess at a ball, Tess held out her hand, let Ben pull her out of the heap of muddy snow. She wanted to shudder at what she was going to see in the mirror but managed a cool smile. "Thank you. And," she added, aiming the smile at Willa, "I'd say that the matter is now settled. Friday morning, and pack a decent dress for dinner."

Too furious to speak, recognizing the danger in uttering a single word, Willa spun on her heel and stalked into the pole barn. The laughter inside instantly cut off into silence.

"She'll go." Ben said it quietly, took out a bandanna, and gently dabbed at the blood at the corner of Tess's mouth. "You got her on pride and honesty. She can buck just about anything but those."

"Ouch." She closed her eyes a moment, then gingerly fingered the rising lump on her temple. "It cost me more than I bargained for. That's the first real fight I've been in since ninth grade, when Annmarie Bristol called me Wide Load. I cleaned her clock, then I went on a diet-and-exercise program."

"It worked." He bent down and picked up her crushed hat. "All around."

"Yeah." Tess set the hat on her dirty, wet hair. "I'm in damn good shape. Never figured she'd be so hard to take down."

"She's lean, but she's tough."

"Tell me about it," Tess murmured, nursing her swollen lip. "She needs to get away from here. More than I do, more than Lily does."

"I think you're right about that."

"I don't know when she sleeps. She's up before anyone else in the morning, spends half the night in the office, or out here." Then she shrugged. "What the hell do I care?"

"I think you know."

"Maybe." She looked back at him, arched a brow. "I tell you what else she needs. A good sweaty, mind-emptying bout of sex. What the hell are you waiting for?"

It wasn't something he cared to discuss. But even as propriety urged him to shut up, instinct tugged in a different direction. He glanced back toward the barn, took Tess's arm, and led her farther away.

"Willa, you know . . . she's never . . . she's never," he repeated, and then shut his mouth.

"Never what?" The narrowed, impatient look in his eyes tipped her off. Tess stopped dead. "She's never had sex? Good God." She blew out a breath, readjusted her thoughts. "Well, that puts a different light on the matter, doesn't it?"

Despite her throbbing lip, she pressed a light kiss to his cheek. "You're a patient, considerate man, Ben McKinnon. I think that's lovely, and very sweet."

"Hell." He shuffled his feet. "I'm thinking maybe she never had anybody to talk to about, to explain things to her."

Tess caught the drift instantly and shook her head. "Oh, no, uh-uh. No way."

"I just thought maybe, you know, being sisters—"

"Oh, yeah, Will and I are like this." Sarcasm dripping, Tess crossed two fingers. "Just how do you think she'd take to me giving her a crash course in Sexual Relations one-oh-one?"

"Yeah. You're right."

And you're a frustrated, hungry man, Tess thought, and patted his cheek. "Just keep working on her, big guy. And maybe I'll think of something. I'm going to go soak in the

Jacuzzi for a day or two." With a hand pressed to her sore
ass, Tess limped off to the house.

"Oh, my." IT WAS ALL LILY COULD SAY. ALMOST ALL SHE'D
managed to say since they'd driven to the Mountain King
Spa and Resort.

She'd never seen anything like it.

The main lodge spread for acres, glass and wood and
clever pebbled paths through snow-dipped evergreens and
heated pools where steam curled in dreamy mists.

She'd clutched the strap of her purse tightly as they
checked in, her head swiveling in wonder around the plush
lobby with its double fireplace, atrium ceiling, and lush
plants. Her heart had begun to thunder as she'd thought of
the expense, for surely any place so beautiful, so quietly
sumptuous, would cost the earth even for an overnight stay.

But Tess had greeted the desk clerk with a friendly smile,
called him by name, and chatted easily about how much she
and her companion had enjoyed their stay earlier in the season.

He'd all but simpered over her, calling up a bellman to
take care of their luggage and guide them to their private
cabin nestled on a ridge behind curtaining pines.

Then the cabin itself had simply wiped her mind clean.

A huge wall of glass opened up the living area to the
majesty of the mountains, offered a tempting peek at the
private hot tub built cleverly into the rocks.

There was a fire already set and burning in a stone hearth,
flowers, fresh and dewy, exploding out of pottery vases, a
deep, curving seating area in buff, accented by jewel-toned
pillows in front of an entertainment center complete with
big-screen TV, VCR, and stereo.

A charming dining room set in dark wood was arranged
conveniently near a sleek little kitchenette.

"Oh, my," she said, but under her breath this time, as
the bellman led the way into a bedroom with its own glass
doors leading to a stone terrace. Two double beds were
made up neatly with thick pillows and quilts, and the bath
beyond—she only managed a quick look—had a mile of

ivory counter, an oversized jet tub, and a separate glassed-in shower. And surely that was a bidet.

A bidet. Imagine it.

She could barely think as Tess instructed the bellman. "These bags in here, thank you. You can take hers . . ." Tess sent Willa a steely look. "In the other bedroom. You don't mind sharing the room with me, do you, Lily?"

"What? No, no, of course not, I—"

"Good. Go ahead and get settled. Our first treatment's in an hour."

"Treatment? But what—"

"Don't worry," Tess said, as she sailed out after the bellman. "I took care of it. You'll love it."

All Lily could do was sink down on the side of the bed and wonder if she'd wandered into someone else's dream.

"WHAT HAPPENED TO YOUR EYE, HONEY?"

The technician, therapist, consultant, whatever the hell she was called, made a long, sympathetic study of Willa's shiner. Willa didn't shrug. It was tough shrugging when you were buck naked on a padded table in a small, dim room.

"Wasn't watching where I was going."

"Ummm. Well, we'll see what one of our skin consultants can do about it. Just relax," she ordered, and began to wrap Willa in something warm and damp. "Is this your first visit to Mountain King Spa?"

"Yeah." And her last, she promised herself.

The claustrophobia came quickly, unexpectedly, as the wrappings snugged her arms close to her body. She felt her heart pound, her breathing shorten, and she began to struggle.

"No, no, just relax, take slow, quiet breaths." A warm, heavy blanket went over the wrappings. "A lot of clients have that initial reaction to an herbal wrap. It'll pass if you just clear your mind, let yourself go. Now, these cotton balls are soaked in our Eye-Lax solution. It'll probably help a bit with that swelling as well as the puffiness. You haven't been sleeping enough."

Swell. Now she was blind as well as trapped. Willa won-

dered if she would be the first client to tear herself free of
herb-soaked restraints and run naked and screaming out of
the Ladies' Treatment Center.

Since she didn't want the distinction, she fought to relax,
let herself go. It was no more than she deserved, she supposed, for keeping her mouth so stubbornly shut on the drive
down.

Music was playing, she realized. Or it wasn't music really, but the sounds of water falling into water and birds
chirping. She took one of those slow, quiet breaths and reminded herself she only had just over forty-eight more hours
to suffer.

In less than five minutes, she was sound asleep.

She awoke groggily twenty minutes later with the consultant murmuring to her.

"Huh? What? Where?"

"We're getting all those toxins out of your system." Efficiently the consultant removed the layers of herbal wrap.
"I want you to be sure to drink plenty of water. Nothing
but water for the next few hours. You have a gommage in
ten minutes. So relax. I'll help you with your robe and slippers."

Still half asleep, Willa let herself be bundled into her robe
and slid her feet into the plastic slippers the spa provided.
"What's a gommage?"

"You'll love it," the consultant promised.

So she was naked again, on yet another table with yet
another woman in a pale pink lab coat fiddling with her. At
the first rough swipe with a damp loofah over bare skin
slicked with a fine sandy cream, Willa yelped.

"Was I too rough? I'm terribly sorry."

"No, it just caught me by surprise."

"Your skin's going to be like silk."

Willa shut her eyes, mortified, as the woman rubbed her
bare butt. "What the hell is that stuff you're putting on
me?"

"Oh, it's our special exfoliator. Skin-Nu. All our products
are herbal-based and available in our salon. You have fab-

ulous skin, the coloring . . . but where did you get all these bruises?''

"Pulling calves.''

"Pulling . . . oh, you work on a ranch. That's exciting, isn't it? Is it a family operation?''

Willa gave up, let the layers of skin be scraped away. "It is now.''

THE NEXT TIME WILLA SAW TESS, SHE, WILLA, WAS FLAT ON her back again, naked again, unless you counted the warm, thick brown mud that was being slowly smoothed all over her. Tess poked a head in the door, took one look, and burst into deep, bubbling laughter.

"You're going to pay for this, Hollywood.'' Christ, the woman was painting hot mud on her tits. On her tits!

"Correction, Mercy's already paying. And you've never looked lovelier.''

"I'm sorry, ma'am,'' the new consultant said, "these are private rooms.''

"It's okay, we're sisters.'' Tess leaned against the door-jamb, looking right at home in her white terry-cloth robe and plastic slippers. "I've got a facial in five. Just thought I'd see how you were holding up.''

"I've been lying down since I got here.''

"You really want to try the steam room if you have time between treatments. What have you got on next?''

"I have no idea.''

"I believe Ms. Mercy is scheduled for a facial next as well. The one-hour Bio Treatment.''

"Oh, that's a honey,'' Tess remembered. "Well, enjoy. Lily's getting the full-body facial in the next room. She's whimpering in pleasure right now. See you.''

"You came with your sisters,'' the consultant said when Tess closed the door.

"So to speak.''

The consultant smiled and painted mud on Willa's face. "Isn't that nice.''

Willa gave up and closed her eyes. "So to speak.''

•   •   °

WILLA GOT BACK TO THE SUITE AFTER SIX, ALL BUT crawling, as her legs were so limp and loose they didn't seem willing to hold weight. She could have whimpered herself and hated to admit that it, too, would have been from pleasure. Her body felt so light, so pampered, so relaxed that her mind simply had no choice but to follow suit.

Maybe the fifteen-minute steam bath with a bunch of other naked women after her full hour massage had been a bit of overkill. But she'd lost her head.

"There you are." Tess was just popping the cork on a bottle of champagne when Willa walked in. "Lily and I had just decided we wouldn't wait for you."

"Oh, you look wonderful." Still wrapped in her robe, Lily got up from the sofa and clasped her hands together. "You're positively glowing."

"I don't think I can move. That guy, that massage guy, Derrick, I think he did something to me."

"You had a man?" Eyes wide, Lily hurried over to lead Willa to the couch. "For a full-body massage?"

"Wasn't I supposed to?"

"My massage therapist was a woman, I just assumed . . ." She trailed off as Tess handed her a flute.

"I ordered a female for you, Lily. I thought you'd be more comfortable." She passed another flute to Willa. "And I requested a male for Willa because I thought she should start getting used to what it feels like to have a man get his hands on her—even in perfectly professional surroundings."

"If I wasn't afraid I'd melt if I tried to stand up again, I'd punch you for that."

"Honey, you should be thanking me." With her own glass, Tess eased onto the arm of the sofa. "So was it great or what?"

Willa sipped the wine. She'd downed enough water to sink a battleship and the change to bubbles with a kick was glorious. "Maybe." She sipped again, let her head fall back. "He looked like Harrison Ford, and he rubbed my feet. God. And there was this place just above my shoulder blades."

She shuddered. "He used his thumbs. He had incredible thumbs."

"You know what they say about thumbs on a man." Smirking, Tess lifted her glass, toasted when Willa bothered to open one eye. "I've noticed that Ben has very . . . large . . . thumbs."

"Isn't noticing Nate enough for you?"

"Sleeping with Nate's enough for me. But I'm a writer. Writers notice details."

"Adam has wonderful thumbs." The minute Lily heard herself say it, she choked and went beet-red. "I mean, he has good hands. That is, I mean, they're very . . ." She snickered at herself, gave up. "Long. Could I have some more?"

"You bet." Tess bounced up, grabbed the bottle. "A couple more and maybe you'll tell us all about Adam's wonderful long thumbs."

"Oh, I couldn't."

"I've got another bottle."

"Don't tease her about it," Willa said, but there wasn't any sting in the words. "Not everybody likes to brag about their bedroom activities."

"I'd like to," Lily said, and flushed again. "I'd like to brag and strut and tell everyone because it's never been like this for me. I never knew it could. I never knew I could." Though she had no head for liquor, she knocked back her second glass with abandon. "And Adam is so beautiful. I mean his face and his heart, but his body. Oh, my God."

She pressed a hand to her breast and held out her glass, which Tess obligingly filled. "It's like something carved out of amber. It's perfect, and I get all loose and fluttery inside just looking at him. And he's so gentle when he touches me. And then he's not, and I don't care because I want him, and he wants me, and everything goes wild and I feel so strong, as if I could make love with him for hours, for days. Forever. And sometimes I have three or four orgasms before we're finished, and with Jesse I hardly ever had even one, and then—"

She broke off, blinked, swallowed. "Did I just say that?"

Tess took a slow, labored breath, a long drink. "Are you sure you want to stop? Another few minutes, and I might just come myself."

"Oh." Hurriedly, Lily set her glass down, clasped her hands to her hot cheeks. "I've never said things like that to anyone. I didn't mean to embarrass you."

"You didn't." Willa's own stomach was fluttering as she reached over to pat Lily's arm. "I think it's wonderful for you, and for Adam."

"I couldn't say things like that to anyone before." Lily's voice broke, and the tears swam. "I couldn't to anyone except the two of you."

"Now, Lily, don't—"

"No." Lily cut off Tess's concern with a shake of her head. "Everything's changed for me. It started changing when I first met both of you. I started changing. Even with all the horrible things that have happened, I'm so happy. I found Adam, and both of you. I love all of you so much. I love you so much. I'm sorry," she said, and sprang up to rush to the bathroom.

Moved, flummoxed, Willa sat where she was and listened to the sound of water rushing into the bathroom sink. "Should one of us go in there?"

"No." Feeling misty-eyed herself, Tess filled Willa's glass again, then dropped onto the couch beside her. "We'll give her a minute." Thoughtfully she selected a perfect Granny Smith apple from the complimentary basket on the table. "She's right, you know. As bad as things are, there's a lot of good stuff trying to balance the scales."

"I guess." Willa looked down into her glass, then lifted her gaze to Tess's. "I guess I'm glad I got to know you. I don't have to like you," she added before things got sloppy. "But I'm glad we got to know each other."

Tess smiled, tapped her glass to Willa's. "I'll drink to that."

NINETEEN

"WHAT'S THE POINT?" WILLA ASKED AS SHE FROWNED down at her toenails, currently being painted Poppy Pink by a technician. "Nobody sees them but me, and I don't pay much attention to my toenails."

"Which was quite obvious," Tess returned, pleased with her Ravage Red polish. "Before Marla worked her magic on you, your toenails looked like they'd been groomed with a lawn mower."

"So?"

Willa hated the fact that she was actually enjoying most of the process—which had included her new favorite, foot massage. She turned to the opposite side of the padded pedicure bench where Lily was beaming down at her half-painted toes.

"You really think Adam's going to go for—what is it"—Willa cocked her head to read the label on the bottle of polish—"Calypso Coral?"

"It makes me feel pretty." Smiling, Lily admired her nails, already shaped and slicked with matching lacquer. "Grown-up and pretty." She looked over at Tess. "I guess that's the point, isn't it?"

"There." As if after a long classroom lecture a student had finally grasped the formula, Tess clapped, careful to guard her nails against smears. "At last some simple common sense. A smart woman doesn't dress up and decorate herself for a man. She does it for herself first. Then for other women, who are the only species that really notices the details. Then, coming up in the rear, for men, who, if a woman's lucky, see the big picture."

Amused at all of them, Tess wiggled her brows, lowered her voice an octave. "Ugh. Looks good. Smells good. Me wanna mate."

She was rewarded for this insight by a snorting chuckle from Willa. "You don't think much of men, do you, Hollywood?"

"*Au contraire*, dimwit, I think a great deal about men and find them, on the whole, an interesting diversion from the day-to-day routine of life. Take Nate."

"You appear to have already done that."

"Yes." Tess's smile turned smug and feline. "Nathan Torrence, an enigma at first. The slow-talking Montana rancher with the law degree from Yale who likes Keats, Drum tobacco, and the Marx brothers. A combination like that, well, it presents both a challenge and an opportunity."

She lifted her completed foot and preened. "I like challenges, and I never miss an opportunity. But I'm getting my toenails painted because it makes me feel good. If he gets a charge out of it, that's just a bonus."

"It makes me feel exotic," Lily put in, "like—what was the name of that woman in the sarong? The one in the old black-and-white movies?"

"Dorothy Lamour," Tess told her. "Now take Adam, a different type of man altogether."

"He is?" Since they'd moved to her favorite topic, Lily perked up. "How?"

"Don't encourage her, Lily. She's playing at expert here."

"I don't have to play at it, when it comes to men, champ. Adam," Tess continued, wagging a finger. "Serious, solid, and yet vaguely mysterious. Probably the most gorgeous man I've ever seen in my short, if illustrious, career of male tracking, with this—the only word I can think of is 'goodness'—sort of beaming out of those yum-yum eyes.''

"His eyes," Lily said with a sigh that made Willa roll her own.

"But—'' Tess made her point with a shake of her finger. "It doesn't make him boring, as goodness sometimes can, because there's this simmering, controlled passion in there too. And as far as you're concerned, Lily, you could shave your head and paint your face Calypso Coral, and he'd still adore you.''

"He loves me," Lily said with a foolish grin.

"Yes, he does. He thinks you're the most beautiful woman in the world, and if you woke up some morning and some wicked witch had put a spell on you and turned you into a hag, he'd still think you were the most beautiful woman in the world. He sees past the physical, appreciates it but sees past it to everything you are inside. That's why I think you're the luckiest woman in the world.''

"Maybe that wasn't such a bad take," Willa commented, "for a Hollywood writer.''

"Oh, I'm not done. We have to complete our triad.'' Delighted with herself, Tess leaned back. "Ben McKinnon.''

"Don't start," Willa commanded.

"Obviously you're hot for him. We'll just sit here a minute and dry,'' she told the technicians, then reached for her glass of sparkling mineral water. "A woman would have to be dead two weeks not to have a pulse spike around Ben McKinnon.''

"How much has your pulse been spiking?''

Pleased with the reaction, Tess moved a lazy shoulder. "I'm otherwise involved. If I wasn't . . . In any case, I haven't been dead for two weeks.''

"Could be arranged.''

"No, don't get up and stalk around yet, you'll smear.'' Tess put a restraining hand on Willa's arm. "Back to Ben—his sexuality is right out there, striding along a foot in front of him. Raw, hot, unapologetic sex in a tough male package. You watch him ride a horse and you just know he'd ride a woman with the same power. He's also intelligent, loyal, honest, and looks fabulous in Levi's. As a student of such matters, I'd have to say Ben McKinnon has the best buns in denim east or west of the Pecos. Not a bad distraction,'' she finished, taking a slow sip of water, ''from the day-to-day routine.''

''I don't know why you're looking at his butt when you've already got a guy,'' Willa muttered.

''Because it's a fine butt, and I have excellent eyesight.'' Tess skimmed her tongue over her teeth. ''Of course, a woman would have to be brave enough, strong enough, and smart enough to match him in power and style.''

There, Tess thought, as Willa sulked beside her, challenge issued, Ben. That's the best help I can give you.

It WASN'T UNTIL WILLA WAS BACK AT MERCY AND UN-packing that she realized that through the last twenty-four hours of her stay at the spa, she hadn't thought of the ranch, of her troubles, her responsibilities at all. And now that she did realize it, there was a quick wash of guilt that it should have been so easy to leave it all behind, to immerse herself in the pampering and pleasure.

Like walking into an alternate reality, she supposed, and grimaced as she tumbled pretty gold boxes onto her bed. Which might explain why she'd barely put up a struggle when Tess and Lily had urged her to buy creams, lotions, scents, shampoo.

Christ Almighty, hundreds of dollars' worth of female foolishness that she was unlikely to remember to use.

So she'd give the lot of them to Bess, she decided, to go with the fancy perfumed soaps and bubble bath she'd bought her.

In any case, it was good to be getting back into jeans, she thought, tugging them on. It was better to have Adam tell her there'd been no whisper of trouble over the weekend. The men were starting to relax again, though the round-the-clock guard remained in effect. Calf-pulling season was winding down, and the calendar insisted that spring was on the way.

You wouldn't know it, she mused, trailing her shirt from her fingers as she walked to the window. The air swooping down from Canada was as bitter as an old woman with gout. There was no snow in the sky, and for that she was grateful. Still, Willa knew the vagaries of March—and April, for that matter. The reality of spring remained as distant as the moon.

And she longed for it.

That surprised her as well. Normally she was content in any season. Winter was work, certainly, but it also offered, even demanded, periods of rest. For the land, for the people on it.

Spring might be a time of rebirth and rejoicing, but it was also a time of mud, of drought or impossible driving rain, of aching muscles, fields to be planted, cattle to be separated and led to range.

But she longed for it, longed to see even one single bud bloom—the flower of the bitterroot, triumphing out of the mud; a laurel, springing up miraculously in the thickening forest; wild columbine teasing a mountain ridge.

Amazed at herself, she shook her head and stepped back from the window. Since when had she started dreaming of flowers?

It was Tess's doing, she imagined. All that talk about romance and sex and men. Just a natural segue into spring, flowers—and mating season.

Chuckling, she studied the scatter of gold boxes over the simple quilt on her bed. And what were those, she admitted, but expensive mating lures?

At the sound of footsteps she called out and began to gather the boxes up. "Bess? Got a minute? I've some other things in here you might want. I don't know why I—"

She broke off as Ben, not Bess, stepped into the room.

"What the hell are you doing here? Don't you knock?"

"Did. Bess let me in." His brows went up, and the eyes under them lit with appreciation. "Well, hell, Willa, look at you."

She was grateful she'd pulled on jeans at least and also very aware she was shirtless but for the thin, clinging silk of her thermal undershirt. Her nipples hardened traitorously even as she snatched up the flannel shirt she'd tossed aside.

"I'm not back an hour," she complained as she punched her arms through shirtsleeves, "and you're in my face. I don't have time to chat or go over reports. I've already lost a whole weekend."

"Doesn't appear you lost a thing." He was understandably disappointed when she buttoned up the plaid shirt but intrigued by the busy, businesslike way her fingers executed the task. Eventually he'd like to see them go in reverse.

"You look fine." He came closer. "Rested. Pretty." And lifted a hand to the spiraling curls raining over her shoulders. "Sexy. I had a couple of bad moments when Nate told me about the place you were going. Figured you might come back with your face all tarted up and your hair chopped off like one of those New York models trying to look like a teenage boy. Why do you suppose they want to do that?"

"I couldn't say."

"How'd they get all that hair of yours into those corkscrews?"

"You hand those people enough money, they'll do anything." She tossed back the curls, faintly embarrassed by them. "What do you want, Ben, to stand here and talk about salon treatments?"

"Hmm?" It was the damnedest thing, he mused, toying with her hair again. All those wild curls, and it was still as soft as duck down. "I like it. Gives me ideas."

She was getting that picture clearly enough, and slipped strategically out of reach. "It's just hair curls."

"I like it curled." His grin spread as he maneuvered her toward the wall. "I like it straight too, the way it just swings down your back, or when you twist it back in a pigtail."

She knew the dimensions of her room well enough to judge she'd be rapping into the wall in another two steps. So she held her ground. "Look, what do you think you're doing?"

"Is your memory that poor?" He took hold of her, pleased that she'd stopped retreating. "I didn't figure a few days away would have you forgetting where we left off.

Hold still, Willa,'' he said patiently when she lifted her arms to push him off. "I'm just going to kiss you."

"What if I don't want you to?"

"Then say, 'Get your hands off me, Ben McKinnon.' "

"Get—"

That was as far as she got before he cut off her opportunity. And his lips were hungry, not nearly as patient as his voice had been. The arms that held her tightened possessively, stole her breath, had her parting her lips to gasp for air. . . .

And her mouth was invaded by his quick and clever tongue.

It was like being swallowed, she thought hazily. Like being eaten alive with a greed that incited greed. Hearts pounding. That was his, she realized, as well as hers. Racing wild. Dangerously fast. And she wondered if they continued to ride this course, at this speed, how soon one or both of them would fly headlong over the saddle and into the air.

"Missed you."

He said it so quietly as his lips trailed down to sample her throat that she thought she'd imagined it.

Missed her? Could he?

Those lips cruised up again, along the side of her throat, behind her ear, doing things to her skin that made her giddy and weak inside.

"You smell good," he murmured.

He'd said she looked good, she remembered, as her knees trembled. Smelled good. Did that mean he had the big picture? And what came next was . . . She thought of Tess's lightly cynical remark and swallowed hard.

"Wait. Stop." She couldn't have pushed a mound of feathers away, much less an aroused man, but at her breathy voice and the flutter of her hands he changed the tone.

"Okay." He still held her, but easy now, his hand stroking up her back to soothe. She was shaking, he realized, and cursed himself for it. Innocent, innocent, he repeated like a mantra, until his breathing began to level.

He'd only meant to indulge in a couple of teasing tastes, not a flurry of half-mad gulps. But days, weeks—hell, years—of frustration and wanting, he admitted, were boiling up and threatening to blow.

And what he wanted to do, what he'd imagined doing to her in that room, on that bed, wasn't the way a civilized man should initiate a virgin.

"Sorry." He eased back to study her face. Fear and confusion and desire swirled in her eyes. He could have done without the fear. "I didn't mean to spook you, Will. I forgot myself a minute." To lighten the mood, he flicked a finger at a curl. "Must be the hairdo."

He was sorry, she realized, more than a little stunned. And something else was in his eyes. It couldn't be tenderness, not from him, but she was certain it was a softer emotion than lust. Maybe, she thought—and smiled a little—maybe it was affection.

"It's okay. I guess I forgot myself for a minute too. Must have been the way you were gulping me down like two quarts of prime whiskey."

"You've got a tendency to be as potent," he muttered.

"I do?"

The stunned female response got his blood moving again. "Don't get me started. I really came up to let you know that Adam and I are riding up into high country to take a look around. Zack says the north pass is blocked by snow. And he thought some hunters might be making use of your cabin."

"Why does he think that?"

"On one of his flyovers he caught sight of tracks, other signs." Ben shrugged it off. "Wouldn't be the first time, but since I want to see how bad the pass is blocked, Adam and I thought we'd swing up and check it out."

"I'll go with you. I'll be ready in fifteen minutes."

"We're getting a late start. Odds are we won't make it back tonight. We can radio you from the cabin."

"I'm going. Ask Adam to saddle Moon for me, and I'll pack my gear."

IT WAS GOOD TO RIDE, WILLA THOUGHT. GOOD TO BE IN the saddle, out in the air that crisped with the climb. Moon loped easily through the snow, apparently pleased to be out herself. Her breath plumed ahead and her harness jingled.

The sun shone bright, dazzling light off the untrod snow, adding glitter to the draped trees. Here in high country, spring would come late and last hardly more than a precious moment.

A falcon called, a scream in the silence, and she saw signs of deer, of other game, of predators that hunted the hills. Perhaps she had enjoyed her weekend of pampering, but this was her world. The higher she climbed, the more thrilled she was to be back.

"You look pleased with yourself." Ben flanked her left and, keeping an easy hand on the reins, studied her face. "What did they do to you up there at that fancy spa?"

"All sorts of things. Wonderful things." She tilted her head, sent him a sly smile. "They waxed me. All over."

"No kidding?" He felt a pleasant little thrumming in his loins. "*All* over?"

"Yep. I've been scraped down, oiled up, waxed and polished. It was pretty good. You ever had coconut oil rubbed over your entire body, Ben?"

The thrumming increased considerably. "You offering, Willa?"

"I'm telling you. At the end of the day this guy would rub—"

"Guy?" He shot straight arrow in the saddle. The sharp tone of his voice had Charlie scampering back from his scouting mission and whining. "What guy?"

"The massage guy."

"You let a guy rub your—"

"Sure." Satisfied with his reaction, she turned to Adam. The gleam in his eye assured her that her brother knew just what game she was playing. "Lily had something called aromatherapy. It seemed to me to be a lot like our mother's people have been doing for centuries. Using herbs and scents to relax the mind, and the body. Now they've slapped on a fancy name and charge you an arm and a leg for it."

"White men," Adam said with a grin. "Always seeking profit from nature."

"That was my thought. In fact, I asked Lily's massage therapist why she figured—"

"She?" Ben interrupted. "Lily had a woman massage lady?"

"That's right. So I asked her why it was she figured her people had come up with all these treatments when the Indians had been using mud and herbs and oils before there were whites within a thousand miles of the Rockies."

"How come Lily had a woman and you didn't?"

Willa glanced over at Ben. "Lily's shy. Anyway, some of the treatments seemed very basic. And the oils and creams not unlike what our grandmother would have brewed up in her own lodge."

"They put it in fancy bottles and make it theirs," Adam added.

Ben knew when his chain was being pulled, and now he shifted in the saddle. "They use bear grease on you, too?"

Willa bit off a smile. "Actually I suggested they look into it. You should tell Shelly to take a weekend there when the baby's weaned. Tell her to ask for Derrick. He was amazing."

Adam coughed into his hand, then clucked to his horse and took the lead, with Charlie trotting happily in his wake.

"So you let this guy, this Derrick guy, see you naked?"

"He's a professional." She flicked back her curling hair, no longer embarrassed a bit. "I'm thinking of getting regular massages. They're very . . . relaxing."

"I bet." Reaching over, Ben put a hand on her arm, slowing both their mounts. "I've just got one question."

"What is it?"

"Are you trying to drive me crazy?"

"Maybe."

He nodded. "Because you figure it's safe since we're out here and Adam's just up ahead."

The smile got away from her. "Maybe."

"Think again." He moved fast, leaning into her, dragging her into him and fixing his mouth hard on hers. When he let her jerk back, control her frisking mount, he was smiling.

"I'm going to buy me some coconut oil, and we'll see how you look in it."

Her heart stuttered, settled. "Maybe," she said again. She started to kick Moon into a trot.

The shot crashed and echoed, a high-pitched, shocking sound. Too close, was all Willa had time to think before Adam's horse reared, nearly unseating him.

"Idiots," she said between her teeth. "Goddamn citified idiots must be—"

"Take cover." Ben all but shoved her out of the saddle, swinging his mount to her other side as a shield. He had his rifle out in a lightning move even as he plunged knee-deep into the snow. "Use the trees, and stay down."

But she'd seen now, the blood that stained the sleeve of Adam's jacket. And seeing it, she was running toward her brother, in the open. Ben swore ripely as he tackled her, used his body to cover hers as another shot exploded.

She fought bitterly, bucking and clawing in the snow. Terror was a hot, red haze. "Adam—he's shot. Let me go."

"Keep down." Ben's face was close to hers, his voice cold and calm as he held her under him. Charlie barked like thunder, quivering for the signal to hunt. He subsided only when Ben gave him the terse order to stay.

Still covering Willa, Ben shifted his eyes as Adam bellied toward them. "How bad?"

"Don't know." The pain was bright, a violent song up his arm to the shoulder. "I think he got more of the coat than me. Will, you're not hit?" He rubbed a snow-coated glove over her face. "Will?"

"No. You're bleeding."

"It's okay. His aim was off."

She closed her eyes a moment, willing herself to calm. "It was deliberate. It wasn't some stupid hunter."

"Had to be a long-range rifle," Ben murmured, lifting his head enough to scan the trees, the hills. He slid a hand over his dog's vibrating back to calm him. "I can't see anything. From the direction, I'd guess he's holed up in that gulch, up there in the rocks."

"With plenty of cover." Willa forced her breath slowly in, slowly out. "We can't get to him."

Trust her, Ben thought, to think first of attack. He slid off Willa, steadied his rifle. "We're almost to the cabin. You and Willa make for it, keep to the trees. I can draw his fire here."

"The hell with that. I'm not leaving you here." She started to scramble up, but Ben pushed her flat again. In the seconds that his eyes held Adam's, the men agreed how to handle it.

"Adam's bleeding," Ben said quietly. "He has to be looked after. You get him to the cabin, Will. I'll be right behind you."

"We can make a stand in the cabin if we have to." Blocking out the pain, Adam walked his way through the details. "Ben, we can cover you from up ahead. When you hear our fire, start after us."

Ben nodded. "Once I get to that stand of rocks where we used to have that fort, I'll fire. That'll give you time to make it to the cabin. Fire again so I'll know you made it."

Now she had to choose, Willa realized, between one man and the other. The blood staining the snow gave her no choice at all. "Don't do anything stupid." She took Ben's face in her hands, kissed him hard. "I don't like heroes."

Keeping low, she grabbed the reins of her horse. "Can you mount?" she said to Adam.

"Yeah. Stay in the trees, Willa. We're going to move fast." With one last look at Ben, Adam swung into the saddle. "Ride!"

She didn't have time to look back. But she would remember, she knew she would remember always, the way Ben knelt alone in the snow, the shadows of trees shielding his face and a rifle lifted to his shoulder.

She'd lied, she thought when she heard him fire once, twice, three times. She had an open heart for heroes.

"There's no return fire," she called out as she and Adam pulled up behind a tower of rock. "Maybe he's gone."

Or maybe he was waiting, Adam thought. He said nothing as Willa unsheathed her rifle. She fired a steady half dozen rounds. "He'll be all right, won't he, Adam? If the sniper tries to circle around and—''

"Nobody knows this country better than Ben." He said it quickly to reassure both of them. He'd left his brother behind, was all he could think. Because it was all that could be done. "We've got to keep moving, Willa. We can give Ben the best cover from the cabin."

She couldn't argue, not when Adam's face was so pale, not when the cabin, warmth, and medical supplies were only minutes away. But she knew what none of them had said: There was no cover for the last fifty yards. To get inside, they would have to ride in the open.

The sun was bright, the snow dazzling. She had no doubt that they stood out against that white like deer in a meadow. In the distance she could hear the frigid sound of water forcing its way over ice and rock and, closer, the rapid sound of her own breathing.

Rocks punched out of snow, trees crouched. She rode with her rifle in her hand, prepared for some faceless gunman to leap out at any moment and take aim. Overhead an eagle circled and called out in triumph. She counted the seconds away by her heartbeats, and bit down hard on her lip when she heard the echo of Ben's rifle.

"He made it to the stand of rocks."

She could see the cabin now, the sturdy wooden structure nestled on rocky ground. Inside, she thought, was safety. First aid for Adam, a radio to signal for help. Shelter.

"Something's wrong." She heard herself say it before it became completely clear. A picture out of focus, a puzzle with pieces missing. "Someone's shoveled a path," she said slowly. "And there are tracks." She took a deep breath. "I can still smell smoke." Nothing puffed from the chimney, but she could catch the faint whiff of smoke in the air. "Can you?"

"What?" Adam shook his head, fought to stay conscious. "No, I . . ." The world kept threatening to gray on him. He couldn't feel his arm now, not even the pain.

"It's nothing." Moving on instinct, Willa shoved her rifle back in its sheath, took Adam's reins with her free hand. In

the open or not, they would have to move quickly before
he lost any more blood. "Nearly there, Adam. Hold on.
Hold on to the horn."

"What?"

"Hold on to the horn. Look at me." She snapped it out
so that his eyes cleared for a moment. "Hold on."

She kicked Moon into a gallop, shouting to urge Adam's
mount to keep pace. If Adam fell before they reached safety,
she was prepared to leap down, drag him if necessary, and
let the horses go.

They burst into a flash of sunlight, blinding. Snow flew
up from racing hooves like water spewing. She rode straight
in the saddle, using her body to defend her brother's. And
every muscle was braced for that quick insult of steel into
flesh.

Rather than taking the cleared path, she drove the horses
toward the south side of the cabin. Even when the shadow
of the building fell over them, she didn't relax. The sniper
could be anywhere now. She dragged her weapon free,
jumped the saddle, then fought the nearly waist-high snow
to reach Adam as he swayed.

"Don't you pass out on me now." Her breath burned in
her lungs as she struggled to support him. His blood was
warm on her hands. "Damned if I'm carrying you."

"Sorry. Hell. Just give me a second." He needed all his
concentration to beat back the dizziness. His vision was
blurred around the edges, but he could still see. And he
could still think. Well enough to know they wouldn't be
safe until they were inside the cabin walls. And even
then . . .

"Get inside. Fire off a shot to let Ben know. I'll get the
gear."

"The hell with the gear." Willa steadied him against her
side and dragged him toward the door.

Too warm, she thought the minute she was inside the
door. Pulling Adam toward a cot, she glanced at the fireplace. Nothing but ash and chunks of charred wood. But she
could smell the memory of a recent fire.

"Lie down. Hold on a minute." Hurrying back to the

door, she fired three times to signal Ben, then closed them in. "He'll be right along," she said, and prayed it was true. "We have to get your coat off."

Stop the bleeding, get a fire started, clean the wound, radio the ranch, worry for Ben.

"I haven't been much help," Adam said, as she removed his coat.

"Next time I'm shot you can be the tough one." She choked off a gasp at the blood that soaked the sleeve of his shirt from shoulder to wrist. "Pain? How bad?"

"Numb." With a tired and objective eye, he studied the damage. "I think it passed through. I don't think it's so bad. Would've bled more if it hadn't been so cold."

Would've bled less, Willa thought, ripping the sleeve aside, if they hadn't been forced to ride like maniacs. She tore through the thermal shirt as well, felt her stomach heave mightily at the sight of torn and scored flesh.

"I'm going to tie it up first, stop the bleeding." She pulled out a bandanna as she spoke. "I'm going to get some heat in here, then we'll clean it out and see what's what."

"Check the windows." He laid a hand on hers. "Reload your rifle."

"Don't worry." She tied the makeshift bandage snugly. "Lie back down before you faint. You're beginning to look like a paleface."

She tossed a blanket over him, then rushed to the wood-box. Nearly empty, she noted, while her heart thudded. With trembling hands she set the kindling, arranged logs, set them to blaze.

The first aid kit was in the cupboard over the sink. Setting it on the counter, she flipped the lid to be sure it was fully stocked. With that small relief, she crouched down to the cabinet below for bandages, pushed through containers of cleaning supplies.

And felt her bowels turn to water.

The bucket kept below the sink was just where it should have been. But it was heaped with rags and stiffened towels. And the rusty stain coating all of them was blood. Old blood, she thought, as she gingerly reached out. And much too much blood to have been the result of some casual kitchen accident.

Too much blood to be anything but death.

"Will?" Adam struggled to sit up. "What is it?"

"Nothing." She closed the cupboard door. "Just a mouse. Startled me. I can't find bandages." Before she turned back, she schooled the revulsion out of her face. "We'll use your shirt."

She clattered a basin into the sink, filled it with warm water. "I'd say this is going to hurt me more than it's going to hurt you, but it won't."

She set the basin and first aid kit beside him, then went into the bathroom for clean towels. She found one, only one, and indulged herself by pressing her clammy face against the wall.

When she came back, Adam was up, swaying at the window. "What the hell are you doing?" she barked, pulling him back to the cot.

"Can't let our guard down yet. Will, we've got to call the ranch." There were bees buzzing in his ears, and he shook his head to scatter them. "Let them know. He could head down there."

"Everyone at the ranch is fine." Willa removed the bandanna and began to clean the wound. "I'll call as soon as I've got you settled. Don't argue with me." Her voice took on a trembling edge. "You know I don't do well with blood to begin with, and this is my first gunshot. Give me a break here."

"You're doing fine. Shit." He hissed through his teeth. "I felt that."

"That's probably good, right? Looks like it went in here just under the shoulder." Nausea churned, was ignored. "And came out here in the back." Raw, torn flesh with blood still seeping. "You must have lost a pint, but it's slowing down. I don't think it hit bone. I don't think." She gnawed her lip as she opened the bottle of alcohol. "This is going to burn like hellfire."

"Indians are stoic in pain, remember. Holy shit!" He

yelped once, jerked, and his eyes watered as the antiseptic seared.

"Yeah, I remember." She tried to chuckle, nearly sobbed. "Go ahead and yell all you want."

"It's okay." His head spun, stomach churned. He could feel the clammy sweat pop out in small beads on his skin. "I got it out. Just get it done."

"I should have given you pain pills first." Her face was as white as his now, and she spoke quickly, words tumbling out to keep them both from screaming. Tears were falling. "I don't know if we have anything but aspirin anyway. Probably like trying to piss out a forest fire. It's clean, Adam, it looks clean. I'm just going to smear this stuff on it now and wrap it up."

"Thank Christ."

They sweated their way through the last of it, then each sighed heavily and studied the other. Their faces were dead pale and sheened with sweat. Adam was the first to smile.

"I guess we didn't do half bad, considering it was the first gunshot wound for both of us."

"You don't have to tell anybody I cried."

"You don't have to tell anybody I screamed."

She mopped her damp face, then his. "Deal. Now lie back and I'll . . ." She trailed off, buried her face against his leg. "Oh, God, Adam, where's Ben? Where's Ben? He should be here."

"Don't worry." He stroked her hair, but his eyes were trained on the door. "He'll be here. We'll radio the ranch, get the police."

"Okay." She sniffled, lifted her head. "I'll do it. Just sit there. You've got to get your strength back." She rose and walked to the radio, switched it on. There was no familiar hum, no light. "It's dead," she said, and her voice reflected her words. A cursory look made her stomach drop. "Someone's pulled out the wires, Adam. The radio's dead."

Tossing down the mike, she strode across the room, hefted her rifle. "Take this," she ordered, and laid the gun across his knees. "I'll use yours."

"What the hell are you doing?"

She picked up her hat, wound the scarf around her throat again. "I'm going after Ben."

"The hell you are."

"I'm going after Ben," she repeated. "And you're in no shape to stop me."

His eyes on hers, he rose, steadied himself. "Oh, yes, I am."

It was a matter for debate, but at that moment they both heard the muffled sound of hooves in snow. Unarmed, Willa whirled toward the door and dragged it open. With Adam only steps behind her, she raced out. Her knees didn't buckle until Ben slid out of the saddle.

"Where the hell have you been? You were supposed to be right behind us. We've been here nearly thirty minutes."

"I circled around. Found some tracks but—Hey!" He dodged the fist she'd aimed at his face, but misjudged the one to his gut. "Jesus, Will, are you crazy? You—" He broke off again when she threw her arms around him. "Women," he muttered, nuzzling her hair. "How you holding up?" he asked Adam.

"Been better."

"Me too. I'll tend to the horses. See if there's any whiskey around here, would you?" He gave Willa a friendly pat on the back and turned her toward the door. "I need a drink."

TWENTY

"CAMPSITE A LITTLE NORTH OF WHERE WE GOT AM-bushed was cold. Signs somebody dressed some game. Looked like three people on horseback, with a dog." He patted Charlie on the head. "Two days, maybe three. Tidied the place up, so I'd say they knew what they were doing."

He dug into the canned stew Willa had heated. "Anyhow, there were fresh tracks. One rider, heading north. My guess is that would be our man."

"You said you'd be right behind us," Willa said again.

"I got here, didn't I? Charlie and I wanted to poke around first." He set what was left of the stew on the floor for the grateful dog and resisted rubbing his hand over his stomach where her fist had plunged. "The way I see it, the guy takes a couple of shots, then rides off. I don't think he waited around to see what we'd do."

"He may have been staying here," Adam put in. "But that doesn't explain why he sabotaged the radio."

"Doesn't explain why he tried to shoot us, either." Ben shrugged his shoulders. "The man we've been worried about for the past few months uses a knife, not a gun."

"There were three of us," Willa pointed out. At Charlie's thumping tail she managed a small smile. "Four. A gun's a safer bet."

"You got a point." Ben reached for the coffeepot, topped off all three cups.

Willa stared at hers, watched the steam. They had food in their bellies, the kick of caffeine in their blood. It was all the time she could give the three of them to recover.

"He's been here." Her voice was steady. She'd been working on that. "I know the police checked the cabin after that woman was killed, and they didn't find anything to indicate she'd been held here. But I think she was. I think she was held right here, killed right here. And then he cleaned up after himself."

She got up, went to the base cupboard, dug out the bucket. "I think he mopped up her blood with these, then stuck it back under the sink."

"Let me have that." Ben took the bucket from her, then eased her into a chair. "We'd better take this back with us." He set it aside near the woodbox, out of her range of vision.

"He killed her here." Willa was careful to keep her voice from bobbing along with her heart. "He probably tied her to one of the bunks. Raped her, killed her. Then he cleaned up the mess so if anybody checked in, things would look just as they should. He'd have had to bring her down on horseback, most likely at night. I guess he could have hidden the body somewhere for a few hours, even a day, then he dumped what was left of her at the front door. Just dumped her there with less care than you would a butchered deer."

She closed her eyes. "And every time I begin to think, to hope, that it's over, it comes back. He comes back. And there's no figuring the why."

"Maybe there is no why." Ben crouched in front of her, took her hands in his. "Willa, we've got two choices here. It's going to be dark in an hour. We can stay until morning, or we can use night as a cover and head back. Either way it's a risk. Either way it's going to be hard."

She kept her hands in Ben's, looked at Adam. "Are you up to the ride?"

"I can ride."

"Then I don't want to stay here." She drew a deep breath. "I say we head out at dusk."

IT WAS A COLD, CLEAR NIGHT WITH JUST A HINT OF FOG crawling low on the ground. A hunter's moon guided them. Just, Willa thought, as that same hunter's moon spotlighted them for whatever predator stalked them. The dog trotted ahead, his ears pricked up. Beneath her, Moon quivered as her nerves were transmitted to the mare.

Every shadow was a potential enemy, every rustle in the brush a whispered warning. The hoot of an owl, the quick whoosh of wings on a downward flight, and the scream of something hunted well and killed quickly were no longer simply sounds of the mountains at night but reminders of mortality.

The mountains were beautiful with the pale blue cast that moonlight made on snow, the dark trees outlined in fluffy ermine, the unbowed rock jutting up to challenge the sky.

And they were deadly.

He would have come this way, she thought, riding steadily east with his trophy strapped over his saddle. Wasn't that what that poor girl had been to him? A trophy. Something to show how skilled he was, and how clever. How ruthless.

She shuddered, hunched her shoulders against the kick of the wind.

"You okay?"

She glanced at Ben. His eyes gleamed in the dark like a cat's. Sharp, watchful. "I thought, on the day of my father's funeral when Nate read off how things were, would be, I thought nothing would ever be as hard, as hurtful as that. I thought I'd never feel that helpless, that out of control. That it was the worst that could happen to me."

She sighed, carefully guided her horse down an uneven slope where the shadows were long and the ground began to show through in patches. Thin fingers of mist parted like water.

"Then when I found Pickles, when I saw what had been done to him, I thought that was the worst. Nothing could be more horrid than that. But I was wrong. I just keep being wrong about how much worse it can get.''

''I won't let anything happen to you. You can believe that.''

There in the distance, the first glimmer of light that was Mercy. ''You were a damn fool today, Ben, going out tracking on your own. I told you I didn't like heroes, and I think less of fools.'' She nudged her horse forward, toward the lights.

''Guess she told me,'' Ben murmured to Adam.

''She was right.'' Adam tilted his head at Ben's quick frown. ''I wasn't any good to you, and she was too busy making sure I didn't bleed to death to do anything else. Going looking on your own didn't help things.''

''You'd have done the same in my place.''

True enough. ''We're not talking about me. She cried.''

Uncomfortable now, Ben shifted, shot a look toward Willa as she rode a few paces ahead. ''Oh, hell.''

''Promised I wouldn't tell, and I wouldn't have if all the tears had been for me. But there were plenty for you. She was about to go out after you.''

''Well, that's just—''

''Foolish.'' Adam's lips curved. ''I'd have tried to stop her, but I doubt I'd have managed it. Maybe you'd better think of that next time.''

He tried to ease his stiffening shoulder. ''There's going to be a next time, Ben. He isn't finished.''

''No, he isn't finished.'' And Ben quietly closed the distance to Willa.

THE DAMN SIGHT ON THE RIFLE HAD BEEN OFF. STINKING expensive biathlon sight, and it had been defective.

That's what Jesse told himself as he relived every moment of the ambush. It had been the rifle, the sight, the wind. It hadn't been him, hadn't been his aim, hadn't been his fault.

Just bad fucking luck, that was all.

He could still see the way the half-breed, wife-stealing bastard's horse had reared. He'd thought, oh, for one sweet moment he'd thought he nailed the target.

But the sight had been off.

It had been impulse, too. He hadn't planned it out. If he'd planned it out instead of having it all just happen, Wolfchild would be cold and dead—and maybe McKinnon would be dead too. And maybe he'd have taken a taste of Lily's half sister for good measure.

Jesse blew out smoke, stared into the dark, and cursed.

He'd get another chance, sooner or later, he'd get another chance. He'd make sure of it.

And wouldn't Lily be sorry then?

EVERY NIGHT FOR A WEEK WILLA WOKE IN THE GRIP OF A nightmare, drenched in sweat, with screams locked in her throat. Always the same: She was naked, wrists bound. Night after night she struggled to free herself, felt the cord bite into her flesh as she whimpered and writhed. Smelled her own blood as it trickled down her bare arms.

Always, just before she pulled herself awake, there was the glint of a knife, that shimmering arc as the blade swept down to work on her.

Every morning she shoved it away, knowing that, like a rat, it would gnaw free in the night.

The signs of spring, those early hesitant signs, should have thrilled her. The brave glint of crocus her mother had planted scattered such hopeful color. There was the growing spread of earth where the snow melted back to thinning patches, the sounds of young cattle, the dance of foals in pasture.

The time to turn the earth was coming, to plant it and watch it grow. And the time when the cottonwoods and aspens and larches would take on a lovely haze of green. The lupine would bloom, and even the high meadows would be bright with it, with the neon signs of Indian paintbrush, with the sunny faces of buttercups.

The mountains would show more silver than white, and the days would be long again and full of light.

It was inevitable that winter would whisk back at least once more. But spring snows were different; they lacked the brutal harshness of February's. Now that the sun was smil-

ing, bumping the temperature up to the balmy sixties, it was
easy to forget how quickly it could change again. And easy
to cherish every hour of every bright day.

From the window of her office, Willa could see Lily. She
was never far from Adam these days, had rarely left his side
since the night they had come back from high country. Willa
watched Lily touch Adam's shoulder, as she often did, fussing with the sling he wore.

He was healing. No, she thought, they were healing each
other.

How would it be to have someone that devoted, that much
in love, that blind to everything but you? How would it be
to feel exactly that same way about someone?

Scary, she thought, but maybe it would be worth those
jiggles of fear and doubt to experience that kind of unfet-
tered emotion. It would be an exhilarating trip, that wild
ride on pure feeling, pure need. And more, she realized,
beyond the moment, the promise and permanence that was
so easily read on the faces of Lily and Adam when they
looked at each other.

The little secret smiles, the signals that were so personal.
So *theirs*. What a thrill, she mused, and what security to
know there was someone who would be there for you, always. To have someone who thought of you first, and last.

Silly, she told herself, and turned away from the window.
Daydreaming this way with so much to be done, so much
at stake. And she would never be the kind of woman a man
thought of first. Even her own father hadn't thought of her
first.

She could admit that now, here in his office that still held
so much of him trapped in the air, like a scent ground into
the fibers of carpet. He had never thought of her first, and
he had certainly not thought of her last.

And what was she? Deliberately Willa sat in the chair
that was still his, laid her hand on the smooth leather arms
where his had rested countless times. What had she ever
been to him? A substitute. A poor one at that, she thought,
certainly by Jack Mercy's standards.

No, not even a substitute, she thought as her hands curled

into fists. A trophy, one of three that he hadn't even bothered to keep a memento of. Something easily discarded and forgotten, not even worth the space of a snapshot on his desk.

Not worth as much as the heads of the game kills mounted on the walls.

The fury, the insult of it was rising up in her so quick, so huge, she didn't fully realize what she was doing until she'd done it. Until she was up and yanking the first glassy-eyed head from the wall. The left antler of the six-point buck cracked as it hit the floor, and the sound, almost like a gunshot, mobilized her.

"The hell with it. The hell with him. I'm not a fucking trophy." She scrambled onto the sofa, tugged at the bighorn sheep that stared at her with canny eyes. "It's my office now." Grunting, she heaved the head aside and attacked the next. "It's my ranch now."

Later, she might admit she went a little insane. Pulling, pushing, dragging at the mountings, a macabre task, stripping the walls of those disembodied heads, breaking nails as she pried them loose. Her lips were peeled back in a snarl matching that of the mountain cat she wrestled from its perch.

For a moment Tess just watched from the doorway. She was too stunned to do much more as she saw the grisly heap growing on the floor, and her sister muttering oaths as she muscled the towering grizzly out of its corner.

If she hadn't known better, Tess would have said Willa was locked in a life-and-death battle, with the bear in the lead. Since she did know better, she wasn't certain whether she should laugh or run away.

Instead of either, she pushed the hair back from her face, cleared her throat. "Wow. Who opened the zoo?"

Willa whirled, her face contorted in rage, her eyes alive with it. The bear lost the edge of gravity and toppled like a tree. "No more trophies," Willa said, and panted to get her breath. "No more trophies in this house."

Sanity seemed called for. Hoping to instill it, Tess leaned negligently against the doorjamb. "I can't say that I've ever cared for the decor in here, or elsewhere. *Field and Stream* isn't my style. But what brought on this sudden urge to redecorate?''

''No more trophies,'' Willa repeated. Desperation had cemented into conviction. ''Not them. Not us. Help me get them out.'' She took a step, held out a hand. ''Help me get them the hell out of our house.''

When realization came, it was sweet. Stepping forward, Tess rolled up her sleeves, and there was a gleam in her eyes now. ''My pleasure. Let's evict Smokey here first.''

Together they heaved and dragged the stuffed and snarling bear to the doorway, then through it. They'd made it to the top of the steps before Lily came running up them.

''What in the world—For a minute I thought—'' She pressed a hand to her speeding heart. ''I thought you were about to be eaten alive.''

''This one had his last meal some time ago,'' Willa managed to say, and tried for a better grip.

''What are you doing?''

''Redecorating,'' Tess announced. ''Give us a hand with this bastard. He's heavy.''

''No, screw it.'' Willa blew out a breath. ''Back off,'' she warned, and when the stairs were clear she began to shove. ''Come on, help me push.''

''Okay.'' Tess made a show of spitting on her hands, then put her back into it. ''Push, Lily. Let's dump this big guy together.''

When he went, he went with a flourish, tumbling down the staircase with the noise of a thunderclap, dust puffing, claws clattering. At the din, Bess came rushing out from the kitchen, her face red with the effort and her hand on the .22 Baretta she'd taken to keeping in her apron pocket.

''Name of God Almighty.'' Huffing for air, Bess slapped her hands on her hips. ''What are you girls up to? You've got a bear in the foyer.''

''He was just leaving,'' Tess called out, and began to whoop with laughter.

''I'd like to know who's going to clean up this mess.''

Bess nudged the trophy with her toe, considering it every bit as nasty dead as alive.

"We are." Willa swiped her palms over her jeans. "Just consider it spring cleaning." She turned on her heel and marched back into the office.

Now, with the first thrust of fury deadened, she could see clearly what she'd done. Heads and bodies were strewn all over the room like bomb victims after a blast. Wooden mountings were cracked or chipped where she'd thrown them. Eerily, a loosened glass eye stared up at her from the beautiful pattern of the carpet.

"Oh, my God." She let out one long breath, then another. "Oh, my God," she said again.

"You sure showed them, pal." Tess gave her a light thump on the back. "They didn't have a chance against you."

"It's—" Lily pressed her lips together. "It's horrible, isn't it? Really horrible." She hiccuped, turned away, pressed her lips tighter. "I'm sorry. It's not funny. I don't mean to laugh." She struggled to hold it back by crossing her arms hard over her stomach. "It's just so awful. Like a wildlife garage sale or something."

"It's hideous." Tess lost her slippery hold on composure and began to giggle. "Hideous and morbid and obscene, and—oh, Jesus, Will, if you'd seen yourself when I first walked in. You looked like a madwoman doing the tango with a stuffed bear."

"I hate them. I've always hated them." Her own laughter bubbled up until she simply sat on the floor and let it go.

Then the three of them were sprawled on the floor, howling like loons amid the decapitated heads.

"They're all going," Willa managed, and pressed a hand to her aching side. "As soon as I can stand up, they're all going."

"Can't say I'll miss them." Tess wiped her streaming eyes. "But what the hell are we going to do with them?"

"Burn them, bury them, give them away." Willa moved her shoulders. "Whatever." She took a cleansing breath and pushed herself to her feet. "Clean sweep," she announced, and hauled up a mounted elk's head.

They carted them out—elk, moose, deer, sheep, bear. There were stuffed birds, mounted fish, lonely antlers. As the pile in front of the porch began to build, the men wandered over to make a fascinated and baffled audience.

"Mind if we ask what you ladies are doing?" As unofficial liaison, Jim stepped forward.

"Spring cleaning," Willa told him. "You think Wood can fire up the backhoe and dig a hole big enough to dump these in, give them a decent burial?"

"You're just going to dump them in a hole?" Shocked, Jim turned back as the men began to mumble. It took only a few minutes in a huddle to come to an agreement. This time Jim cleared his throat. "Maybe we could have a few for down to the bunkhouse and thereabouts. It's a shame just to bury 'em. That buck there'd look fine over the fireplace. And Mr. Mercy, he put store by that bear."

"Take what you want," Willa said.

"Can I have the cat, Will?" Billy hunkered down to admire it. "I sure would appreciate it. He's a beauty."

"Take what you want," she repeated, and shook her head as the men began to argue, debate, and lay claim.

"Now you've done it." Ham moseyed over while four of the men muscled the bear into the back of a rig. "I'm going to have that damn ugly bastard staring at me every morning and every night. They'll be storing what don't fit on the walls in one of the outbuildings, too, mark my words."

"Better there than in my house." Willa cocked her head. "I thought you liked that bear, Ham. You were with him when he took it down."

"Yeah, I was with him. Don't mean I harbor an affection for it. Jesus. Billy, you're going to break that rack you keep that up. Have a care, for God's sake. Be hanging their hats from it," he muttered as he stalked over to supervise. "Damn idiot cowboys."

"Now everybody's happy," Tess observed.

"Yep. Library's next."

"I can give you an hour." Tess glanced at her watch. "Then I've got to get ready. I've got a hot date."

She had some new lingerie, delivered just that afternoon from Victoria's Secret. She wondered how long it would take Nate to get her out of it.

Not long, she speculated. Not long at all.

She let her thoughts circle back to Will. "And isn't this the night for you and Ben to take in your weekly picture show?" she said with her tongue in her cheek.

"I guess it is."

"Lily's fixing a fancy dinner for Adam tonight."

Distracted, Willa glanced back. "Oh?"

"Well, it's sort of the anniversary of when we first . . . first," Lily finished, and blushed.

She'd gotten a delivery from Victoria's Secret too.

"And it's Bess's night off." Casually, Tess studied her nails. Evicting wildlife had been tough on her manicure. "I heard she was going down to Ennis to spend the night with her gossipmate Maude Wiggins. Since I'm planning on staying at Nate's, you'll have the house all to yourself."

"Oh, you shouldn't be alone," Lily jumped in. "I can—"

"Lily." Tess rolled her eyes. "She won't be alone unless she's incredibly slow or incredibly stupid or just plain stubborn. A quick woman, a smart one, a flexible one, would get herself all polished and perfumed and suggest a quiet evening in."

"Ben would think I'd lost my mind if I got all dressed up, then said I wanted to stay in."

"Wanna bet?"

At Tess's slow smile, Willa felt her own lips curving. "Things are too complicated now. I've got too much on my mind to be thinking of wrestling with Ben."

"When aren't things complicated?" Tess took Willa's arms, turned her face-to-face. "Do you want him or not? Yes or no."

Willa thought of the flutter that had been in her stomach all day. Because he'd been on her mind. "Yes."

Tess nodded. "Now?"

"Yeah." Willa let out a breath she hadn't been aware of holding. "Now."

"Then leave the rest of the spring cleaning for tomorrow. It'll take Lily and me at least an hour to find something halfway sexy in that closet of yours."

"I didn't say I wanted you to dress me again."

"It's our pleasure." Mind on her mission, Tess pulled Willa back inside. "Isn't it, Lily? Hey, where are you going?"

"Candles," Lily called out as she dashed across the road. "Willa doesn't have nearly enough candles in her room. I'll be right there."

"Candles." Willa dragged her feet. "Fancy clothes, pretending I don't want to see a movie, candles in my bedroom. It feels like I'm setting a trap."

"Of course it does, because that's exactly what you're doing."

At the doorway of Willa's room, Tess stopped, put her hands on her hips. There was work to be done here, she determined, if the scene was to be properly set. "And I guarantee, he's not only going to love being caught, he's going to be grateful."

TWENTY-ONE

"I FEEL LIKE AN IDIOT."

"You don't look like an idiot." Tess tilted her head and studied Willa from top to toe.

Yes, the hair swept up was a good touch—Lily's. With only a few pins anchoring all that mass, it would tumble down satisfactorily at a man's impatient handling.

Then there was the long dress—simple, full-skirted, nipped just a bit at the waist. Too bad it wasn't white, Tess mused, but Willa's limited wardrobe hadn't run to long white dresses. And the pale gray was quiet, almost demure. Except that Tess had left the long line of front buttons undone to the thigh.

The tiny silver hoops at Willa's ears were Lily's contribution again. The makeup was Tess's, and she knew Willa had been relieved that she'd used a light hand. But she didn't think Willa understood the power of innocence on the verge.

"You look," Tess finally decided, "like a virgin eager to be sacrificed."

Willa rolled her eyes. "Oh, God."

"That's a good thing." Woman to woman, she patted Willa's cheek. "You'll destroy him."

Then the guilt hit. Had she pushed this moment? Tess wondered. Had she finagled it before Willa was ready? It was easy to forget that Willa was six years younger than she. And untouched.

"Listen . . ." Tess caught herself wringing her hands and dropped them to her sides. "Are you sure you're ready for this? It's a natural step, but it's still a big one. If you're not absolutely sure, Nate and I can stay. We can make it a double date, keep things simple. Because—"

"You're more nervous than I am." Since that was such a surprise, and oddly sweet, Willa grinned.

"Of course not. I'm just—hell." It wasn't just Lily, who had left half an hour before blinking back tears, who was sentimental, Tess discovered. While Willa's eyes widened in shock, Tess leaned forward and kissed her gently on both cheeks.

Absurdly touched, Willa felt her stomach flutter and her color rise. "What was that for?"

"I feel like a mommy." And she was going to start bawling in a minute, so she turned quickly for the door. "I put condoms in your nightstand drawer. Use them."

"For heaven's sake, he'll think I'm—"

"Prepared, smart, self-aware. Damn it." Even as she heard the sound of the rig pull up outside, Tess gave up. Turning back, she rushed up to Willa and hugged her hard. "See you tomorrow," she managed, and raced out.

Grinning hugely, Willa stayed where she was. She heard Tess's voice rise, and Nate, who'd been waiting downstairs, answered. Then the door, and Ben's easy greeting. Her stomach jumped again, so she sat on the edge of the bed and pressed her hand to it. The conversation trailed off, then the door opened and closed again. An engine roared to life.

She was alone with Ben.

She could always change her mind, she reminded herself. There was no obligation here. She would play it by ear. She made herself rise. Starting now.

He was in the great room, studying the newly blank stone

above the fireplace. "I took it down," she said, and he turned, and he studied her. "We took it down today," she corrected. "Lily, Tess, and I. We haven't decided what we want to put up in place of his portrait, so we're living with nothing for a while."

She's taken down Jack Mercy's portrait, Ben thought. By the tone in her voice, he knew she understood just what a step she'd taken. "It changes the room. The focus of it."

"Yes, that was the idea."

He stepped forward, stopped. "You look great, Will. Different."

"I feel different." She smiled. "Great. And how are you?"

He'd been feeling easy before he turned and saw her in that long mist-colored dress, the flowing skirt with the teasing hint of leg. That slim neck revealed by the pinned-up hair. She looked too soft, too touchable, too everything.

"Fine. The same. Seems like I should take you to something fancier than a movie, the way you look."

"Lily and Tess get a charge out of going through my closet and criticizing my wardrobe. I'm told this is about the only decent thing I own." She plucked at the skirt and his blood pressure spiked as the unbuttoned material gave way to more leg. "They've threatened to take me shopping."

Stop babbling, she ordered herself, and moved behind the bar. "Want a drink?"

"I'm driving."

"Actually, I was thinking we could just stay in." There, now she'd done it.

"In?"

"Yeah, I don't get the house to myself often anymore. Bess is staying with a friend tonight, and Tess and Lily are . . . well."

"Nobody's here?" Something lodged in his throat, something hot and not easily swallowed.

"Nobody's here." She opened the cold box behind the bar, found the champagne Tess had directed her to serve. "So, I thought we could just . . . stay in. Relax." The bottle clinked hard on wood when she set it down. "Tess has a suitcase full of videos if we want a movie, and there's food."

Since he made no move to do so, Willa tore off the foil, twisted the wire free. "Unless you'd rather go out."

"No." He focused on the bottle when she popped the cork. "Champagne? Are we celebrating?"

"Yeah." If she could just manage to get a grip on the glasses. "Spring. I saw wildflowers today, and the bulbs are sprouting. Birds are building a nest in the pole barn again." She passed him his glass. "We'll start inseminating cows soon."

His lips twitched as he took the glass. "Yeah, it's that time of year."

"Oh, the hell with this." She muttered it, then downed the bubbly wine in her glass in two long gulps. "I'm no good at games. This is Tess and Lily's idea, anyway." Debating another, she set her empty glass down, looked him dead in the eye. "Look, the point is, Ben, I'm ready."

"Okay." Baffled, he took a sip of champagne. "You want to go out after all?"

"No, no." She pressed her fingers against her eyes, took a breath. "I'm ready to have sex with you."

He choked, managed to wheeze in air, sputter it out. "Excuse me?"

"Why dance around all this?" She came out from behind the bar. "You want me to go to bed with you, and I'm ready to. So, let's go to bed."

He took another drink—a mistake, as each individual bubble took on an edge and ripped its way down his throat. "Just like that?"

The horror in his voice had her fumbling. What if he'd just been stringing her along, teasing her the way he had since childhood?

Why, then, she thought, he'd have to die.

"It's what you said you wanted," she snapped at him. "So?"

"So." She'd always done him in with angry eyes and impatience. Made him want to bite her—in all sorts of interesting places. But she was changing the game, he thought. And the rules. "Just, I'm ready now so yippee?"

"What's wrong with that?" She jerked a shoulder. "Unless you've changed your mind."

"No, I haven't changed my mind. It's not a matter of changing my mind, it's . . . Jesus, Will." He set the glass on the bar before he could bobble it and make a fool of himself. "You've thrown me off stride."

"Oh." The confusion faded from her eyes and her mouth curved into a smile. "Is that all?"

"What do you expect?" His voice shot out, filled with male frustration. "You stand there all prettied up, shove champagne at me, and tell me you want to have sex. How am I supposed to keep my rhythm?"

Maybe he had a point, though she couldn't quite see it. But he looked sort of cute, all flustered and embarrassed. So she'd humor him.

"Okay." She closed the distance, wound her arms around his neck. "Let's see if we can get your rhythm back." Pressed her mouth hard to his.

His reaction was quick, and satisfying. The way his arms came up, banded her, the way his mouth angled and fed, the quick intake and release of his breath. Then, when his lips gentled, the way he murmured her name.

"Your gait seems steady enough to me." Now her voice was shaky. The muscles in her thighs were vibrating like harp strings. "I want you, Ben. I really want you." She proved it by locking her mouth to his again, then tearing it away to rain kisses over his face. "We don't have to go upstairs. The couch."

"Hold on. Slow down." Before I rip your clothes off and ruin it. "Slow down," he repeated, holding her close before the last of the blood could drain out of his head. "I've got to get my feet back under me, and you've got to be sure. It's going to be really tough to back off if you change your mind."

With a laugh, she boosted herself up, wrapped her legs around his waist. "Do I look like I'm going to change my mind?"

"No, guess not." But if she did, it was on him to hold himself back. He thought such an eventuality might kill him. "I want you, Willa." He brushed his lips over hers. "I really want you."

Her heart did a neat somersault. "Sounds like a deal."

"Upstairs." He managed to walk even as she tightened her grip and started nibbling at his jaw. "The first time should be in a bed."

"Was yours?"

"No, actually." He got to the stairs, wondered why he'd never noticed how long they were. "It was in a rig in the middle of winter and I nearly froze my . . . never mind."

She chuckled, nuzzled at his throat. "This'll be better, won't it?"

"Yeah." For him, without a doubt. For her . . . he was going to do his best. He stopped in the doorway of her room. He wasn't sure how many more shocks he could survive in one night.

Candles burned everywhere, and the fire glowed low. The bed was turned down, inviting with dozens of pillows.

"Tess and Lily," Willa explained. "They really got into this."

"Oh." Nothing like being showcased, Ben thought as his nerves jumped. "Did they . . . has anyone talked to you about . . . things?"

"McKinnon." She eased back to grin at him. "I run a ranch."

"It's not exactly the same." He set her on her feet, backed off a step. "Listen, Willa, this is kind of a first for me, too. I've never—the others weren't—" He had to shut his eyes a minute, gather his scattered wits. "I don't want to hurt you. And I, well, I haven't had anyone in a while. I set my sights on you damn near a year ago, and I haven't had anyone else since."

"Really?" That was interesting. "Why?"

He sighed, sat on the edge of the bed. "I have to get my boots off."

"I'll give you a hand." She obligingly turned her back to him, hefted one booted foot between her legs. He nearly groaned. "A year?" She glanced over her shoulder as she tugged.

"Maybe more, if it comes down to it." Struggling to be amused, he planted a foot on her butt and pushed.

"You were never particularly nice to me." She took his other foot, pulled at the boot.

"You scared the hell out of me."

She stumbled forward as the boot came off, then turned, still holding it. "I did?"

"Yeah." Irritated with himself, he pushed a hand through his hair. "And that's all I'm going to say about it."

It was enough to think about, she supposed. "Oh, I forgot." She hurried to the table by the window and fiddled with Tess's CD player. "Music," she explained. "Tess claims it's mandatory."

He couldn't hear anything over the knocking of his own heart. Her hair was falling down, just a little, and the firelight streamed through that long, thin skirt every time she moved.

"That should do it. Unless we should have the champagne up here."

"That's all right." His throat was closing again, snapping like a bear trap. "Later."

"Okay." She lifted her hands, began to undo the buttons of the dress while his mouth fell open. Her busy fingers flipped open six before he could get his tongue off his toes.

"Hold it. Slow down. If you're going to strip for a man, you should pace yourself."

"Is that so?" Intrigued, she stopped, watched his gaze dip to her fingers, then began again. "I'm not wearing a stitch under here," she said conversationally. "Tess said something about contrast and impact."

"Oh, good Jesus." He wasn't sure how he got to his feet when he couldn't feel them. But he stepped to her. "Don't take it off." His voice had thickened, and the sound of it had her eager fingers pausing, trembling. "Let me finish it."

"All right." Odd, her arms were so heavy now. She let them fall to her sides as he slipped the rest of the buttons free. It was a lovely sensation, she thought, the skim of his knuckles over her skin. "Shouldn't you be groping me or something?"

A laugh, even a weak one, soothed some of the nerves. "I'll get to it." The dress was open now, with light and shadow playing over that lovely line of bare flesh. "Just stand there," he said quietly, and touched his mouth to hers. "Can you do that?"

"Yeah. But my knees are going to start knocking."

"Just stand there," he repeated, touching only mouth to mouth as he undid his shirt. "Let me taste you awhile. Here." His lips cruised over her jaw. "Here." Up to her ear. "You can trust me."

"I know." Now her eyes were heavy, she felt the lids drooping as his mouth toyed with hers. "Whenever you chew on my lip that way, I can't get my breath."

"Want me to stop?"

"No, I like it." She said it dreamily. "I can breathe later."

He tossed his shirt aside. "I want to see you, Willa. Let me look at you."

Slowly, he slid the dress from her shoulders, let it drift to the floor. She was long and slim, subtle curves and strong angles, her skin glowing gold in the dancing light. "You're beautiful."

It was an effort not to lift her hands to cover herself. No one had ever said that to her. Not once in her life. "You always said skinny."

"Beautiful." He cupped a hand to the back of her neck, drew her slowly toward him. His fingers combed up, her hair tumbled down. He experimented with the weight of it, lifting it, letting it fall while his mouth rubbed over hers. "I always wanted to play with your hair, even when you were a kid."

"You used to pull it."

"That's what boys do when they want girls to pay attention to them." He gathered it, gave it a tug, and had her head jerking back. "Mmm." He sampled the exposed line of her throat, nibbled lazily where the pulse was rabbiting. "Paying attention?"

"Yeah." She shuddered, couldn't stop. "Or I'm trying to, but I keep losing my focus. All this stuff's happening inside me."

"I want to be inside you." Her eyes opened at that, and in them he saw nerves gloriously mixed with needs. "But there's more first. I have to touch you."

He skimmed a hand down to her breast, circled with a fingertip, forced a moan through her lips as his thumb scraped over her nipple. She felt an answering tug, deep inside. An echo of shock and pleasure. Then his hand slid down, over her hip, his fingers trailing lightly toward her center, brushing, awakening, then retreating.

Her eyes were huge, focused on his. Her hands came to his shoulders for balance and found smooth skin, taut muscles, an old scar. Her fingers dug in once as she tried to absorb and analyze the sensation of those callused hands stroking her flesh.

She hadn't expected this. She'd thought it would be fast, a grappling match full of grunts and howls. How could she have known there would be tenderness mixed with the heat? And the heat was huge.

"Ben?"

"Hmm?"

"I don't think I can stand up anymore."

His lips curved against her shoulder. "Just another minute. I haven't quite finished."

So this was what it was like to awaken a woman. To know that your hands were the first hands. To know you were the first to bring that flush to the skin, that weakness to the limbs, that quiver to the muscles. He could be careful with her, would be careful with her, no matter how that very innocence made his blood surge.

When her eyes drooped this time, he lifted her into his arms, laid her on the bed.

"You still have your pants on."

He covered her, letting her grow accustomed to his

weight. "It'll be better for both of us if I keep them on awhile yet."

"Okay." His hands were roaming again, and she was beginning to float. "Tess—in the drawer there—condoms."

"I'll take care of it. Let go for me, Will." He trailed a line of kisses down her throat. "Just let it all go." And with a shudder of his own he took her breast in his mouth.

She arched, the breath exploding through her lips. Sensation careened through her system, flashing with heat, urging her hips to grind with the rhythm he set. He bit lightly, but the sensation was no kin to pain. Her hands were fisted in his hair, urging him to feed.

He heard her sigh, and gasp and murmur. Her response to every touch was as free and open as any man could wish. Beneath his her body was agile, limber one moment, taut the next as she flowed with him. The flavor of her filled him, threatened to drive him mad if he didn't stop, if he didn't take more. Her scent—soap and skin—aroused him more than any perfume.

He took her mouth again, needed it like he needed breath. Her tongue tangled with his in an avid dance. Somewhere in the back of his mind, he could hear the quiet thrum of music.

He stroked a hand up that long length of leg, stopping just short of the heat, retreating. Her breath came quickly now, fast and shallow while her nails bit into him.

"Look at me." He brushed her, lightly, found her erotically hot, wet. But even as she arched, he retreated again. "Look at me. I want to see your eyes the first time. I want to see what it does to you."

"I can't." But her eyes were open, wide and blind. Her body was on the edge of something, like a high cliff where the wind both pulled and pushed. "I need—"

"I know." God, that voice of hers—straight sex. And now even throatier, rustier, and quivering with little gasps. "But look at me." He cupped her, watched her eyes go dark with fear and passion.

The first time, he thought. "Let go."

What choice did she have? His fingers stroked her to flash

point, and everything happened at once. Her body tightened like a fist. Lights whirled in front of her eyes, spinning to the roar of sound in her head that was her own frantic heartbeat.

And this pleasure was kin to pain, an eruption that had her helplessly crying out while her body bucked, shuddered, then went slack.

Her skin was dewed with sweat now, her lips soft with surrender when he sought them again. Weakness warred, then gave way to fresh energy as he patiently, ruthlessly worked her back into a frenzy. Her system overcharged, reeled, imploded. She rocked against him, wildly greedy for more. And he gave more until she was pliant again, body still quivering in reaction, breath coming slow and thick.

When he rolled off her she couldn't even manage a protest, but lay sprawled in the hot, tangled sheets.

He had to pray he wouldn't fumble now, though his hands shook when he tugged at the snap of his jeans. He'd wanted her sated and satisfied before he took her, wanted her to remember the pleasure if he was unable to prevent the pain.

"I feel like I'm drunk," she murmured. "I feel like I'm drowning."

He knew the feeling. His blood was singing a siren's song in his head, and his loins were screaming for release. Stripping away his jeans, he tossed them aside before he remembered what he carried in his wallet, snugged into the back pocket.

Blessing Tess, he dug into Willa's nightstand drawer.

"Don't fall asleep," he begged as he heard her sigh. "For God's sake don't fall asleep."

"Uh-uh." But this state of floaty relaxation was the next best thing. She stretched, and the firelight danced over her, rippling golds and reds and ambers. Ben tore his gaze away and finished the business at hand. "Are you going to touch me again?"

"Yeah." He had to get the nerves under control. The hunger was one thing, he could keep it chained, but the nerves fluttered through his stomach as he ranged himself over her. "I need you." It wasn't an easy admission, not the same as want, and he gave it to her as his mouth closed over hers. ''Let me have you, Willa. Hold on to me and let me have you.''

And her arms came around him as he slid into her.

Oh, God, so tight, so hot. He had to use every ounce of control not to plunge mindlessly into her like a stallion covering a ready mare. Battling to go slowly, he fisted his hands on either side of her head, watched her face. Watched it so intently, so closely that he saw those first flickers of shock, of acceptance, and finally, that lovely glaze of dark pleasure.

''Oh, it's wonderful.'' She breathed the words out as he moved inside her. ''Really wonderful.''

She gave up her innocence without regret, with a smile bowing her lips as she matched him stroke for slow stroke. In his eyes she saw the need he had spoken of, the need focused only and fully on her. When she looked deeper, she saw herself reflected back in them, lost in them.

And this, she thought, when he finally buried his face in her hair and emptied himself into her, was beauty.

''I DIDN'T KNOW IT WOULD BE LIKE THAT.'' STILL PINNED beneath him, still joined, Willa lazily played with his hair. ''I might have been ready sooner.''

''I'd say the timing worked just fine.'' He had fantasies already working. Pouring champagne over that lovely golden body and licking it off. Drop by drop.

''I always thought people set too much store by sex. I guess I've changed my mind.''

''It wasn't sex.'' He turned his head, nibbled at her temple. ''We'll have sex some other time. This was making love. And you can't set too much store by either.''

She stretched her arms up, then lowered them so that her hands could knead his bottom. ''What's the difference?''

He was still half aroused, and well aware it wouldn't take much to finish the job. ''You want me to show you?'' Lifting his head, he grinned down at her. ''Right now?''

She chuckled and, feeling sentimental, stroked his cheek. ''Even a bull needs recovery time.''

''I ain't no bull. Just stay right there.''

"Where are you going?" My, oh, my, she thought, she hadn't taken nearly enough time to look at that body of his. It was . . . an education.

"I'll be right back," he told her, and strode out without bothering with his jeans.

Well, well. She stretched again, then shifted so that she was cradled by pillows. It seemed the night wasn't over. Experimentally, she laid a hand on her breast. Her heart was bumping along at a normal rate now rather than with that snare drum riff it had reached when he'd nuzzled just there.

It was an odd feeling, she thought, to have a man suckling you, to have him pull you inside him. And to experience those mirror tugs in the womb.

Everything he'd done had made her body feel different— tighter then looser, lighter then heavier.

She wondered if she looked different—to herself, to him. There was no denying that she felt different.

With all the pain, all the grief and fear in her life over the past months, she had found an oasis. For tonight, if only for tonight, there was only this room. Nothing outside of this room mattered. No, not even murder. She wouldn't let reality in.

Tomorrow was soon enough for worries, for the fear of what was haunting her ranch, her mountains, her land. Just for tonight she would be only a woman. A woman, she decided, who, this once, would be content to let a man hold the reins.

So she was smiling when he walked back in. And for a moment, just looked.

She'd seen him shirtless before, countless times, and knew those broad shoulders, that strong back. One memorable day she'd caught him and Adam and Zack skinny-dipping in the river, so she'd seen him naked.

But she'd been twelve then, and she wasn't thinking like a twelve-year-old now. And she wasn't looking at a teenager, but a man. A powerful one. One that had her stomach flopping around in delighted reaction.

"You look good naked," she said conversationally.

He stopped pouring the glass he'd brought in with him,

turned to stare at her. "You don't look so bad yourself."

The fact was, she looked stunning, sprawled over the rumpled sheets without a hint of modesty. Her hair was tumbled, her eyes glowed in the candlelight, and she had one hand low on her belly, idly tapping along with the music.

"You sure as hell don't look like a novice," he told her.

"I learn fast."

Now his smile came, slow, dangerous. "I'm counting on that."

"Yeah?" She loved a challenge. "So, what have you got there, McKinnon?"

"Your champagne." He set the bottle on her dresser, where candles flickered. "Have a glass." The one he brought her was full to the rim. "You may want to be a little drunk for this."

"Really?" The smile widened into a grin, but with a shrug, she sipped. "Aren't you having any?"

"After."

She chuckled, sipped again. "After what?"

"After I take you. That's what I'm going to do this time." He trailed a finger from her throat down to her quivering belly. "I'm going to take you. And you're going to let me."

The breath backed up in her lungs and it took an effort to push it out. He didn't look tender now, or flustered. Now with those eyes so dark, so green, so focused. He looked ruthless. Exciting.

"Am I?"

"Yeah." He could see that pulse in her throat begin to beat and flutter. "It's not going to be slow, but it's going to take a long time. Drink the champagne down, Willa. I'll taste it on you."

"Are you trying to make me nervous?"

He climbed onto the bed, straddled her, watched her blink in surprise. "Darling, I'm going to make you crazy." He took the glass, dipped a finger in the wine, then traced it over her nipple. "I'm going to make you scream. Yeah." He nodded slowly, repeating the process on her other breast.

"You should be afraid. In fact, I like you being just a little afraid this time."

He trickled the last few drops over her belly, then set the glass aside. "I'm going to do things to you that you can't even imagine. Things I've been waiting to do."

She swallowed hard as a new and fascinating chill ran over her skin. "I think I am afraid." She shuddered out a breath. "But do them anyway."

TWENTY-TWO

It WASN'T EASY TO TRACK WILLA DOWN ONCE APRIL HIT its stride, and with it the spring breeding season. As far as Tess could see, everything was focused on mating, people as well as animals. If she hadn't known better, she would have sworn she'd caught Ham flirting with Bess. But she imagined he had been trying to wrangle a pie.

Young Billy was eye-deep in love with some pretty little thing who worked a lunch counter in Ennis. His former liaison with Mary Anne had hit the skids, left him broken-hearted for about fifteen minutes.

The way he strutted around, Tess could see he thought of himself as a man of the world now.

Jim had some slap and tickle going with a cocktail waitress, and even the longtime-married Wood and Nell were exchanging winks and sly grins.

With nothing disturbing the peace and pastoral quality of the air, everyone seemed ready to fall into a routine of work, flirtations, and giggling sex.

There was Lily, of course, with wedding preparations in full swing. And Willa, when she stood still long enough, had a dopey grin on her face.

It seemed to Tess that the cows were trying to keep pace with the humans. Though she couldn't see anything particularly romantic about a man shooting bull sperm into a cow.

She sincerely doubted the bull was thrilled with the arrangement either, but he was allowed to cover a few, just to keep him happy. And the first time Tess witnessed the coupling was enough of a shock to make her wish it her last. She refused to believe that the bull's chosen *innamorata* had been mooing in sexual delight.

She'd watched Nate and his handler breed his stallion too. She had to admit there had been something powerful, elemental, and a little frightening in that process as well. The way the stallion had trumpeted, reared, and plunged. The way the mare's eyes had rolled in either pleasure or terror.

She wouldn't have called the process romantic, and it certainly hadn't been anything to giggle about. The smells of sweat and sex and animal had been impetus enough for Tess to drag Nate off at the first decent opportunity and jump him.

He hadn't seemed to mind.

Now it was another glorious afternoon, with the temperature warm enough for shirtsleeves. The sky was so big, so blue, so clear, it seemed that Montana had stolen every inch of it for itself.

If she looked toward the mountains—as she often caught herself doing—she would see spots of color bleeding through the white. The blues and grays of rock, the deep, dark green of pine. And if the sun angled just so, a flash that was a river tumbling down fueled with snowmelt.

She could hear the tiller running behind Adam's house. She knew Lily was planning a garden and had cajoled Adam into turning the earth for the seedlings she'd started. Though he'd warned Lily it was too early to plant, he was indulging her.

As, Tess mused, he always would.

It was a rare thing, she decided, that kind of love, devotion, understanding. With Adam and Lily, it was as solid as the mountains. As often as she wrote about people, watched them so that she could do just that, she'd never grasped the simple and quiet power of love.

She could write about it, make her characters fall in or out of it. But she didn't understand it. She thought perhaps it was like this land that she'd lived on, lived with for so many months now. She had learned to value and appreciate it. But understand it? Not a bit.

Cattle and horses dotted the hills where grass was still dingy from winter, and men worked in the mud brought on by warming weather to repair fencing, dig posts, and drive cattle to range.

They would do it over and over again, year after year, season after season. That, too, she supposed, was love. If she felt a stir herself, she blocked it off, reminded herself of palm trees and busy streets.

She had, Tess thought with a sigh, survived her first—and she hoped last—Montana winter.

"There you are." Tess started forward, but Willa rode straight past her toward the near pasture. "Damn it." Refusing to give up, Tess broke into a trot and followed. She was only slightly out of breath by the time she caught up. "Listen, we've got to get into town tomorrow. Lily's fitting our attendant dresses."

"Can't." Willa uncinched Moon, hauled off the saddle. "Busy."

"You can't keep avoiding this." She winced as Willa thoughtlessly tramped on the infant wildflowers perking up around the fence posts.

"I'm not avoiding it." After dropping the saddle over the fence, Willa removed the saddle blanket and bit. "I've resigned myself to the fact that I'm going to be wearing some lame dress, probably have posies in my hair. I just can't take off for the day right now."

Pulling a pick out of her pocket, she leaned into Moon, lifted the mare's near hind leg, and went to work on her hoof.

"If you don't go, Lily and I will have to choose the dress for you."

Willa snorted, skirted Moon's tail, and lifted the next

hoof. "You're going to pick it out anyway, so it doesn't matter if I'm there or not."

True enough, Tess thought, and with an ease she wouldn't have believed possible even a few months before, she stroked and patted Moon. "It would mean a lot to Lily."

This time Willa sighed and moved to the foreleg. "I'd like to oblige her. Really. I'm swamped right now. There's a lot to get done while the weather holds."

"Holds what?"

"Holds off."

"What do you mean holds off?" Tess frowned up at the clear, perfect blue of the sky. "It's the middle of April."

"Hollywood, we can get snow here in June. We ain't done with it yet." Willa studied the western sky, the pretty, puffy clouds that clung to the peaks. She didn't trust them. "A spring snow's a fine thing, gives us moisture when we need it and melts off quick enough. But a spring blizzard." She shrugged, pocketed the pick. "You never know."

"Blizzard, my butt. The flowers are blooming." Tess looked down at the trampled blooms. "Or were."

"We grow them hardy here—those that we grow. I wouldn't put that long underwear away just yet. Hold, Moon." With that order, she hefted the saddle again and carried it toward the stable.

"There's other things." Determined to finish, Tess dogged her heels. "I haven't had a chance to talk to you alone in days."

"I've been busy." In the dim stable, Willa stored her tack and took up a grooming brush.

"With this and that."

"Which means?"

"Look, so you're making up for lost time with Ben. That's fine, glad you're happy. And you're busy impregnating unsuspecting cows all day, or ruining your hands with barbed wire, but I need to know what's going on."

"About?"

"You know very well." Cursing under her breath, Tess walked back outside, where Willa began brushing Moon. "It's been quiet, Will. I like it quiet. But it's also making me edgy. You're the one who talks to the cops, to the men, and you haven't been passing things along.''

"I figured you were too busy playing with one of your stories and talking to your agent all day to worry about it.''

"Of course I'm worried about it. All Nate says is there's nothing new. But you still have guards on.''

Willa blew out a breath. "I can't take any chances.''

"And I don't want you to.'' To soothe herself, Tess stroked Moon's cheek. "Though I admit I've had a few bad moments waking up at night hearing people walking around outside. Or you pacing around in.''

Willa kept her eyes on Moon's smooth coat. "I have nightmares.''

More surprised by the admission than the fact, Tess moved closer. "I'm sorry.''

She hadn't been able to talk about it, and wondered now if that was a mistake. So she would see. "They've gotten worse since going up to the cabin. Realizing that girl was killed there. No doubt of that now that they've matched her blood to the towels and rags I found under the sink.''

"Why the hell didn't the cops find them?''

Willa shrugged her shoulders and continued to groom her horse. "It's not the only cabin, the only shelter in the hills. They looked around, saw nothing out of place, everything as it should be. They didn't see any point in poking into dark corners and overturning buckets, I guess. They sure as hell have gone over the place now, every inch. Hasn't helped. Anyway, I think about that, and the time up in the hills with Adam shot, and bleeding, and not knowing.''

She gave Moon a slap on the flank to send her into the pasture. "Just not knowing.''

"Maybe it is over,'' Tess put in. "Maybe he's gone off. Sharks do that, you know. Cruise one area for a while, then go off to another feeding ground.''

"I'm scared all the time.'' It wasn't hard to admit it, not when she watched Lily walk around the side of the house laughing up at Adam. Fear and love, she'd discovered, went hand in hand. "Work helps, keeps the fear in the back of the mind. Ben helps. You can't think at all when a man's inside you.''

Yes, you can, Tess mused. Unless it's the right man.

"It's that three o'clock in the morning thing," Willa continued. "When there's nobody there, and nothing to hold it off. That's when the fear creeps up and snaps at my throat. That's when I start wondering if I'm doing the right thing.''

"About?"

"The ranch." It spread out around her, her life. "Having you and Lily stay on when we can't be sure if it's safe.''

"You don't have any choice." Tess hooked a boot in the fence, leaned back into it. She couldn't see the land through Willa's eyes, doubted she ever would. But she'd come to admire the pull of it, and the power. "We have minds of our own. Agendas of our own.''

"Maybe.''

"I'll tell you what mine is. When my time's up here, I'm going back to LA. I'm going shopping on Rodeo Drive and I'm having lunch at whatever the current hot spot is.'' Which, she knew, would certainly not be the hot spot she'd lunched in that past autumn. "And I'm taking my share of the profits from Mercy and putting it toward a place in Malibu. Near the ocean so I can hear the waves day and night.''

"Never seen the ocean," Willa murmured.

"No?" It was hard to imagine. "Well, maybe you'll come visit sometime. I'll show you what civilized people do with their days. Might just add a chapter to my book. Willa in Hollywood.''

Grinning, Willa rubbed her chin. "What book? I thought you were writing another movie.''

"I am." Flustered, Tess dipped her hands in her pockets. "I'm just playing with a book. Just for fun.''

"And I'm in it?"

"Pieces of you.''

"It's set here, in Montana? On Mercy?''

"Where else am I going to set it?" Tess muttered. "I'm stuck here for a year. It's nothing." Her fingers began to drum against the rail. "I haven't even told Ira. It's just something I'm fooling around with when I'm bored.''

If that was true, Willa thought, she wouldn't be so embarrassed. "Can I read it?"

"No. I'm going to go tell Lily you're dodging the shopping trip tomorrow. And don't complain if you have to wear organdy."

"The hell I will." Willa turned around and studied the mountains again. Her mood had lifted considerably, but as she watched more clouds roll in, gather, and cling, she knew it wasn't over. Not winter, not anything.

THE DINNER PARTY WAS LILY'S IDEA. JUST A SMALL, INTImate, casual dinner, she'd promised. Just the three sisters, and Adam, Ben, and Nate. Her family, as she thought of them now.

Small, intimate, and casual perhaps, but exciting for her. She would be hostess, a position she'd never held in her life, at a party in her own home.

Her mother had always planned and managed social events when Lily was growing up. And so efficiently, so cleverly that Lily's input or assistance simply hadn't been necessary. During the brief time she'd lived on her own, she hadn't had the funds or the means to host dinners. And her marriage certainly hadn't been conducive to social occasions.

But now things had changed. She had changed.

She spent all day preparing for it. Cleaning the house was hardly a chore. She loved every inch of it, and Adam wasn't a man to toss clothes everywhere or leave beer bottles cluttering the tables. He didn't mind the touches she'd added— the little brass frog she'd ordered from a catalogue, the pretty glass ball of melting blues she'd fallen in love with at first sight in a shop in Billings. In fact, he seemed to appreciate them. He often said the house had been too simple, too empty, before she'd come to him.

She'd pored over recipes with Bess and settled on a rib roast, which she was just sliding into the oven when Bess poked her head in the kitchen doorway.

"Everything under control in here?"

"Absolutely. I prepared it just as you told me. And

look.'' Proud as a mother with twins, Lily opened the refrigerator to show off her pies. ''Didn't the meringue turn
out nice? All those pretty sugar beads.''

''Most men got a fondness for lemon meringue.'' Bess
approved them with a nod. ''You did just fine there.''

''Oh, I wish you'd change your mind and come.''

Bess waved a hand. ''You're a sweet girl, Lily, but when
I got a choice between putting my feet up and watching my
movies and sitting around with a roomful of young people,
I'm putting my feet up. Now, you want a hand, I'll give
you one.''

''No. I want to do it myself. I know that sounds silly,
but—''

''Doesn't.'' Bess wandered over to the window where
Lily had herb pots started from seed. Coming along well,
she thought, just like Lily. ''A woman's got a right to lord
it over her own kitchen. But you call me if you run into any
problem.'' She winked. ''Nobody has to know you had a
little help.''

Bess turned as the back door opened again. ''Wipe your
feet,'' she ordered Willa. ''Don't you be tracking mud in
here on this clean floor.''

''I'm wiping them.'' But under those eagle eyes, Willa
gave them a few extra swipes on the mat.

''Oh, aren't those lovely!'' Lily pounced on the wildflowers Willa was clutching. ''That was so sweet of you to think
of it, to pick them for me.''

''Adam did.'' Willa passed them over and considered her
mission complete. ''One of the horses pulled up with a
strain, so he's busy treating it. He didn't want them to wilt.''

''Oh, Adam did.'' Lily sighed, and her heart melted as
she buried her nose in the tiny blooms. ''Is the horse all
right? Does he need help?''

''He can handle it. I've got to get back.''

''Couldn't you come in for a minute, have coffee?
There's fresh.''

Before Willa could refuse, Bess jabbed an elbow in her
ribs. ''Sit down and have coffee with your sister. And take
off your hat in the house. I've got laundry to do.''

"Bossy old thing," Willa complained when Bess shut the door behind her. But she already had her hat off. "I guess I've got time for a cup, if it's already hot."

"It is. Please, sit down. I just want to put these in water."

Willa sat at the round maple table, drummed her fingers on the wood. The dozens of chores still on her list raced through her head. "Smells good in here."

"It's the herbs, and this potpourri I made."

"Made it?" Willa drummed a little faster. "You're a regular little homemaker, aren't you?"

Lily kept her eyes on the stems she carefully slid into an old glass bottle. "It's all I'm good at."

"No, it's not. And I didn't mean it to sound that way." Annoyed with herself, Willa squirmed in her chair. "You've made Adam so happy he looks like he could float. And it's so neat and pretty in here." She scratched the back of her neck and felt like an awkward rube. "I mean, like that big white bowl there with the shiny red and green apples. I'd never think of something like that. Or putting stuff in those bottles you've got on the counter. What is that stuff?"

"Flavored vinegars." Lily glanced toward the long-necked bottles where sprigs of basil and rosemary and marjoram floated. "You use them for cooking, for salad. I like the way they look."

"Shelly does stuff like that too. I could never figure it."

"That's because you have to look at the big picture, the foundation and not the fancywork. I admire you so much."

Willa stopped frowning at the bottles and gaped. "Huh?"

"You're so smart and strong and capable." Lily set a pretty blue cup and saucer on the table. "You scared me to death when I first came here."

"I did?"

"Well, everything did. But especially you." Lily took her own cup, added a hefty measure of cream to make it palatable to her taste. Then she sat, deciding it was time to confess all. "I watched you the day of the funeral. You'd lost your father, and you were hurting, but you were also coping. And later, when Nate read the will, and everything that was yours, that should have been yours, was taken out of your control, you dealt with it.''

Willa remembered, too. Remembered she hadn't been kind. "I didn't have much choice.''

"There's always a choice,'' Lily said quietly. ''Mine was usually running away. I'd have run that day if there'd been any place left to go. And I don't think I would have had the courage to stay when the horrible things started to happen if not for you.''

"I didn't have anything to do with it. You stayed for Adam.''

"Adam.'' Everything about Lily softened—voice, eyes, mouth. "Yes. But I wouldn't have had the courage to go to him, to let myself feel for him. I looked at you, at everything you were doing, had done, and thought, She's my sister and she's never run from anything. There must be something inside me that matches what's in her. So I dug for it. It's the first time in my life I've stuck when things got rough.''

Willa pushed her coffee aside and leaned forward. "Look, I grew up the way I wanted to, did what I wanted to. I never found myself trapped in a relationship where someone used me for a punching bag.''

"Didn't you?'' Lily gathered her courage again when Willa said nothing. "Bess told me how hard our father was on you.''

Bess talked too damn much, was all Willa could think. "An occasional backhand from a parent isn't the same as a fist in the face from a husband. Running from that wasn't cowardly, Lily. It was right and it was smart.''

"Yes. But I never fought back. Not once.''

"Neither did I,'' Willa murmured. "I may not have run from my father, but I never fought back either.''

"You fought back every time you got on a horse, pulled a calf, rode a fence.'' Lily kept her eyes steady when Willa's flicked over her face. "You made Mercy yours. That's how you fought back. You dug your roots. I didn't know him, and he never chose to know me. But, Willa, I don't think he knew you either.''

"No." Her voice was soft and slow with the realization. "I don't suppose he did."

Lily drew a deep breath. "I'd fight back now, and that's in very large part because of you, because of Tess, because of the chance I've had here. Jack Mercy didn't give me that chance, Will. You did. You should have hated us. You had every right to hate us. But you don't."

She'd wanted to, Willa remembered. It just hadn't been possible. "Maybe hate just takes too much energy."

"It does, but not everyone understands that." Lily paused, toyed with her cup. "When Tess and I were shopping the other day, I thought—for a minute I thought I saw Jesse. Just a flash, just a glimpse."

"You saw him in Ennis?" Willa bolted straight up in her chair, fists curled.

"No." Dazzled by her, Lily smiled a little. "See, that's your first reaction, fight back. Mine was to run. I used to think I saw him everywhere, I could imagine him everywhere. It hasn't happened in a while. But the other day, some face in the crowd, the tilt of a head . . . But I didn't run. I didn't panic. And I think if I ever had to, really had to, I'd fight back. I owe that to you."

"I don't know, Lily. Sometimes running's a fine choice."

IT WENT SO WELL LILY COULD HARDLY BELIEVE IT WAS HER life. Her new life. People she had grown to love were sitting in the cozy dining room, taking second helpings of food she'd prepared, laughing with each other like friends. Arguing with each other like family.

It was Tess who had started that, quite deliberately, Lily realized, by telling Willa the dress they'd picked out for her was a fuchsia organdy with a six-flounce skirt and puffed sleeves. With a bustle.

"You're out of your mind if you think you'll get me into something like that. What the hell is fuchsia anyway? Isn't that pink? No way I'm wearing pink flounces."

"You'll look so sweet in it," Tess purred. "Especially with the hat."

"What hat?"

"Oh, it's adorable, matching color, enormous floppy brim decked in a garden of spring flowers. English primroses. And the crown's cut out so we can dress your hair up high. Then there's the gloves. Elbow length, very chic."

Because Willa had gone dead pale, Lily took pity on her. "She's just teasing you. The dress is lovely. Pale blue silk with pearl buttons at the back and just a touch of lace on the bodice. It's very simple, very classic. And there's no hat or gloves."

"Spoilsport," Tess muttered, then grinned at Willa. "Gotcha."

"At this rate, Will's going to have a dress on more times this year than I've seen in her whole life." Ben toasted her. "I used to figure she slept in Levi's."

"Like to see you drive cattle in a dress," Willa tossed back.

"So would I." With a chuckle, Nate nudged his plate aside. "Lily, that was a fine meal. Adam's going to have to start buying bigger belts with you cooking for him."

"You have to have room for pie." Beaming with pleasure, Lily rose. "Why don't we have it in the living room?"

"That girl can cook," Ben commented as he settled into a wing chair in the living room. "Adam's a lucky son of a bitch."

"Is that how you gauge a man's fortune in a wife, McKinnon?" Willa chose the floor in front of the fire and folded her legs. "By how she cooks?"

"Couldn't hurt."

"A clever woman hires a cook." Tess groaned a little as she sat with Nate on the sofa. "And only eats this way once a year. I'm going to have to do fifty extra laps in the pool tomorrow."

Willa thought of several snide comments, but let them pass. She shot a quick look toward the kitchen, where Adam and Lily were busy readying dessert. "Before they come in, did Lily say anything to you about seeing her ex while you were shopping the other day?"

"No." Tess sat up quickly. "Not a word."

"In Ennis?" Nate's eyes narrowed, and he stopped playing with Tess's fingers.

"She said she was mistaken. Said it was an old habit to imagine him wherever she went, but it worried me."

"She got quiet for a while." Pursing her lips, Tess thought back. "We were window-shopping at a lingerie store, and I thought she was dreaming of her wedding night. She seemed nervous for a couple minutes, but she never said a thing."

"You ever get that picture of him?" Ben asked Nate.

"Just a couple of days ago. There was some sort of holdup back East." He, too, sent a cautious look toward the kitchen. "Looks like a frigging altar boy. Pretty face and a jarhead haircut. I haven't seen him around. I should have brought it over with me, got it to Adam."

"I want to see it," Willa said. "We'll talk about it later," she added, when she heard Adam's voice. "I don't want to spoil this for her."

To cover the gap, Ben rose and strolled over as Lily carried in a tray. "Now, that's pie." He leaned over, sniffed, like a man who had nothing more on his mind than his next bite. "So what have you got for everybody else?"

They kept the evening light, and when Nate gave Tess a subtle signal by a quick squeeze of her hand, he rose. "I'd better head on before you have to roll me out the door. Lily." He bent to kiss her. "You set one fine table."

"I'm so glad you came."

"I'll walk out with you." Tess feigned a yawn. "All that food, I'm going to sleep like a log."

By tacit agreement Ben and Willa gave them five minutes after hugs and good-byes before they made their own exit.

When they were alone, Adam turned Lily into his arms. "Who do they think they're fooling?"

"What do you mean?"

Finding her incredibly sweet, he pressed a kiss to her brow. "Did you hear a rig start up?"

She blinked, understood, and laughed. "No, I don't suppose I did."

"I think they've got the right idea." He swept Lily up, headed for the steps.

"Adam, all the dishes."

"They'll still be here in the morning." He kissed her again. "And so will we."

IN HER BED, IN THE DARK, WILLA LET OUT A LONG throaty moan. The sound of that always aroused him, spurred him to quicken the pace. He loved to watch her when she rode him, the way her hair rained down off her shoulders, so lush and dark. He could see those flashes, those flickers of pleasure on her face as she lost herself. And when he took her breasts in his hands, when he reared up to replace his hands with his hungry mouth, she wrapped herself around him like a silky vine, all clinging arms and legs so he could feast on her.

No matter how much she gave, he wanted more.

"Go over." He panted out the demand, pressed his hand where they joined, and found her, drove her.

Her moan came again, a rusty sound of delight that pumped through his blood like good whiskey. He felt her give, and flood, then sob again before her teeth closed over his shoulder.

So he let her set the pace now, let her shudder back into control. Now she leaned over him, her hair curtaining his face, her hands braced on either side of it.

"I want to make you crazy." She lowered her head until her lips were a breath from his. "I want to make you beg."

Her pace was slow, torturous, and her mouth took his in quick, nipping kisses that gradually deepened and heated. When his hands were fisted in her hair, his breath heaving, she released his mouth, eased back. Quickened the rhythm, skimmed her hands over him, watched his eyes.

She saw what she wanted. They were wild and blind and desperate, mirroring the emotions raging inside her. His hands had moved, gripped her hips now, gripped them hard. She'd have bruises. Branding, she thought in triumph.

Her body bowed back, shuddered while Ben's fingers dug into her pumping hips. She knew what to expect now, that explosion of pleasure ramming into pleasure, the assault on the system that could come like lightning or linger like dew. Yet still it was always a shock, this violent intimacy and the need that always, always bloomed.

She felt him erupt, the final hard drive of him into her, and the glorious burst of heat. The orgasm struck like an arrow winging through her system, and pinned to him, filled with him, she welcomed it.

"Willa." Ben drew her down so they could tremble, slick flesh to slick flesh. When he could speak more than her name, he turned his lips to her throat. "I've wanted to hold you like this all night."

A little foolishness like that always warmed her, and tied her tongue. "You were too busy eating to think about this."

"I'm never to busy to think about this. Or you. I do think about you." He lost his hands in her hair as he turned her mouth to his. "More all the time. And I worry about you."

"Worry?" Beautifully relaxed, she braced herself on her elbows and looked down at him. She loved to find his face in the dark, pick out feature by feature. "About what?"

"I don't like not being right on hand with all this going on."

"I can take care of myself." She brushed the hair back from his face. Funny, she thought, how the tips of it always looked as if they'd been dipped in wet gold dust. Funnier still how her fingers always itched to touch it these days. "And I can take care of the ranch."

"Yeah." Almost too well, he thought. "But I worry anyway. I could stay tonight."

"We've been through that. Bess likes to pretend she doesn't know what's going on up here. I like to let her. And . . ." She kissed him before she rolled lazily to her back. "You've got your own ranch to run." She stretched. "Saddle up, McKinnon. I'm done with you."

"Think so?" He rolled atop her to prove her wrong.

WHEN A MAN TIPTOES OUT OF A DARKENED HOUSE, HE mostly feels like a fool. Or very lucky. Nate was debating which course to take when he opened the front door and came face-to-face with Ben.

They stared at each other, cleared throats. "Nice night," Nate said.

"One of my best." Ben gave up, flashed a grin. "So, where'd you park your rig?"

"Back of the pole barn. You?"

"Same. Don't know why we bother. There's not a man on this spread who doesn't know what we're up to with those women." They stepped off the porch, headed toward the barn. "I keep wondering if I'm going to get shot at."

"Adam and Ham have this shift," Nate pointed out. "I try to time it that way. They're not so trigger-happy." He glanced back toward the main house, Tess's window. "And it might be worth dodging a couple bullets."

"I worry about a man who says that."

"I'm thinking I'll marry her."

Ben stopped dead. "Something's buzzing in my ear. I don't think I heard you right."

"You heard me right enough. She's banking on going back to California in the fall." Nate shrugged. "I'm banking she won't."

"You tell her that?"

"Tell Tess." Amused at the thought, Nate let out a muffled hoot of laughter. "Hell, no. You have to be cagey with a woman like that. Used to running the show. So you make her think everything's her idea. She doesn't know she's in love with me, but it'll come to her."

Talk of love and marriage was making Ben's gut churn. "What if it doesn't? Come to her. What if she packs up and goes? You just going to let her?"

"Can't lock her up, can I?" Nate took out his keys, jiggled them in his palm. "But I'm betting she stays. And I've got some time yet to work on it."

Ben thought of Willa, and how he'd react if she suddenly got it in her head to pull up stakes. He'd have her hog-tied in record time. "Don't think I could be as reasonable."

"Well, push hasn't come to shove yet. I've got court the next day or two," he added when he climbed into his rig.

"Soon as I'm able, I'll swing by with that picture."

"You do that." Ben paused by his own rig, looked back toward the main house. No, he didn't think he could be reasonable if he was in love. On the drive home he told himself, several times, that it was a good thing he wasn't.

TWENTY-THREE

JESSE HAD IT ALL WORKED OUT. OH, HE'D BEEN WILLING to wait, be patient. Be reasonable. After all, if he held out till fall, he could sweep up a lot of money along with his wife.

But now the little bitch thought she could go off and marry that Indian bastard. He'd studied on it and knew that if he let that happen, legally he'd get zilch. So he couldn't let it happen.

If his aim had been a little more true, he'd have taken care of Adam Wolfchild already. The opportunity had been there, but the son of a bitch had gotten lucky. And since Wolfchild hadn't been alone, Jesse hadn't risked waiting around for another chance at him.

He was sure there'd be another opportunity. Just a little window of luck was all he'd need. But spring work, and that damn slave driver Ben McKinnon, kept him tied at Three Rocks while his adulterous wife was out buying wedding finery.

So if he couldn't get to Wolfchild, he would damn well get to Lily. He'd have to make her sorry she'd messed with him and ruined his plans for cashing in on her inheritance, but that would be a pleasure.

He'd hoped to cash in on a lot of things, he thought as he drew another queen to go with his other two ladies. But it was time to move on. And he was taking Lily with him.

"I'll see your five," Jesse said, smiling easily at Jim across the poker table. "And bump it five."

"Too rich for me." Ned Tucker tossed in his cards, belched, and got up to get a fresh beer. He was comfortable at Mercy; he found Willa a fair boss and enjoyed the company of the men. He gave the bear the men had wrestled into the corner a rub on the head for luck. Not, Ned thought, that it had done him a damn bit of good at the table that night.

He shook his head as Jesse pulled in another pot. "Sumbitch can't seem to lose," he said to Ham.

"Got enough luck to shit gold nuggets." But Ham decided to try his own. "Deal me in this hand. I've gotta take over for Billy outside in an hour. Might as well lose some money first."

An hour, Jesse thought, as he took his turn at deal. Billy and that know-it-all college boy were on shift now. Neither one of them would be much challenge to him. He would give the game another ten minutes, then make his move.

He lost one hand, folded on another, then pushed back from the table. "Deal me out. Gonna get some air."

"Make sure Billy don't shoot you," Jim called out. "That boy's mind's on town pussy and he spooks easy."

"Oh, I can handle Billy," Jesse said, and shrugging into his jacket, he strolled out.

He checked the time. He'd studied the workings of Mercy carefully enough to know that Adam would be giving his horses a final look for the night. The main house would be settled down, and Lily would be alone. He took the Colt out from under the seat of his rig. You could never be too careful. Tucked it into his belt and moved through the shadows toward the pretty white house.

It would go like clockwork, he mused. Lily would cry and plead, but she'd come easily enough. She always did what she was told. If not quick enough, after the first smack.

He was looking forward to that first smack. It had been much too long.

He tapped his belt, moved quietly toward the rear of the house.

"That you, J C?" Cheered by the prospect of company on his shift, Billy came forward, rifle lowered and on safety. "You skinning the guys back at the bunkhouse again? What are you doing out here?"

Jesse smiled at him, slid the gun from his belt. "Taking what's mine," he said, and smashed the butt of the Colt down. "No reason to shoot you," Jesse said as he dragged Billy into the bushes. "And it makes too much noise. You just stay out of my way now, or I might change my mind."

He crept to the back door, quiet as a snake, and looked through the glass.

And there she was. Sweet little Lily, he thought. Sitting at the table drinking tea and reading a magazine. Waiting for her Indian lover to come stick it to her. Faithless bitch.

The rumble of thunder threw him off a moment, made him look up at the starless sky. Even the weather was on his side, he thought with a grin. A nice rain would be fine cover on the trip south.

He turned the knob slowly, stepped in.

"Adam, there's an article in here about wedding cakes. I wonder . . ." She trailed off, her gaze still glued to the page, but her heart thudding. Beans was growling under the table. And she knew, even before she gathered the courage to turn, she knew.

"Keep that dog quiet, Lily, or I'll kill him."

She didn't doubt it. He looked the same—even with the darker hair, the length of it, the moustache, he looked exactly the same to her. Those beautiful eyes slitted mean, his mouth frozen in a dangerous smile. She managed to get to her feet, put herself between Jesse and the dog.

"Beans, hush now. It's all right." When he continued to growl, she watched in horror as Jesse took a gun from his belt. "Don't, please, Jesse. He's just an old dog. And they'll hear you. They'll hear if you shoot. People will come."

He wanted to kill something, felt the urge bubbling up. But he wanted it quiet more. "Then shut him up. Now."

"I—I'll put him in the other room."

"You move slow, Lily, and don't try to run." He liked the feel of the gun in his hand, the way the butt curled neatly into his palm. "I'll hurt you bad if you do. Then I'll sit right here and wait for that Indian you've been spreading your legs for. And I'll kill him when he walks in."

"I won't run." She took Beans by the collar, and though his pudgy body was tense and he strained against her, she dragged him to the door and through it. "Please put the gun away, Jesse. You know you don't need it."

"Guess I don't." Still smiling, he slid it back in his belt. "Come here."

"This is no good, Jesse." She struggled hard to remember everything she'd learned in therapy, to stay calm, to think clearly. "We're divorced. If you hurt me again, they'll put you in jail."

He laid a hand on the butt of the gun again. "I said come here."

Closer to the door, she thought. There might be a way to get through. She had to get through to warn Adam, everyone. "I'm trying to start over," she said as she walked toward him. "We can both start fresh. I never did anything but disappoint you, and—" She cried out, not in shock but in pain, when he slapped her backhanded across the face.

"I've been waiting to do that for more than six months." And since it felt so good, he did it again, hard enough to send her to her knees. "I've been right here, Lily." He gripped her hair, yanked her to her feet by it. "Watching you."

"Here?" The pain was too sickeningly familiar, made it too hard to think. But she did think. Of murder, of madness. "You've been here. Oh, God."

Now the fear was paralyzing. He used his fists, she told herself. Just his fists. He wouldn't rip people apart.

But all she saw when she looked in his eyes was blind rage.

"Now you're coming with me, and you're going to be

quiet and do just what I say.'' In case she didn't understand his meaning, he gave her hair another vicious yank. ''You mess with me, Lily, I'll hurt you and anybody else that gets in the way.'' He continued to talk, his face close to hers. In the other room the dog was barking wildly, but neither paid attention. ''We're going to take a nice long trip. Mexico.''

''I'm not going with you.'' She took the next blow, reeled from it, then shocked them both by leaping forward, attacking with nails, teeth, fists.

The force of her headlong rush rammed him back against the counter, and pain bloomed in his hip where it struck the edge. He howled when she drew blood from his cheek, too stunned to strike back until she'd raked his face a second time. ''Fucking cunt!'' He knocked her back into the table, sent her pretty teacup flying.

The dogs howled like wolves and scratched madly at the door.

''I'll kill you for that. I'll fucking kill you.''

And he nearly did. The gun was in his hand, his finger on the trigger vibrating. But she was staring up at him, not with fear, not with pleading in her eyes. But with hate.

''Is that what you want?'' He dragged her up again, held the barrel to her temple. ''You want me to kill you?''

There had been a time she might, out of sheer weariness, have said yes. But she thought of her life here, with Adam, with her sisters. Her home and family.

''No, I'll go with you.'' And wait, she promised herself, for the first chance to escape, or to fight.

''Damn right you will.'' He closed a hand over her throat, shook her as blood stung his eyes. ''I haven't got time to make you pay now, but you wait. You just wait.''

He was trembling as he pulled her to the door. The shock of her hurting him, actually hurting him until the blood ran down his face, had rocked him badly. The time he'd wasted dealing with her when she could have come along docile as a cow left him jittery.

He barely noticed that it wasn't rain falling from that dark sky, but snow. While the thunder still raged. Thick, heavy flakes danced in front of his eyes so that he didn't see Adam until they were nearly face-to-face and he was looking at a rifle.

"Let go of her." Adam's voice was calm as a lake, without any of the fury or fear rippling the surface. "Lily, step away from him."

Jesse shifted his grip to her throat, his arm over her windpipe. The gun, still in his hand, was at her head. There was no calm in him. He was screaming, "She's my goddamn fucking wife! Get the hell out of my way. I'll kill her. I'll put a bullet in her brain."

He heard a gun cock and saw Willa step forward, coatless, snow covering her hair. "Take your hands off my sister, you son of a bitch."

It was wrong, everything was wrong, and the panic made Jesse's finger tremble. "I'll do it. Her brains'll be splattered on your shoes if you take one step. You tell them, Lily. Tell them I'll kill you here and now."

She could feel the steel pressed into her temple. Imagine the flash of explosion. She could barely breathe through the grip on her throat. To stay alive, she kept her eyes on Adam. "Yes, he will. He's been here, all the time, he's been here."

Jesse's eyes fired. He looked like a monster with the blood oozing down his face and his lips peeled back in a wide, challenging grin. "That's right. I've been here, right along. You want me to do to her what was done to the others, you just stay in my way." His lips curved in a dazzling smile. He was in charge again. He was in control. "Maybe I won't gut her, I won't lift her hair, but she'll still be dead."

"So will you," Adam said, and sighted.

"I can snap her neck like a twig." Jesse's voice rolled and pitched. "Or put a bullet in her ear. And maybe I'll get lucky." He increased the pressure on Lily's throat so that her hands came up in defense to drag at the obstruction. "Maybe I'll get off one more shot, right into your sister's gut."

"He's bluffing, Adam." Willa's finger twitched on the trigger. She'd put a bullet in his brain, she thought grimly. If Lily would just move her head another inch, just shift over an inch, she could risk it. But the damn snow was blowing like a curtain. "He doesn't want to die."

"I'm a fucking Marine!" Jesse shouted. "I can take two of you out before I go down. And Lily's first."

Yes, Lily was first. "You won't get away." But Adam lowered his rifle. Rage, pride, weren't worth Lily's life. "And you'll pay for every minute she's afraid."

"Back off, bitch," he ordered Willa, and tightened his grip so Lily's eyes rolled up white. "I can break her neck as easy as blinking."

Helpless, every instinct raging against it, Willa stepped back. But she didn't lower the gun. One clear shot, she promised herself. If she had one clear shot, she'd take it.

"You get in the rig." He pulled Lily with him, moving backward, his eyes jumping from side to side. "Get in the fucking rig, behind the wheel." He pushed her in, shoved her across the seat, keeping the gun high and in plain sight. "You come after us," he shouted, "I kill her, slow as I can. Start the goddamn thing and drive."

Lily had one last look at Adam's face as she turned the key. And she drove.

With hands that trembled, Willa lowered the rifle. She hadn't taken the shot. There'd been a moment, just an instant, and she'd been afraid to risk it.

"God. Dear God. They're heading west." Think, she ordered herself. Think. "The cops can put up a roadblock, stop them if he tries for the main road. If he's smart, he'll figure that and go into the hills. We can be after them inside twenty minutes, Adam."

"I let her go. I let him take her."

Willa gave him a hard shake. "He'd have killed her, right in front of us. He was panicked and crazy. He'd have done it."

"Yes." Adam drew in a breath, let it out. "Now I'll find them. And I'll kill him."

Willa nodded once. "Yes. You call the police, I'll get the men. Those of us going into the hills will need horses and gear. Hurry."

She started off in a spring, nearly tripped over Billy,

who'd managed to crawl, groaning, onto the road. "Jesus." The blood covering his face made her certain he'd been shot. "Billy!"

"He hit me. Hit me with something."

"Just sit tight. Stay right here." She headed toward the main house at a dead run. "Bess! Get the first aid kit. Billy's over in front of Adam's. He's hurt. Get him in here."

"What the hell's going on?" Annoyed at having her evening session at her computer interrupted, Tess came to the head of the stairs. "First dogs barking like maniacs, now you yelling down the roof. What happened to Billy?"

"Jesse Cooke. Hurry," she ordered as Bess scooted by her. "I don't know how bad he's hurt."

"Jesse Cooke." Alarmed, Tess raced down the stairs. "What are you talking about?"

"He's got Lily. He's got her," Willa repeated, overriding Tess's babbled questions. "My guess is he's taking her into high country. We've got a thunder blizzard in the works, and she didn't even have a coat." The first bubble of hysteria was her last as Willa clamped down hard on emotion. "He's panicked and he's got to be half crazy, more. You call Ben, Nate, anyone else you can think of, tell them we need a search party and fast. We're riding after them."

"I'll get warmer gear together." Tess's fingers stayed white on the newel post. "And for Lily. She'll need it when we find her."

"Make it fast."

Within ten minutes Willa was organizing the men. They were armed, prepared to set out in rigs or on horseback with supplies to last two days.

"He doesn't know the area like most of us," she continued. "He's only had a few months. And Lily will throw him off, slow him down as much as she can. We'll spread out. There's a chance he'll take her up to the cabin, so Adam and I will head there. The weather's going to make it rough on him, but it isn't going to help us either."

"We'll get the son of a bitch." Jim slapped his rifle into its sheath. "And we'll get him before morning."

"There won't be any tracking in this, so . . ." She trailed

off as she saw Ben's rig drive recklessly into the ranch yard. She wanted to buckle then, needed to, so she stiffened her spine. "So we spread out over a wide area. You all have your targets. The cops are covering the main roads, and they're sending more men. Search and Rescue will be out at first light. I want her back by then. As for Cooke—" She drew a breath. "Whatever it takes. Let's move."

"Which are you taking?" It was the only question Ben asked.

"I'm going with Adam, up the west face toward the cabin."

He nodded. "I'm with you. I need a horse."

"We've got one."

"I'm going too." Eyes ready to brim over with tears, Tess stepped next to Adam. "I can ride."

"You'll slow us down."

"Goddamn you." Tess gripped Willa's arm and spun her around. "She's my sister too. I'm going."

"She can ride" was all Adam said. He swung into the saddle and, with his young hound beside him, galloped off.

"Wait for Nate," Willa ordered. "He knows the way." She mounted quickly. "He'll need someone to fill him in on the rest of it."

Knowing she had to be satisfied with that, Tess nodded. "All right. We'll catch up with you."

"We'll bring her home, Tess," Ben murmured as he hoisted into the saddle, whistled for Charlie.

"Bring them both home," Tess said, as she watched them ride away.

ADAM SAID NOTHING UNTIL THEY FOUND THE ABAN-doned rig. His mind was too dark for words, his heart too cold. They stopped long enough to look carefully for signs. The rig was plunged to the wheel wells in snow, leaning drunkenly against a tree.

The thick, wet snow covered everything, and the dogs scouted through it, noses buried.

"He'd hit her." Adam wrenched open the driver's-side door, terrified that he'd find blood. Or worse. "There were bruises already on her face where he'd hit her.''

The rig was empty, with a few drops of blood near the far door. Not Lily's, he thought. Cooke's.

''There was blood running down his face,'' Willa reminded him. ''She'd given it back, in spades.''

When Adam turned, his eyes were blank as a doll's. ''I told her, I promised her, no one would ever hurt her again.''

''There was nothing you could do. He won't hurt her now, Adam. She's his only way out of this. He won't do to her what—''

''What he did to the others?'' Adam bit the words off, buried the thought. Without another word he mounted and rode ahead.

''Let him have some distance.'' Ben laid a hand over Willa's. ''He needs it.''

''I was standing right there too. I had a gun on him. I'm a better shot than Adam, better than anyone on Mercy, but it didn't do any good. I was afraid to risk—'' Her voice broke and she shook her head.

''What if you'd risked it, and she'd moved, jerked? You might have hit her instead.''

''Or she might be safe now. If I had it to do over again, I'd shoot the son of a bitch right between the eyes.'' She made herself shake it off. ''Doubling back on it doesn't help either. It could be he's heading toward the cabin, the direction's right enough. He'd think he could make a stand there.''

Willa swung onto her horse. ''She tried to fight him this time. Maybe running would have been better.''

LILY WOULD HAVE RUN IF SHE COULD HAVE. SHE WAS freezing, her shirt soaked through, but she would have taken her chances with the storm and the hills if running had been an option.

He'd put the gun away, but after she ran the rig into the tree, he changed strategies. She'd aimed for the tree, hoping the impact on his side would jar him enough to buy her a lead. It had only earned her a headlong toss into the snow.

And then he tied her hands and looped the slack around

his waist so that she was tethered to him. She stumbled a lot, deliberately at first to slow him down. But he only jerked her upright again.

The snow was monstrous. The higher they climbed, the more vicious it became, with bellowing bursts of thunder following the eerie sky-cracking lightning. And the wind was so fierce she could barely hear him cursing her.

The world was white—swirling, howling white.

He had a knapsack over his shoulders. She wondered if there was a knife in it, and what he might do to her in the end.

The cold had sapped her strength, leached into her bones so that they felt like brittle sticks, ready to snap. Fighting him was no more than a fantasy now, running a fading hope. Where could she run when there was nothing but a blinding wall of snow?

All she could do was survive.

"Thought they had me, didn't they?" He jerked the rope so she fell against him. He had the collar of his sheepskin jacket turned up, but still the wet snow snuck in and down his neck and irritated him. "Your horseshit shoveler and half-breed bitch of a sister thought they had the upper hand. I got what I wanted." He squeezed her breast hard through her shirt. "Always did, always will."

"You don't want me, Jesse."

"You're my fucking wife, aren't you? Took vows, didn't you? Love, honor, and obey. Till death." He pushed her into the snow for the hell of it and rode on the power of that. "They'll come after us, but they don't know what they're up against, do they, Lily? I'm a goddamn Marine."

He could plow through this snow just like he'd plowed through basic training, he thought. He could plow through anything and still kick ass.

"I've been planning this for a long time." He took out a cigarette, flicked on the Zippo he'd turned up to maximum flame. "I've been taking the lay of the land. I've been working at Three Rocks since I got here, practically right on your skinny ass."

"At Three Rocks. For Ben."

"Ben Bigshot McKinnon." He let smoke pour out between his teeth. "The same who's been bouncing on your sister lately. I've given some thought to that myself." He studied Lily, shivering in the snow. "She'd be a hell of a lot more interesting in bed than you. A fucking tree would be, but you're my wife, right?"

She pushed herself up. It would be too easy to just lie there and give up. "No, I'm not."

"No lousy piece of paper's going to tell me different. You think you can run out on me, go to some freaking lawyer, call out the cops? They put me in a cell because of you. I got a lot of payback coming."

He studied her again. Pale, beaten. His. Taking one last drag, he flicked his cigarette into the snow. "You look cold, Lily. Maybe I'll just take a minute or two to warm you up. We got time," he continued, pulling the rope to drag her to him. "The way they're going to be tripping over themselves trying to track me. Couldn't track an elephant in this."

He pushed his hand between her legs. When all he saw in her eyes was revulsion, he pushed harder until the first flicker of pain bloomed. "You like to pretend you don't like it rough, but you're a whore like all the rest. You used to tell me it was just fine, didn't you? 'That's just fine, Jesse. I like what you do to me.' Didn't you used to say that, Lily?"

She stared into his eyes, fought to ignore the humiliation of his hand on her. "I lied," she said coolly. She didn't wince from the pain as he dug into her. Wouldn't let herself.

"Castrating bitch, I can't even get a hard-on with you." She'd never used to back-talk him. Not after the first couple licks. Unsettled, he shoved her back, then shifted his pack. "No time for this anyway. When we get to Mexico, it'll be different."

Changing directions, he took her south.

SHE LOST TRACK OF TIME, AND DISTANCE, AND DIRECTION. The snow had slowed, though the occasional boom of thunder still rolled over the peaks. She put one foot in front of the other, mechanically, each step a survival. She was certain now that he wasn't going to the cabin, wondered where Adam was, where he was looking, what he was feeling.

She'd seen murder in his eyes at that last glimpse of his face. He would find her, she knew he would find her. All she had to do was live until he did.

"I need to rest."

"You'll rest when I say." Worried that he'd lost his way in the storm, Jesse took out his compass. Who could tell where the hell they were going in this mess?

It wasn't his fault.

"Not much farther anyway." He pocketed the compass and headed due east now. "Just like a woman—bitch, moan, and complain. Never known you not to whine about something."

She'd have laughed if she'd had the strength left. Perhaps she had whined once upon a time about the paychecks that had gone missing, the whiskey bottles, the forgotten promises. But it seemed a far cry from whining about dying of exposure in the Rockies.

"It'll be harder for you if I collapse from exhaustion, Jesse. I need a coat, something hot to drink."

"Shut up. Just shut the hell up." He stared through the dark and the lightly falling snow, shielding his flashlight with his hand. "I've got to think."

He had his direction. He had that, all right. But the distance was another matter. None of the landmarks he'd been careful to memorize seemed to materialize. Everything looked different in the dark. Everything looked the same.

It wasn't his fault.

"Are we lost?" She had to smile. Wasn't that just like him? Big-talk Jesse Cooke, ex-Marine, lost in the mountains of Montana. "Which way is Mexico?"

And she did laugh, weakly, even when he whirled on her, fists raised. He would have used them, just to relieve his frustration, but he saw what he was looking for. "You want to rest? Fine. This is as far as we go for now."

He pulled her again through a snowdrift that reached the top of her thighs and toward the mouth of a small cave.

"This was Plan B. Always have a Plan B, Lily. I scouted

this place out more than a month ago.'' And he'd meant to lay in extra supplies, just in case, but hadn't had the chance. ''Hard to spot. Your Indian isn't going to find you here.''

It was still cold, but at least it was out of the wind. Lily sank to her knees in relief.

Delighted now that he'd reached the next stage of his plan, Jesse shrugged off his pack. ''Got us some jerky in here. Bottle of whiskey.'' He took that out first, drank deeply. ''Here you go, sweetheart.''

She took it, hoping that even false heat would slow the shivering. ''I need a blanket.''

''So happens I got one. You know I'm always prepared, don't you?''

He was pleased with the survival gear he'd packed—the food and the flashlight, the knife, the matches. He tossed her a blanket, amused when she gathered it awkwardly with her bound hands and struggled to wrap it around herself. He crouched on the floor of the cave.

''We'll get a little sleep. Can't risk a fire, though I imagine those boys are way north of here.'' He took out another cigarette. God knew a man deserved a drink and a smoke after putting in a long day. ''In the morning, we'll head out. I figure we get to one of these bumfuck towns and I can hot-wire a car. Then we're on our way to sunny Mexico.'' In celebration, he blew smoke rings. ''Can't be soon enough for me.'' He bit off a piece of jerky, chewed thoughtfully. ''Montana sucks.''

He stretched out his legs, rested his back on the wall of the cave while she let herself drowse in the stingy warmth of the blanket. ''I'm going to make me a pile of money down there. I wouldn't have had to worry about that if you'd behaved yourself. Your share of Mercy, that was big bucks for me, Lily, and you had to fuck it up by thinking you could go off and get married. We're going to talk about that later. A lot.''

He took the bottle back and drank deeply again. ''But a smart man like me, one who's got luck at cards, he can do just fine down there with those greasers.''

She needed to sleep, had to sleep to pull her strength back

until Adam found her. Until she could get away. She curled against the side wall, as far away as the tether would allow, and wrapped the blanket tight around her.

He would drink now. She knew the pattern. He would drink until he was drunk, and then she'd have a better chance of getting away from him.

But she had to sleep. It was closing in on her like a fog and the chills were racking her so hard she thought her bones would crack. She listened to the whiskey slosh in the bottle as he lifted it, felt herself drift.

"Why did you kill those people, Jesse? Why did you do all those things?"

The bottle clinked, sloshed. He chuckled a little, as if at a small private joke. "A man does what he's got to."

It was the last thing she heard him say.

TWENTY-FOUR

ON A COLD, WINDY RIDGE, ADAM STOOD, STARING INTO the dark, trying to see into it as he might a mirror. The only relief from that dark was the strong beam of the flashlight in his hand and the beams behind him.

"He's veered off from the cabin." Ben studied the sky, measured the hours until dawn. He wanted the sun, damn it. The morning might bring signs other than the scent the dogs were pursuing. Morning would bring the planes, and his own brother would be up, scanning every tree and rock.

"He's got someplace else he's taking her." Adam kept his face to the wind, as if it might tell him something. Anything. "He knows someplace else. He'd have to be past crazy to take the mountain on foot at night without a shelter."

The man who had ripped two people to pieces was past crazy, Ben thought grimly. But it wasn't what Adam needed to hear. "He's gone to ground somewhere. We'll find him."

"Snow's let up some. Storm's moved east. She wasn't dressed for a night in the cold." Adam stared straight ahead, had to stare into the dark and make himself breathe no matter how his insides shook. "She gets cold at night. Bird bones. Lily's got little bird bones."

"He can't be that far ahead of us." Because it was all he could do, Ben laid a hand on Adam's shoulder, left it there. "They're on foot. They'll have to stop and rest."

"I want you to leave me alone with him. When we find them, I want you to take Lily and Will, and leave him to me." Adam turned now, and the eyes that were always so gentle, so quiet, were hard and cold as the rock on which he stood. "You leave him to me."

There was civilized, Ben thought, and there was justice. "I'll leave him to you."

From her post by the horses, Willa watched them. She had lived and worked and survived in a man's world her entire life. Perhaps she understood better than most that there were times a woman couldn't cross the line. Whatever they spoke of wasn't for her, and she accepted that. What was between them on that ridge wasn't just between men, but between brothers.

Her sister's fate was in their hands. And hers.

When they started back toward her, she took Lily's blouse and gave both dogs the scent fresh. Shuddering with excitement, they whined and headed due south.

"Sky's clearing," she said, as they mounted and Adam rode ahead. She could see stars, just a sprinkle of them glinting through. "If the clouds move off we'll have a half-moon and some light."

"It'll help." Ben gave her a quick study. She rode straight as an arrow with no sign of flagging. But he couldn't see her eyes, not clearly enough. "You holding up?"

"Sure. Ben . . ."

He slowed a bit, thinking she might be close to breaking, need him to comfort. "You need a minute, we can hang back."

"No, no. Damn it, it's been working at my mind for hours. There was something familiar about the bastard. Something . . . like I'd seen him somewhere before. But it was dark, and there was blood all over his face where Lily

must have scratched him.'' She pushed her hat back, suddenly irritated by the weight of it. ''I dumped Billy on Bess
so fast. I didn't take time to ask him any questions. I should
have. Maybe we'd have a better idea of his moves.''

''You had other things on your mind.''

''Yeah.'' But it nagged at her, that memory that circled,
then dipped just out of reach. ''Doesn't matter now.'' She
settled her hat back on her head, nudged Moon into a quick
trot. ''Finding Lily's what matters.'' Finding her alive, she
thought, but couldn't say it.

T HE CAVE WAS DARK. SHE WAS BURNING UP, THEN FREEZ-
ing, then burning again, tossed in fever and dreams and ter-
rors. Her hands were cold, sore to numbness at the wrists
where the rope abraded her skin. She curled tight into herself, dreamed of curling tight into Adam, having his arm
drape over her as it did during the night to pull her close.
And warm. And safe.

She whimpered a little as the rocks scattered across the
floor of the cave bit into her shoulder, her back, her hip.
Every time she shifted, she hurt, but it was a distant pain,
a dream pain. No matter how she struggled she couldn't
quite bring herself to the surface of it.

When the light burned over the back of her eyelids, she
turned away from it. She so wanted to sleep, to drop away
from everything. She murmured a little, as the fever began
to brew inside her.

Footsteps, she thought dimly. Adam's home. He'd crawl
into bed beside her now. His body would be a bit chilled
but would warm quickly. If she could just turn, just wake
enough to turn to him, his mouth would be soft on hers, and
he would make love to her, slow and sweet, as he often did
when he came in late from his shift.

They wouldn't even have to speak, just sigh perhaps.
They wouldn't need words, just touch and taste and that
steady rhythm of bodies finding each other. Then sleep
again . . .

As she started to drift again, she thought she heard a
scream, cut quickly off. Like a mouse caught in a trap.

Adam would take it away before she saw it. He understood things like that.

Sinking into unconsciousness, she never felt the knife slip between her wrists to cut the rope, or the heavy warmth of Jesse's coat spread over her. But she said Adam's name as the man who stood over her, blood dripping from his hands, sheathed his knife.

It had been quick work, and he regretted that. He hadn't had time for finesse. He'd gotten lucky finding them before any of the others did. Luckier still to find the bastard drunk and stupid. He'd died easier than he deserved. Like a pig slaughtered with only one surprised squeal.

But he'd taken the hair nonetheless. It was traditional now, and he'd even thought to bring a plastic bag to hold it. In case he got lucky.

He'd have to leave the woman as she was, for others to find. Or circle around, stumble across the cave a second time when there was someone with him, to make it seem all nice and proper.

He scanned the light around the cave again, then smiled when it shone on a small stack of twigs. Well, he could take time for that, couldn't he? A little fire close to the opening, smoke to bring one of the search parties along quicker.

What a picture they'd find, he thought, chuckling. He simply couldn't help but laugh as he built the fire quickly, set it to flame. Couldn't help but laugh as the flames danced over the body slumped against the wall of the cave and the blood pooling like a red river.

When he rode off, he rode east, zigzagging through the trees and picking his way down and up rock until he caught the flash of another searcher's light. All he had to do then was turn his mount and melt in among the men who fanned out over the hills, looking to be heroes.

He was the only one who knew a hero's work was already done.

"SMOKE." WILLA WAS THE FIRST TO CATCH THE SCENT. HER saddle creaked as she rose in it, concentrated. "There's smoke.'' And with it the first true tug of hope pulled at her heart. ''Adam?''

''Up ahead. I can't see it, but it's there.''

''He built a fire,'' Ben murmured. ''Stupid bastard.''

Though they hadn't discussed it, they moved into a trot and now rode three abreast. And the first thin light broke in the east.

''I know this place. Adam, we did some rock climbing in the ravine near here.'' Ben's jaw tightened. ''Caves, lots of little caves. Decent shelter.''

''I remember.'' Only the memory of the gun against Lily's temple kept Adam from breaking into a gallop. His eyes had grown accustomed to the dark, and they narrowed now against the gently growing dawn. And they were sharp. ''There!'' He pointed ahead at the thin gray column of smoke just as Charlie's high, frantic barking echoed.

''Found them.'' Before Willa could speak, Ben blocked her mount with his. ''Stay here.''

''The hell I will.''

''Do what you're told for once, goddamn it.''

He knew that bark. It wasn't the excitement of a find, it was the signal for a kill. He could already tell from the set of her chin that she wasn't going to obey any order. But she might listen to a plan.

''He's armed,'' Ben reminded her. ''Maybe we can flush him. If we do, we need you back here, with your rifle. You're a better shot than Adam. Damn near as good as me. Odds are he's not expecting we brought a woman, so he'll be focused on us.''

Because it made sense, she nodded. ''All right. We try it that way first.'' She looked over at Adam as she pulled out her gun. ''I'll cover you.''

He dismounted, met Ben's eyes. ''Remember'' was all he said.

They parted there, one to the left, one to the right to flank the opening of the cave where the small fire was down to fading smoke. Willa steadied Moon with her knees and waited, watched them. They moved in sync, men who had hunted together since childhood and knew each other's thoughts. A hand signal, a nod, and the pace changed, quick, but not rushed.

Her heart began to knock against her ribs as they neared the cave. Her breath caught in her lungs, clogged there as she braced for the shattering sound of gunfire, of screams, or of the horrific sight of blood splattering over snow.

She prayed, the words repeating over and over in her head in English, in her mother's tongue, then in a desperate mixture of both as she pleaded with any god who would listen to help.

Then she drew a breath, forced it out. Steadying herself, she lifted her rifle and drew a bead on the mouth of the cave.

It was Lily who stumbled out into the crosshairs.

"My God." She forgot her duty, her post, and kicked Moon forward in a gallop. Lily was already in Adam's arms, being rocked in the trampled snow, when Willa slid off her horse. "Is she hurt? Is she all right?"

"She's burning up. Fever." Desperate, Adam pressed his face to hers as if to cool it. Even thoughts of vengeance vanished as she shuddered against him. "We've got to get her back quickly."

"Inside," Lily managed, and burrowed into Adam. "Inside. Jesse. Oh, God."

"Inside?" Willa's head whipped up, and all the fear came roaring back. "Ben?" She said his name the first time, then shouted it as she ran toward the cave.

He was quick, but not quite quick enough to stop her from getting in, from seeing what was spread out on the floor of the cave.

"Get out." He blocked her view with his body, took her hard by the shoulders. "Go out now."

"But how?" Blood, a sea of it. The gaping throat, the split belly, the brutal lifting of the trophy of hair. "Who?"

"Get out." He turned her roughly, shoved her. "Stay out."

She made it as far as the opening, then had to lean on the rock. Sweat had popped cold to her skin, and her stomach heaved viciously. She sucked in air, each breath a rasping sob until she was sure she wouldn't faint or be sick.

Her vision cleared, and she watched Adam bundling Lily into his coat. "I have a thermos of coffee in my saddlebags. It should still be warm." Willa straightened, ordered her legs to hold her weight. "Let's try to get some into her, then we'll take her home."

Adam rose, lifting Lily into his arms. When his eyes met Willa's, the sun flashed into them as it would on the edge of a sword. "He's already dead, isn't he?"

"Yes, he's already dead."

"I wanted it on my hands."

"Not like that you didn't." Willa turned and went to her horse.

WILLA PACED THE LIVING ROOM OF ADAM'S HOUSE. SHE was useless in a sickroom and knew it. But she felt worse than useless out of it. They'd barely been back an hour, and she'd already been dismissed. Bess and Adam were upstairs doing whatever needed to be done for Lily. Ben and Nate were dealing with the police, and her men were taking the rest of the morning to recover after the long night.

Even Tess had been given an assignment and was in the kitchen heating up pots of coffee or tea or soup. Something hot and liquid anyway, Willa thought, as she paced past the window again.

At least she'd had something to do before. Streaking down from the high country to alert the police, to call off Search and Rescue, to tell Bess to ready a sickbed. Now there was nothing but useless waiting.

So when Bess came down the stairs, Willa pounced. "How is she? How bad is it? What are you doing for her?"

"I'm doing what needs to be done." Worry and lack of sleep made her voice sharp and testy. "Now go on home and go to bed your own self. You can see her later."

"She should be in a hospital," Tess replied, as she came in with a tray, the bowl of soup she'd been ordered to heat steaming in the center.

"I can tend her well enough here. Fever doesn't break before long, we'll have Zack fly her into Billings. For now

she's better off in her own bed, with her man beside her.''
Bess snatched the tray away from Tess. She wanted both of
these girls out of her hair, where she wouldn't have to worry
about them as well as the one upstairs in bed. ''Go about
your business. I know what I'm doing here.''

''She always knows what she's doing.'' Tess scowled after Bess, who flounced back up the stairs. ''For all we know
Lily might have frostbite, or hypothermia.''

''Wasn't cold enough for either,'' Willa said wearily.
''And we checked for frostbite anyway. It's exposure. She's
caught a bad chill and she's banged up some. If Bess thinks
it's worse, she'll be the first to send her to the hospital.''

Tess firmed her lips and said what she'd been harboring
in her heart for hours. ''He might have raped her.''

Willa turned away. It had been one more fear, a woman's
fear, that she'd lived with during the long night. ''If he had,
she would have told Adam.''

''It isn't always easy for a woman to talk about it.''

''It is when it's Adam.'' Willa rubbed her gritty eyes,
dropped her hands. ''Her clothes weren't torn, Tess, and I
think there was more on his mind than rape. There'd have
been signs of it. Bess would have seen them when she un-
dressed her. She'd have said.''

''All right.'' That was one hideous little terror she could
put aside. ''Are you going to tell me what happened up
there?''

''I don't know what happened up there.'' She could see
it, perfectly. It was imprinted on her mind like all the others.
But she didn't understand it. ''When we found them Lily
was delirious, and he was dead. Dead,'' she repeated, and
met Tess's eyes, ''like the others were. Pickles and that
girl.''

''But—'' Tess had been sure that Adam had killed him.
That they would put a spin on it for the police, but that
Adam had done it. ''That doesn't make any sense. If Jesse
Cooke killed the others . . .''

''I don't have any answers.'' She picked up her hat, her
coat. ''I need air.''

"Willa." Tess laid a hand on her arm. "If Jesse Cooke didn't kill the others?"

"I still don't have any answers." She shook her arm free. "Go to bed, Hollywood. You look like hell."

It was a weak parting shot, but she wasn't feeling clever. It felt as though her legs were filled with water as she trudged across the road. She would have to talk to the police, she thought. She would have to bear that one more time. And she would have to think, to get her mind in order and think of what to do next.

Too many rigs in the yard, she thought, and paused to study the official seals on the sides of the cars flanking Ben's truck. If there had ever been a police rig on the ranch when her father had been alive, she couldn't recall it. She didn't care to count how many times one had been there since his death.

Gathering her forces, she climbed the steps to the porch and went inside. By the time she'd removed her hat, hung it on the hall rack, Ben was coming down the stairs.

He'd seen her from the office window, watched her almost staggering progress toward the house, her deliberate squaring of shoulders as she saw the police cars.

And he'd had enough.

"How's Lily?"

"Bess won't let anyone but Adam near her." Willa took her coat off slowly, certain that any sudden move would bang her aching bones together. "But she's resting."

"Good. You can follow suit."

"The police will want to talk to me."

"They can talk to you later. After you've gotten some sleep." He took her arm and towed her firmly up the stairs.

"I've got responsibilities here, Ben."

"Yeah, you do." When they reached the top of the stairs and she turned in the direction of the office, he simply picked her up bodily and carried her toward her room. "The first is not to end up in a sickbed yourself."

"Let go of me. I don't appreciate the caveman routine."

"Neither do I." He kicked her door shut behind him, strode to the bed, and dumped her. "Especially when you're playing the caveman.'' She bounced up, he shoved her down again. ''You know I've got you outmuscled, Will. I'm not letting you out of here until you've had some sleep.''

Maybe she couldn't outwrestle him, but she thought she could outshout him. ''I've got cops in my office, a sister too sick to say two words to me, a bunkhouse full of men who are speculating on just what the hell happened up in high country, and a ranch nobody's running. What the hell do you expect me to do, let it all go to hell while I take a nap?''

''I expect you to bend.'' She'd been wrong, he could outshout her too. The explosion might have knocked her back if she hadn't already been down. ''Just once in your damn life, bend before you break. The cops can wait, your sister's being taken care of, and your men are too damn tired to speculate on anything but who's snoring the loudest. And the ranch isn't going to fall apart if you turn off for a couple hours.''

He grabbed her boot, wrenched it off, then heaved it across the room. She reached for the second, gripped the top in what would have been a comic struggle if his eyes hadn't been so raw with temper. ''What the hell crawled up your butt?'' she demanded. ''Just cut it out, Ben.''

The second boot slid out of her fingers and went flying. ''You think I didn't see your face when you walked into that cave? That I don't know what it did to you, or how you were holding yourself together by your fingernails all the way back down?'' He grabbed her shirtfront, and for a moment she was certain he intended to haul her off the bed and toss her after her boots. ''I'm not having it.''

She was stunned enough that she didn't react until he'd unbuttoned her shirt and yanked it off her shoulders. ''Just take your hands off me. I can undress myself when I'm ready. You're an overseer around here, McKinnon, but you don't run my life, and if you don't—''

''Maybe you need somebody to run it.''

He lifted her off the bed—clean off, she thought in wonder, as her feet dangled inches above the polished wood floor. And she realized he was as furious as she'd ever seen him, and she'd seen him red-eyed furious plenty. She'd never seen him like this.

He added a quick, teeth-rattling shake. "Maybe you need to listen to somebody besides yourself now and again."

It was the shake that snapped it. The humiliation of it. "If I do, it won't be you. And the only place you're going to be running is for cover if you don't turn me loose—" Her hand was fisted and ready when he dropped her onto her feet.

"Take a swing at me." He ground out the dare. "Go ahead, but you're going to bed if I have to tie you to the headboard."

She grabbed the hands that grabbed at her shirt. "I'm warning you—"

"He worked for me."

That stopped her, stopped them both as they struggled with her thermal shirt. "What?" Now her hands covered his, dug in. "Jesse Cooke?"

And her hands went limp as she remembered. That day on the road to Three Rocks, that pretty, smiling face at the window of her rig. They'd been that close, as close as Ben and she were now, with only that thin shield of glass between them.

What would he have done, she wondered, if her door hadn't been locked, her window up?

"That's where I saw him." She shuddered when she thought of how he'd flashed that grin at her, called her by name. "I couldn't put it together. He was right there all along. He's been here, playing poker with the men. Right down in the bunkhouse playing cards."

She shook herself, looked at Ben, and saw the weight he was carrying. Not anger so much as guilt, she thought. And she knew the sharp edge of it too well. "It's not your fault." She touched his face, and her words were as gentle as fingertips. "You couldn't know."

"No, I couldn't know." He'd chewed over that until it had made him as ill as spoiled beef. "But it doesn't change it. I had him work on Shelly's rig. She had him in for coffee—her and the baby alone with him. He fixed my mother's bathroom sink. He was in the house with my mother.''

"Stop." She did bend, enough to put her arms around him, to draw him down until he sat beside her. "He's done now."

"He's done, but it's not." He took her by the shoulders, turning her so they faced each other on the edge of the bed. "Whoever killed him, Willa, works for you, or for me."

"I know that." She'd thought of it, thought of it constantly on the racing ride back from the cave, during her helpless pacing of Adam's living room. "Maybe it was payback, Ben, for the others. Maybe Jesse killed the others, and whoever found him did it for them. Lily wasn't hurt. She was alone, and sick, but he didn't touch her."

"And maybe one at a time's enough for him. Will, the chances that we've got two men who do that with a knife are slim. Cooke carried a small boot knife, a four-inch blade hardly bigger than a toy. You don't do that kind of damage with an undersized blade."

"No." It all played back in her head. "No, you don't."

"Then there's that first steer we found, up toward the cabin. No way he did that. I'd barely signed him on. He didn't know his way around high country then."

She had to moisten her lips, they'd become so dry. "You've told all this to the police."

"Yeah, I told them."

"Okay." She rubbed her fingers dead center of her brow. There wasn't a headache there yet, just intense concentration. "We go on the way we have. Keep the guards, the men working in teams and shifts. I know my men." She rapped a fist on her knee. "I know them. The two new ones I just hired on—Christ, I shouldn't have taken on any new hands until this was done."

"You have to stop riding out alone."

"I can't take a damn bodyguard every time I've got cattle to check."

"You stop riding out alone," he said evenly, "or I'll use the old man's will to block you. I'll put down that I consider you incompetent as operator. I can convince Nate to go along with me.''

What little color she had left drained out of her face as she got to her feet. "You son of a bitch. You know goddamn well I'm as competent as any rancher in the state. More."

He rose as well, faced her. "I'll say what I need to say, and I'll do what I have to do. You butt against me on this, you risk losing Mercy."

"Get the hell out of here." She whirled away, balled fists at her sides. "Just get the hell out of my house."

"You want to keep it your house, you don't ride out without Adam or Ham. You want me out, you get into bed and get some sleep."

He could have forced her down again. It would have been easier than saying what he had to say. "I care about you, Willa. I've got feelings for you, and they go pretty deep." It was harder yet when she turned and stared at him. "Maybe I don't know what the hell to do with them, but they're there."

Her heart hurt all over again, but in a way she didn't expect. "Threatening me is sure a damn fool way of showing them."

"Maybe. But if I asked you nice, you wouldn't listen."

"How do you know? You never ask nice."

He dragged a hand through his hair, regrouped. "I've got to get through my day too. Worrying about you's putting a hitch in my stride. If you'd do this one thing for me, it'd make it easier."

This was interesting, she thought. When her mind was clear again, she'd have to ponder it. "Do you ride out alone, Ben?"

"We're not talking about me."

"Maybe I've got feelings too."

That was unexpected—and something worth considering. So he considered it, sticking his hands in his pockets and rocking back on his heels. "Do you?"

"Maybe. I don't want to punch you every time I see you these days, so maybe I do.''

His mouth curved up. "Willa, you do have a way of flushing a man's ego and then shooting it down. Let's take it forward a step." He came toward her, tilted her face up with his finger under her chin, and brushed his lips against hers. "You matter to me. Some."

"You matter to me too. Some."

She was softening. He knew she wasn't aware of it, but he was. Under different circumstances it would have been time to make gentle love to her, perhaps say more. Perhaps say nothing. Because he knew that was just what she'd expect, he kissed her again, let it deepen, let himself sink into her, into that sensation of intimate isolation.

Her arms came up, circled his neck. Her body went pliant as he gathered her closer. The muscles he stroked, kneaded, began to relax under his hands. This time, when he lifted her onto the bed, she sighed.

"You'd better lock that door," she murmured. "We could have the cops in here. Get ourselves arrested."

He kissed her eyes closed as he unfastened her jeans. He kissed her curved lips as he drew the jeans down her legs. Then he threw a blanket over her, got up, and lowered the shades. Her eyes were heavy, smiling lazily as she watched him move back to her, bend down, touch that warm mouth to hers again.

"Get some sleep," he ordered, then straightened and strode to the door.

She popped up like a string. "You son of a bitch."

"I love it when you call me that." With a chuckle, he closed the door.

Steaming, she plopped back on the pillows. How was it he always seemed to outmaneuver her? He'd wanted her flat on her back in bed, and by God, that's just where she was. It was mortifying.

Not that she was staying. In just a minute she would get up, take a bracing shower. Then she'd get back to work.

In just a minute.

She wasn't closing her eyes, wasn't going to sleep. If she did, she was certain she'd be back in that cave, back in the horror. But that wasn't the reason, she assured herself as she struggled to force her eyelids open again. It wasn't fear that was pushing her along. It was duty. And as soon as she got her second wind, she was getting up to fulfill that duty.

She wasn't going to sleep just because Ben McKinnon told her to. Especially since he'd told her to.

She fell like a rock and slept like a stone.

PART FOUR

SUMMER

Rough winds do shake the darling buds of May,
And summer's lease hath all too short a date.

—Shakespeare

TWENTY-FIVE

There wasn't a dish in the sink, not a crumb on the counter or a scuff mark on the floor. Lily stared at the spotless kitchen. Adam had beaten her to it. Again. She stepped to the back door, through it. The gardens she'd planned were tilled, with the hardier vegetables and flowers already planted.

Adam and Tess. Lily hadn't even gotten soil on her garden gloves. And oh, how she'd wanted to.

She struggled not to resent it, to remember that they were thinking of her. She'd been ill for two weeks, and for another, too weak to handle her regular chores without periodic rests. But she was recovered now, fully, and growing weary of being worried over and pampered.

She knew the freezer was stuffed to overflowing with dishes that Bess or Nell had prepared. Lily hadn't cooked a meal since the night Jesse had come through the door where she now stood looking out at the tender green buds on the trees, feeling the gentle warmth of the May air on her face.

It seemed like years since that cold and bitter night. And there were blank spots still, areas of gray she didn't care to explore. But she was to be married in three short weeks, and her life was more out of her control than it had ever been before.

She hadn't even been permitted to address her own wedding invitations. It had been discovered, to everyone's surprise, that Willa possessed the neatest handwriting among them. So Tess had assigned the job to Willa, with Lily playing only a minor role.

They'd let her lick the stamps.

The flowers were ordered, the photographer and music settled on. And she'd let them, all of them, lovingly step over and around her to handle the details.

It had to stop. It was going to stop. Closing the door firmly at her back, she marched toward the stables. Or she began in a march and ended up with dragging feet. Every time she ventured toward stables or pasture, Adam found a way of whisking her home again. Never touching her, she thought. Or touching her so dispassionately it was more like doctor to patient than lover to lover.

He stepped out of the stables as she approached, which made her think, not for the first time, that he had some sort of radar where she was concerned. He smiled, but she saw that his eyes remained sober, and searching.

"Hi. I'd hoped you'd sleep longer."

"It's after ten. I thought I'd work with a couple of the yearlings today, on the longe line."

"There's plenty of time for that." As usual, he guided her away from the stables, his hand barely touching her elbow. "Did you have breakfast?"

"Yes, Adam, I had breakfast."

"Good." He resisted picking her up and carrying her back to the house, tucking her away where she'd be safe and close. "Did you finish that new book I brought you? It's a pretty morning, maybe you could sit on the porch and read. Get a little sun."

"I nearly finished it." Had barely started it. It made her guilty, knowing he'd made a special trip into town to buy her books, magazines, the little candied almonds she was so fond of.

And she hated the book, the magazines, the almonds. Even the flowers he was constantly bringing home to cheer her.

"I'll bring the radio out for you. And a blanket. It can get cool when you're just sitting." He was terrified she'd catch a chill, lie shivering in bed again with her hand limp in his. "I'll make you some tea, then—"

"Stop it!" The explosive shout stunned them both. In the time he stared at her, she realized she'd never really shouted at anyone before. It was a powerful and thrilling experience. "Stop it, Adam. I'm tired of this. I don't want to sit, I don't want to read. I don't want you bringing me tea and flowers and candy and treating me like a piece of cracked glass."

"Lily, there's no need to get upset. You'll make yourself sick again, and you're barely out of bed."

For the first time in her life she understood the wisdom of counting to ten before speaking. Another time, she decided, she might even try it.

"I am out of bed. I would have been out of bed days before I was if you hadn't been hovering around me. And I am sick. I'm sick of not being allowed to wash my own dishes or plant my own garden or run my own life. I'm sick to death of it."

"Let's go inside." He treated her as he would a fractious mare, with great patience and compassion. "You just need to rest. With the wedding only weeks away you've got a lot on your mind."

That tore it. She whirled on him. "I do not need to rest, and I do not need to be placated like a cranky child. And there isn't going to be any wedding, not until I say differently."

She stalked off, leaving him stunned, speechless, and staggered.

She rode on the temper, the unfamiliar and exciting kick of it all the way to the main house, up the stairs, and into the office, where Willa was arguing with Tess.

"If you don't like the way I'm setting things up, why the hell did you dump the job on me? I've got enough to do without fussing with this reception."

"I'm dealing with the flowers," Tess shot back. "I'm dealing with the caterer—if you can call some bucktoothed jerk whose specialty is pigs in a blanket a caterer." She threw up her hands, then fisted them on her hips. "All you have to do is arrange for tables and chairs for the alfresco buffet. And if I want striped umbrellas, then the least you can do is find me striped umbrellas."

Now Willa's fists rode her hips as well, and she went nose to nose with Tess. "And where in God's name am I supposed to come up with fifty blue-and-white-striped umbrellas—much less this canopy thing you're so hot for. If you'd just . . . Lily, aren't you supposed to be resting?"

"No. No, I am not supposed to be resting." She was surprised sparks didn't fly from her fingertips as she marched to the desk and swept all the lists and folders and invoices onto the floor in an avalanche of paper. "You can toss every bit of paper that has to do with the wedding in the trash. Because there's not going to be any wedding."

"Honey." Tess broke out of her shock, slid an arm around Lily's shoulder, and tried to nudge her into a chair. "If you're having second thoughts—"

"Don't 'honey' me." Lily wrenched away, fuming. "And don't pretend you give me credit for having second thoughts when no one gives me credit for having the first ones. It's my wedding, damn it. Mine. And you've all just taken it over. If you want to plan a wedding so badly, then *you* get married."

"I'll get Bess," Tess murmured, and sent Lily into a fresh tantrum.

"Don't you dare get Bess and have her up here clucking over me. The next person, the very next person who clucks over me, I'm slapping them. I mean it. You." She jabbed a finger at Tess. "You planted my garden. And you." She spun on Willa. "You addressed my wedding invitations. Between the two of you, you've taken everything. And what slips through your fingers, Adam snaps up so quickly I can't even grab for it."

"Well, fine." Willa threw up her hands. "Excuse us for trying to help you through a difficult time. I can't tell you how much I enjoyed getting writer's cramp with this one here breathing down my neck."

"I was not breathing down your neck," Tess said between her teeth. "I was supervising."

"Supervising, my butt. You've got your nose in everything and sooner or later someone's going to pop you in it."

"Oh, and that would be you, I suppose."

"Shut up, both of you. Just shut the hell up."

They did, though their mouths hung open when Lily lifted a vase and sent it flying. "The two of you can argue till your tongues fall out, but not over my business. Not over me. Do you understand? I'm not going to be used anymore. I'm not going to be controlled. I'm not going to be brushed aside. I want everyone to stop looking at me as if I'm going to fall to pieces at any moment. Because I'm not. I'm *not!*"

"Lily." Adam stepped into the doorway. He wasn't sure how to approach her now, so he stood back and hoped a soothing tone would work. "I didn't mean to upset you. If you need time to—"

"Oh, don't you start on me." Vibrating with fury, she kicked at the papers scattered at her feet. "That's just what I'm talking about. Don't anyone upset Lily. Don't anyone treat Lily like a normal woman. Poor thing, poor Lily. She might shatter."

She spun around so she could fire a stream of frustrated rage at all of them. "Well, I'm the one Jesse abused. He held a gun to *my* head. I'm the one he dragged into the hills and kicked into the snow and pulled along on a rope like a dog. And I got through it. I survived it. It's about time you did too."

It was Adam who shattered, at the image that flashed into his brain. "What do you want me to do? Forget it? Pretend it never happened?"

"Live with it. I am. You haven't asked any questions." Her voice hitched, but she steadied it. No, she promised herself, she wasn't going to shatter. And she wasn't going to cry. "Maybe you don't want the answers. Maybe you don't want me the way things are."

"How can you say that?"

Now she drew herself up, made her voice as cool and

reasonable as she could with her heart pounding so hard it hurt her ribs. "You haven't touched me, Adam. Not once since it happened have you touched me." She shook her head as Willa and Tess started to leave the room. "No, stay. This isn't just between Adam and me. That's only part of it. You haven't talked about it either, so let's talk about it now. Right now."

She wiped a tear from her cheek. Damn it, that would be the last one that fell. "Why haven't you touched me, Adam? Is it because you think he did, and you don't want me now?"

"I don't know how." He stepped forward, stopped. His hands felt clumsy, outsized, as they had for weeks. "I didn't stop him. I didn't protect you. I didn't do what I promised you. And I don't know how to touch you, or why you'd want me to."

She closed her eyes a moment. Why hadn't she seen that before? He was the fragile one now. He was the lost one. "You came for me." She said it softly, hoping he could understand just how much that mattered. "Yours was the first face I saw when I stumbled out of that cave, away from . . . away from it. You were the first thing I saw, and that's one of the reasons I can live with it."

She took one unsteady breath, tried again, and found that the next one came more easily. "And all the time he had me, I knew you'd come. That's one of the reasons I got through it. And I fought back."

She looked at her sisters. They, too, had to know how much it mattered. "I fought back and I held on just as you would have done. He had the gun, and he was stronger, but he didn't have control. Not really. Because I didn't give up. I drove into that tree. To slow him down, to make it harder for him."

"Oh, Lily." Undone, Tess sat down and began to weep. "Oh, God."

"And when he tied my hands, I kept falling down." A calm settled over her now, a calm that came from surviving the worst. "Because that would slow him down too. I knew he wouldn't kill me. He'd hurt me, but he wouldn't kill me.

But then it was so cold, and I couldn't fight back anymore. But I held on."

Saying nothing, Willa walked over, poured a glass of water, and brought it to Tess. Lily took a deep breath. She would finish now, say it all, everything that hadn't been said.

"I thought he might rape me, and I could survive that. He'd done it before. But he wasn't in control this time, and he was afraid. Every bit as much as I was, maybe more. When we got to the cave, I was so tired, and I knew I was sick. Nothing he did to me then would have mattered because all I had to do was get through it. And get back here."

She walked to the window, looked out. And gathering her strength because she had gotten back, she had made it through, she turned around once more. "He had whiskey, and I took some because I thought it might help. He drank a lot. I fell asleep, or passed out, listening to him drinking and boasting, just like he used to. I listened to the whiskey sloshing in the bottle, and in part of my mind I thought he might get drunk enough, just drunk enough, and I might be strong enough, just strong enough, to get away. Then someone came."

She crossed her arms over her chest, hugged her elbows. "It's not clear." If any part of the ordeal still frightened her, it was this. The nebulous, fever-soaked memories. "I must have had a fever by then and I suppose I was delirious. I thought it was you," she told Adam. "I thought I was home, in bed, and you were coming in, sliding in next to me. I could almost feel it. And feeling it, I fell asleep again, and slept while whoever was there killed Jesse and cut the rope on my hands. I was only a few feet away, but—"

That quick, high-pitched scream that had snapped off. She could still hear it if she let herself. "When I woke up," she continued, steadily, "Jesse's coat was over me. There was blood on it, all over it. So much blood. I saw him. The light was just coming in through the opening of the cave, and I could see him. Seeing Jesse like that was worse somehow than when he'd held the gun to my head. The need to get away from him was worse. Every time I took a breath, I breathed in the smell of him, and what had been done to him while I'd been a few feet away, sleeping. And I was more frightened in those few moments than I'd been through all the rest of it.''

She stepped forward, just one step, toward Adam. ''But then I crawled out into the sunlight, and you were there. You were there when I needed you most. And I knew you would be.''

Purged, she walked over, poured a glass of water for herself. ''I'm sorry I shouted at all of you. I know everything you've done was out of concern. But I need to take my life back now. I need to go on.''

''You should've yelled sooner.'' Composed again, Tess rose. ''You're right, Lily. You're absolutely right about all of it. I got carried away planning things for you. I'm sorry. I'd have hated being shoved to the background this way.''

''It's all right. It's been a bad habit of mine to let myself be shoved. And I might ask for help planting the rest of the garden.''

''Maybe I should plant my own. I didn't know I'd like it so much. I'll be downstairs.'' She started out, shot a telling glance at Willa.

''If you want to start taking things back,'' Willa said, nudging the papers with her foot. ''You can start by picking these up and getting them out of here.'' She smiled. ''I don't like hunting up printed cocktail napkins.''

Taking a chance, she grasped Lily's shoulders, leaned in close so that her whisper could be heard. ''He'd have crawled through hell if that's what it took to get you back. Don't punish him for loving you too much.''

Easing back, she glanced at Adam. ''You've got a couple hours off,'' she told him, ''to get your life straightened out.'' Walking out, she closed the door behind her.

''I must seem ungrateful,'' Lily began, but he only shook his head, so she crouched down and began to gather the papers. ''I threw a vase. I've never done anything like that before. I didn't know I'd want to. It was difficult to go back to feeling unnecessary.''

''I'm sorry I made you feel that way.'' He crossed to her,

gathered papers himself. He picked up the list of accep-
tances for the wedding, then lifted his eyes to hers. "Nothing in my life is more necessary than you, or more precious.
If you want to call off the wedding . . ." No, he couldn't be
patient or reasonable about this. All he could say was
"Don't."

And nothing he could have said, Lily realized, could have
been more perfect. "After Tess and Will have gone to all
this trouble? That would be rude." She started to smile,
nearly did, but he covered his face with his hands. Covered
it, but not before she'd seen the stricken look in his eyes,
and the hurt she'd put there.

"I let him take you."

"No."

"I thought he would kill you."

"Adam."

"I thought if I touched you it would make you think of
it, of him."

"No, no, Adam. Never." So it was she who held him.
"Never. Never. I'm sorry. I'm sorry. I didn't mean to hurt
you. I was just so angry, so frustrated. I love you, I love
you, I love you. Oh, hold me, Adam. I won't break."

But he might. Even as his arms came around her, his grip
tightened convulsively, he thought he might shatter like thin
glass. "I wanted to kill him." His voice was muffled against
her throat. "I would have. And living with the wanting isn't
nearly as hard as living with the fact that I didn't. And worse
is living with the thought that I nearly lost you."

"I'm here. And it's over." When his mouth found hers,
she poured herself into it, her hands soothing him as he had
always soothed her. "I need you so much. And I need you
to need me back."

He framed her face. "I do. I always will."

"I want to plant gardens with you, Adam, and raise
horses, paint porches." Cupping his face in turn, she drew
his head back and said what was trembling in her heart. "I
want to make children. I want to make a child with you,
Adam. Today."

Staggered, he lowered his brow to hers. "Lily."

"It's the right time." She lifted his hand, pressed it to her lips. "Take me home, Adam, to our bed. Make a child with me today."

FROM THE SIDE WINDOW, TESS WATCHED LILY AND ADAM walk toward the white house. It made her think of the first time she'd seen them walk together, on the day of the funeral. "Check it out," she called to Willa.

"What?" A little impatient, Willa joined her at the window, then smiled. "That's a relief." Moments later, the shades on the bedroom windows of the white house came down, and she grinned. "Looks like we've still got a wedding going."

"I still want those striped umbrellas."

"You're such a bitch."

"Ah, that's what they all say. Will." In a surprising move, she laid a hand on Willa's shoulder. "Are you still driving cattle up to high country tomorrow?"

"That's right."

"I want to come."

"Very funny."

"No, I mean it. I can ride, and I think it might be an interesting experience, one I can use in my work. And since Adam's going, Lily should too. It's important that we stick together. It's safer that way."

"I was going to have Adam stay behind."

Tess shook her head. "You need people you can trust. Adam won't stay behind even if you ask him. So Lily and I go too."

"Just what I need. A couple of greenhorns." But she'd already thought of it herself, and had weighed the pros and cons. "The McKinnons will be moving their herd up as well. We'll take one man with us, leave Ham in charge of the rest. Better get your beauty sleep tonight, Hollywood. We ride out at dawn."

THE ONLY THING MISSING, TESS THOUGHT AS SHE YAWNED in the saddle at daybreak, was the theme from *Rawhide*. So she hummed it to herself, struggled to remember the words

that were vaguely familiar only because of the bar scene in
The Blues Brothers.

Was it "Cut 'em in" or "Head 'em out"?

"Head 'em out" was the obvious winner, as that was
exactly what Willa called into the misty morning air.

It was rather magnificent, Tess mused. The sea of cattle
swarming forward, the riders skimming the edges of the
herd on horses fresh and eager. All of them surged through
the curtain of mists, the low-lying river of fog, tearing it
into delicate fingers while the sun glinted off dewy grass.

And westward, the mountains rose like gods, all silver
and white.

Then Willa turned in the saddle, shouted out for Tess to
move her ass. Why, Tess thought with a grin, that just completed a perfect picture. Belatedly she kicked her horse forward to catch up as the drive began.

No, something was still missing, she realized as the noise
of hooves on hard-packed dirt, of braying moos, of riders
clucking and calling filled the air. Nate. For once she wished
he had cattle as well as horses; then maybe she'd be riding
along with him.

"Don't just ride," Willa called out as she trolled up
alongside. "Keep 'em in line. You lose one, you go after
it."

"Like I could lose a big fat cow," Tess muttered, but she
tried to mimic Willa's herding whistle and the way her sister
slapped her looped rope on the saddle.

Not that Tess had been given a rope, or would know what
to do with one, but she used her hand, then as the hundreds
of marching hooves kicked up dust, her bandanna.

"Oh, for Christ's sake." Rolling her eyes, Willa circled
back. "Not like that, you idiot. You may need that hand."
She took the bandanna from Tess, who was holding it over
her nose, and after a few quick trips, leaned over to tie it
on. "That's an improvement," she decided when it was secured and hung down over half of her sister's face. "Never
seen you look better."

"Just go play trail boss."

"I am trail boss." With that Willa kicked Moon into a

gallop and rode to the rear of the herd to check for stragglers.

It was an experience, Tess decided. Maybe not quite like driving longhorns north from Texas or whatever cowboys had once done. But there was a kind of majesty in it, she supposed. A handful of riders controlling so many animals, driving them along past pastures where other cattle watched the procession with bored eyes, nipping potential strays back in with a quick movement of horse.

Season after season, she mused, year after year and decade after decade, in a manner that changed little. The horse was the tool here, as it had always been. A four-wheeler couldn't travel the forests, over the rivers, up and down the rocky ravines.

The pastures of the high country were rich, and so the cattle were taken up to graze on thick meadow grass, to laze through the summer and into the early fall under the wide sky with eagle and mountain sheep and each other for company.

And summer was coming, like a gift. The trees grew greener, the pines lusher, and she could hear the cheerful bubble of water moving quick and cool. Wildflowers dotted a near meadow, a surprising shower of color, teased out by the strong sun. Birds darted through the trees like arrows, over the hills like kites. And the mountains rose, creamy white at the peaks, with the deep green belt of trees darkening, and the ridges and folds that were valleys and canyons shimmering shadowlike.

"How you holding up?" Jim paced his horse beside her and made her grin. He looked as cocky and raw as anything that had ridden out of the Wild West.

"Holding. Actually it's fun."

He winked. "Be sure to tell that to your back end at the end of the day."

"Oh, I stopped feeling that an hour ago." But she stretched up just to check. No, her butt was as dead as a numbed tooth. "I've never been up this high before. It's gorgeous."

"There's a spot just up ahead. You look out thataway"—
he gestured—"it's a picture."

"How long have you been doing this, Jim? Taking the
herd up in the spring?"

"For Mercy? Shit, about fifteen years, give or take." He
winked again, saw Willa riding up, and knew she'd give
him the look that meant he was lollygagging. "Keeps me
outta pool halls and away from wild women." He trotted
back to point, leaving Tess chuckling.

"Don't flirt with a cowboy on a drive," Willa told her.

"We were having a short, civilized conversation. When
I flirt I—oh, oh, my God." Tess reined in her horse, looked
out in the direction Jim had just indicated. Understanding,
Willa stopped behind her.

"Nice view."

"It's like a painting," Tess whispered. "It doesn't seem
real." It couldn't be real, the way the colors and shapes, the
size and scope all swept together.

The peaks shot up against the sky, tumbled down to a
wide, silvery canyon where a river ran blue and trees grew
thick and green. Somewhere along the way, it seemed miles
to Tess, the river took a curve and vanished into rock. But
before it vanished it spewed white, crashed over rock, then
settled to serene.

A hawk circled in the distance, arching around and around
that curving river, amid rugged rocks, under spearing silver
peaks, above green trees.

"Good fishing there." Willa leaned on her saddle horn.
"People come from all over hell and back to fly-fish in this
river. Me, I'm not big on it, but it's a sight to see. The way
the lines dance and whip through the air, and land with
barely a sound or a ripple. Farther down, around the curve,
there's some wild white water. People plunk themselves in
rubber rafts and have a high old time riding it. I'll stick with
horses."

"Yeah." But Tess wondered what it would be like. It
surprised her that she wondered not in cool writer's fashion
but in hot, thrilling anticipation of what it would feel like
to chase that river, to fly down it.

"It'll be here when we come back." Willa turned her horse. "Montana's funny that way. It mostly stays put. Come on, we're falling behind."

"All right." Tess carried that view with her, along with countless others, as they drove the herd on.

The air cooled to a snap, and patches of snow appeared under the trees, around rocks. And still there were flowers, the sprawl of mountain clematis, the sassy purple of wild delphinium. A meadowlark sang a spring song.

When they stopped to rest the horses and grab a quick lunch, jackets came out of saddlebags.

"For Christ's sake, don't tie your horse." With another roll of the eyes for the greenhorn, Willa took the reins from Tess, gave her mount an easy slap that sent it trotting away.

"What the hell did you do?" Tess took two running steps before she realized the horse would outdistance her. "Now what am I supposed to do? Walk?"

"Eat." Willa shoved a sandwich in her face.

"Oh, fine, just fine. I'll have a little roast beef while my horse goes trotting back home."

"He's not going far. You can't go tying your horse up around here, then wandering off to sit under a tree and have your lunch." Then she grinned as she spotted Ben riding up. "Hey, McKinnon, haven't you got enough to do without looking for handouts?"

"Thought there might be an extra sandwich." He slid off his horse, gave it the same absent pat as Willa had given Tess's. Speechless, Tess watched his mount mosey off.

"What, are you all crazy? There won't be a horse left to ride at this rate."

Ben took the sandwich Tess held, bit into it, and winked at Willa. "She try to tie hers up?"

"Yep. Tenderfoot."

"You don't tie horses up in high country," he said between bites. "Cats. Bears."

"What are you—cats?" Eyes popping, Tess spun around in a circle, trying to look everywhere at once. "You mean mountain lions? Bears?"

"Predators." Willa took what was left of the sandwich

from Ben, finished it off. "A horse hasn't got a chance if it's tethered. How far back's your herd, Ben?"

"About a quarter mile."

"But—" Tess thought of her rifle that was still in her saddle holster. "What chance have *we* got?"

"Oh, fair to middling," Ben drawled, and Willa roared with laughter.

"Lily's probably got that coffee hot by now."

He tugged Willa's hat over her eyes. "How do you think I found you, kid? I followed the scent."

Tess stood frozen to the spot as they wandered toward the little campfire where Lily heated the pot. At a faint rustle in the brush behind her she sprinted forward like a runner off the mark. "Wait. Wait for me."

"Your sister's got a powerful love for coffee," Ben commented as Tess barreled by.

"You should have seen her face when I set her horse loose. It was worth bringing her along just for that."

"Everything all right otherwise?"

"Quiet." She slowed her pace. "Normal. Or as quiet and normal as you'd expect with wedding plans gearing up."

"I wouldn't like to see anything spoil that."

"Nothing's going to." She stopped completely now, turned her back on the group by the fire so that she faced only Ben. "I talked to the police again," she said quietly. "They're investigating my men. Every one of them."

"Mine too. It's necessary, Willa."

"I know it. I left Ham back, and it worries me, not knowing. He and Bess, Wood's two boys. As far as it goes, Ben, they're alone."

"Ham can handle himself, so can Bess if it comes to that. And nobody's going to hurt those kids, Will."

"I wouldn't have thought so before. Now I just don't know. I wanted Nell to take them, go stay with her sister for a while. She won't leave Wood. Of course if it is Wood, then she and the boys are probably safe."

Playing back her own words in her head, Willa blew out a breath. "I can't believe what I think sometimes, Ben. If it's Wood, if it's Jim, if it's Billy. Or one of your men. I've known most of them my whole life. And then I think, maybe Jesse Cooke was the last of it. Maybe it'll stop with him and we won't have to deal with it anymore. Thinking that way's like shoving Pickles and that girl aside.''

''Thinking that way's human.'' He touched her cheek. ''I've wondered if it might stop with Cooke.''

''But you don't believe it.''

''No, I don't believe it.''

''Is that why you're here? Is that why you're driving your herd up the same day I'm driving mine?''

He'd been afraid it hadn't been a very subtle move, and now he rubbed a hand over the scar on his chin. ''You could say I've got an investment in you. I look after what's mine.''

Her brows rose. ''I'm not yours, Ben.''

He bent down, gave her a quick, casual kiss. ''Look again,'' he suggested, and went after his coffee.

TWENTY-SIX

F ROM TESS'S JOURNAL:

*Driving cattle is in no way similar to driving a Mercedes
450 SL—which is a little something I believe I'll treat myself
to when I get back to the bright lights and big city.*

*Driving cattle is an adventure perhaps akin to whizzing
along the highway in a spiffy sports car. You go places, you
see things, and the wind is in your hair. But it is also a
painful business.*

*My butt is so sore I've got to sit on a pillow to write. I
suppose, all in all, it was worth it. The Rockies are a grab-
ber, absolutely. Even finding snow underfoot this late in the
year couldn't spoil it. The air's different in high country.
Purer is the closest I can come to describing it. It's like the
clearest of spring waters in a fine crystal glass.*

*We stopped on a rocky plateau and I swear I thought I
could see all the way to Nate's ranch.*

*It made me miss him a little—well, more than a little. An
odd feeling. I can't recall ever missing a man before. Sex,
sure, but that's a different matter.*

In any case, the cattle seem to drive themselves for the most part, trudging along with only the occasional complaint. Adam says it's because many of them have made the trip before and know the drill, and the others just tag along. Still, they make quite a noise with all that clopping and mooing, and the occasional maverick has to be rounded up.

I watched Will rope a cow and I was impressed. The woman looks more natural on horseback than she does on her own two feet. I'd have to say regal, though I'd never say it to her. Her head's quite big enough as it is. She's a natural boss, and I'd have to admit that's a necessary attribute in her position. She works like a stevedore, again admirable, but I don't appreciate her cracking the whip in my direction.

I suspect we meandered a bit on our way up. I have to give her credit for that as well. I have no doubt she lengthened the route for my and Lily's benefit. It was quite a trip. We saw elk and mule deer, moose, bighorn sheep, and huge, gorgeous birds.

I did not see a bear. I am in no way disappointed by this.

Lily took rolls of pictures. She's recovered so completely you could almost forget all the horror that happened to her. Almost. I think of scales when I think of Lily, with her balancing tragedy and happiness on either end. She's found a way to weight down that happiness end. I admire that, too.

But forgetting all the way just isn't possible. Beneath the tough, focused exterior, Will is a bundle of nerves. We've all homed in on the wedding, all seem determined to have nothing spoil it. But there's worry here. It's in the air.

On another front, I'm whipping through the rewrites on my script. Ira's very pleased with the deal, and the progress. I expect to be inundated with meetings when I get back to LA in the fall. And I finally decided to tell him about the book. He was pretty jazzed, which surprised me, so I shot off the first couple chapters to him to give him a taste. We'll see.

At the moment, I'm squeezing in writing time between wedding preparations. The shower's coming up, and we're

*all pretending Lily doesn't know we're planning one. Should
be a hoot.*

"SO WHAT ARE YOU MEN PLANNING FOR THE BACHELOR
party?" Tess sat on the corral fence at Nate's and watched
him take a yearling through his paces.

"Something dignified, of course."

"How many strippers?"

"Three. Any more isn't dignified." He reined in, backed
the yearling up, then squeezed gently with his knees. The
yearling broke into an easy trot. "That's the way. Smart
boy."

Look at him, Tess thought, all lanky and lean with his
hat pulled low and those long, narrow hands as sexy as a
concert pianist's.

He quite literally made her mouth water. "I ever tell you
how good you look on a horse, Lawyer Torrence?"

"A time or two." It still made heat crawl up his neck.
"But you can tell me again."

"You look good. When am I going to see you in court?"

Surprised, he circled the horse. "Didn't know you wanted
to."

Neither had she. "Well, I do. I like looking at you in
your lawyer suit, all sober and serious. I like looking at
you."

He slid off, looped the reins around the rail, and began
to uncinch the saddle. "Hasn't been much time for looking
or anything else just lately, has there?"

"Busy time. Only ten days until the wedding, and Lily's
parents are coming in tomorrow. After things settle, maybe
you can take me into town, let me watch you ride the court.
Then . . . we could stay in a hotel for the night and play."
She ran her tongue around her teeth. "Wanna play with me,
Nate?"

"Your rules or mine?"

"No rules at all." With a laugh, she hopped off the fence
and grabbed him into a hot, lengthy kiss. "I've missed
you."

"Have you?" That was progress he hadn't expected quite so soon. "That's nice."

She glanced toward the house, thought of bed. "I don't suppose we could . . ."

"I don't think Maria could stand the shock of that, middle of the day and all. Maybe you could stay the night."

"Mmm. Wish I could, but I'm already AWOL. And I don't like to stay away long, after what happened."

His eyes went cold as he turned to lift the saddle off the yearling. "I wish I'd been there sooner that night, to back Adam up."

"It wouldn't have mattered. There was nothing Adam or Will could do to stop it. Nothing you could've done if you'd been there."

"Maybe not." But he'd had some bad moments thinking of it, imagining it. Wondering what he would have done if it had been Tess with a gun at her head. Because the light had gone out of her eyes as well, he moved on impulse and swung up on the horse's bare back. "Come on, take a ride with me."

"Without a saddle?" She blinked, then laughed and stepped back. "I don't think so. I like having the horn to grab onto."

"Tenderfoot." He held out a hand. "Come on. You can grab me."

Intrigued but wary, Tess eyed the horse. "He's awfully big for a yearling."

"Just a baby and anxious to please." Nate cocked his head and waited for her to take the offered hand.

"All right. But I really hate falling off." She let him grip her hand and with little grace clambered on behind him. "Different," she decided, but found a definite advantage in being able to snuggle close behind Nate, her arms circling his waist. "Sexy. Adam rides bareback quite a lot. He looks like a god."

Nate chuckled, clucked the horse into a walk. "Puts you more in tune with your mount."

It also, Tess realized when they slid into a trot, put her more in tune with her lust. And when they smoothed out into a gallop she was grinning like a fool. "This is great. More."

"That's what you always say." He circled the corral again, enjoying the sensation of those firm, generous breasts pressed into his back. His eyes crossed when she slid her hands down below his belt.

"Figured as much," she said, when she found him hard. "Ever do it on horseback?"

"Nope." The idea provided a fascinating visual—Tess laid back in front of him on the horse's neck, her legs wrapped tight around his waist as they mated to the rhythm of the horse. "We'd break our necks when he caught the scent of sex and bucked us off."

"I'm ready to risk it. I really want you, Nate."

He stopped, steadied the horse, then turning, hauled her in front of him with a great deal of gasping and groping. "No." He could barely get the word out of his busy mouth as her fingers zoomed in on his belt buckle. "This'll have to hold us for now. Just hold on to me, Tess. Just hold on and let me kiss you awhile."

She would have been reckless, but he held her close, pinning her arms to her sides as he assaulted her mouth. Her hat fell off, landed in the dirt, and her heart went wild, the echoes of it pounding everywhere at once. Then it changed, everything changed and became gentle, sweet, pure as the air in high country.

From desperation to tenderness he eased her until her pulse slowed and went thick, until her throat ached from it and her eyes stung.

"I love you." He hadn't meant to say it, but it was too much, too huge to keep trapped inside. His lips formed the words against hers, slowly.

"What?" Dazed, dreaming, she stared into his eyes. "What did you say?"

"I'm in love with you."

She dropped out of her floaty state and hit reality with a thud. She'd heard the words before. They were easy for some to toss off, just another line. But not from him, she realized. Not from a man like Nate.

"That's getting a little carried away." She wanted to smile, keep it light. Couldn't. "Nate, we're just . . ."

"Lovers?" he added, and didn't bother to curse himself for finishing her sentence. "Convenient bed partners? No, we're not, Tess."

She took a steadying breath and spoke firmly. "I think we'd better get down."

Instead he took her chin in his hand so that her eyes stayed level with his. "I'm in love with you, have been for a while now. I'll make what adjustments I have to to make it work for you, but it comes down to this: I want you to stay with me, marry me, raise a family with me here."

The first shock paled beside the rest of it. "You know I can't possibly—"

"You got a while to get used to the idea." With this, he dismounted. "There's not much I've wanted in life," he said, studying her stunned face. "My law degree, this place, a good string of horses. I got them. Now I want you."

It helped, she thought, the unmitigated insult and arrogance of that helped shift shock into temper. "You may want to take notes, Lawyer Torrence. I'm not a law degree, a ranch, or a brood mare."

"No, you're not." A smile flirted around his mouth as he plucked her off the horse. "You're a woman, a tough-minded, ambitious, and frustrating woman. And you're going to be mine."

"Would you care to hear what I think of this sudden cowboy mentality of yours?"

"I've got a pretty good picture." He slid the bridle off the yearling, slapped its flank to send it trotting away. "You'd better get home, take some time to think it through."

"I don't need time to think it through."

"I'll give it to you anyway." He looked up at the sky. The sun was just beginning to drop toward the western peaks, blushing red against blue. "Going to rain tonight." He said it casually as he leaped over the fence and left Tess gaping after him.

· · ·

"I DON'T KNOW WHAT BUR'S UP YOUR BUTT," WILLA MUT-tered, "but yank it out. Lily's going to be back here with her folks any minute."

"You're not the only one who's allowed to have things on her mind." Tess crammed a petit four in her mouth.

The house was full of chattering women, gaily wrapped gifts, and white streamers. It had been Tess's idea to serve champagne punch for the wedding shower, and though Bess had clucked her tongue over it for the sake of form, she was enjoying a cup herself while she gossiped with neighbors.

Everybody's happy as clowns, Tess thought, and snagged another petit four. Celebrating the ridiculous idea of two people chaining themselves together for the rest of their lives. She pouted, debated another cake, then went for a cigarette instead.

No way was Nate Torrence going to make her split an-other pair of jeans. She grabbed a cup of punch and decided to get drunk instead.

By the time the bride-to-be came in, Tess had gulped down three cups and was feeling more celebratory. She got a kick out of the way Lily feigned surprise. The shower hadn't been a secret since the first invitation had been sent. Now there were gifts to be oohed and aahed over, every-thing from whisk brooms to peignoirs.

Tess watched Lily's mother blink back tears and slip out-side.

An interesting woman, Tess decided, pouring herself an-other cup. Attractive, well presented, well spoken. What the hell had she ever seen in a son of a bitch like Jack Mercy?

When Bess poured two cups and slipped out too, Tess shrugged and tried to work up the proper enthusiasm for a set of embroidered napkins.

"Here you go, Adele." Bess settled herself on the glider, handed Adele a cup while the woman dabbed at her eyes. "Been some time since we sat here."

"I didn't know how I would feel coming back. It's hardly changed."

"Oh, here and there. You haven't changed much your-self."

Vanity was a small weakness, and Adele automatically touched a hand to her carefully groomed hair. It was cut sleek and short, kept a subtle shade of deep blond.

"Lines," she said with a weak laugh. "I never know where they come from, but there are new ones in my mirror every morning."

"Just life." Bess took stock. Adele still had a pretty, almost delicate face, the features small and well proportioned. She'd kept in shape, too, Bess mused. Trim, easing toward lanky, and her eye for color and line hadn't changed either. She looked good in the rose-toned slacks and ivory blouse.

"You've got a fine daughter, Adele. You did a good job with her."

"I could've done better. I should have. Seeing her now, I look back to when she was a little girl. The hours I should have spent with her that I didn't."

"You had work, and your own life too."

"I did." To soothe herself, Adele sipped her drink. "And a lot of pain, the first few years anyway. I hated Jack Mercy more than I ever loved him, Bess."

"That's natural. He didn't do right by you or the girl. But I'd say you found the better man."

"Rob? He's a good man. Set in his ways, he always has been. But they're good ways." Her lips softened. They'd had a good life, she thought. "Rob's not, well, overtly affectionate, but he loves Lily. I wonder now if we didn't expect too much from her. If we both didn't. But we love her."

"It shows."

She rocked awhile in silence. "God, the view. I've never forgotten it. I missed this place. I've been happy back East—the green, the gentleness of the land. But I have missed this place."

"You'll come back, now that Lily's living here."

"Yes. We'll come back. Rob's enchanted. He loves to travel. We've avoided this part of the country, but now . . . He's down with Adam, looking at the horses." She sighed, smiled. "He's a good man too, isn't he, Bess? Lily's Adam."

"One of the finest I know, and he'd walk through fire for her."

"She's been through so much. When I think about it—"

"Don't." Bess covered Adele's hand with hers. "It's behind her now. Just like Jack Mercy's behind you. She's going to be a beautiful bride, and a happy wife."

"Oh." It brought the tears again. They were falling down her cheeks when Willa stepped out.

"Excuse me." Automatically, she started back inside.

"No, don't." Sniffling, Adele rose, reached out a hand. "I'm just being sentimental. I haven't had a chance to really talk to you. Every letter Lily wrote me was full of you, and Tess."

A woman's tears always disarmed her. Willa shifted, tried to smile. "I'm surprised there was room with Adam in there."

"You have the same eyes, you and your brother." Dark and wise, Adele thought. And steady. "I knew your mother, a little. She was a beautiful woman."

"Thank you."

"I've been frightened." Adele cleared her throat. "I realize this isn't a good time to bring it up, but I've been so worried. I know Lily toned down a great deal of what's happened here in her letters and calls to me. But when Jesse—when those things happened with Jesse, there were reports back East. I wanted to say that I'm still worried, but I feel easier now that I've met you, and Adam."

"She's stronger than you think. Than any of us thought."

"You may be right," Adele agreed, then braced herself. "And I want to thank you for your hospitality, for inviting Rob and me to stay here in your home. I know it must be awkward for you."

"I thought it would be. It's not. My sister's parents are always welcome at Mercy."

"Not much of Jack in you." Adele paled, appalled at herself. "I'm sorry."

"Don't be." Willa's eyes shifted as she spotted the gleam of sun on chrome. And her lips curved slowly. "And here comes the next surprise.'' She flicked a glance at Adele. ''I hope this one's not awkward for you.''

''What have you done, girl?'' Bess asked.

Willa only continued to smile, and poked her head back inside. ''Hey, Hollywood, come on out here a minute.''

''What?'' Carrying a cup in one hand, Tess wandered to the door. ''We're playing parlor games. How many words can you make out of 'honeymoon'? I think I'm ahead. There's a basket of bath stuff riding on it.''

''I've got a better prize for you.''

Tess looked over, cleared her fuzzy eyes enough to recognize Nate's rig as it pulled up. ''Don't wanna talk to him now. Arrogant cowboy lawyer. Just tell him I'm . . . Oh, Jesus bleeding Christ.''

''Don't you blaspheme at a wedding shower,'' Bess ordered, then popped up with a mile-wide grin as the side door of the rig opened and a vision burst out. ''Louella Mercy, as I live and breathe, you're a sight for sore eyes.''

''I'm a sight, period.'' With a braying laugh, Louella raced forward on red stiletto heels and embraced her staggered daughter. ''Surprise, baby.'' She kissed Tess, smudged away the smear of lipstick from her cheek, then whirled to catch Bess in a bear hug. ''Still kicking butt around here?''

''As best I can.''

''And this must be Jack's youngest.'' She twirled to Willa, squeezed hard enough to crack her ribs. ''Lord, you look just like your mama. Never saw anyone to match Mary Wolfchild for straight good looks.''

''I—thanks.'' Dazzled, Willa only stared. Why, the woman looked like a glamour queen and smelled like a perfume counter. ''I'm so glad you could come,'' she added, and meant it. ''I'm so glad to meet you.''

''That goes double for me, honey. Could've knocked me over with a feather when I got your letter inviting me out.'' Keeping an arm tight around Willa's shoulders, she turned and beamed at Adele. ''I'm Louella, wife number one.''

A little stunned, Adele stared. Was the woman actually

wearing a gold lamé blouse in the middle of the afternoon? "I'm Lily's mother."

"Wife number two." With another earsplitting laugh, Louella embraced Adele like a sister. "Well, the bastard had good taste in women, didn't he? Where's your girl? Must take more after you than Jack, as Tess tells me she's pretty as a picture and sweet as they come. I've got presents."

"Should I take them in for you, Louella?" At the base of the steps, Nate stood grinning, Louella's wriggling pocket dogs in his arms.

Focusing on him fully for the first time, Tess all but writhed in horror. "Oh, God, Mom, you didn't bring Mimi and Maurice!"

"Of course I did. Couldn't leave my precious babies at home all alone." She took them from Nate and made kissy noises. "Is this a prime hunk, ladies?" She gave Nate a proprietary kiss on the cheek and left a clear imprint of her lips behind. "I swear my heart's been going pitty-pat ever since I laid eyes on him. You just take everything right on inside, sweetie."

"Yes, ma'am." He shot Tess a quick, amused look before he turned back to unload the rig.

"So what are we all doing out here?" Louella demanded. "I hear there's a party going on, and I could sure use a drink. You don't mind if I take a look around the place, do you, Willa?"

"Not at all. I'd love to show you around myself. Nate, Louella's things go in the room next to Tess's. The pink room."

"Wait until Mary Sue sees you," Bess began as she led Louella inside. "You remember Mary Sue Rafferty, don't you?"

"Is she the one with the buck teeth or the one with the lazy eye?"

Carefully Tess set her empty cup on the porch rail. "Your idea?"

"Mine and Lily's." Willa beamed. "We wanted to surprise you."

"You did. You definitely did. And we'll have a nice talk

about it later.'' Tess grabbed Willa by the shirtfront. "A nice, long talk about it.''

"Okay. I'm going to make sure she gets that drink.''

"Your ma sure packs for the duration.'' Nate hauled the last of five suitcases out of the back of the rig. Each one of them weighed like a yard of wet concrete.

"She packs nearly that for a weekend in Vegas.''

"She sure makes a statement.''

Mortification aside, Tess squared her shoulders and prepared to defend her mother. "Meaning?''

"Meaning she's right there, no pretenses. It's all Louella. After five minutes, I was crazy about her.'' Curious, he angled his head. "What did you think I meant?''

She moved her tense shoulders but couldn't quite relax them. "People have varying reactions when it comes to my mother.''

He nodded slowly. "Apparently you do. You ought to be ashamed of yourself.'' And while she was gaping, he carried two of the suitcases past her.

With a snarl, Tess hauled one up herself and followed him. "Just what was that supposed to mean?'' She huffed her way up the stairs. Louella didn't believe in packing light.

"I mean you've got one in a million there.'' He set the cases on the bed, turned, and walked out.

Tess dumped the third case on the bed, flexed her arms, and waited. "I know what I've got,'' she said the minute he walked back in with the rest of the luggage. "She's my mother. Who else would come to a wedding shower in Montana wearing Capri pants and gold lamé? Oh, wipe that lipstick off your cheek. You look like an idiot.''

She struggled with the straps of a suitcase, flipped the top back, and rolled her eyes at the contents. "Who else would pack twenty pairs of high heels to spend a couple weeks on a cattle ranch? And this.'' She pulled out a sheer lavender robe trimmed in purple feathers. "Who wears things like this?''

He eyed the robe as he tucked his bandanna back in his pocket. "Suits her. You're too concerned with appearances, Tess. That's your biggest problem.''

"With appearances? For God's sake, she paints her dogs' toenails. She has concrete swans in her front yard. She sleeps with men younger than I am."

"And I imagine they consider themselves lucky." He leaned against one of the bed's four posts. "Zack flew her to my spread and nearly wrecked his plane, he was laughing so hard. He told me she kept him howling since they took off from Billings. She asked me if she could come back and see my horses later. She wanted to see them, but she couldn't wait to get here and see you first. Thirty seconds after she hugged the life out of me, we were friends. She talked about you most all the way here, made me tell her half a dozen times that you were all right, safe. Happy. I guess it took her about ten miles to figure out I was in love with you. Then I had to stop so she could fix her makeup because it made her cry."

"I know she loves me." And she was ashamed. "I love her. It's just—"

"I'm not finished," Nate said coolly. "She told me she didn't hold anything against Jack Mercy because he'd given her something special. And having you changed her life. It made her a mother and turned her into a businesswoman. She was glad to be coming back, to take another look, to meet your sisters. To see you here and know you were getting what you had a right to."

He straightened, kept his eyes on hers. "So I'll tell you what my reaction is to Louella Mercy, Tess. Pure admiration—for a woman who took a kick in the face and stood right back up again. Who raised a daughter on her own, made a home for her, ran a business to see that her child never went without. Who gave that daughter backbone and pride and a heart. I don't care if she wears cellophane to church, and neither should you."

He walked out on her. Tess sat on the edge of the bed feeling a little drunk and very weepy. Carefully she laid the robe over the bed, then rose and began to unpack for her mother.

When Louella bounced in fifteen minutes later, the chore

was nearly half done. "What in the world are you fooling with this for? We're having a party."

"You never finish unpacking. I thought I'd give you a head start."

"Don't fuss with it now." Louella grabbed her hands. "I'm working on getting Bess plowed. She'll sing when she's plowed."

"Really?" Tess set aside a sundress in eye-popping cerise. "I wouldn't want to miss that." Then she turned and laid her head on Louella's shoulder. A shoulder, she thought, that had always been there, without question, without qualification. "I'm glad to see you, Mom. I'm glad you came." Her voice hitched. "Really glad."

"What's all this?"

"I don't know." Tess sniffed and stood back. "Stuff. Things. I don't know."

"It's been a scary time for you." Louella took out a lace-trimmed hanky and dried her daughter's face.

"Yeah, in a lot of ways. I guess I'm shakier than I realized. I'll get through it."

"Of course you will. Now come on down and join the party." With her arm around Tess's waist, Louella started out. "Later, we'll pop open a bottle of French bubbly and catch up."

"I'd like that." Tess's arm slid around Louella's waist in turn. "I'd like that a lot."

"Then you can fill me in on that long, cool drink of water you've got your eye on."

"Nate doesn't like me very much right now." It was going to make her weepy again to think of it. "I'm not sure I like me very much either."

"Well, that can be fixed." Louella paused on the stairs, listened to the sounds of women. "I like both of you."

"I should have asked you to come," Tess murmured. "I should have asked you to visit months ago. It shouldn't have been Willa inviting you. Partly I didn't because I thought you'd be uncomfortable. And partly I didn't because I thought I would be. I'm sorry."

"Sweetie, you and me, we're as different as Budweiser

and Moët. Doesn't mean they don't both have their points. God knows, I've scratched my head over you as often as you've scratched yours over me.''

Louella gave Tess a quick squeeze. "Listen to that hen chatter. Reminds me of my chorus girl days. I've always had a fondness for women carrying on. Can't be uncomfortable with that, or with a wedding in the works. And I sure do like your sisters, honey.''

"So do I.'' Tess firmed her chin. "Nothing's going to spoil the wedding for us.''

H E WAS THINKING THE SAME THING. HE COULD HEAR THE sound of women's laughter, of women's voices, pretty as music. It made him smile. He liked to think of Lily inside, in the center of it, soft and sweet. She'd be dead if not for him, and he'd been hugging his secret heroics to his heart for weeks.

He'd saved her life, and he wanted to see her married.

When those pretty images paled, he could always bring the picture of what he'd done to Jesse Cooke to the front of his mind. Sometimes he liked to fall asleep with that replaying through his head. A fine, colorful dream, scented with blood.

He'd been very careful since then, and when the lust for killing became overpowering, he cooled it in the hills and buried his prey. It was odd how much stronger that lust was now, more than the need for food, for sex. Soon, he knew, soon, it wouldn't be satisfied by rabbit or deer or a calf from pasture.

It would have to be human.

But he would hold it back, he would control it until after Lily was safely married. He was bound to her now, and where he was bound, he was loyal.

He feared she was worried that something would happen. But he had fixed that as well. He'd printed the note with great care, pondered the words like an exercise. Now that he had written it, now that he had slipped it under her kitchen door, he was lighter of heart.

She wouldn't worry now. She would know someone was

looking out for her. Now he could relax and enjoy the
sounds of the female ritual. Now he could dream of wedding
bells that would herald the breaking of his fast for blood.

As the sky washed with red over the western peaks and
the party broke up, some of the women who drove past
waved. He lifted a hand in return. And he wondered whom
he would choose to hunt when the time was right.

TWENTY-SEVEN

"I THINK YOU SHOULD SEE THIS."

Her brow arched, Willa took the sheet of notepaper from Lily's hand. She'd been ready to turn in after a long day of socializing when Lily had come to her room. It took only the first glance to wash the fatigue away.

I don't want you to worry. I won't let anything happen to you, or Adam, or your sisters. If I had known what J C was up to, I would have killed him sooner, before he scared you. You can rest easy now and have a nice wedding. I'll be there, looking out for you and yours. Best wishes, a friend.

"Christ." The chill sent a shudder through her. "How did you get this?"

"It was under the door in the kitchen."

"You showed it to Adam?"

"Yes, right away. I don't know how to feel about this, Will. The person who sent this killed Jesse. And the others." She took the paper back from Willa, folded it. "Yet he seems to be trying to reassure me. There's no threat here, and yet I feel threatened."

"Of course you do. He was practically in your house." She began to pace, her stockinged feet soundless. "Goddamn it. Goddamn it! We're back to the center again. This was put there today, dozens of people coming and going. It could have been anyone. No matter what I do I can't narrow it down."

"He doesn't mean to hurt me, or you, or Tess." Lily drew a calming breath. "Or Adam. I'm holding on to that. But, Will, he'll be at the wedding. He'll be there."

"You're to let me worry about this. I mean it," she continued, putting her hands firmly on Lily's shoulders. "Give me the note. I'll deal with it, see that it gets to the police. You're getting married in a few days. That's all you have to think about."

"I'm not going to tell my parents. I thought about it, talked it over with Adam, and decided not to tell anyone but you. Whoever you think should know is fine with me. But I don't want to upset my mother and father."

"This won't touch them." Willa took the note, set it on her dresser. "Lily, the wedding means almost as much to me as it does to you. I've got, I guess you could say, a double interest." She tried to smile, but it wouldn't quite gel. "Not everyone can say their brother and sister are getting married. At least not in Montana. Just concentrate on being a bride. It'd mean a lot to me."

"I'm not afraid. I don't seem to be afraid of much anymore." She pressed her cheek to Willa's. "I love you."

"Yeah. Same goes."

She closed the door behind Lily, then stared at the folded note. What the hell was she going to do now? The answer wasn't going to bed for a good night's sleep. Instead, she picked up her boots and walked to the phone.

"Ben? Yeah, yeah, we saved you some cake. Listen, I need a favor. You want to call that cop who's working this case and ask him to meet me at your place? I have something I need to show him, and I don't want to do it here. No." She cradled the phone between her ear and shoulder, tugged on a boot. "I'll explain when I get there. I'm on my way. I don't have time for that," she said when he started to argue. ''I'll lock the doors of the rig and carry a loaded rifle on the seat, but I'm leaving now.''

She hung up before he could shout at her.

''DAMN, STUBBORN, PIGHEADED WOMAN.''

Willa had stopped counting the number of times Ben had called her that, or a similar name, over the past two hours. ''It had to be dealt with, and it's done.'' She appreciated the wine he'd poured her, though it had been a surprise. She hadn't thought Ben went in for wine, or that he would be playing host after the session with the police.

''I'd have come for you.''

''You damn near did,'' she reminded him. ''You were nearly halfway to Mercy when I ran into you. I told you I'd be all right. You read the note yourself. It wasn't a threat.''

''The fact that it was written at all is threat enough. Lily must be frantic.''

''No, actually, she was very calm. More concerned that her parents not be upset by it. We're not telling them about it. I guess I'll have to tell Tess. She'll tell Nate, but that's as far as we'll take it.''

She sipped again while he paced. She supposed his quarters suited a muscle-flexing type of man. The walls were paneled in honey-toned wood, the floors matching and uncluttered by carpet or rug. The furniture was big, heavy, and deeply cushioned in unadorned navy. There wasn't a single fussy pillow or feminine knickknack in sight.

There were, though, framed photos of his family crowding the pine mantel over the fireplace, a set of antique spurs, and a pretty hunk of turquoise on a shelf where books leaned against each other drunkenly.

There was a hoof pick tossed on a table along with a bone-handled pocketknife and some loose change.

Simple, basic. Ben, she decided, then decided further that she had let him pace and complain long enough.

''I appreciate you helping me handle this right away. We could get lucky and the cops could do cop things with the note and figure out who wrote it.''

''Sure, if this was a Paramount production.''

"Well, it's the best I can do for now." She set the half-full glass aside and rose. "I've got a wedding in less than a week and a houseful of company, so—"

"Where do you think you're going?"

"Home. Like I said, I've got a houseful of company, and morning comes early." She took out her keys; he snatched them out of her hand. "Look, McKinnon—"

"No, you look." He tossed her keys over his shoulder, and they rattled into a corner. "You're not going anywhere tonight. You're staying right here where I can keep an eye on you."

"I've got the midnight shift."

He merely picked up the phone, punched in numbers. "Tess? Yeah, it's Ben. Willa's here. She's staying. Call Adam and tell him to adjust guard duty accordingly. She'll be back in the morning." He hung up without waiting for an assent. "Done."

"You don't run Mercy, Ben, or me. I do." She took a step toward her keys and found the room revolving as she was slung over his shoulder. "What the hell's gotten into you?"

"I'm taking you to bed. I handle you better there."

She swore at him, kicked, and when that failed wiggled into position to take a bite out of his back. He hissed through his teeth, but kept going.

"Girls bite," he said when he dumped her on his bed. "I expected better from you."

"If you think I'm going to have sex with you when you treat me like a maverick calf, you're dead wrong."

His back throbbed where her teeth had dug in just enough to make him mean. "Let's see about that." He shoved her back, pinned her, and handcuffed her hands over her head. "Fight me." It was a pure dare delivered in steel tones. "We never tried that before. I might like it."

"You son of a bitch." She bucked, twisted, and when he lowered his mouth to hers, bit again. He rolled with her, careful to keep her hands—and nails—away from his exposed flesh.

Her aim with her knee was off just enough to make him grateful, close enough to make him sweat.

He used his free hand to rip her shirt, then the thin cotton beneath, but didn't touch her. It was the grapple, the excuse for violence he thought they both needed to scare away the fears.

And when she lay still beneath him, panting, her eyes closed, he thought he knew what they both needed next.

"Turn me loose, you coward."

"I'll tie you to the headboard if I have to, Willa, but you're staying. And when we're done, you'll sleep. Really sleep." He touched his lips to her temple, then her cheek, her jaw in a sudden shift to tender.

"Let me go."

He lifted his head. Her hair was tumbled over the dark green corduroy spread of his bed. There were flags of angry color riding high across her cheekbones. Her eyes burned so hot he was surprised his skin didn't blister.

"I can't." He lowered his forehead to hers, wondering if either of them would be able to accept it. "I just can't."

His mouth found hers again, quietly, slowly, deeply, until she felt something inside of her quake to the point of shivering apart. "Don't." She turned her face away, tried to struggle back to level. "Don't kiss me that way."

"It's rough on both of us." He turned her face back, saw her eyes were damp and dark now, the heat burned out of them. "It may get rougher yet." His mouth met hers again, lingered so that the shock swept through him. "God, I need you, Will. How the hell did this happen?"

He dragged her where he was bound to go, making her head reel and her heart break open to pour out secrets she'd kept even from herself. She sobbed out his name, then simply lost her grip on the slippery ledge she'd clung to for longer than she'd known.

When he lifted his head again, she stared into his face, one she'd known her whole life, and saw fresh and new. "Let go of my hands, Ben." She didn't struggle, didn't shout, but only said again, "Let go of my hands."

So he did, gentling his grip, then releasing it. When he

started to lever himself away, those hands came to his face, framed it, and brought him back. "Kiss me again," she murmured. "The way I told you not to."

So he did, deepening the moment, then drowning in it.

He pushed aside her tattered shirt to find her, claim her, his hands sure and slow. She surrendered to it, the sensation of those hands gliding, scraping, stroking. Gave in to it, the taste of that mouth drawing and drinking from hers. Yielded against it, the heat of that body, the hard angles pressed into the curves of hers.

Whatever he wanted tonight, she would give. Whatever he seemed to need, she'd find. The quiet, unspoken desperation seeped from him into her, and the pleasure of knowing she possessed whatever it was he searched for.

The violence was spent. Now there were only sighs and murmurs, the whisper of flesh sliding over flesh, the quick moans of surprised delight.

The moon rose, unnoticed, and the night birds sang to the light. Wind, gentle with full spring, teased the curtains and wafted like water over their heated skin.

There was the long, long groan of that first lazy climax, one that shimmered through her as silver as the moonlight and left her glowing. He drew her up so they were torso to torso, so that he could lose his hands in her hair, sweep the weight of it back from her face. When her lips curved, so did his.

He held her like that, just held her, with their hearts pounding together, her head on his shoulder, his hands in her hair. And still holding her, he laid her back and slipped inside her.

Slow and deep, so that each thrust was like a velvet slap. He watched her come, watched it happen, the darkening eyes, the trembling lips, the sudden racking shudder. The silky movements quickened, driving them both toward the brink.

This time when she fell, he let her drag him with her.

IT WAS A PERFECT DAY FOR A WEDDING, LACED WITH WARM breezes that teased the scent of pine down to the valley, stirred the perfume of the potted flowers Tess had ordered arranged in banks around the porches and terraces of the main house, Adam and Lily's house, even the outbuildings.

There wasn't a hint of rain, or the hail that had come so fiercely forty-eight hours before and sent Tess and Lily into a tailspin of worry. The willow tree by the pond that Jack Mercy had ordered built, stocked with Japanese carp, then forgotten, was delicately green.

There were tables with striped umbrellas, a snowy white canopy to shade the wedding feast, and a wooden platform that the men had cheerfully constructed to stand as a dance floor.

It was a perfect day, Willa mused, if she ignored the fact that cops would be sprinkled among the guests.

"Gosh, look at you." Misty-eyed, Willa reached up to adjust the tie of Adam's tux. "You look like a picture out of a magazine." Unable to keep her hands off him, she brushed at his shirtfront. "Big day, huh?"

"The biggest." He caught a tear off her lashes, pretended to put it in his pocket. "I'll save it. You hardly ever let them fall."

"The way they keep backing up on me, I have a feeling plenty are going to fall today." She took the tiny lily of the valley boutonniere—his own request—and carefully pinned it on for him. "I know I'm supposed to let your best man do all this, but Ben's got those big hands."

"Yours are shaking."

"I know." She laughed a little. "You'd think I was getting married. This whole thing didn't make me nervous until this morning when I had to put this getup on."

"You look beautiful." He took her hand, laid it on his cheek. "You've been in my heart, Willa, since before you were born. You'll always be there."

"Oh, God." Her eyes welled again. She gave him a hasty kiss, then whirled. "I've got to go." In her blind rush out the door, she barreled into Ben. "Move."

"Just hold on, let me look." Ignoring the teary eyes, he turned her in a circle, admiring the flow and fit of the slim blue gown. "Well, well, well. Pretty as a bluebell in a meadow." He brushed a tear from her cheek. "With dew still on it."

"Oh, save your fancy talk and go do what you're supposed to do with Adam. Make man noises and tell bad jokes or something."

"That's what I'm here for." He kissed her before she could wriggle free. "The first dance is mine. And the last," he added, as she dashed away.

It wasn't fair, Willa told herself as she hurried toward the main house. It wasn't fair that he had her stirred up this way. She had too much on her mind, too much to do. She damn well didn't want to be in love with Ben McKinnon.

Probably wasn't, she thought, and swiped a hand under her nose.

It was just so embarrassingly female, this reaction of hers. Imagining herself in love with him just because they went to bed together, because he said those fancy words now and again or looked at her in a certain way.

She'd have to get over it, that was all. Get herself back in gear before she made herself the biggest joke in the county. Or crowded her mind with it so she started doing something stupid like pining away, or dogging his heels, or picturing herself in a wedding dress.

She stopped outside the door, pressed a hand to her fluttering stomach. As composed as possible, she strode inside and was met by the sight of Adele weeping and leaning on Louella's arm as they came down the steps.

"What's wrong? Did something happen?" Willa was braced to rush to the gun rack when Louella smiled.

"Nothing's wrong. Adele's just having a mother-of-the-bride moment."

"She looked so beautiful, didn't she, Louella? Like an angel. My baby."

"The most beautiful bride I've ever seen. You and me, honey, we're going to open a bottle of that bubbly early and drink to her." She patted Adele as they walked. "Will, you go on up. Lily asked if you would when you came back."

"I should find Rob."

"Men just don't get moments like this, Addy." Louella

steered her toward the kitchen. "We'll hunt him up after we've toasted the bride. A time or two. Get upstairs, Will. Lily's waiting for you."

"All right." But she had to shake her head a moment, baffled and amused by the bond that these two very different wives of Jack Mercy had forged.

She was still shaking it when she opened the door to Lily's temporary bedroom and was struck dumb.

"Isn't it great?" Tess bubbled over as she fussed with the veil. "Isn't she fabulous?"

"Oh, my—oh, Lily. You look like a fairy tale. Like a princess."

"I wanted the white gown." Dazzled by herself, Lily turned in front of the cheval glass. The woman who beamed back at her was beautiful, draped in billowing skirts of white satin, nipped into a bodice romantic with lace and tiny gleaming pearls. "I know it's my second marriage, but—"

"No, it's not." Tess brushed a hand down the long, snug sleeves of the bridal gown. "It's the only one that matters, so it's your first."

"My first." Lily smiled, touched her fingers to the veil that drifted over her shoulders. "I'm not even nervous. I was sure I would be, but I'm not."

"I've got something." Nervous enough for all of them, Willa brought out the small velvet box she'd held behind her back. "You don't have to use them. You've probably already got the old and new and all of that stuff taken care of. But when Tess told me there were pearls on your dress, I remembered these. They were my grandmother's. Our grandmother's," she corrected, and held the box out.

Lily could only sigh as she opened the lid. The pearls were fashioned into fragile eardrops with old-fashioned and lovely filigree settings. Without hesitation she removed the earrings she'd bought to match the dress and replaced them with the gift.

"They're so beautiful. They're so perfect."

"They look good." Made for the delicate, like Lily, she thought with a tangle of pride and envy. Not the sturdy like herself. "I figured she'd like you to have them. I didn't know her or anything, but . . . hell, I'm going to start leaking again.''

''We all are, but I can fix that.'' Tess stuffed a tissue into Willa's hand. ''I stole a bottle of champagne and hid it in the bathroom so Bess wouldn't know. I'd say we deserve a glass.''

Willa chuckled as Tess hurried into the adjoining bath. ''Takes after her ma.''

''Thank you, Willa.'' Lily touched the drops at her ears. ''Not just for these, for everything.''

''Don't start on me, Lily. I'm running out of fingers to plug the dam. I've got a reputation around here, and it's not as a sniveler.'' She heard the pop of the cork echo off the bathroom tile with great relief. ''The men figure out I'm a soft touch, there'll be no living with them.''

''Here we go.'' Tess brought in three flutes and a bottle foaming at the lip. ''What'll we drink to?'' She poured generously, passed out glasses. ''To true love and connubial bliss?''

''No, first . . .'' Lily lifted her glass. ''To the ladies of Mercy.'' She touched her glass to Willa's, Tess's. ''We've come a long way in a short time.''

''That I can drink to.'' Tess lifted a brow. ''Will?''

''So can I.'' Willa bumped the rim of her flute against Tess's, grinned at the celebratory ring of crystal. Leave it to Hollywood to pick the best glasses.

Smiling, Lily touched the glass to her lips. ''But I can only take a sip. Alcohol isn't good for the baby.''

''Baby?'' Tess and Will choked in unison.

Savoring the moment, Lily wet just the tip of her tongue with the champagne. ''I'm pregnant.''

LATER, WILLA WOULD THINK SHE'D NEVER SEEN ANYTHING more magical than Lily gliding across the dusty ranch road in her fairy-tale dress on the arm of the man who had become her father, toward the man who became her husband.

And as the vows were said and the promises made, she let herself forget there was anything in the air but beauty. And as the first kiss was exchanged between husband and wife and the cheers rose up, she cheered along.

She thought of the child, and the future.

"How far'd you travel this time?" Ben murmured in her ear.

Startled, she looked up and nearly stumbled over his feet. "What?"

"You keep going away."

"Oh. You know I have to concentrate when I'm dancing. I lose the count."

"Wouldn't if you'd let a man do the leading and just go along. Anyway, that's not it." He eased her closer. "You worried about him being here?"

"Of course I am. I keep looking at faces that I know, people I think I know, and wondering. If it wasn't for this damn will, Adam and Lily could go off for a couple weeks on a real honeymoon. I'd have two less to worry about."

"If it wasn't for the damn will they might not have gotten as far as postponing a honeymoon," he reminded her. "Put it aside, Will. Nothing's going to happen here today."

"I mostly have. They look so happy." She turned her head so that she could see the bride and groom again, circling in each other's arms. "Funny, a year ago they'd never met. And now they're married."

"And starting a family."

This time she did trip. "How do you know?"

"Adam told me." He grinned and, since he was tired of having his feet trounced on, led her over to the buffet table. "I think if he was any happier he'd have to split in two parts to hold it."

"I want them to stay that way." She resisted reaching down to pat the derringer she had strapped to her thigh. It was a pitiful, girlish weapon, but she felt better knowing it was there. "You'd better start spreading yourself out, Ben, dancing with some of the ladies here. People are going to talk otherwise."

He chuckled, lifted her chin. For someone as clear-eyed as Willa, she was dead blind when it came to herself. "Darling, people already are." He enjoyed the way she scowled at that, scanning the crowd as if she would catch someone whispering behind a hand. "Doesn't bother me any."

"I don't like people gossiping over their fences about me." She jerked her chin toward Tess and Nate. "What are they saying about that?"

"That Nate's caught himself a slippery one, and he'll have to be sure-handed to hold on. Now, there's a woman who can dance." He snagged two glasses from a passing waiter, gestured with one toward Louella.

She was poured into a hot-pink dress and kicking up her skyscraper heels with Ben's father. At least a dozen cowboys pounded their feet and waited their turn. "That's your father."

"Yep."

"Look at him go."

"He'll be sore for a week, but he'll be happy."

Laughing, Willa grabbed Ben's hand and hustled over for a better view. As they watched, a cowboy from a neighboring ranch cut in and spun Louella into a spirited two-step. Stu McKinnon took out his bandanna and mopped his flushed face.

"She'll outlast all of them," Tess predicted.

Nate winked at Ben and watched Stu hobble off for a beer. "She teach you how to dance like that?"

"I haven't had enough to drink yet to dance like that." Taking Willa's glass, Tess drank deep, handed back the empty. "Give me time."

"Oh, I'm a patient man. Best wedding I've been to in my life, Will. You and the ladies have done yourselves proud." Then he grunted when Louella slammed into him.

"Your turn, handsome."

"Louella, I couldn't keep up with you if I had four feet. You must keep everything hopping at that restaurant of yours."

"Restaurant, hell." She howled and grabbed his hands. "I run a strip joint, honey. Now, let me show you some moves."

"A strip joint?" Willa arched an eyebrow as Nate was dragged onto the dance floor.

"Oh, shit." Tess sighed long and hard. "Get me another drink, Ben. I need it."

"Coming up."

"A strip joint?" Willa repeated.

"So what? It's a living."

"What's it like? I mean, do they take everything off and dance around buck naked?" Her eyes popped wide, not in shock but fascination. "Does Louella—"

"No." Tess grabbed the glass from Ben, drank again. "At least, not since she bought her own place."

"I've never been to one." And wouldn't it be interesting, Willa mused. "Does she have men, too? Naked dancing men?"

"Oh, good God." Tess passed the drink to Willa. "Only on ladies' night. I'm going to rescue Nate before she puts him in traction."

"Ladies' night." The very idea was marvelous to Will. "I guess I'd pay to see a man dance naked." Speculating, she turned her head, shot Ben a look.

"No, not for any amount of money."

She thought she could come up with another kind of payment and, laughing, slid an arm around his waist and watched the show.

HE WATCHED TOO. AND WAS HAPPY. THE BRIDE WAS BEAUtiful, glowing, just as a bride should be in her white gown and veil. The music was loud, and food and drink were plentiful.

It made him feel sentimental, heart strong and proud all at once.

The day had happened because of him, and he hugged that knowledge, and the giddy pleasure of it, to himself. There had been so much out of his control, all of his life, just beyond his reach. But he'd accomplished this.

Perhaps no one could ever know. He might have to keep the secret all of his life. Like a hero in a book—a kind of Robin Hood who took no personal credit.

They'd see about that.

Saving Lily had changed his direction, his purpose. But not his means.

It amused him that the police were wandering through the crowds of guests. Looking for him. Thinking they could spot him.

They never would.

He imagined himself going on for years, forever. Killing for pleasure. Strictly for pleasure now. Revenge, even harbored resentments, seemed very pale and weak beside pleasure.

Someone bumped into him. A pretty woman, flirting. He flirted back, making her laugh and blush, leading her into a dance.

And thinking, all the while wondering if she might be the next one.

Her pretty red hair would make a nice trophy.

TWENTY-EIGHT

He got a redheaded whore because she reminded him of the pretty redheaded girl he'd danced with at Lily's wedding. A whore wasn't much of a challenge, and he was disappointed in that.

But he'd waited so long.

He'd waited, considerately, until Lily's parents and Tess's mother had gone on home. It hadn't seemed right to him to cause all that excitement with company around.

Lily's folks had stayed on a week after the wedding, and Louella ten days. Everybody agreed they were going to miss Louella particularly with her big, wide laugh, her knee-slapping jokes.

And those tight skirts she liked to wear.

The woman was a caution, and he hoped she came back to visit real soon. He felt a tie to her now, to all of them. The in-laws and the outlaws, as his ma used to say. That had always made him laugh.

The in-laws and the outlaws.

But now the company had cleared out, and the ranch was back to routine. The weather was holding fine, and he was pleased by it. The crops were coming along well, though they could use some rain. But God knew, and so did he, that rain in Montana was usually feast or famine.

There'd been some thunder headed to the west a time or two, but June had stayed bone-dry thus far. The streams were running well, and the snowmelt was plentiful, so he wasn't worried.

The cattle were fattening in pasture, with the spring calves coming along just as they should. There'd been some elk nosing around, which was always a worry. Damn varmints tore up the fences and could carry disease into the herd, but Willa stayed on top of those matters.

He'd studied on her new ideas, the reseeding of natural grass, the gradual cutting back of chemicals and growth hormones and found that he approved. He'd decided that most anything she did that the old man hadn't, he approved of.

It had taken him some time, and some hard soul-searching, but he now believed it had been right and just that she'd been given the reins of Mercy. It still burned that McKinnon and Torrence had a say in things, at least for a few more months, but Willa handled them well enough, too.

He'd come to care for Lily and Tess, but blood was thicker than water, he'd always said. He now visualized both of them settled on Mercy, all the family rooted on the ranch.

Family stuck by family. He'd been taught that from the cradle, had done his best to live by it. It had only been grief and rage that had caused him to want to bring them pain, as he had pain. But now he'd put that solidly at the old man's door, where it belonged.

He'd left a sign there too, one that had made him weep and laugh all at once.

Now it was time for bigger game, so he hunted the red-headed whore.

He picked her up in Bozeman, a twenty-dollar street hooker he didn't figure would be missed. She was bone-thin and dumb as a post, but she had a mouth like a suction cup and knew how to use it. When they were in the cab of his rig and her face was buried in his lap she worked off the first twenty, and he ran his fingers through her long red hair.

It was probably dyed, but that didn't matter. It was a fine bright color, and it was clean. Dreaming of what was to come, he laid his head back, closed his eyes, and let her earn her keep.

"You're hung like a bull, cowboy," she said when it was done. "I shoulda charged you by the inch." It was her standard line after a blow job and usually earned a quick grin if not a modest tip. She wasn't disappointed when he flashed his teeth and bumped his hips up to reach for his wallet.

"I got another fifty here, sweetheart. Let's take a little ride."

She was cautious, a woman in her profession had to be. But her gaze latched greedily on the dead president he held between forefinger and thumb. "Where to?"

"I'm a country boy, towns crowd me. Let's find us a nice quiet spot and we'll set the springs in this old rig creaking." When she hesitated, he reached out, twirled her hair around his finger. "You sure are pretty. What'd you say your name was?"

Mostly johns didn't care about names, and she liked him better for asking. "It's Suzy."

"How about it, Suzy Q? Want to take a ride with me?"

He seemed harmless, and she did have the loaded twenty-five-caliber pistol in her bag. She smiled, her thin face going sly. "You gotta wear a slicker, cowboy."

"Sure." He'd no more have dipped his wick into a street whore without protection than slit his own wrists. "Can't be too careful these days."

With a wink, he watched his fifty disappear into her shiny vinyl handbag. He started the engine and drove out of Bozeman.

It was a pretty night, and the road was clear, tempting him to push the gas pedal to the floor. But he drove moderately, humming along with Billy Ray Cyrus on the radio. And as the dark became country dark, he was a happy man.

"This is far enough for fifty." It made her nervous, the quiet, the lack of light and people.

Not far enough, he thought, and smiled at her. "I know a little place, just a couple miles up." Steering with one hand, he reached under the seat, amused at the way she shrank back and reached for her bag. He pulled out a bottle of the cheap wine he'd doctored. "Drink, Suzy?"

"Well . . . maybe." Her johns didn't usually offer her wine, or call her pretty, or use her name. "Just a couple more miles, cowboy," she said, and tipped back the bottle. "Then we'll ride."

"Me and my pal here are more than ready." He patted his crotch, turned up the radio. "Know this one?"

She drank again, giggled, and sang along with him and Clint Black.

She was a little thing, barely a hundred pounds. It took less than ten minutes for the drug to work. He nipped the bottle neatly from her limp fingers before it could spill. Whistling now, he pulled to the side of the road.

She was slumped in the corner, but he lifted an eyelid to be certain, then nodded. Climbing out, he dumped the rest of the drugged wine out, then heaved the bottle, sending it in a long, flying arc into the dark.

He heard it shatter as he walked to the bed of the rig and got out the rope.

"YOU DON'T HAVE TO DO THIS, WILL." ADAM STUDIED HIS sister as they walked their horses through a narrow stream.

"I want to. For you." She paused, let Moon drink. "For her. I know I haven't come to her grave very often. I let other things get in the way."

"You don't have to go to our mother's grave to remember her."

"That's the problem, isn't it? I can't remember her. Except through you."

She tipped back her head. It was a gorgeous afternoon and she was pleasantly tired, her shoulders just a little achy from unrolling wire and hammering fence.

"I didn't come, very often, because it always seemed morbid. Standing there, looking down at a piece of earth and a carved stone, having no memories of her to pull out and hold on to." She watched a bird flit by, chasing the breeze. "I've started thinking of it differently. It was seeing

Lily with her mother, and Tess with hers. It's thinking of the baby Lily's carrying. The continuity.''

She turned to him, and her face was relaxed. "It was always the land that was continuity to me, the seasons, the work that had to be done in each one of them. When I thought of yesterday or of tomorrow, it was always the ranch.''

"It's your heart, Willa, your home. It's you.''

"Yeah, that'll always be true. But I'm thinking of the people now. I never really did before—except for you.'' She reached out, closed a hand over his. "You were always there. My memories are of you. Picking me up, me riding your hip, your voice talking to me and telling me stories.''

"You were, and always will be, a joy to me.''

"You're going to be such an amazing father.'' She gave his hand a last squeeze, began to walk Moon again. "I've been thinking. It's not just the land that continues, not just the land we owe. I owe her my life, and I owe her you, and I owe her the child I'll be aunt to.''

He was silent a moment. "It's not just her you owe.''

"No, it's not.'' Adam would understand, she thought. He always did. "I owe Jack Mercy, too. The anger's gone now, and so is the grief. I owe him my life, and the lives of my sisters, and so the child I'll be aunt to. I can be grateful for that. And maybe, in some way I owe him what I am. If he'd been different, so would I.''

"And what about the tomorrows, Will? What about your tomorrows?''

She could only see the seasons, and the work that had to be done in each one of them. And the land, waiting endlessly. "I don't know.''

"Why don't you tell Ben how you feel about him?''

She sighed and wished for once there could be some corner of her heart secret from Adam. "I haven't made up my mind how I feel.''

"Your mind has nothing to do with it.'' His lips curved as he kicked his horse into a trot. "Neither does his.''

And what the hell was that supposed to mean? she wondered. Her brow knit, she clicked to Moon and galloped after him. "Don't start that cryptic business with me. I'm only half Blackfoot, remember. If you have something to say—"

She broke off as he held up a hand. Without question she pulled up and followed his gaze toward the tilting stones of the cemetery. She smelled it too. Death. But that was to be expected here; it was another of the reasons she so rarely came.

But then she knew, even before she saw, she knew. Because old death had a quiet and dusty murmur. And new death screamed.

They walked the horses slowly again, dismounted in silence with only the wind in the high grass and the haunting song of birds.

It was her father's grave that had been desecrated. What rose up in her was disgust, chased by superstition. To mock and insult the dead was a dangerous matter. She shuddered, found herself murmuring a chant in her mother's tongue to calm restless spirits.

Then to calm her own, she turned away and stared over the land that rolled and waved to forever.

Not a very subtle message, she thought, as the healing rage took over. The mutilated skunk had been spread over the grave, its blood staining the mound of new grass. The head had been removed, then placed carefully just under the headstone.

The stone itself had been smeared with blood, going brown now in the sun. And words had been printed over the deep carving:

Dead but not forgotten

She jerked when Adam laid a hand on her shoulder. "Go back to the stream, Willa. I'll take care of this."

Her weak legs urged her to do as he asked, to crawl back onto her horse and ride. But the rage was still here, and beneath that, the debt she had come to acknowledge.

"No, he was my father, my blood. I'll do it." Turning,

she fumbled with the clasps on her saddlebags. "I can do it, Adam. I need to do it."

She took out an old blanket, spent some of her temper ripping it. After digging for her gloves, she tugged them on. Her eyes were bright and hard. "Whatever he was, whatever he'd done, he didn't deserve this."

She took a piece of the blanket and, kneeling beside her father's grave, began the filthy task of removing the corpse from it. Her stomach revolted, but her hands stayed steady. Her gloves were stained with gore when she finished, so she stripped them off, tossed them into the heap. Tying the blanket securely, she set it aside.

"I'll bury it," Adam murmured.

She nodded, rose. Using her canteen, she soaked another piece of the blanket, then knelt again to wash the stone.

She couldn't get it clean, no matter how she scrubbed. She would have to come back with something more than water and a makeshift rag. But she did her best and sat back on her heels, her hands raw and cold.

"I thought I loved you," she murmured. "Then I thought I hated you. But nothing I ever felt for you was as deep or as deadly as this." She closed her eyes and tried to clear her lungs of the stench. "It's been you all along, I think. Not me, but you it's been aimed at. Dear God, what did you do, and who did you do it to?"

"Here." Adam reached down to lift her to her feet. "Drink a little," he said, and offered her his canteen.

She drank, gulping deep to wash the nasty taste from her throat. There were flowers blooming on her mother's grave, she realized. And blood staining her father's.

"Who hated him this much, Adam? And why? Who did he hurt more than me, and you? More than Lily and Tess? Who did he hurt more than the children he ignored?"

"I don't know." He worried only about Willa now, and gently led her back to her horse. "You've done all you can do here. We'll go home."

"Yes." Her legs felt brittle, like ice ready to crack. "We'll go home."

They rode west, toward Mercy and a sky stained red as the grave.

THE FOURTH OF JULY MEANT MORE THAN FIREWORKS. IT meant roping and riding, bronco busting and bull riding. For more than a decade, Mercy and Three Rocks had held a competition for cowboys on their ranches and any of the neighboring spreads who didn't choose to go farther afield for holiday entertainment.

It was Mercy's turn to host. Willa had listened to Ben's request that they move the competition to Three Rocks that year, to Nate's advice that they cancel it altogether. She'd considered, then ignored.

She was Mercy, and Mercy continued.

So people crowded corral fences, cheering on their picks. Cowboys brushed off their butts as they were tossed out of the saddle, into the air, and onto the ground. In a near pasture, the barrel-racing competition entered its second phase. Near the pole barn, hooves thundered and ropes flew through the air.

A bandstand was set up, draped with bunting of red, white, and blue. Music was interrupted periodically as names and places were announced. Gallons of potato salad, truckloads of fried chicken, and barrels of beer and iced tea were consumed.

Hearts were broken, along with a few bones.

"I see we're up against each other in the target shooting," Ben commented, slipping an arm around Willa's waist.

"Prepare to lose."

"Side bet?"

She angled her head. "What do you have in mind?"

"Well." He tucked his tongue in his cheek, leaned down close so their hats bumped, and whispered something that made her eyes round.

"You're making that up," she decided. "No one could live through that."

"Not chicken, are you?"

She straightened her hat. "You want to risk it, McKinnon,

I'll take you on. You're in this round of bronc busting, aren't you?''

"I'm on my way over."

"I'll go with you." She smiled sweetly. "I've got twenty on Jim."

"You bet against me?" He wobbled between insult and shock. "Hell, Willa."

"I've been watching Jim practice. Ham's been coaching him." She sauntered away. No point in telling him she'd bet fifty on Ben McKinnon. It would just go to his head.

"Hey, Will." A little blood drying on his chin, his arm around a blonde in girdled-on jeans, Billy beamed at her. "Jim's in the chute."

"That's what I'm here for." She propped a boot on the rail beside his. "How'd you do?"

"Aw, shit." He rolled a sore shoulder.

"That good, huh?" With a laugh she squeezed over to make room for Ben. "Well, you're young yet, kid. You'll still be breaking bronc when geezers like McKinnon here are riding their rocking chairs. You get Ham to work with you."

She looked up, saw her foreman was standing on the outside wall of the chute, snapping last-minute instructions to Jim.

"I was thinking maybe you could. You ride better'n anybody on Mercy except for Adam. And he won't bust broncs."

"Adam's got a different way of taming them. We'll see," she added, then let out a whoop as the chute opened and horse and rider shot out. "Ride that devil, Jim!"

He careened by in a cloud of dust, one hand thrown high.

When the eight-second bell clanged, he jumped clear, rolled, then gained his feet to the wild cheers of the onlookers.

"Not bad," Ben said. "I'm coming up." With manhood and pride at stake, he cupped his hands under Willa's elbows, lifted her up, and kissed her. "For luck," he said, then swaggered off.

"Think he'll take our Jim, Will?" Billy wanted to know.

She thought Ben McKinnon could take damn near anything. "He'll have to ride like a hellhound."

Though the blonde shifted under his arm in a bid for attention, Billy tugged Willa's sleeve. "You're up against him in the target shooting, aren't you?"

"That's right."

"You'll take him, Will. We all put money on you. All the boys."

"Well, I wouldn't want you to lose it." She watched Ben climb over the chute. He tipped his hat to her, a cocky move that made her grin back at him.

When his horse leaped out of the door, her heart did a foolish little roll in her chest. He looked . . . magnificent, she decided. Riding straight on that furious horse, one hand grabbing for the sky, the other locked to the saddle. She caught a glimpse of his eyes, the dead-focused concentration in them.

They look like that when he's inside me, she realized, and her heart did another roll, quicker. She didn't even hear the bell clang, but watched him jump down, the horse still kicking furiously. He stayed on his feet, boots planted. And though the crowd cheered, he looked straight at her. And winked.

"Cocky bastard," she muttered. And I'm hip-deep in love with him.

"Why do they do that?" Tess asked from behind her.

"For the hell of it." Grateful for the excuse to think of something else, Willa turned. Tess had turned herself out for the day. Tight jeans, fancy boots, a bright blue shirt with silver trim that matched the band on her snowy-white hat. "Well, ain't you a picture. Hey, Nate. Ready for the race?"

"It's a tight field this year, but I'm hopeful."

"Nate's helping out with the pie-eating contest." Tess chuckled and tucked an arm through his. "We were hunting up Lily. She wanted to watch, since she helped make the pies."

"I saw her . . ." Willa narrowed her eyes and searched the crowds. "I think she and Adam were helping out with the kids' games. Egg toss, maybe, or the three-legged races.''

''We'll find her. Want to tag along?''

''No, thanks.'' Willa shrugged off Tess's invitation. ''I may catch up later. I need a beer.''

''You're worried about her,'' Nate murmured as they zigzagged through the crowd.

''I can't help it. You didn't see her the day she came back from the cemetery. She wouldn't talk about it. Usually I can goad her into talking about anything, but not this.''

''It's been over two months since Jesse Cooke was murdered. That's something to hang on to.''

''I'm trying.'' Tess shook herself. There was music, people, laughter. ''It's a hell of a party. You do throw amazing parties out here.''

''We can start throwing our own anytime you say.''

''Nate, we've been there. I'm going back to LA in October. There's Lily.'' Desperate for the distraction, Tess waved wildly. ''I swear, she glows all the time now. Pregnancy certainly agrees with her.''

Nate thought it might agree with Tess as well. That was something else they could start—once he'd finished pecking away at this stubborn idea of leaving.

THE FIRST FIREWORKS EXPLODED AT TWENTY MINUTES PAST dusk. Color leaped over the sky, shadowed the stars, then bled down like tears. Willa let herself be cuddled back against Ben to watch the show.

''I think your daddy likes sending those bombs off more than the kids like to watch.''

''He and Ham argue over the presentation and order every blessed year.'' Ben grinned as a gold starburst bloomed overhead with a crackling boom. ''Then they cackle like hens, taking turns lighting fuses. Never would let Zack or me have a hand in it.''

''It's not your time,'' she murmured. That, too, would come. That, too, was continuity. ''It was a good day.''

''Yeah.'' He covered her hands with his. ''Real good.''

''Not miffed 'cause I beat you shooting?''

It still stung, a little, but he shrugged his shoulders. The two of them had whittled away the rest of the competitors until they'd gone head to head in the final round. Then head to head in two tie-breaking rounds. And there she'd squeaked past him.

"By a lousy half an inch, tops."

"Doesn't matter by how much." She looked over, up at him, and grinned. "Matters who won. You're a good shot." She wiggled her brows. "I'm better."

"Today you were better. Anyway, I cost you twenty when I beat out Jim. Serves you right."

Laughing, she turned in his arms. "I made back the fifty I put on you." When his brow lowered, she laughed again. "Do I look like a fool?"

"No." He tipped her face up. "You look like a smart woman who knows how to hedge her bets."

"Speaking of bets." Despite the crowd that gasped and cheered at every burst of light, she wrapped herself around him, pressed her mouth warm and firm to his. "Let's go inside and see if we live till morning."

"You going to let me stay till morning?"

"Why not? It's a holiday."

LATER, WHEN THE FIREWORKS WERE DONE, THE CROWDS gone, and the night quiet, they turned to each other again. Her dreams hadn't been full of blood and death and fear this time. Finding him there, warm, solid, ready to hold her, she knew there'd be no shaking dreams that night.

SOMEONE ELSE DREAMED OF A REDHEADED WHORE AND shivered, thrilled with the memory. It had been so easy, so smooth, and every detail played back so clearly.

He'd watched her come back to consciousness, the glassy eyes, the muffled whimper. He'd driven her far from Bozeman, into the sheltering dark of trees.

Not on Mercy land. Not this time, and never again. He was done with punishing Mercy. But he couldn't be done with killing.

He'd tied her hands behind her back, and he'd gagged

her. He wouldn't have minded hearing her scream, but he didn't want her to be able to use her teeth on him. He'd cut her clothes away but had been careful, very careful, not to cut her flesh.

He was very, very good with a knife.

While she'd slept, he had taken his money back, and the rest of hers, which had been pathetically little. He'd bided his time, toying with her little pistol, her tube of red lipstick.

Now that she was awake, now that her eyes were wide and she was struggling in the dirt, making noises like a trapped animal, he took the tube back out of her cheap purse.

"A whore should be painted up proper," he told her, and aroused himself by stroking the lipstick over her nipples until they were bright, blood red. "I like that. Yes, indeed." Since her cheeks were pale, he colored them as well, in round circles like a doll's happy blush.

"Were you going to shoot me with this toy of yours, sweetheart?" He pointed the pistol playfully at her heart and watched her eyes roll white. "Guess a woman in your line a work's gotta protect herself in more ways than one. Told you I'd wear a rubber."

He set the pistol aside, then tore open the foil package. "Love to have you suck me off again, Suzy Q. I do believe that was the finest blow job I ever paid for. But you might bite this time." He pinched her red nipples painfully. "We can't have that, can we?"

He was already hard, throbbing hard, but made himself slide the condom on slowly. "I'm going to fuck you now. You can't rape a whore, but since I ain't going to pay for it, I guess technically we could call it that. So we'll say I'm going to rape you now." He levered himself over her, smiling as she tried to draw her legs up to protect herself. "Now, honey, don't be shy. You're going to like it."

In two rough jerks, he pulled her legs straight, spread them, locked them. "You're damn well going to like it. And you're going to tell me how much you love it. You can't say much with that rag stuffed in your whore-sucking mouth, but you're going to moan and groan for me. I want you to groan now. Like you can't wait for it. Now.''

When she didn't respond, he released one of her legs and slapped her. Not hard, he thought, just enough to let her know who was boss. ''Now,'' he repeated.

She managed a sob, and he settled for it. ''You make noise for me, plenty of noise. I like plenty of noise with my sex.''

He rammed himself into her. She was dry as dust and as unwelcoming as a tomb, but he pumped furiously, working up a sheen of sweat that gleamed on his back under the scatter of stars. Her eyes rolled in pain and fear, the way a horse's did when you dug in spurs and drew blood.

When he was finished, he rolled off her, panting. ''That was good. That was good. Yeah, I'm going to do that again in just a minute or two.''

She was curled into a ball and, weeping, tried to crawl. Lazily, he picked up the gun, fired a shot at the sky. It stopped her cold. ''You just rest there, Suzy Q. I'm going to see if I can work up the gumption for another round.''

He sodomized her this time, but it wasn't as good. It took him too long to get hard, and the orgasm was small and unsatisfying. ''Guess that's it for me.'' He gave her a friendly slap on the rump. ''And for you.''

He thought it was a shame he couldn't keep her a couple days like he had little Traci with an *I*. But that kind of game was too risky now.

And there would always be another whore.

He opened his pack, and there it was, waiting. Lovingly he slipped the knife from its oiled-leather sheath, admired the way the starlight caught the metal and glimmered.

''My daddy gave me this. Only thing he ever gave me. Pretty, ain't it?'' After shoving her onto her back, he held it in front of her face so that she could see it. He wanted her to see it.

And smiling, he straddled her.

And smiling, he went to work on her.

Now there was a trophy of red hair in his box of secrets. He doubted anyone would find her where he'd left her. Or if they did, if they would be able to identify what was left of her once the predators had done with what he'd left behind for them.

He didn't need the fear and the fame any longer. It was enough that he knew.

TWENTY-NINE

Summers in Montana were short and fierce, and August could be cruel. Sun baked the dirt and dried the trees to kindling and made men pray for rain.

A match flicked the wrong way or a well-aimed bolt of lightning would turn pasture into fire, crops into tears.

Willa sweated through her shirt as she surveyed a field of barley. "Hottest summer I remember."

Wood merely grunted. He spent most of his time scowling at the sky or worrying over his grain. His boys should have been there worrying with him, but he'd gotten tired of their spatting and sent them off to bother their mother.

"Irrigation's helping some." He spat, as if that drop of moisture would make a difference. Mercy was both joy and worry to him, and had been for too many years to count. "Water table's dead low. Couple more weeks of this, we'll be in trouble."

"Don't sugarcoat it for me," she said wearily, and remounted. "We'll get through it."

He grunted again, shook his head at her as she rode off. The ground bounced heat back at her relentlessly. The cattle she passed stood slack-legged, with barely enough energy to swish tails. Not even the stingiest breeze stirred the grass.

She saw a rig well out along a fence line, and the two men unrolling wire. Changing directions, she galloped out.

"Ham, Billy." She dismounted, walked over to the two-gallon jug in the bed of the rig, and poured herself a cup of icy water.

"Ham says this ain't hot, Will." Sweating cheerfully, Billy strung wire. "He says he recollects when it was so hot it fried eggs still in their shells."

She smiled at that. "I expect he does. You get as old as Ham here, you've seen everything twice." She took off her hat, wiped an arm over her brow. She didn't like Ham's color. The red flush that stained his face looked hot enough to explode. But she knew to tread carefully.

Pouring two cups, she walked over, held them out. "Hot work. Take a break."

"Be done soon," Ham said, but his breath was puffing.

"You got to keep the fluid in. You told me that often enough that I have to take it as truth." She all but shoved the cup into his hand. "You boys take your salt tablets?"

"Sure we did." Billy gulped the water down, his Adam's apple bobbing.

"Ham, I'm going to finish here with Billy. You take Moon back for me."

"What the hell for?" His eyes were running from squinting into the sun. Under his soaked shirt, his heart pounded like a hammer on an anvil. But he finished any job he started. "I said we're about done here."

"That's fine, then. I need you to take Moon back and get me those stock reports. I'm falling behind, and I want to catch up on them tonight."

"You know where the damn reports are."

"And I need them." Casually, she took her gloves out of her saddlebags. "And see if you can sweet-talk Bess into making some peach ice cream. She'll do it for you, and I've got a yen for some."

He wasn't a fool, knew just what she was doing. "I'm stringing wire here, girl."

"No." She hefted the roll as Billy watched, wide-eyed and fascinated. "I'm stringing wire here. You're going to take Moon back in, get those stock reports in my office, and see about peach ice cream."

He tossed his cup on the ground, planted his feet. "The hell with that. Take her back yourself."

She set the roll down. "I run Mercy, Ham, and I'm telling you what I want you to do. You got a problem with that, we'll take it up later. But now, you ride back and do what I'm telling you."

His face was redder now, making her pulse skittish, but she kept her eyes cool and level with his. After ten humming seconds, with the heat crippling both of them, he turned stiffly away and mounted.

"You think I can't do the job this half-assed boy can do, then you get my paycheck ready." He kicked the horse, sent Moon into a surprised rear, then galloped off.

"Jeez" was all Billy could think of.

"Damn it, I should have handled that better." She rubbed her hands over her face.

"He'll be all right, Will. He doesn't mean it. Ham'd never leave you or Mercy."

"That's not what I'm worried about." She blew out a breath. "Let's get this damn wire strung."

SHE WAITED UNTIL NIGHTFALL, CANCELED A DATE WITH Ben, and sat out on the front porch. She heard the thunder, watched lightning flash, but the sky was too clear for rain.

Despite the heat she had no taste for the ice cream Bess had churned. Even when Tess came out with a bowl heaped full of it, Willa shook her head.

"You've been sulking since you came in today." Tess leaned against the porch rail and tried to imagine cool ocean breezes. "Want to talk about it?"

"No. It's a personal problem."

"They're the most interesting." Philosophically, Tess spooned up some ice cream and sampled it. "Ben?"

"No." Willa gave an irritated shrug. "Why is it people think every personal thought in my head revolves around Ben McKinnon?"

"Because women usually do their best sulking over a man. You didn't have a fight with him?"

"I'm always fighting with him."

"I mean a real fight."

"No."

"Then why did you cancel your date?"

"Jesus Christ, can't I choose to stay home on my own porch one night without answering a bunch of questions?"

"Guess not." Tess dug out another spoonful. "This is great stuff." Licked the spoon clean. "Come on, try it."

"If it'll get you off my back." With little grace, Willa grabbed the bowl and scooped some up. It was sheer heaven. "Bess makes the best peach ice cream in the civilized world."

"I tend to agree with you. Want to eat ice cream, get drunk, and take a swim? Sounds like a great way to cool off."

Willa's eyes slitted with suspicion. "Why are you so friendly?"

"You look really bummed. I guess I'm feeling sorry for you."

It should have annoyed her. Instead it touched her. "I had words with Ham today. He was out stringing wire and I got spooked. He looked so old all of a sudden, and it was so blasted hot. I thought he'd have a stroke or something. A heart attack. I made him come back in, and that slapped his pride flat. I just can't lose anybody else," she said quietly. "Not right now. Not yet."

"His pride will bounce back. Maybe you dented it a little, but he's too devoted to you to stay mad for long."

"I'm counting on it." Soothed, she handed the bowl back to Tess. "Maybe I'll come in shortly and take that swim."

"All right." Tess opened the screen, shot back a grin. "But I'm not wearing a suit."

Chuckling, Willa eased back in the rocker, let it creak. Thunder rumbled, a little closer now. And she heard the crunch of boots on stone. She sat up, one hand going under the chair where her rifle rested. She brought it back up, laid it in her lap when Ham stepped into the light.

"Evening," she said.

"Evening. You got my check?"

Stubborn old goat, she thought, and gestured to the chair beside her. "Would you sit down a minute?"

"I got packing to do."

"Please."

Bandy legs stiff as a week-old wishbone, he climbed the steps, lowered himself into the next rocker. "You took me down in front of that boy today."

"I'm sorry." She folded her hands in her lap, stared down at him. It was the sound of his voice, raw with hurt and wounded pride, that scraped at her. "I tried to make it simple."

"Make what simple? You think I need some girl I used to paddle coming out and telling me I'm too old to do my job?"

"I never said—"

"Hell you didn't. Plain as day to me."

"Why do you have to be so stubborn?" She kicked at the porch rail out of sheer frustration. "Why do you have to be so hardheaded?"

"Me? Never in my life did I see a more rock-headed female than the one I'm sitting beside right now. You think you know it all, girl? You think you got all the answers? That every blessed thing you do is right?"

"No!" She exploded with it, leaped up. "No, I don't. I don't know half the time if it's right, but I have to do it anyway. And I did what I had to do today, and it *was* right. Goddamn you, Ham, you were going to have heatstroke in another ten minutes, and then where the hell would I be? How the hell could I run this place without you?"

"You're already doing just that. You took me off the job today."

"I took you off the fences. I don't want you riding fence in this heat. I'm telling you I'm not having it."

"You're not having it." He rose too, went nose to nose

with her. "Who the hell do you think you are, telling me you're not having it? I've been riding fence in every kind of weather since before you were born. And you nor no-body's telling me I can't do it until I say I'm done."

"I'm telling you."

"Then cut me my last check."

"Fine." She swung to the door, pushed by temper. Her hand fisted on the edge, then whipped it back in a slam that shook the wood under her feet. "I was scared! Why can't I be allowed to be scared?"

"What in hell are you scared of?"

"Losing you, you mule-headed son of a bitch. You were all red-faced and sweaty and your breath was puffing like a bad engine. I couldn't stand it. I just couldn't. And if you'd just gone in like I asked you, it would've been fine."

"It was hot," he said, but his voice was weak now, and a little ashamed.

"I know it was hot. Goddamn it, Ham, that's the point. Why'd you make me push you that way? I didn't want to embarrass you in front of Billy. I just wanted you to get out of the sun. I know who my father was," she said furiously, and made his head come up, his eyes meet hers again. "And I haven't buried him yet. Not the one who really counted when I needed him to count. I don't want to bury him for a long time."

"I could've finished." He bumped his toe on the rail, stared at it. "Hell, Will, I was making the boy do most of the work. I know my limits."

"I need you here." She waited for her system to calm again. "I need you, Ham. I'm asking you to stay."

He moved his shoulders, kept his eyes on his feet. "I guess I got no place better to be. I shouldn'ta bucked you. I guess I knew you were thinking of me." He shifted his feet, cleared his throat. "You're doing a fine job around here, all in all. I'm, ah . . . I'm proud of you."

And that's why he was the one who counted, she thought. The father of her blood had never said those words to her. "I can't do it alone. You want to come in?" She opened the door again. "Have some of that peach ice cream. You can tell me all the things I'm doing wrong.''

He scratched his beard. "Maybe. I guess there's a few things I could straighten you out on.''

WHEN HE LEFT, HIS BELLY WAS FULL AND HIS HEART CON-siderably lighter. He strolled toward the bunkhouse, light of step. He heard the sounds, the disturbed braying of cattle, the click of boot heels.

Who the hell was on guard duty? He couldn't quite place it. Jim or Billy, he thought, and decided to wander over to check things out.

"That you, Jim? Billy? What are you playing with the penned head for this time of night?''

He saw the calf first, bleeding, eyes rolling in fear and pain. He'd taken two running steps before he saw the man rise up out of the shadows.

"What the devil's this? What the hell have you done?''

And he knew, before he saw the knife arch up, but there was no time to scream.

The panic came first. With the knife dripping in his hand, he stared down at Ham, the blood. Wiped a hand over his mouth. He'd just needed a quick fix, that was all. One calf. He'd meant to drag it away from the ranch yard, but the knife had just leaped into his hand.

And now Ham. He'd never meant to hurt Ham. Ham had trained him, worked with him, paid attention when attention needed to be paid. He'd always felt Ham had known the truth about where he'd come from and who he was.

And Ham was loyal.

But now there was no choice. It had to be finished. He crouched down, prepared, just as Willa rushed out of the night.

"Ham? Is that you? I forgot to tell you about the—'' Her boots skidded. Lightning flashed, bursting light onto the men all but at her feet. "Oh, sweet God, what happened to him? What happened?'' She was already on her knees, turn-ing him over into her arms. "Did he—'' And there was blood on her hands.

"I'm sorry, Will. I'm sorry.'' He turned the knife on her,

held it to her throat. "Don't call out. I don't want to hurt you. I swear I don't want to hurt you." He took a deep, shuddering breath. "I'm your brother."

And bringing his fist up, he knocked her cold.

H AM WOKE TO PAIN. FIERY, BLINDING PAIN. HE COULDN'T pinpoint it, couldn't find the source, but he tasted blood in his mouth. Groaning, he tried to sit up, but couldn't move his legs. He turned his head, saw that the calf had bled out. Its eyes were dead.

Soon, he thought, he'd bleed out too.

There was something else on the ground that caught his eye. He stared at it a long time, watched it come and go as his vision cleared and blurred. Then hissing, he crawled toward it, brushed the tip with his fingers.

Willa's hat.

H E HAD TO CARRY HER. HE SHOULD HAVE GONE FOR A rig, knew he should have, but he'd been so shaken he hadn't been able to think clearly. Now he laid her as gently as he could on the ground near the pasture and with a trembling hand rattled a bucket of oats.

They'd go on horseback. It was probably best. He wanted to get her away, into the hills a ways so that he could explain everything to her. She'd understand once he had.

Blood was thicker than water.

He saddled the paint pony that nosed into the bucket, then the roan that tried to nuzzle through.

Oh, he hated to do it, even temporarily, but he tied Willa's hands, tied her feet, then strapped her across the saddle. She'd come to shortly, he thought, and she'd try to get away before he could explain.

She had to understand. He prayed she'd understand as he vaulted into the saddle, took both pairs of reins. If she didn't, he'd have to kill her.

Thunder stalked closer as he rode into the hills.

H AM CLUTCHED THE HAT IN HIS HAND, STAGGERED TO his feet. He managed two drunken steps before he went to his knees. He called out, and though his voice boomed in his ears, it was barely a whisper.

He thought of Willa, hardly more than a baby with a milky mouth, grinning at him as he plopped her into the saddle in front of him. A little girl, all braids and eyes, begging him to let her ride out to pasture with him. An adolescent, gawky as a colt, running wire with him and chattering his ears off.

And the woman who had looked at him tonight, her heart in her eyes when she'd told him he was the one who counted.

So he bit back the pain that was eating through him like cancer and fought his way to his feet again.

He could see the main house, the lights in the windows circling in front of his eyes. Blood dripped through his fingers and onto her hat. He didn't feel the ground when it jumped up to meet him.

SHE CAME TO SLOWLY, HER JAW THROBBING. HER EYES FOcused on the ground bumping and falling beneath her. She tried to shift, found herself snugly secured, lying across the saddle with her head dangling. She must have moaned, or made some sound, for the horses stopped quickly.

"It's okay, Will. You're okay." He loosed the straps, the restraints on her legs, but kept her hands secured. "Need to ride a little further. Can you handle it?"

"What?" Still groggy, she felt herself lifted, then she was sitting in the saddle, shaking her head to clear it while her hands were strapped tight to the horn.

"You just catch your breath. I'll lead your horse."

"What are you doing?" It leaped back into her mind but refused to root there. "Ham?"

"Couldn't help it. Just couldn't help it. We'll talk this through. You just—" He broke off, dragging her down by the hair when she sucked in her breath. "Don't you scream. Nobody's going to hear you, but I don't want you screaming." Mumbling to himself, he tugged out his bandanna, tied it quickly over her mouth. "I'm sorry I have to do it this way, but you just don't understand yet."

Trying not to be angry with her, he strode back to his horse, swung on, and rode into the trees.

WELL, WILLA HAD MISSED HER SWIM, TESS THOUGHT AS she tied the belt of a short terry robe. She ran her fingers through her hair to smooth it back and wandered out of the pool house toward the kitchen.

Probably still sulking, she decided. Willa took everything in and worried over it. It might be a good idea to try to teach her a few relaxation techniques—though Tess couldn't quite visualize Willa meditating or experimenting with imaging.

Rain would make her happy, Tess supposed. Lord, everyone around here lived their life by the weather. Too wet, too dry. Too cold, too hot. Well, in two months, she would say farewell, scenic Montana, and hello, LA.

Lunch alfresco, she mused. Cartier's. God knew, she deserved to treat herself to some ridiculously expensive bauble after this yearlong banishment from the real world.

The theater. Palm trees. Traffic-choked highways and the familiar haze of smog.

God bless Hollywood.

Then she pouted a little because it didn't sound quite as wonderful as it had a month before. Or a month before that.

No, she'd be glad to get back. Thrilled. She was just feeling broody, that was all. Maybe she'd buy a place up in the hills rather than on the beach, though. She could have a horse up there, and the trees, the grass. That would be the best of both worlds, after all. A brisk, exciting drive from the excitement and crowds of the city home to the pleasure she'd come to enjoy of the country.

Well, not exactly country, by Montana standards, but the Hollywood hills would do just fine.

She could probably persuade Nate to come out and visit. Off and on. Their relationship would fade after a while. She expected and, damn it, accepted that. So would he. This wild idea of his to have her settle down here, get married, and start breeding was ridiculous.

She had a life in LA. A career. She had plans, big, juicy

plans. She would be thirty-one years old in a matter of weeks, and she wasn't tossing those plans aside at this stage of her life to be a ranch wife.

Any kind of a wife.

She wished she had brought down a cigarette, but she swung into the kitchen in search of other stimulation.

"You've had your share of ice cream."

Tess wrinkled her nose at Bess's back. "I didn't come in for ice cream." Though she would have enjoyed one or two spoonfuls. She went to the refrigerator, took out a pitcher of lemonade.

"You been skinny-dipping again?"

"Yep. You ought to try it."

Bess's mouth twitched at the idea. "You put that glass in the dishwasher when you're finished. This kitchen's clean."

"Fine." Tess plopped down at the table, eyed the catalogue Bess was thumbing through. "Shopping?"

"I'm thinking. Lily might like this here bassinet. The one we used for you girls wasn't kept after Willa. He got rid of it."

"Oh." It was an interesting thought, the idea of her and Lily and Willa sharing something as sweet as a baby bed. "Oh, it's adorable." Delighted, Tess scraped her chair closer. "Look at the ribbons in the skirt."

Bess slanted her eyes over. "I'm buying the bassinet."

"All right, all right. Oh, look, a cradle. She'd love a cradle, wouldn't she? One to sit by your chair and rock."

"I expect she would."

"Let's make a list."

Bess's eyes softened considerably and she pulled out a pad she'd stuck under the catalogue. "Got one started already."

They made cooing noises over mobiles and stuffed bears, argued briefly over the right kind of stroller. Tess rose to get them both more lemonade, then glanced at the kitchen door when she heard footsteps.

"I wasn't expecting anyone," she whispered, her nervous hand going to her throat.

"Me either." Calm as ice, Bess pulled her pistol out of her apron pocket and, standing, faced the door. "Who's out there?" When the face pressed against the screen, she laughed at herself. "God Almighty, Ham, you nearly took a bullet. You shouldn't be sneaking around this time of night."

He fell through the door, right at her feet.

The pistol clattered as it hit the table. Tess was on the floor with her before Bess could lift Ham's head in her lap. "He's bleeding bad here. Get some towels, press them down hard."

"Bess . . ."

"Quiet now. Let's see what's what here."

Tess ripped the shirt aside and pressed down hard on the wound. "Call for an ambulance, a helicopter. He needs help quickly."

"Wait." Ham grabbed for Bess's hand. "He's got . . ." He squeezed until he could find the breath to speak again. "He's got her, Bessie. He's got our Will."

"What?" Straining to hear, Tess pushed her face close. "Who has Will?"

But he was unconscious. When her eyes lifted, latched onto Bess's, they were ripe with fear. "Call the police. Hurry."

HE WAS READY TO STOP NOW. HE'D CIRCLED, BACK-tracked, followed a stream down its center, then moved onto rock. He had no choice but to tether the horses, but he kept them close.

Willa watched his every move. She knew the hills, and he wouldn't find the hunt easy even if she had to go on foot once she got loose.

He hauled her down first, retied her ankles. After getting his rifle, he sat across from her, laid it across his lap. "I'm going to take the gag off now. I'm sorry I had to use it. You know it won't do any good to scream. They may come after us, but not for a while, and I covered the trail."

He reached over, put his hand on the cotton. "We're just

going to talk. Once you hear me out, we'll get back to the way things were.'' He tugged the gag down.

"You murdering bastard."

"You don't mean that. You're upset."

"Upset?" Fury carried her, had her pulling furiously to try to break her bonds. "You killed Ham. You killed all the others. You slaughtered my cattle. I'll kill you with my own hands if I get the chance."

"Ham was an accident. I'm as fond of him as I can be, but he saw me." Like a boy caught with the shards of a cookie jar at his feet, he lowered his head. "The cattle was a mistake. I shouldn't have done that to you. I'm sorry."

"You're—" She shut her eyes, balled her helpless hands into fists. "Why? Why have you done these things? I thought I could trust you."

"You can. I swear you can. We're blood, Willa. You can trust your own blood."

"You're no blood of mine."

"Yes, I am." He knuckled a tear away, such was his joy in being able to tell her. "I'm your brother."

"You're a liar and a murderer and a coward."

His head snapped up, his hand flew out. The sting of flesh striking flesh sang up his arm, and he regretted it immediately. "Don't say things like that. I got my pride."

He rose, paced, worked himself back under control. Things didn't go well when you lost control, he knew. But stay in charge, stay on top, and you could handle anything that came along.

"I'm as much your brother as Lily and Tess are your sisters." He said it calmly as the sky split and fractured with swords of electric light. "I want to explain things to you. I want to make you see why I did what I did."

"Fine." The side of her face burned like hellfire. He'd pay for that too, she promised herself. He would pay for everything. "Okay, Jim, explain it to me."

BEN SLAMMED HIS RIFLE INTO ITS SHEATH, SNAGGED HIS gunbelt, strapped it on. The .30 carbine he shot into the holster was a brute of a revolver, and he wanted a mean gun. He wouldn't allow himself to feel, or he might sink shaking to his knees. He could only allow himself to move.

Men were saddling up fast, with Adam shouting orders. Ben wasn't giving any orders, not this time. Nor was he taking them. He took Willa's hat, gave it to Charlie to scent. "You find her," he murmured. "You find Willa." Stuffing the hat in his saddlebag, he swung into the saddle.

"Ben." Tess grabbed the bridle. "Wait for the others."

"I'm not waiting. Move aside, Tess."

"We can't be sure where—or who." Though there was only one man missing.

"I'll find the where. I don't have to know who." He jerked his horse's head out of her grip. "I just have to kill him."

Tess raced over to Adam, put both arms around Lily, and held tight. "Ben rode off. I couldn't stop him."

Adam merely nodded, gave the signal to ride. "He knows what he's doing. Don't worry." Turning, he embraced them both. "Go inside," he told Lily, and laid his hand on her gently rounded belly. "Wait. And don't worry."

"I won't worry." She kissed him. "You found me. You'll find her. Bring her back safe." It was a plea as much as a statement, but she stepped back to let him mount.

"Take Lily inside, Tess." Nate reined in, steadied his eager mount. "Stay inside."

"I will." She laid a hand on his leg, squeezed. "Hurry" was all she could say.

The horses drove west, and she and Lily turned, started back toward the house to begin the painful process of waiting.

THIRTY

"My mother served drinks in a bar down in Bozeman." Jim sat cross-legged as he told his tale, like a true storyteller should. "Well, maybe she served more than drinks. I expect she did, though she never said. But she was a good-looking woman, and she was alone, and that's the kind of thing that happens."

"I thought your mother came from Missoula."

"Did, original. Went back there, too, after I was born. Lots of women go home after something like that, but it never worked out for her. Or me. Anyhow, she served drinks and maybe more for the cowboys who passed through. Jack Mercy, he passed through plenty back in those days, looking to kick ass, get piss-faced drunk, find a woman. You ask anybody, they'll tell you."

He picked up a stick, ran it over the rock. Behind her back Willa twisted her wrists, working them against the rope. "I've heard stories," she said calmly. "I know what kind of man he was."

"I know you do. You used to turn a blind eye to it. I saw that too, but you knew. He took a shine to my mother back then. Like I said, she was a good-looking woman. You see the ones he married. They all had something. Looks, sure. Louella, she had flash. And Adele, seemed to me, seeing her, she'd have been classy and smart. And your ma, well she was something. Quietlike, and special, too. Seemed she could hear things other people couldn't. I was taken with your ma.''

It made her blood chill to hear it, to think of him anywhere near her mother. "How did you know her?"

"We paid some visits. Never stayed long in the area, never at Mercy either. I was just a kid, but I got a clear memory of your ma, big and pregnant with you, walking with Adam in the pasture. Holding his hand. It's a nice picture.'' He mused on it for a while. "I was a bit younger than Adam, and I skinned my knee or some such, and your ma, she came up and got me to my feet. My mother and Jack Mercy were arguing, and your ma took me into the kitchen and put something cool on my knee and talked real nice to me.''

"Why were you at the ranch?"

"My ma wanted me to stay here. She couldn't take care of me proper. She was broke and she got sick a lot. Her family'd kicked her out. It was drugs. She had a weakness for them. It's because she was alone so much. But he wouldn't have me, even though I was his own blood.''

She moistened her lips, ignored the pain as the rope bit in. "Your mother told you that?"

"She told me what was.'' He pushed back his hat, and his eyes were clear. "Jack Mercy knocked her up one of the times he was down in Bozeman and looking for action. She told him as soon as she knew, but he called her a whore and left her flat.'' His eyes changed, went glassy with rage. "My mother wasn't a whore. She did what she had to do, that's all. Whores are no damn good, worthless. They spread their legs for anybody. Ma only went on her back for money when she had to. And she didn't do it regular until after he'd planted me and left her without a choice.''

Hadn't she told him that, tearfully, time and time again throughout his life? "What the hell was she supposed to do? You tell me, Will, what the hell was she supposed to do? Alone and pregnant, with that son of a bitch calling her a filthy lying whore."

"I don't know." Her hands were trembling now from the effort, from the fear. Because his eyes weren't clear any longer, nor were they glassy. They were mad. "It was difficult for her."

"Damn near impossible. She told me time and time again how she begged and pleaded with him, how he turned his back on her. On me. His own son. She could've gotten rid of me. You know that? She could've had an abortion and been done with it, but she didn't. She told me she didn't because I was Jack Mercy's kid and she was going to make him do right by both of us. He had money, he had plenty, but all he did was toss a few lousy dollars at her and walk out."

She began to see, too well, the bitterness of the woman planting the bitter seeds in the child. "I'm sorry, Jim. Maybe he didn't believe her."

"He should've!" He slammed his fist on the rock. "He'd done it with her. He'd come to her regular, promised her he'd take care of her. She told me how he promised her, and she believed him. And even when she had me, took me to him to show him I had his eyes, and his hair, he turned her away so she had to go back to Missoula and beg her family to help her out. It's because he was married to Louella then, snazzy Louella, and he'd just got her pregnant with Tess. So he didn't want me. He figured he had a son coming. But he was wrong. I was the only son he was going to get."

"You had a chance to hurt Lily. In the cave, when Cooke had her." He was too good with a rope, she thought. She couldn't budge the knots. "You didn't."

"I wouldn't hurt her. I thought about it, sure. Early on when I first found out what he'd done in his will. I thought about it, but they're kin." He drew a deep breath, rubbed the side of his hand where he'd bruised it on the rock. "I promised my ma I'd come back to Mercy, I'd get what was mine by right of birth. She was sickly, having me made her sickly. That's why she needed the drugs to help her get through the day. But she done her best for me. She told me all about my father, all about Mercy. She'd sit for hours and tell me about all of it, and what I'd do when I was old enough to go right up to his face and tell him I wanted what was mine.''

"Where's your mother now, Jim?"

"She died. They said the drugs killed her, or she used them to kill herself. But it was Jack Mercy who killed her, Will, when he turned her away. She was dead from then on. When I found her lying there, cold, I promised her again I'd come to Mercy and do what she wanted."

"You found her." There was sweat pouring down her face now. The heat had eased from the air, but sweat ran and dribbled into the raw skin of her wrists to sting. "I'm sorry. So sorry." And she was, desperately.

"I was sixteen. We were in Billings then, and I did some work at the feedlots when I could. She was stone dead when I came home and found her, lying there in piss and vomit. She shouldn't have died that way. He killed her, Will."

"What did you do then?"

"I figured on killing him. That was my first thought. I'd had a lot of practice killing. Stray cats and dogs mostly. I used to pretend they had his face when I carved them up. Only had a pocketknife to work with back then."

Her stomach rolled, rose up to her throat, and was swallowed down. "Your family, your mother's family?"

"I wasn't going to go begging there, after they'd pushed her aside. Hell with them." He picked up the stick, stabbed it at the rock. "Hell with them."

She couldn't hold off the shudders as he stabbed the rock, over and over, repeating that phrase while his face twisted. Then he stopped, his face cleared, and he tapped the stick musically like a man keeping time.

"And I'd made a promise," he continued. "I went to Mercy, and I faced him down. He laughed at me, called me the bastard son of a whore. I took a swing at him, and he knocked me flat. He said I wasn't no son of his, but he'd give me a job. If I lasted a month, he'd give me a paycheck. He turned me over to Ham.''

A fist squeezed her heart. Ham. Had someone found him? Was anyone helping him? ''Did Ham know?''

''I always figured he did. He never spoke of it, but I figured it. I look like the old man, don't you think?''

There was such hope, such pathetic pride in the question. Willa nodded. ''I suppose you do.''

''I worked for him. I worked hard, I learned, and I worked harder. He gave me a knife when I turned twenty-one.'' He slid it out of its sheath, turned it under the moonlight. A Crocodile Bowie, with an eight-inch blade. The sawtooth top glittered like fangs.

''That means something, Willa, a man gives his son a fine knife like this.''

And the sweat on her skin turned to ice. ''He gave you the knife.''

''I loved him. I'd have worked the skin off my hands for him, and the bastard knew it. I never asked him for a thing more, because in my heart I knew when the time came he'd give me what was mine by right. I was his son. His only son. But he gave me nothing but this knife. When the time came, he gave it all to you, to Lily and to Tess. And he gave me nothing.''

He inched forward, closer to her, the knife gleaming in his hand, his eyes gleaming in the dark. ''It wasn't right. It wasn't fair.''

She closed her eyes and waited for the pain.

CHARLIE RACED THROUGH THE HILLS, NOSE TO THE ground, ears at alert. Ben rode alone, grateful for the moonlight, praying that the clouds that gathered thick in the west would hold off. He couldn't afford to lose the light.

He could almost swear he smelled her himself. That scent of hers, soap and leather and something more that was only Willa. He wouldn't picture her hurt. It would cloud his mind, and he needed all his senses sharp. This time his quarry knew the land as well as he. His quarry was mounted and knew all the tricks. He couldn't depend on Willa slow-

ing him down or leaving signs, because he couldn't be sure
she was . . .

No, he wouldn't think of that. He would only think of
finding her, and what he would do to the man when he did.

Charlie splashed into a stream and whined as he lost the
scent. Ben walked his horse into the water, stood for a moment listening, plotting, praying. They'd follow the water
for a while, he decided.

That's what he would have done.

They walked through the stream, the water level stingy
from the lack of rain. Thunder rumbled, and a bird
screamed. Ben clamped down on the urge to hurry, to kick
his horse into a run. He couldn't afford to rush until they'd
picked up the trail again.

He saw something glint on the bank, forced himself to
dismount. Water ran cold over his boots as he walked
through the stream, bent, picked it up.

An earring. Plain gold hoop. The breath whooshed out of
his lungs explosively as his fist clutched it. She'd taken to
wearing baubles lately, he remembered. He'd found it
charming and sweet, that little touch of female added to her
denim and leather. He'd enjoyed telling himself it was for
his benefit.

He tucked it into his front pocket, swung back on his
horse. If she was clearheaded enough to leave him signs, he
was clearheaded enough to follow them. He took his horse
up the bank and let Charlie pick up the trail.

"HE SHOULDN'T HAVE DONE WHAT HE DID." VOICE SHAK-
ing, Jim sawed at the rope tying her ankles. "He did it just
to show me he didn't give a rat's ass about me. About you,
either."

"No." The tears that sprang to her eyes weren't pity, but
sheer relief. With her bound hands she reached forward to
massage her legs. They were horribly cramped. "He didn't
care about either of us."

"It made me crazy at first. Me and Pickles were up at
the cabin when I heard, and I just went crazy. That's why
I killed the steer that way. I had to kill something. Then I

started thinking. I had to get back at him, Will, make him pay. I wanted you to pay too, at first. You and Tess and Lily. I didn't figure they had any right to what was mine. What he should've left to me. I thought I'd scare them off. Nobody'd get anything if I scared them off. I left the cat on the porch. I liked seeing Lily scream and cry over it. I'm sorry about that now, but I wasn't thinking of her as kin then. I just wanted her to go away, back where she'd come from. And for Mercy to go to hell.''

"Can you cut my hands loose, Jim? Please, my arms are cramped.''

"I can't. Not yet. You just don't understand it all.''

"I think I do.'' The feeling was back in her legs. They were stinging as the blood surged back, but she could run if she saw an opening. "He hurt you. You wanted to hurt him back.''

"I had to. What kind of man would I be if I took that from him? But the thing is, Will, I like killing things. I figure that's from him too.'' He smiled and a flash of lightning haloed him like a fallen saint. "Nothing much you can do about what comes down through the blood. He liked killing too. Remember that time he had you raise that calf, right from pulling it clear of its mother? You raised it up like a pet, even named it.''

"Blossom,'' she murmured. "Stupid name for a cow.''

"You loved that dumb cow, won blue ribbons with it. I remember how he took you out that day. You were twelve, maybe thirteen, and he made you watch while he killed it for beef. Teaching you ranch life, he said, and you cried, and you went off and got sick. Ham damn near came to blows with the old man over it. You never had a pet since.''

He took out a cigarette, struck a match. "You had an old dog then, died about a year after all that. You never got another.''

"No, I never did.'' She brought her knees to her chest, pressed her face to them as the memory washed over her.

"I'm just telling you so you'll see, so you'll understand what's in the blood. He liked being the boss, making people dance to his tune. You like being the boss too. It's in the blood.''

She could only shake her head, will herself not to break. ''Stop it.''

''Here now.'' He rose, got the canteen he'd filled at the stream, and brought it to her. ''Drink a little. I didn't mean to get you so worked up. I'm just trying to make you understand.'' He stroked her hair, his baby sister's pretty hair. ''We're in this together.''

CHARLIE SURGED FORWARD, CLAMORING OVER ROCKS. HE didn't bark or howl, though his body vibrated often. Ben listened for the sounds of men, of horses, more dogs. If he was on track, then so was Adam. He could be sure of that. But he heard nothing but the night.

He found the second earring lying on rock where wildflowers struggled through cracks. He retrieved it, touched it to his lips before tucking it away. ''Good girl,'' he whispered. ''Just hang on a little longer.''

He looked toward the sky. The clouds were sneaking toward the moon, and half the stars were gone. Rain, so long prayed for, was coming too soon.

SHE DRANK, WATCHED HIS EYES. THERE WAS AFFECTION IN them. Terrifying. ''You could have killed me, months ago. Before anyone else.''

''I never wanted to hurt you. You'd gotten the shaft, just like me. I always figured that one day, we'd run Mercy. You and me. I didn't even mind you being in charge. You've got a real knack for it. I do better when someone else points the way.''

He sat back again, took a drink himself, capped the canteen. He'd lost track of time. It was soothing, sitting here with her, under the wide sky, reminiscing.

''I didn't plan on killing Pickles. Didn't have a thing against him, really. Oh, he could be a pain in the butt with his complaining and argumentative ways, but he didn't bother me any. He just happened along. I never figured he'd come rolling up there just then. Thought I had more time.

I'd just planned on doing another steer, leaving it out where one of the boys would come across it and get things heated up. Then I had to do it. And, Will, to tell the truth and shame the devil, I got a taste for it.''

"You butchered him."

"Meat's meat when it all comes down to it. Damn, I could go for a beer right now. Wouldn't a beer go down smooth?'' He sighed, took off his hat to fan his face. "Cooled off some, but goddamn, it's close. Maybe we're in for that rain we've been waiting for.''

She looked up at the sky, felt a jolt of alarm. They were going to lose the moon. If anyone was coming after her, they'd be coming blind as bats. She tested her legs again and thought they would do.

And he tapped the knife on the toe of her boot. "I don't know why I scalped him. Just came to me. Kind of a trophy, I guess. Like hanging a rack on the wall of the den. I've got a whole box of trophies buried east of here. You know where those three cottonwood trees stand across from the far pasture?''

"Yeah, I know." She fought to keep her eyes on his, and off the knife.

"I did all those calves that night. Seemed to me that would send those city girls running off, and that would be that. But they stuck. Had to admire that. Started me thinking a little, but I just couldn't get past the mad of it.'' He shook his head at his own stubbornness. "So when I picked up that kid, hitchhiking, I used her. I wanted to do a woman.''

He moistened his lips. Part of him knew it wasn't proper to talk of it with his little sister, but he couldn't stop himself. "I'd never done a woman before. I had a yen to do Shelly, you know, Zack's wife.''

"Oh, my God.''

"She's a pretty thing, pretty hair. Couple times I went over to Three Rocks to play poker with the boys there, I studied on it. But I did that girl, and I left her there, right at the front door, just to show Jack Mercy who was boss. That was before the calves,'' he said dreamily. "I remember now. That was before. They get all mixed up in my head, until Lily they do. It was Lily that changed things. She's my sister. I got that into my head when J C treated her like that, hurt her like that. She might've died if I hadn't taken care of her. Isn't that right?''

"Yes." She wouldn't be sick, refused to be. "You didn't hurt her."

"I wouldn't have harmed a hair on her head." He caught the joke, slapped the rock, and howled. "A hair on her head. Get it? That's a good one." He sobered, the change abrupt and frightening. "I love her, Will. I love her and you and Tess just like a brother should. And I'll look out for you. And you have to look out for me. Blood's thicker than water."

"How do you want me to look out for you, Jim?"

"We got to have a plan, get our stories together here. I figure I'll take you back and we'll tell everybody that somebody dragged you off. You didn't see, but I went off after you. Didn't have time to send out the alarm. We'll say I chased him off, scared him off. I'll fire a couple of shots." He patted the rifle. "He ran off into high country, and I got you away safe. That'll work, won't it?"

"It could. I'll tell them I never saw his face. He hit me. I've probably got a bruise anyway."

"I'm sorry about that, but it works out real good. We'll go back to the way things were, all right. Couple months more and the ranch is free and clear. I can be foreman now." He saw her eyes flicker, her instinctive cringe. "You don't mean it. You're lying."

"No, I'm just thinking it over." Her heart began to thud at the rapid change of his moods. "We have to make sure it sounds right or else—"

"You're lying!" He screamed it so that the rocks echoed. "You think I can't see it? You think I'm too stupid to see what's going on in your head? I take you back, you'll tell them everything. You'll turn me over, your own brother. Because of Ham."

Wild with fury, he sprang to his feet, the knife in one hand, the rifle in the other. "It was an accident. There wasn't anything I could do. But you'll turn me over. You care more about that old man than your own family.''

He'd never let her go. And he'd kill her before she got two yards. So she pushed herself to her feet, teetered once until she could brace them apart, and faced him. ''He was my family.''

He tossed the rifle down, grabbed her by the shirtfront with his free hand, and shook her. ''I'm your blood. I'm the one who matters. I'm a Mercy, same as you.''

Out of the corner of her eye she saw the knife wave. And the clouds smothered the moon and killed the glint. ''You'll have to kill me, Jim. And once you do, you won't be able to run fast enough or hide deep enough. They'll hunt you. If Ben or Adam finds you first, God help you.''

''Why won't you listen?'' His shout boomed over rock and hill and hung in the heavy air. ''It's Mercy that counts. I just want my share of Mercy.''

She closed her aching hands into fists, stared into his desperate eyes. ''I haven't got any mercy to give you.'' Rearing back, she thrust her stiffened hands into his stomach and whirled to run.

He caught her by the hair, yanking back until stars erupted in front of her eyes. Sobbing in pain, she rammed back with her elbow, caught him hard. But his grip stayed firm. Her feet slid out from under her and she would have gone down but for the hold on her hair.

''I'll make it quick,'' he promised. ''I know how.''

Ben stepped out of the shadows. ''Drop the knife.'' His pistol was cocked, aimed, ready. ''You so much as break the skin on her, I'll blow you to hell.''

''I'll do more than break skin.'' Jim angled the knife under her chin. His voice was dead calm again. He felt the control seep back into him, the command. He was in charge. The woman pressed against him was no longer his sister but just a shield. ''All I do is jerk my wrist, and she's dead before she hits the ground.''

''So are you.''

Jim's eyes flickered over. His rifle was just out of reach. Cautious, he moved back a step, keeping the knife edge at

Willa's throat. "You give me five minutes' start, and when I'm clear, I'll let her go."

"No, he won't." She hissed as the knife bit in and the first trickle of blood oozed down her throat. "He'll kill me," she said calmly, kept her eyes on Ben's. "It's just a matter of when."

"Shut up, Will." Jim flicked the knife under her chin. "Let the men handle this. You want her, McKinnon, you can have her. But you put down the gun, and you step back until we're mounted. Otherwise, I do her here, and you watch her die. Those are your choices."

Ben skimmed his gaze from Jim's face to Willa's. Lightning shot overhead like lances, illuminated the three of them standing on silvered rock.

He held the look until he saw her nod slowly in acknowledgment. And he hoped, in understanding.

"Are they?" He pulled the trigger. The bullet hit just where he'd aimed it, dead between the eyes. God bless her, he thought, as his hand finally shook. She didn't flinch. Even when the knife clattered to the ground, she didn't flinch.

She felt herself sway and rock now that no one was holding her up. She saw the sky reel just as rain started to fall. And she saw Ben rushing toward her.

"Good shot," she managed, and to her mortification and relief, she fainted.

She came to in his arms, with her face wet and his mouth rushing over it. "Just lost my balance."

"Yeah." He was kneeling in the dirt, rocking her like a baby as rain flooded down on them. "I know."

Her ears were ringing like church bells. Though she knew it was cowardly, she turned her face into his shoulder rather than turn it toward the body that must be sprawled beside them. "He said he was my brother. He did it because of Mercy, because of my father, because of—"

"I heard him clear enough." He pressed his lips to her hair, then took off his hat and put it on her in a fruitless attempt to keep her dry. "Damn idiot woman, you were begging him to kill you. I lost three lives listening to you goading him while I was climbing up."

"I didn't know what else to do." Fear she'd battled back opened wide and devoured her. "Ham?"

"I don't know." She was shaking now, and he gathered her closer. "I don't know, darling. He was alive when I rode out."

"Okay." Then there was hope. "My hands. Oh, Jesus, Ben, my hands."

He began to curse then, hard and fast, as he pulled out his knife and cut the rope away from the raw flesh. "Oh, baby." It broke his heart and left him shattered. "Willa."

He was still rocking her, kneeling in the pouring rain, when Adam found them.

THIRTY-ONE

"You're going to eat when I tell you to eat, and eat what I tell you to eat." Bess stood over the bed and scowled.

"Can't you leave me be for five damn minutes?" Huddled in the bed, as miserable as a scalded cat, Ham shoved at the tray she set over his lap.

"I do, and you're climbing out of bed. Next time you do, I'm stripping you naked so you can't get past the door."

"I spent six weeks flat on my back in the hospital. And I've been out of that cursed hospital for over a week. I'm alive, for Christ's sake."

"Don't you use the Lord's name to me, Hamilton. The doctor said two full weeks of bed rest, with one hour, twice a day, of walking." Her chin jutted, her head angled, and she looked down her pug nose at him. "Need I remind you you had a knife stuck in your thick hide and you bled all over my clean kitchen floor?"

"You remind me every time you walk in here."

"Well, then." She looked over in approval as Willa stepped in. "Good. You can try dealing with him. I've got work to do."

"Giving her grief again, Ham?"

He glowered as Bess flounced out of the room. "The woman doesn't stop fussing over me, I'm tying these sheets together and climbing out the window."

"She needs to fuss just a little while longer. We all do." She sat on the edge of the bed, gave him a thorough study. He had good color again, and some of the weight he'd lost in the hospital was coming back on. "You look pretty good, though."

"I feel fine. No reason I couldn't be up in the saddle." His hands fumbled when she laid her head on his chest and cuddled. Awkward, he patted her hair. "Come on now, Will, I ain't no teddy bear."

"Grizzly bear's more like it." She grinned and kissed his whiskered cheek despite his embarrassed wriggles.

"Women, always after a man when he's down."

"It's the only time you're going to let me pet you." She sat back, took his hand. "Has Tess been in?"

"She was in a while back. Came to say good-bye." She'd been blubbering over him too, he remembered. Hugging and kissing. He'd nearly blubbered himself. "We're going to miss seeing her strut around here in those fancy boots."

"I'm going to miss her too. Nate's already here to take her to the airport. I've got to go see her off."

"You okay . . . with everything?"

"I'm living with everything. Thanks to you and Ben, I'm living." She gave his hand a last squeeze before going to the door. "Ham." She didn't turn back, but spoke, staring out into the hallway. "Was he Jack Mercy's son? Was he my brother?"

He could have said no, and just let it die. It would've been easier for her. Or it might have been. But she'd always been a tough one. "I don't know, Will. The God's truth is, I just don't know."

She nodded and told herself she would live with that, too. The never knowing.

When she got outside, she saw Lily, already in tears and holding on to Tess for dear life.

"Hey, you'd think I was going to Africa to become a

missionary." Tess squeezed back her own tears. "It's only California. I'll be back for a visit in a few months." She patted Lily's growing belly. "I want to be here when Junior comes."

"I'll miss you so much."

"I'll write, I'll call, hell, I'll send faxes. You'll hardly know I've left." She closed her eyes and hugged Lily fiercely. "Oh, take care of yourself. Adam." She reached out for his hands, then went into his arms. "I'll see you soon. I'll be calling you for advice in case I end up buying that horse." He murmured something. "What did that mean?"

He kissed her cheeks. "My sister, in my heart."

"I'll call," she managed to choke out, then turned and nearly bumped into Bess.

"Here." Bess pushed a wicker basket into her hands. "It's a ride to the airport, and with that appetite of yours, you'll never make it."

"Thanks. Maybe I'll lose this five pounds you put on me."

"It doesn't hurt you any. You give my best to your ma."

"I will."

With a sigh, Bess touched her cheek. "You come back soon, girl."

"I will." She turned blindly and stared at Willa. "Well," she managed, "it's been an adventure."

"Sure has." Thumbs tucked in her front pockets, Willa came the rest of the way down the stairs. "You can write about it."

"Some of it." She swallowed hard to steady her voice. "Try to stay out of trouble."

Willa lifted a brow. "I could say the same to you, in the big, bad city."

"It's my city. I'll, ah, drop you a postcard so you can see what the real world looks like."

"You do that."

"Well." She turned. "Hell." Shoved the basket at Nate and spun to walk into Willa's open arms. "Damn it, I'll really miss you."

"Me too." Willa tightened her grip, clung. "Call."

"I will, I will. God, wear some lipstick once in a while, will you? And use that lotion I left you on your hands before they turn into leather."

"I love you."

"Oh, God, I've got to go." Weeping, Tess stumbled toward the rig. "Go castrate a cow or something."

"I was on my way." With a little hitching breath, Willa took out her bandanna and blew her nose as the rig rumbled away. " 'Bye, Hollywood."

TESS WAS SURE SHE'D GOTTEN HOLD OF HERSELF BY THE time she'd checked her bags in the terminal. An hour-long cry was good enough for anyone, she thought, and Nate had been considerate enough to let her indulge in it.

"You don't have to come to the gate." But she kept his hand clutched in hers.

"I don't mind."

"You'll keep in touch."

"You know I will."

"Maybe you'll fly in for a weekend, let me show you around."

"I could do that."

Well, he was certainly making it easy, she thought. It was all so easy. The year was up, she had what she wanted. Now it was back to her life. The way she wanted.

"You'll keep me up with the gossip. Fill me in on Lily and Willa. I'm going to miss them like crazy."

She looked around, busy people coming and going, and wished desperately for her usual excitement at the prospect of getting into the air and flying.

"I don't want you to wait." She made herself look up at him. Into those patient eyes. "We've already said good-bye. This only makes it harder."

"It can't be any harder." He put his hands on her shoulders, ran them down her arms, up again. "I love you, Tess. You're the first and last for me. Stay. Marry me."

"Nate, I . . ." Love you too, she thought. Oh, God. "I

have to go. You know I do. My work, my career. This was
only temporary. We both knew that."

"Things change." Because he could read her feelings on
her face, he shook her gently. "You can't look me in the
eye and tell me you're not in love with me, Tess. Every
time you start to say you're not, you look away and don't
say anything."

"I have to go. I'll miss my plane." She broke away,
turned, and fled.

She knew what she was doing. Exactly what she was
doing. She rushed past gate after gate telling herself that.
How was she supposed to live on a horse ranch in Montana?
She had her career to think of. Her laptop bumped against
her hip. She had a new screenplay to start, a novel to work
on. She belonged in LA.

Swearing, she spun around and ran back, pushing through
other people who rushed in the opposite direction. "Nate!"
She saw his hat, on the downward glide of the escalator,
and doubled her pace. "Nate, wait a minute."

He was already at the bottom when she clambered her
way down. Out of breath, she stood in front of him, a hand
pressed to her speeding heart. She looked into his eyes.
"I'm not in love with you," she said without a blink,
watched his eyes narrow. "See that, smart guy? I can look
right at you and lie."

And with a laugh, she jumped into his arms. "Oh, what
the hell. I can work anywhere."

He kissed her, set her on her feet again. "Okay. Let's go
home."

"My bags."

"They'll come back."

She looked over her shoulder and said a spiritual good-
bye to LA. "You don't seem very surprised."

"I'm not." He scooped her out the door, then up into his
arms and into a wild circle. "I'm patient."

BEN FOUND WILLA RUNNING WIRE ALONG THE FENCE
line that separated Three Rocks from Mercy. It made him
realize he should have been doing the same. Still, he dis-

mounted, strolled over to her. "Need a hand?"

"No, I've got it."

"I was wondering how Ham was getting on."

"He's cranky as a constipated bear. I'd say he's coming along fine."

"Good. Let me do that for you."

"I know how to run fence."

"Just let me do it for you." He yanked the wire from her.

Stepping back, she set her hands on her hips. "You've been coming around here a lot, wanting to do things for me. It's got to stop."

"Why?"

"You've got your own land to worry about. I can run Mercy."

"Run every damn thing," he muttered.

"The term of the will's done, Ben. You don't have to check things over around here anymore."

His eyes weren't friendly when they flickered under the brim of his hat. "You think that's all there is to it?"

"I don't know. You haven't been interested in much else lately."

"What's that supposed to mean?"

"What it says. You haven't exactly been a regular visitor in my bed the last few weeks."

"I've been occupied."

"Well, now I'm occupied, so go run your own wire."

He braced his legs apart much as she'd braced her own and faced her between the fence posts. "This line's as much mine as yours."

"Then you should've been checking it, same as me."

He tossed the wire down between them, like a boundary between them, between their land. "Okay, you want to know what's going on with me, I'll tell you." He tugged two thin gold hoops out of his pocket and shoved them into her hand.

"Oh." She frowned down at them. "I'd forgotten about them."

"I haven't." He'd kept them—God knew why, when

every time he looked at them he relived the night, the dark, the fear. And each time he looked at them he wondered if he'd have found her in time if she hadn't been smart enough, strong enough, to leave a trail.

"So, you found my earrings." She tucked them in her own pocket.

"Yeah, I found them. And I climbed up that ridge listening to him screaming at you. Saw him holding a knife to your throat. Watched a line of blood run down your skin where he nicked you."

Instinctively she pressed her hand to her throat. There were times when she could still feel it there, the keen point of the knife her father had put in a killer's hand.

"It's done," she told him. "I don't much like going back there."

"I go back there plenty. I can see that flash of lightning, your eyes in that flash of lightning when you knew what I was going to do. When you trusted me to do it."

She hadn't closed her eyes, he remembered. She'd kept them open, level, watching as he squeezed the trigger.

"I put a bullet in a man about six inches from your face. It's given me some bad moments."

"I'm sorry." She reached for his hand, but dropped her own when he pulled back, stayed on his own land. "You killed someone for me. I can see how that would change your feelings."

"That's not it. Well, maybe it is. Maybe that's what did it." He turned away, paced, looked up at the sky. "Maybe it was always there anyway."

"All right, then." She was grateful his back was to her so he couldn't see the way she had to squeeze her eyes tight, bite down on her lip to keep from weeping. "I understand, and I'm grateful. There's no need to make this hard on either of us."

"Hard, hell, that doesn't come close." He tucked his hands in his back pockets and contemplated the long line of fence. It was all that separated them, he mused, those thin lines of barb-edged wire. "You've been underfoot and causing me frustration most all of my life."

''You're on my land,'' she shot back, wounded. ''Who's under whose feet?''

''I guess I know you better than most. I know your flaws well enough. You've got a bundle of them. Ornery, mean-tempered, exasperating. You've got brains, but your guts get in the way of them half the time. But knowing the flaws is half the battle.''

She kicked him, hard enough to make him stumble into his own horse. He picked up the hat she'd knocked off his head, brushed it over the leg of his jeans as he turned. ''Now I could wrestle you down for that, and it'd probably turn into something else.''

''Just try it.''

''You see, that's the damnedest thing.'' He shook a finger at her. ''That look right there, the one you're wearing on your face right now. When I think it through, that's the one that did it to me.''

''Did what?''

''Had me falling in love with you.''

She dropped the hammer she'd picked up to hit him with. ''In what?''

''I figure you heard me the first time. You got ears like a damn alley cat.'' He scratched his chin, settled his hat back into place. ''I think you're going to have to marry me, Willa. I don't see a way around it. And I tell you, I've been looking.''

''Is that so?'' She bent down, picked up the hammer again, and tapped it against her palm. ''Have you?''

''Yeah.'' He eyed the hammer, grinned. He didn't think she'd use it. Or if she tried, he figured he'd be quick enough to avoid a concussion. ''I'd have found one if there'd been a way. You know''—he started toward her, circling—''I used to think I wanted you to distraction because you were so contrary. Then when I had you, I decided I still wanted you because I didn't know how long I'd keep you.''

''Keep coming on,'' she said coolly, ''and you'll have a dent in your big head.''

He kept coming on. ''Then it kept creeping up on me, why no one ever pulled at me the way you do. Ever made me miss them five minutes after I walked out the door the way you do. When you weren't safe, I was crazy. Now that you are, I figure the only way to handle things is to marry you.''

''That's your idea of a proposal?''

''You've never had better. And with your prickly attitude, you won't get better.'' He timed it, grabbed the hammer out of her hand, and tossed it over the fence. ''No point in saying no, Will. I've got my mind set on it.''

''That's what I'm saying.'' She crossed her arms. ''Until I get better.''

He sighed, heavily. He'd been afraid it would come to this. ''All right, then. I love you. I want you to marry me. I don't want to live my life without you. Will that do?''

''It's some better.'' Her heart was so full she was surprised it wasn't spilling over. ''Where's the ring?''

''Ring? For God's sake, Will, I don't carry a ring around with me riding fence.'' Perplexed, he pushed back his hat. ''You never wear rings anyway.''

''I'll wear the one you give me.''

He opened his mouth to complain, shut it again, and grinned. ''Is that a fact?''

''That's a fact. Damn, Ben, what took you so long?''

She stepped over the wire and into his arms.

New in Hardcover

NORA ROBERTS

Author of MONTANA SKY

Sanctuary

PUTNAM